I0840616

# A THORN IN EVERY HEART

# ALSO BY KATE KING

**WILDE FAE**

Lords of the Hunt

Lady of the Nightmares

The Last Heir of Elsewhere

A Kingdom of Monsters

**THE GENTLEMEN**

Red Handed

Thieves Honor

Damned Souls

**THE BLISSFUL OMEGAVERSE**

Pack Origin

Pack Bound

Pack Bliss

**STANDALONES:**

By Any Other Name: A Deliciously Dark Romeo and Juliet Retelling

ENCHANTED LEGACIES
BOOK ONE

# A THORN IN EVERY HEART

USA TODAY & INTERNATIONAL BESTSELLING AUTHOR

## KATE KING

This book is a work of fiction. All characters, names, places, and incidents, either are the product of the author's imagination or are used fictitiously. Any resemblance to real persons, living or dead, events, or locales, is purely coincidental.

A Thorn in Every Heart © 2025 by Kate King

All rights reserved.

No part of this book may be reproduced in any form or by any electronic or mechanical means, including information storage and retrieval systems, without written permission from the author, except for the use of brief quotations in a book review. For more information, please email hello@katekingauthor.com.

First Cover edition April 2025

Standard Paperback: 979-8-9917934-3-8

Standard Hardcover: 979-8-9917934-4-5

Barnes and Noble Editions: 979-8-9917934-5-2 , 979-8-9917934-6-9

Cover design and typography: Flowers and Forensics

Development and Copy Editing: The Blue Couch Edits

Edge Design: Painted Wings Publishing Services

Chapter Art: Emmanuelle Bövel (@emmabovel)

Published by Wicked Good Romance

*For anyone who has ever wanted to escape*

*And for the girlies who read dedications and now know that this book contains explicit NSFW artwork...I'm not telling you how to live, but I'd maybe keep an eye on who's reading over your shoulder. Enjoy!*

DYASPORA
THERMIA
VERNALLIS

LLENDER
N
W
E
S
SOLISTINE
HYDRATTA

# PROLOGUE
## THE LAND OF ELLENDER

DAEMON

There are no locks in Dyaspora prison.

Perched on a bleak, snow-covered island in the middle of an unforgiving ocean, the frigid prison is the only structure for a thousand miles.

There are no locks because there doesn't fucking need to be. After a few weeks, every man realizes that escape is impossible. Even if someone managed to slip away in the night, there's no chance of getting off this island. If the monsters that roam the ice planes don't catch you, the sirens lurking beneath the frigid waters will.

Dyaspora is the dumping ground where the four Fae kingdoms exile their undesirables—criminals, rebels, and, most frequently, the *poor* and *impoverished*.

I don't fit any of those labels, yet I'm trapped here like everyone else, with no hope of ever escaping alive.


"If you could have brought one thing with you to Dyaspora, what would it be?"

I slam my heavy pickaxe against the stone cliff and the shards of rock and debris tumble into the snow. "What the fuck are you talking about?"

Beside me, Jett grins and leans against his own pickaxe. "If you knew you were going to be banished here and could bring one thing, what would it be?"

"Release papers," I growl, lifting my axe again.

Jett's black eyes glint with humor. "Come on, Ashwater, that's cheating."

"Cheating at fucking what?" I snap. "Fine, I'd bring a knife. Happy?"

"Not particularly," he replies, completely at odds with his cheerful tone. "You're too practical. Ask me what I'd bring."

I shoot him a withering look. "You're going to get whipped for standing around so long without working."

He ignores me and continues as if I'd played along. "I'd bring a barrel of ale. If I can't be warm, I may as well be drunk."

In spite of myself, I chuckle. Jett's right about that—I'd give almost anything to be drunk right now.

Jett and I are standing in line with our fellow prisoners, our bodies frozen and our feet shackled together by heavy iron chains. Every step, the iron scrapes against my skin, leaving fiery trails of pain—the only hint of warmth in this hellish place.

Eighteen hours a day, we prisoners move as one, raising heavy pick-axes and slam them against the icy cliffs, mining for nothing but exhaustion and broken bones. Every night, the guards cart our sorry asses back to our cells, and that's when the real torture begins.

Fae might be immortal, but we're still going to die here—sooner or later.

For me, it will be sooner. In less than a month, I'm going to die.

And some days, I'm completely fine with that.

"Hello?" a voice echoes down the long stone hallway of the prison. "Can anyone hear me?"

I pause at the sound of the shout, then shake my head and turn back to the cards in my hand. "Must be a new guy, making so much noise."

Across from me, Kastian chuckles. "I pity his cellmate."

"Don't pity him too much. Our room is full enough as it is."

I share my cell with three other men: Jett, who's constantly smiling despite every reason not to. Fox, who almost never talks but is smarter than the rest of us combined. And my best friend, Kastian, who understands what it's like to go from living in a palace to mining ice, day after day.

Tonight, the same as every night, the four of us huddle on the cold, hard stone floor gathered around a makeshift table constructed from a battered wooden crate. Between us lies a deck of well-worn playing cards, stolen from a guard decades ago.

I reach across the table to draw two more cards. "I didn't notice the guards bringing in any new meat."

To my right, Jett leans back against the wall, hands behind his head. "Happened last night while you and Kas were out stealing our dinner."

"Where are they from?" Kastian asks quickly, a note of panic in his voice.

"Solistine, same as me," Jett says, shaking his blue-black hair out of his eyes. "Poor bastards. Most of them have probably never seen snow before."

Kas relaxes. Every time they bring in new prisoners, his reaction is the same. He's always worried about running across someone from his past. But aside from me, no one has ever recognized him.

"It won't matter where they're from," Fox mumbles, tossing his cards on the table. "I grew up in Thermia where the snow never melts, but here is different. I didn't know a cold like this existed."

We all nod in silent agreement.

The Fae cannot die from cold, but we can still fucking feel it.

"Can anyone hear me?" The silence is broken by another shout.

"Yeah!" another voice yells back. "Shut the fuck up!"

There's a long beat before the first man raises his voice again. "Can anyone help me? I'm looking for Daemon Ashwater!"

Jett tosses his cards on the table. "Interesting. It sounds like you've got a customer, Ashwater."

"I hear him." I don't take my eyes off my cards. "He'll figure out soon enough that there are no locks on the doors. No need to waste my time searching for him."

It only takes thirty minutes before my prophecy proves correct. A feeble-looking man with a hunched posture arrives at our door, peering inside. "H-hello?"

I look up, assessing him. His hands shake, and mud splatters his ragged gray cloak. He must have arrived like that, since he hasn't been here nearly long enough for his clothes to be stolen or destroyed. That doesn't bode well for his survival.

"I'm l-looking for Daemon Ashwater," he stammers. "Is he here?"

I turn back to my cards. "Who wants to know?"

"M-me, I'm—" The man's voice quavers again, then he falls into a fit of coughing.

I roll my eyes. "For fuck's sake. Jett, give him something to eat. If he dies on our doorstep, his body becomes our problem."

"Right-o," Jett says, grinning as he jumps up.

"You have f-food?" the beggar stammers.

"Yeah. Isn't that why you're here?"

"N-no, but I'll take it. Thank you."

"It's more for us than for you," I growl. "If you die here, the guards will make it our problem. I don't feel like spending all night digging your grave."

The man blinks, unsure if I'm joking. *I'm not.*

There aren't many deterrents for violence in this place, but the guards keep a loose handle on fighting by forcing any offender to dig their victim's grave all night. Usually, by morning, the graves are unnecessary since both the digger and the body will have been eaten by beasts.

Jett hands the man a loaf of bread and some dried meat from our pile of stolen food and supplies. The beggar's eyes widen, and he accepts the food quickly, shoving them into the pocket of his cloak.

I expect him to leave, but he doesn't. "You? You're Daemon Ashwater?"

"Just 'Ashwater,'" I correct him. "And there's no need to be so shocked."

"I thought you'd be older, that's all."

I raise an eyebrow. "I feel as if I am growing old as we speak. Now, what do you want?"

The man pushes his damp, graying hair out of his eyes. "I heard about you from my neighbor before I...before I came here. She said if anyone could get me off this island, it's you."

I scoff. "If I knew how to escape, do you think I'd be sitting here now?"

"Well...I don't know. But please...I'm i-innocent. At least, I didn't mean to do anything. See, it was daylight—"

I look up, intrigued. "Are you from Vernallis?"

He nods, and I scowl. Unfortunately, I understand all too well what must have happened. The curse on the Kingdom of Vernallis robs its victims of control over their own bodies whenever the sun is out. I don't even want to know what this old man did under the effects of the curse to be sentenced to Dyaspora. I've seen enough of the destruction caused by the curse to guess, and it's not pretty.

"There's only an hour or two of sunlight each day here," I say bitterly. "If you can sleep through it, it's almost like not being cursed at all...at least, until the end of the month."

He blinks, startled, then swallows thickly. "Thank you...but I can't stay here. I need to return to my family. We only have a few weeks left together."

Kastian turns to the man and smiles, almost empathetically. "Every man here claims he's innocent, and we all have families. You'll learn quickly that no one escapes Dyaspora. Make some friends and try your best to live through the night."

"But I heard you could break into anywhere," the man reasons desperately. "You used to sneak over the border into the human realm. You helped my neighbor's daughter escape her husband."

I have no idea who his neighbor is or what daughter he's talking about, but I don't doubt the story. Once, I helped hundreds of people cross into the human realm but not anymore. "That was a long time ago. If you're looking to buy food or steal something from the guards, come back. Otherwise, I can't help you."

"But—" he begins to protest, but his feeble voice is cut off by the sound of commotion in the hall.

"Out of the way!" a guard yells. "Get back! Do not approach the king."

"What the fuck," Kastian says, jumping to his feet. "Did he say 'king?'"

I'm on my feet too, flanked by Kastian, Jett, and Fox.

The feeble beggar scrambles further into the room, flattening himself against the wall in panic. Of course, I forget his presence—all my attention focused on the door and the sound of boots in the hall.

A voice I recognize as the head of the guards echoes over the commotion. "He's in the cell at the end, my lord."

"Good," a high, cold voice replies. "You may leave us."

"But, my lord..."

"Go!"

I breathe heavily as if I'm back at the cliff swinging my axe. I know that voice, and I never thought I'd have the misfortune to hear it again. Part of me wants to run, while another part is frothing at the mouth for the possibility of a fight. *Of revenge.*

A looming shadow turns the corner, and King Thorne of Vernallis steps inside the cell. He carries a leather satchel and wears a tailored blue-and-gold waistcoat that's absurdly clean and looks out of place in this shithole prison. Shaking snow from his blond curls, he smirks at me.

"Hello, brother. I would say it's good to see you, but I'd hate to lie."

My jaw tightens, I ball my hands into fists as I meet my half-brother's challenging gaze.

He's exactly the same height and muscular build as me, but our similarities end there. Thorne looks like his mother, with blond curly hair and pale blue eyes. My darker hair and green eyes are identical to our shared father—which is the entire reason I've spent more than half my life imprisoned in the frozen asshole of the universe.

"What are you doing here?" I demand.

Before Thorne can answer, a rustling in the corner interrupts us. We turn to look at the beggar, still plastered against the wall. His mouth hangs open for a long moment, before he remembers himself and falls onto the floor, performing a comically low bow at Thorne's feet. "Your Majesty!"

Thorne doesn't even spare him a glance. He strolls into the room, stepping over him as if he's garbage.

"What are you doing here?" I ask again. "Come to gloat one more time before the end of the month?"

"I wanted to speak with you," Thorne says, a hint of cruel humor in his voice. "I'd ask you to come to me at court, but given the circumstances..."

My nails bite into the flesh of my palms so hard I'm sure I've broken skin. "Why would you want to speak with me? I thought we'd settled all there was to say ninety years ago when you banished me here."

I know Thorne well enough to see the rage simmering beneath his easy smile. The only question is: is he angry with me? Or angry that he's had to come here and seek me out?

I get my answer immediately.

"I've come to ask for your help," he bites out.

"*You* want *my* help?" I laugh harshly. "With what?"

He looks toward my friends. For a moment, I'm afraid he'll recognize Kastian, but he doesn't because he only says, "Perhaps we could speak in private."

"Anything you have to say to me, you can say in front of my men."

"Oh?" Thorne's eyes glint with amusement. "Have you been building an army? How quaint."

I ignore him, but don't retract my statement. I won't let him separate me from my friends.

Thorne tosses the leather satchel at me and I catch it instinctively. I pull out a pair of denim trousers, and it takes me a second to recognize them. "These are mine. Where did you get them?"

"I thought you might need them. I want you to cross the border to the human realm and fetch someone for me, brother."

I let out another bark of incredulous laughter and shove the jeans back into the satchel before dropping it on the floor. "Why the fuck would I do that?"

"Because if you do, I'll lift your banishment."

A startled silence lingers in the room. I can't fucking believe it. No one leaves Dyaspora. Ever. Not even kings. Why would he offer this?

Thorne doesn't want me back at court or he never would have banished me in the first place. He doesn't need me to cross into the human realm, either. The gates require a lot of magic, but he's more than powerful enough to use them himself. And if he refused to go, there are plenty of others he could have asked before coming to me.

I straighten my shoulders. "That's a very generous offer. But I know you have never been generous a day in your life. What's the catch?"

"No catch. If I could cross myself, I would, but I cannot leave the kingdom unsupervised for more than a day."

I snort a humorless laugh. He's right about that much; the cursed Kingdom of Vernallis can spiral out of control in the blink of an eye. At least, that was true ninety years ago when I left.

"I need someone I can trust to go in my place," Thorne finishes.

"And you think you can trust *me*?"

"I don't trust anyone, but if I can't have trust, control will do. With you, I can offer an incentive no one can." He gestures around the room. "No one has ever escaped Dyaspora in the history of Ellender. You could be the first."

An ache shoots through my chest, and I bite the inside of my cheek to keep my eyes from betraying my desire. Returning to my former life would mean everything to me. Still, I say, "No."

Jett sucks in a sharp breath while Fox stiffens beside me. Kastian, however, doesn't move. Perhaps he understands better than the other two what I'm thinking. Or perhaps he simply wants to avoid Thorne's notice.

Thorne's face twists in a mixture of confusion and anger. "What did you say?"

I turn away from him and bend as if to return to playing cards. "No. I'll stay here. Thanks for the offer."

"I don't think you're considering this," Thorne says, albeit urgently. "You can finally return home without the shame of banishment hanging over you. I'll restore your title and your lands. I can even make you the captain of my guard, if that's what you want."

"It's not enough. I'd rather stay here than return to your cursed court. At least in Dyaspora, there's so little daylight I hardly have to worry about—"

"Shut the fuck up," Thorne cuts me off with a growl.

I grin, pleased at getting under his famously thin skin. "Whatever you say, Your Highness."

He takes a step closer until we're practically nose to nose. "If freedom isn't enough, then what do you want?"

Ninety years ago, I would have jumped at any opportunity to return to the court. Even twenty years ago, it might have been tempting, but now I have my friends—my true brothers—to think about. I cannot abandon them when they never once abandoned me in Dyaspora. "Free all of us," I demand. "Either my friends come with me, or you can shove your offer up your ass. I don't want it."

Kastian lets out a choked sound. He didn't know what I was planning, and maybe returning to Thorne's kingdom won't be safe for him. But there's no time to discuss it now.

"Fine," Thorne agrees, almost too quickly, then glances at my friends. "They'd make decent enough guards, I suppose, but I don't know what you expect me to do with the old one."

I furrow my brow in confusion, before my eyes fly to the feeble man on the floor in the corner. I'd completely forgotten he was there. I don't even know his name. But when he looks up at me, I can't bring myself to say he's not part of the deal. No matter how much I've tried, I'm not as cruel as the rest of my family.

"He can work in the stables," I say. "Or the kitchen. You have thousands of servants. I'm sure you can take one more."

"Fine."

I blink in shock. Is this really happening? It seems too easy. No, it *is* too easy. Something is wrong here. "Who do you want me to find?"

He sucks in a deep breath. "The woman who will put an end to the curse on my kingdom."

Another long silence stretches between us as disappointment settles in my chest.

I knew there would be a catch. For a moment, I let myself believe I could return to court with my friends at my side. But now, the truth settles in—it was never going to happen. "That's impossible. It's been—"

"Over ninety-nine years," Thorne finishes for me, a note of bitterness creeping over his tone. "The rose moon is coming. According to the astronomers, it's only a month away. It marks one hundred years since the curse was cast. If it rises, our curse will become permanent."

"The curse you brought on all of us, you mean," I hiss. "It's your fault that the kingdom is in this mess, and your fault that time is running out when you've had decades to find someone to end our suffering."

"Which is why I need your help," he insists, huffing. "If you will not do it for me, do it for every person in Vernallis."

I shake my head. "Even if I thought you deserved my help after everything you've done, it's impossible. If no one has found our savior in ninety-nine years, why do you think I will in less than a month?"

"Because I already know who she is."

I recoil, shocked. "If you already know, why would you wait so long?"

Thorne sighs again, sounding weary. "I know because she's been here before. She found her way into Ellender sixty years ago. Her name is Isabelle."

"What happened to her? If she was the one who could break the curse, why the fuck would you allow her to leave?"

Thorne scowls and steps back abruptly. "I don't need to explain myself to you," he growls. "I have attempted to incentivize you with gifts, but I am happy to turn to threats instead."

"Threats of what?" I scoff. "You've already sent me here. That's the worst punishment at your disposal. And in a month, it won't matter, anyway. You won't have the ability to speak your own name, let alone punish anyone."

"True, but a month is more than enough time to make sure you never forget how wrong you were to disobey me. Your mother is still living on the Ashwater Estate, and that servant you call a sister is at court. I could send them here to see you."

I bare my teeth, losing my composure for a moment. Women are rarely sent to Dyaspora, but when they are, it's far kinder to kill them upon arrival. My mother wouldn't last a day, and Odessa...I don't even want to fucking think about what would happen to her or what I'd have to do to protect her.

"You wouldn't," I hiss.

Thorne smirks. "You're correct. I won't, as long as you find my bride for me."

"How the fuck am I supposed to find your missing bride?" I grind out. "And how would I recognize her if I did?"

Thorne appears unfazed, as if he anticipated this argument. "Sixty years ago, Isabelle came through the mountain gate. She lived nearby to the entrance in a town called Ironhill. I remember it, because the name was amusing. *Ironhill*—like the humans hoped to scare us away from their home."

Only Thorne would find it amusing that a town would be so afraid of him they might name themselves after the one thing that resists faerie magic.

"Wait a minute," Jett blurts out behind me. "I don't understand."

"What don't you understand?" I grit out, turning slowly to look at him.

*Please shut the fuck up. Don't say anything that will get you killed.*

Jett, seeming to realize he shouldn't have spoken, runs a hand through his pitch-black hair. "It's only that, if this was sixty years ago, wouldn't your woman be an old granny by now? Humans age much faster than we do."

*That's actually a good point.*

Turning back to Thorne, I raise an eyebrow. "Shockingly, he's right. Do you really want me to drag some poor old lady back here?"

Thorne's expression darkens. "Before Isabelle left, I intended her to be my bride. Obviously, I couldn't allow her to wither with age, so I gave her an enchanted necklace. As long as she wore it, she would remain just as young as she was on the day I met her."

"And you're sure she's still wearing it?" I raise a skeptical brow. "It's been sixty years. That's nearly a lifetime for a human."

Thorne shrugs as if he doesn't care, but his eyes betray him.

He does care about this; he cares entirely too much.

"I can only hope so," he says, "because that's how you'll recognize her. The necklace is gold with a red stone and my coat of arms on the back. A mirror lies inside. It will show you a glimpse of Ellender. That's how you'll know you've found the right woman."

He turns and strides toward the door, pausing on the threshold as if he expects us to follow him.

I stay frozen for one moment longer, my mind racing. "What if she doesn't want to return to Ellender? Or what if she hasn't worn the necklace and has grown old? What will you do if I find her but can't return her to you?"

Thorne, already halfway out the door, doesn't even bother to look at me when he replies, "That's your problem to solve. Remember, the future of the kingdom depends on this. Succeed and you'll have everything you ever wanted, restored. Fail, and I will make sure the last thing I ever do is sentence your friends and family to a lifetime of suffering."

# CHAPTER ONE
## CHICAGO

ALIX

If I could take only one item to a deserted island, I'd bring my violin.
Crazy, I know. A more practical person would bring a knife or a Costco-sized box of protein bars, but not me. I'd willingly starve for my art; which is probably a good thing, considering that while I'll never end up on a deserted island, *literally* starving for my art is starting to look like a real possibility.

I stand on a pedestrian-only street in Chicago, my electric violin hooked up to a portable amplifier to compete with the surrounding noise. The street is bustling with tourists, and the smell of coffee and cinnamon wafts toward me from the nearby cafe.

It's the perfect place to perform—except my case contains only six dollars, a couple of quarters, and one shiny silver *Snapple* cap. Despite playing for an hour, I haven't even made enough money to cover the parking meter, let alone my student loans.

I spot a large group of tourists heading my way and plaster on a fake smile as I start a livelier tune. To my excitement and relief, the tour guide stops, letting the group listen, and they fan out around me in a wide circle.

This isn't exactly the venue I pictured myself performing in when I dedicated my life to becoming a musician. Still, I'd rather play here than be locked in some boring office.

Music is everything to me.

I love the emotion of it.

I love how a song can change someone's mood instantly, turning a bad day into a hopeful one with only a few notes.

I love how a single song can unite strangers.

"Play that song from *A Kingdom of Thorns*!" someone shouts.

*Ugh.* I *do not* love that damn song.

I spot a teenage girl with curly blonde hair in the front of the queue. Her excitement is palpable in her *Kingdom of Thorns* T-shirt. I pretend not to have heard her and begin another familiar tune—the lullaby Nana sang when I was a baby. I close my eyes, swaying slightly to the haunting melody bursting from the strings.

"Yeah, play that *Kingdom of Thorns* song!"

Excited murmurs surround me, and I open one eye, struggling not to make my annoyance visible. The teenager catches my gaze, and I can't keep pretending I don't see her.

"Can you play the theme song?" she asks again, her eyes filled with hope.

I force my mouth to form a wide, fake smile. "Sure! Are you a fan?"

The girl nods vigorously. "Yes! But I like the books better than the movies."

*Oh, thank God.* "Me too."

I stop Nana's lullaby mid-verse and switch to the requested theme song, which I've grown to hate on principle, only because the movies simply can't do justice to the books.

I wonder what that girl would say if I told her that my Nana wrote the book this song is based on, and she hates the movies more than I do.

I play through the first verse of the theme song, but get distracted as my phone vibrates in my pocket. After a moment, the call goes to voicemail. And then it starts vibrating again. *Shit.*

I lower my violin. "Sorry, folks. Five-minute break!"

The teenager looks crestfallen, and several people grumble their displeasure as the crowd disperses. I feel guilty, but I've applied for dozens of jobs this week and can't afford to miss a call from a recruiter. Six dollars and a Snapple cap isn't going to pay my student loans or my car insurance, but a boring office job might. Even if my soul dies a little just thinking about it.

I sigh and dig my vibrating phone out of my pocket. "Hello? This is Alix Knight."

"Hey, hun," my mom says too cheerfully.

*Why? Why did I answer? Why didn't I check the caller ID?* "Hey, Mom. Listen, I'm working right now—"

"Sorry?" my mom interrupts. "I can't hear you. Can you go somewhere quieter?"

I glance around the crowded street. "Not really. I'm actually in the middle of—"

"Your Nana had an incident during her interview today."

I nearly drop my bow in panic and quickly set my violin in its case so I can plug my ear and hear her better. "Oh my God, what happened? Did she fall or something?"

Mom lets out a sharp exhale. "No, nothing like that. She's not physically hurt."

I let out a relieved sigh.

Nana is Isabelle Reading, world-renowned author extraordinaire. The mother of modern fairytales and the peddler of happily ever after. Her most famous book, *A Kingdom of Thorns*, has been a pop culture phenomenon for over forty years and this year is scheduled to be rereleased to coincide with the new movie.

Nana has been on the road for months promoting the film, and I'm constantly worried she's going to collapse from exhaustion. My mother, who often travels with Nana as her assistant and caregiver, isn't exactly the person I would trust to make sure Nana isn't overworking herself.

"So if she's not physically hurt, then what happened?"

Mom sighs. "She had a...mental breakdown, I suppose."

"What!"

"I'm sure you'll see the whole thing on social media later. I'll send you a link. Watch it."

"Okay—"

"Anyway," Mom continues with a long sigh, "I'm really calling because I think it's time to consider moving your Nana into a retirement community."

My head spins and I suck in deep breaths, trying to remain calm. I close my eyes. I need to remember that my mother is dramatic and prone to overreaction. Her idea of a "mental breakdown" could mean almost anything. Plus, Nana might be in her eighties, but she looks and acts like she's barely fifty. There's no need to panic...yet.

Still, this isn't a conversation to have in the middle of a crowded street. It's overwhelming, and I can't even think of the right questions to ask.

*Describe this 'mental breakdown.'*

*What kind of retirement community are we talking about here?*

*Is there anything I can do?*

Instead, I chew the inside of my lip and blurt out, "What about her house?"

"Obviously, we'll have to sell it."

I frown. "And what does Nana think about that? She loves that house."

Mom brushes off the question as if it's nothing. "She'll love a nice beach condo more, I'm sure of it."

"Hmm." I roll my eyes at my mother's blatant narcissism. "If you say so."

"Anyway," Mom continues briskly, "I was hoping you could help out."

"With what?"

"Nana is staying with me for a few days until we can find her a retirement facility, so I can't leave the city right now. Could you head over to the house? Someone needs to feed her cat, and I need to know what kind of condition the house is in before we try to sell it."

"I don't know, Mom. That's not exactly a simple favor. I mean, I'd have to book a last-minute flight and I can't really afford that right now."

"This is exactly why I told you not to move so far from home. If you'd stayed in Philly, you could have driven."

"Yeah," I snap, "and if I'd gone to business school instead of a conservatory, I'd have the money for the ticket, right?"

She clucks her tongue. "You said it, hun, not me."

Frustrated, I huff and squeeze my eyes shut. "Right...but I didn't do that, so right now, I'd have to drive twelve hours or pay some insane last-minute booking fee for an already too expensive plane ticket. If this were about helping Nana, I'd do it, no problem, but I'm not going to drop everything to help you sell her house out from under her."

Mom makes a disapproving noise in the back of her throat. "But what about Sushi?"

The image of Nana's enormous gray cat pops into my mind. "Who's been feeding him while you and Nana have been at the book signing?"

"I got a pet sitter, but they refuse to stay any longer than our initial agreement. The house scares them."

"Can't you do it, then? I have to work."

Mom sucks in a sharp breath and sounds happy for the first time since I picked up the phone. "Oh my God, Alixandria, did you get a new job?"

I close my eyes and hold the phone away for a second, resisting the urge to scream. "No. I've been trying but the market is really tough right now. I've been playing my violin for extra money while looking for another job."

After a long pause, she says, "Well, it's not like you couldn't take time off from that. It can't be all that much money."

I glance at the small amount of change in my violin case and sigh. "I have to go. Please tell Nana I'm thinking of her and I'll call her later."

"But—"

I hang up, cutting her off.

LATER, I DRIVE HOME WITH A MEASLY TWENTY-SEVEN dollars in my pocket, feeling extremely guilty.

Am I the asshole here?

On the one hand, it's absolutely insane for my mother to expect me to fly all the way from Chicago just to check on Nana's house. Especially when she and my stepfather, Kevin, live in Philly a mere hour away. On the other hand, my pathological tendency toward people-pleasing isn't letting me off the hook. I feel like I should be doing more to be helpful.

At a red light, I call my best friend, Jenna, to complain. The ringer echoes through my car's Bluetooth, then goes to voicemail. I hang up without leaving a message.

Shit. I can't think of anyone else to call.

Aside from Jenna and Nana, the only other person I talk to regularly is my husband, Ryan, but it's 3:30PM so he's still at work. It's moments like this that I wish I hadn't let my circle get so small.

In college, I had a huge group of friends, but over the years, we all grew apart. Now, I'm all too aware that I don't have anyone else to text about my day or grab dinner with or invite to my upcoming thirtieth birthday.

A fresh wave of gloom washes over me, and that makes me feel guiltier.

There's nothing actually wrong with my life.

So, I don't have that many friends. So, I got laid off from my shitty sales job which I hated anyway and I can't find another job because a masters in music theory isn't exactly in demand right now. So, my marriage has felt kind of stale for a while now. So what? At least I'm driving to my nice apartment right now. At least I'm not dying. Things could be so much worse.

For the rest of my drive, I intermittently berate myself for being ungrateful and try to think of good things in my life. Unfortunately, all I can come up with is full-fat Wheat Thins and that one hot guy from the *Kingdom of Thorns* movie. I'm still trying to think of a third thing to add to my list as I turn onto my street.

Ryan and I live in the downstairs apartment of a two-family home in Wicker Park. The street is pretty, lined with trees, and though the house is older than the internet, it's been well maintained. Even before I lost my job due to budget cuts, I never could have afforded this place without Ryan.

There, that's something to be grateful for. I love this apartment, and even if my marriage is a bit dull, Ryan's job still keeps us afloat while I'm...figuring things out.

There's an unfamiliar black SUV in my driveway, so I park on the street and grab my violin from the passenger seat. Then I walk over to check out the SUV before going into the house. Upon a second glance, I spot a pink and white friendship bracelet hanging from the rearview mirror. I frown in confusion.

This is Jenna's car.

I can't believe I didn't immediately recognize the car. Then again, it's a nondescript black SUV, and I wasn't expecting to see it here. Jenna didn't tell me she was coming over...maybe she's waiting to surprise me? But why? It's still almost three weeks until my birthday, and my best friend isn't the most spontaneous person.

A strange nervousness creeps over me, and I jog up the porch steps, fumbling with the lock.

The moment I step inside, the hairs on the back of my neck rise. Nothing looks out of place. My pile of shoes is still by the door, the romance novel I was reading over breakfast is on the couch. Even my half-drunk coffee from this morning sits on the coffee table, exactly where I left it. Still, that seems almost weirder. If Jenna wanted to drop by, she'd be waiting outside, sitting on the porch. Or at most, in the living room.

As if on cue, a loud bang echoes down the hall, followed by giggling.

A cold dread washes over me, making my skin clam up and my stomach churn.

*Oh my God.*

Some part of me already knows what I'm about to find, but my mind refuses to process it. It's racing, spiraling—too fast to think, too fast to react.

I can't breathe. Can't move. But I have to.

I tighten my knuckles around the handle of my violin case, not bothering to put it down before I move on autopilot toward my bedroom.

To my horror, the door is open and I'm still feet away when I see exactly what I was afraid of since the moment I walked into the apartment.

Jenna is sitting on my desk, bare legs spread wide. Standing between her thighs with his back to me, my husband is furiously pounding into her, making the desk bang against the wall with rhythmic thumps.

I stop just outside the door and stare at them, completely dumbstruck.

*What the absolute fuck is going on?*

I'm not even angry—at least not yet—I'm just shocked. And weirdly, all I can think about is how they didn't even make it to the bed. Why my desk? They're getting cum all over my keyboard. *Is nothing sacred anymore?*

Suddenly, as if sensing my presence, Jenna looks at me. Our eyes lock over Ryan's shoulder, and for a fraction of a second, she looks just as surprised as I am. Then she gives a little tilt of her head, as if to say "sorry" and looks away, dismissing me.

In a second, my entire world shatters.

I open my mouth to say something, to yell, to do *anything*. But no words come out. Instead, I turn on my heel and sprint down the hallway.

I fling the front door open and stumble outside, doubling over on the porch, gasping for air. My stomach roils, and it's all I can do not to vomit all over my shoes.

Oh my God. *Oh my fucking god.*

If I were the main character in one of my books, I'd march back inside and tell them off. I'd destroy my apartment. At the very least, I'd stand up for myself.

But I don't. I can't. I've become a side character in my own life, and right now, I just want to escape.

Escape looks like a box of room temperature Pinot Grigio and a cheap hotel room.

I lie on top of an ugly red and gold bedspread and stare at a crack in the low ceiling. Rolling over, I reach for the box of wine on the night-stand and I turn the plastic spout on the side of the box, filling my Marriott-branded water glass to the brim before downing it in two gulps.

The wine tastes like depression.

Like "fuck you."

Like three liters for $11.99 at the gas station down the street from my hotel.

I came here to think. To decide how to confront my husband. To untangle how things even got to this point.

I'm twenty-nine, married and childless, broke, and now heading for divorce.

*How the fuck did I get here?*

I've been dreaming of *happily ever after* for as long as I can remember. It's hard not to when my Nana literally wrote the manual on fated love. Unfortunately, the women in my family have notoriously terrible taste in men. My dad was the one exception, but he died, and the cycle continued like he never existed. I thought I'd escaped that generational curse when I married Ryan, but I guess not.

Fumbling drunkenly for my phone, I check if I have any texts or missed calls. Nope. Nothing has changed in the three minutes since I last looked, and I don't know why I thought it would.

I open social media and mindlessly scroll, skimming past all the people I went to high school with, flaunting their perfectly curated *happily ever afters*. Even worse are the relentless ads for strollers and baby toys. My targeted ads are working as hard as the family photos from former friends to remind me that I should be grown up by now. I should have my life together.

I guess no one told the algorithm that what was left of my own happily ever after just came crashing down around me.

Or maybe I never had one to begin with. Maybe I wanted so badly to feel loved and taken care of that I deluded myself into believing a fantasy.

My phone vibrates in my hand, startling me.

Is it Ryan calling to explain himself? Or maybe Jenna wants to apologize? I look at it too fast, causing my head to spin and my wine to slosh out of the glass and onto the ugly bedspread.

A wave of disappointment crashes over me when I see "Mom" flash across the screen.

*Please just kill me.*

I would rather chew glass than tell my mom what happened. Invariably, she will manage to make my devastation about her. As if this is my fault. As if my husband cheating is a reflection on her failure to raise me right.

I'm getting too old for mommy issues, but sometimes I feel like since my dad died, there's no one in my family except for Nana who "gets" me.

That thought jolts my memory, and I fumble with the phone, suddenly remembering why my mother is texting. I'd meant to call Nana this afternoon to make sure she was okay, but I completely forgot. Jenna and Ryan drove her accident from my mind, and now guilt piles on top of everything else.

Mom has sent two texts in quick succession. The first is a link to a video. The second says:

MOM:

This is the incident I was talking about earlier. I really hope you change your mind about coming home to help!

I groan. It's not the most passive aggressive text she's ever sent, but it still skyrockets my guilt.

I click on the link, grimacing as I take in the 3,000+ comments and 1.5 million likes and shares. It's a short video, clearly shot from someone's cell phone.

Across the top, bold text reads:

**I saw Isabelle Reading melt down at Northeast Fantasycon**

*Oh God. This is going to be bad.*

In the video, my grandmother is sitting at a long rectangular table on a small stage. Even in this grainy footage, she looks beautiful. Barely sixty, despite being eighty-eight. Her long silvery hair is pulled back in a low ponytail, her smile wide and warm. The interviewer sits beside her, while in the background, my mother stares at her phone.

Someone taps a microphone, and the interviewer introduces Isabelle Reading, celebrated author of the world's best loved fantasy romance: *A Kingdom of Thorns.*

I fast-forward ten seconds, too anxious to wait.

"I'm sure you get this question all the time," the interviewer starts excitedly. "But where did you get the idea for the world of Ellender?"

"A dream," I mutter automatically.

She had a dream about a beastly prince in a castle made of roses and started writing the book the next day.

It's an answer I know well. One I've heard Nana give at least a hundred times, if not more.

But, this time, she doesn't.

Nana looks out into the crowd, squinting as if she's blinded by the bright lights. Her wide smile falters, and she lifts a hand to shield her eyes. *Is she swaying?* After a long silence, the interviewer repeats the question.

Nana's expression darkens. "I saw it."

The interviewer keeps grinning. "Yes, you first saw Ellender in a dream, right?"

"No." Nana's tone sharpens. "I saw it with my own eyes."

Whispers ripple through the crowd. The interviewer furrows her brow. "Yeah, I'd imagine it must seem real to you after all this time. It's been over forty years since your first ever book was published—that's a whole lifetime!"

Nana glances sideways at the interviewer, but it's as if she's looking through her, not at her. "It was real," she says, more urgently this time. "I barely escaped."

"Right," the interviewer says, her smile faltering as she tries to regain control of the interview. "So—"

Nana stands abruptly, her chair screeching backward across the stage. Her voice rises in panic. "He's coming. He's coming for me."

In the corner of the frame, Mom darts onto the stage. She bends, whispering urgently to Nana before grabbing her arm and trying to pull her away from the microphone.

"You don't understand!" Nana's voice trails off as Mom pulls her further away from the mic. "The fire won't stop him forever. The beasts are coming! He's coming!"

I click out of the video and stare at the dark phone screen in shocked silence. *What the absolute fuck was that?*

I always assumed that to be as creative as Nana, you have to be a little nuts. She's definitely a bit eccentric, but I've never thought she was actually crazy.

But now, other odd things about her pop into my mind.

Like the fact that she talks about her fictional characters as if they're real people. Or the fact that she's still living in Ironhill, PA, despite pressure from her neighbors, family, and the goddamn U.S. government.

Nana is one of the last eight residents of a rural Pennsylvania mining town. It's almost literally a ghost town. Decades ago, a mining accident caused an enormous underground fire that's still burning to this day. It's incredibly dangerous for her to keep living there, but even after my grandfather died, and Nana made millions from her books, she refused to move.

That's the house that my mom wants me to go check on, and the fact that it's in a literal ghost town is certainly the reason Mom doesn't want to go herself. Hell, compared with my own home right now, Nana's weird dangerous house sounds like a paradise—

*Wait a minute.*

I sit up too fast, and my head spins. My glass slips from my fingers, wine splashing across my lap, soaking through my jeans and into my panties. "Fuck!"

I leap out of the puddle pooling on the bed and pace, already unlocking my phone with my wine-free hand. Without thinking, I call my mom.

She answers on the second ring. "Hello?"

"H-hi, Mom."

"Alixandria?" She pauses, and I hear the smack of her lips. "Are you alright? You sound...off."

I sound drunk, is what she means. *Oooph.*

I push a long brunette curl out of my face. "I'm f-fine. I just wanted to tell you that I changed my mind. I'd be happy to go check on Nana's house."

"Really?" All the judgment disappears from my her voice, replaced with equal parts shock and relief. "Are you sure?"

I close my eyes, hearing Nana's terrified voice in the back of my head. *He's coming. The beasts are coming.*

Maybe that should scare me, but it doesn't. Even if her house drives me just as crazy as she is, "beasts" can't be worse than my cheating soon-to-be ex-husband and former best friend.

"I am very sure." I hiccup. "I'll be on the first flight to Ironhill tomorrow morning."

# CHAPTER TWO

ALIX

I walk in a daze through Lehigh Valley International Airport, a blue Gatorade clutched in one hand and the handle of my violin case in the other. I'm hungover, starving, and more exhausted than I've ever been in my life.

*I hate drunk me for thinking this was a good idea. That bitch is trying to kill me.*

There's no chance I'm going to find an Uber willing to drive me ninety minutes into the boonies, so I bite the bullet and go in search of the rental car desk.

By the time I find *Enterprise*, hand over my credit card, and retrieve my shiny silver sedan, it's 8:03PM. My stomach churns with hunger, but I don't stop, even to drive through McDonald's. Between the cost of the car and my absurdly expensive plane ticket, I now have exactly $159 in my only bank account that Ryan doesn't have access to. It's not even enough to cover the minimum payment on my credit card.

A fresh wave of depression washes over me, and heat pricks at the backs of my eyes.

*What the fuck was I thinking coming out here?*

The hum of the engine is the only sound as I speed down the nearly deserted highway. The moon hangs low in the sky, casting an eerie glow through the windshield. The darkness and silence of the empty road make me feel even lonelier than I already did.

I wanted to escape my life, but this doesn't feel like freedom; it feels like exile.

I clench my hands until my knuckles turn white and swallow the lump in my throat. If I was driving to Nana's house to see her, maybe things wouldn't feel so bleak. I wish I could lie on her couch like I did as a teenager and tell her about my shitty day. I wish I could tell her about Ryan and Jenna and hear her curse them out far worse than I have.

*I still will tell her.* Nana isn't dead, she's just…getting old, I guess.

As I pull off the highway, I spot the familiar **"Danger"** signs. A couple of miles further, more warnings appear:

**"Underground Fire."**

**"Warning: Unstable Ground."**

**"Road Closed—Seek Alternate Route."**

I ignore them and continue into the empty town square.

I'm used to seeing the occasional condemned farm house or abandoned car on the side of the road, but Ironhill is on a whole other level. Most of the buildings have either been demolished or fallen on their own, but the occasional dilapidated house remains. There are 80s and 90s-era cars rusting in driveways, and even an abandoned gas station that advertises $0.62 per gallon. *If only.*

Nana's house is one of the very last homes standing that looks lived in and taken care of. She has a huge garden, which flourishes despite the contamination of the soil.

I pull up to the house and immediately feel less alone.

The air is crisp and dry, the heat of summer already turning into fall. The sound of crickets fills the air, and I take a deep breath. The air should be contaminated due to the mining fire, but it smells fresh to me. Far better than the city air in Chicago, at least. I close my eyes and savor the moment.

*It's just so quiet here.*

My phone rings loudly. I yank it out of my pocket without even processing the name flashing on the screen. "Ryan?"

"What?" Mom says. "No, it's me."

I press my palm to my forehead as my heartbeat slows back to normal. "Oh. Hi, Mom. Sorry, what's up?"

"I was just calling to make sure you made it to the house. I thought I'd hear from you hours ago, but I know how the cell service is there."

"Sorry," I repeat, even though there's nothing to be sorry for. "I'm here. Just pulled up to the house, actually."

"What?" she yells as if she's standing on the opposite side of a football field. I repeat myself, even as the line crackles. "Oh, good," she says, her voice sounding slightly far away. "I'll wait for you to head inside. I want to know what we're dealing with."

"What do you mean?"

"You know how your Nana is. Her house is always a disaster, I just want to know how bad it is."

While she talks, I walk across the grass and up the front porch steps. The inside of the house is dark, but the porch light is on. The yellow paint shines brightly in the warm glow, and a crowd of moths and June bugs hover around the hanging lamp.

"I'm sure it's not bad, Mom."

She scoffs. "Maybe not by your standards."

I bite my tongue. She's right, actually. I love Nana's house. It's not dirty; it's just eclectic. If it wasn't built on top of the fucking hellmouth, I'd probably want to live right next door.

I hold the phone between my shoulder and ear as I bend to shift the flower pot beside the welcome mat. The hidden key is exactly where I expect it to be, and I let myself inside. Immediately, the familiar scent hits me—cinnamon, oil paint, and lemon *Pledge*.

I flick on the hall light and smile.

The front door opens into a small entryway. The stairs to the second level are directly ahead, with the living room to the right and the dining room to the left. The dining table is covered in hundreds of books, stacked in messy, teetering piles.

I reach for the nearest book.

Nana's publisher must be changing the covers on her series to coincide with the new movies, because this is the first time I've seen this edition of *A Kingdom of Thorns*. The cover features a blond man with pointed ears, standing shirtless in a field of wild roses. Sighing, I put the book down.

"Well?" Mom demands.

I jump, having almost forgotten she was on the line. Her voice is clearer now that I've moved to the kitchen, and the line sounds *almost* normal. "Sorry. It looks fine, Mom. Just like it usually does."

She sighs. "That's what I was afraid of. We're never going to have the time to go through all her stuff."

"What's the rush?"

"I've been wanting to get the house sold for years. It's dangerous. I don't know why she insists on staying there. I don't want to leave Mom any choice but to move once she feels better."

"Mmm."

I cross the kitchen and open the refrigerator as she keeps ranting about selling the house. My heart sinks. There's almost nothing in here —just a jar of pickles, some ketchup, and a carton of expired eggs. I check the cupboard and it's not much better.

"Mom," I interrupt her musing about the house. "When was the last time Nana was home?"

"Um, a few weeks? We've been traveling for her book signings, remember?"

*Fuck.* I close the fridge and sigh. "Okay, sorry, but I have to go. I haven't eaten all day, and I expected to find something here, but I guess I'll have to go to the store."

My dismay must be evident in my voice, because for once, Mom offers something helpful, "Go down to Ted's."

"Where?"

The line crackles a bit, and I have to strain to hear her. "Ted's place. It's a bar just over the town line. They make great burgers."

I'm so taken aback by this extremely out of character comment I'm silent for a long second. "Are you sure they'd be open?"

"They haven't changed their hours in thirty years."

"Hmm, okay. Thanks."

"Don't forget to feed the cat before you go."

We hang up, and I turn in a circle searching for Nana's cat, Sushi. He hasn't appeared since I've been here, but that's not exactly unusual. He's probably chasing mice in the attic.

I quickly refill the food and water bowls, then turn around and retrace my steps to the door. I don't really have the money to eat out right now, but my stomach isn't giving me any choice. I only hope my mother is right and this mysterious Ted's is still open.

On my way to the car, something glittering catches my eye. I pause for a moment to glance again at the books on the table.

On top of the nearest stack is a large gold and ruby locket, the chain curled beneath the pendent.

*This is Nana's locket.*

When I was younger, she wore it every day, and still brings it out for special occasions even now. Why would she leave it here where it could easily get misplaced? Maybe Nana's memory is really starting to fracture and she forgot she left it here?

I pick up the locket and the blond man on the book cover is revealed once again. It's not a photo, as I first thought—it's a shockingly realistic drawing.

The man is almost unnervingly handsome, his smirk giving the impression that he's admiring the person watching him. But it's his pale blue eyes that unsettle me most.

They look *alive.*

A nervous shiver travels down my spine as I loop the gold chain around my own neck and tuck the pendant into my T-shirt. The cold metal immediately warms against my skin, as if pulsing with life.

As I turn toward the door, another change on the cover catches my attention. Beneath the familiar title, the new tagline reads:

*The Beast is coming.*

Ted's is a small, free-standing one-story brick building with a faded brown roof and a peeling green sign. The parking lot is surprisingly full for a Wednesday night, with at least twenty motorcycles and a handful of rundown cars. Out front, two men and a woman, all wearing leather jackets, are smoking.

I park my car and take a deep breath before getting out. I'm not exactly scared...more like wary. It doesn't look like the kind of place my mother would be caught dead in. Hell, it looks like the kind of place I *will* die in, but I'm so hungry I don't even care.

Inside, I'm immediately hit by the scent of tobacco and fried food. I glance around, taking in the mid-sized room—a long bar on one side, clusters of round wooden tables on the other. At the back, a few pool tables draw a small crowd, while a jukebox in the corner blares an old country song I don't recognize.

Nearly every table is taken, and all eyes turn toward me. Even the pool players stop to stare.

I look down, double checking that Nana's necklace is hidden beneath my shirt. This place probably looks rougher than it is, but there's no need to invite unwanted attention by flashing a five-carat ruby on my chest. Nervously, I pull the hem of my T-shirt down to hide the tiny strip of skin above the waistband of my jeans and brush my curls behind my ears.

The stares linger as I cross the bar and take a seat. Behind the counter, the bartender stops cleaning the glass in his hand and turns to look at me. "Hi, there."

"Hey. Can I get a menu?"

"Sure."

He hands me one and proceeds to rattle off a list of specials. He's cute, I guess, with floppy blond hair and a golden retriever smile. Not that it matters. Even if I had the option, I'm not interested in him. That's not why I'm looking. It's more that I've never had the opportunity to look before.

I've been with Ryan since I was eighteen, and I've never even slept with anyone else. I've resolutely not looked at any other man my entire adult life, to the point that I'm not even sure what I find attractive. How sad is that? Maybe I don't even like what I think I like.

"So, did you want a drink?" the bartender asks.

I shake my head to clear it. "Yeah. I'll take whatever you have on tap and a cheeseburger. No pickles."

He walks away, and suddenly I feel lost again. I don't have anything to do now except sit with my thoughts, and the urge to pull out my phone is almost a compulsion. How did people live with silences before phones?

The downside of coming here is that I probably have decent service now.

It's getting harder to convince myself that Ryan and Jenna haven't called because I was on airplane mode all day—or that the reception here is just shit.

They are ignoring me, and the longer I go without hearing from them, the more I start to gaslight myself.

Did I really see what I thought I did?

Did Jenna actually see me? Maybe they don't even know that I know.

Maybe it wasn't Ryan but some other guy?

"Oh my God, I'm losing my mind," I say out loud, putting my head in my hands.

"I doubt that, Peaches."

The strange voice has a lilt to it—an accent that isn't from Pennsylvania, let alone the United States. I whip my head toward the speaker, my jaw dropping—literally. I have to consciously close it so I don't look even crazier than I already do.

I changed my mind: I *do* know what I find attractive.

Sitting beside me is the most physically gifted man I've ever seen.

Even seated, he's tall and his burnt-honey hair is just slightly too long and falls into his face, half obscuring his bright green eyes. Like almost everyone else in here, he's wearing a leather jacket, but somehow his looks sexy instead of scary. Underneath, he wears a simple white T-shirt, which is thin enough that I can see the shadow of a swirling black tattoo crawling up his chest and the side of his neck.

"What did you say?" I ask, when I remember how to speak.

"I said, I don't think you're crazy, Peaches."

"Peaches?" I ask, raising a skeptical eyebrow. I can't tell whether I should be offended or not.

He nods at my T-shirt, smirking.

My cheeks heat as I remember what I'm wearing. I didn't have time to pack in Chicago, so I'm wearing yesterday's jeans and some cheap Mario Brothers T-shirt from an airport gift shop. The shirt is pink with a picture of Princess Peach. Across my chest, it says "Delicious like peaches and cream."

*That explains the stares.*

"Uh, r-right," I stammer. "Well, that really only proves you wrong. For all you know, I might be certifiably insane."

He gives me a cocky grin, flashing a set of perfect teeth. "I suppose, but if you are, I think crazy girls are sexy."

*Woah.*

The stranger has an aura that screams confidence, and that accent is like phone-sex. My stomach does a weird flip, and I have no idea what to say.

"What's your name?" the handsome man asks.

"Alix."

It might be my imagination, but it almost seems like the man relaxes at the sound of my name.

"I'm Daemon." He holds out his hand for me to shake, and his gaze darkens as he runs his finger over my wedding ring. "Married?"

I snatch my hand back. "Um, sort of. Heading for divorce."

His green eyes flare back to life. "Did he fuck up?"

I laugh, then for some reason, I confess, "He fucked my best friend."

It's the first time I've said it out loud, to anyone, and the words seem to hang in the air for a moment, becoming real all at once. I don't think I've really processed what happened until this moment. Like I've been in a state of shock for the last twenty-four hours, and only now is it really hitting me.

"What a fucking idiot," he growls. "If you were my wife..."

He trails off, leaving his sentence hanging. I lean forward, desperate to hear what he was going to say. If I was his wife, then what?

"So is that why you're here?" he asks instead. "Drowning your troubles?"

"N-not exactly," I stammer.

I tell him why I'm here. About Nana, and coming back to check on the house for my crazy mom. Even as I speak, I'm one hundred percent sure I'm screwing this up. It's been ages since anyone flirted with me, and even longer since I tried to flirt back.

Have I forgotten to blink? *Kill me.*

"You're staying in Ironhill?" Daemon asks when I'm finished.

"Uh huh..."

"Maybe you can answer a question for me, then."

"I can try."

He leans toward me like we're sharing a secret. "What happened here?"

I cock my head at him, confused. "What do you mean?"

"The town—" He waves his hand in the air. "I was led to believe people lived here, but it looks abandoned."

"Yeah...it's been that way for years. Haven't you heard about the mine fire?"

Daemon shakes his head, and I narrow my eyes, looking him up and down again. He's a little older than me, but he looks about thirty. Thirty-five, at most. Ironhill has been abandoned for decades, long before I was born. It's not like everyone would know that, but he's making it sound like he expected the town to still be standing. *Weird.*

I swivel on my stool so my knee brushes against his. "Sixty or seventy years ago, this was a busy mining town, but then a fire broke out in one of the mines."

"Ah." He nods as if that means something to him. "What happened?"

"No one knows how it started, but once the fire got going, they couldn't put it out. The coal in the mine just kept fueling it, and there was nothing anyone could do to get it under control. The miners and the people in the town tried to get the government involved, but they ignored it for so long that eventually the fire had eaten up the entire mine. It spanned miles, and the ground got incredibly unstable. Sinkholes started opening up, like literal portals to hell, and the entire town suffered from carbon monoxide poisoning."

He raises one eyebrow. "What happened to them?"

"The people? Most of them survived, but they all left. Thirty years ago or so, the government finally declared the town uninhabitable."

His lip pulls up in a crooked half-smile. "But your grandmother still lives there?"

"Yeah. The government came to some agreement with the residents that they could stay until they died, but no one else could move in. She's one of only like ten people still living there."

"She sounds stubborn. What does she do all day with only ten other people in the whole town?"

"She's a writer," I answer, fighting not to let any expression cross my face.

I must fail, because Daemon grins and asks, "You don't like her books?"

"No, it's not that. Her books are amazing. I've read them so many times I could probably recite them from memory."

"Then why the frown?"

I sigh. "I guess I'm just not in a happily ever after mood lately. Nana writes these incredible stories about fantasy kingdoms and fated romance. I don't know...I've been in the real world too long to buy into the magic."

Daemon takes a sip from his drink and nods. "In my experience, Peaches, every world is a bitch in its own way and magic only makes things more complicated."

I laugh. "I like that. I'm definitely here for a little nihilism."

He flashes me another grin before finishing his drink in one swallow. "Listen," he says, leaning even closer so his woodsy masculine scent fills my nose.

*Oh, I'm listening.*

"Do you think your grandmother would remember the people who used to live here? Or know where they went?"

"I don't know. Are you looking for someone?"

"I was," he says, pulling back slightly. "But I'm getting the impression that she hasn't lived here in a long time."

An embarrassingly intense wave of disappointment washes over me. He's looking for a woman. Of course he is, because I doubt a guy like him goes a single night without company.

"Is she someone important to you?" I ask, trying and failing to sound casual.

He laughs, a flicker of amusement flashing in his eyes. "No, definitely not. In fact, I've never met her."

"Oh," I say, confused. "Okay..."

Before he can explain further, we're distracted by the buzzing of my phone against the bar. Instinctively, I reach for it, and blanch when I see the name that pops up above the text.

RYAN:

Hey, so I thought you'd want to talk, but I guess you're going to be immature about this and avoid me. Let me know when you plan on getting over yourself and coming home.

I stare at the text in complete disbelief. That's it? Over a day of radio silence, and now, that's all he has to say to me? *What the fuck.*

Even though I know I shouldn't engage, I immediately fire back a text.

ME:

I need to get over myself? I'm not the one who got caught cheating.

For a brief second, I feel satisfied, until three dots appear on my screen. The dots appear and disappear as if he's typing and deleting his message. After a second, my phone rings.

"I need to take this, sorry."

Daemon waves me away. "Go ahead, Peaches. I'm not worried."

"Worried about what?"

He smirks. "You'll be back. I'm not done with you yet."

"Umm..." I begin, but the phone starts ringing and I can't focus on anything else. "Sure. Okay. Yeah, I'll be right back."

I stomp across the bar and answer the phone just as I shoulder open the door. "Hello?"

"Where are you?" Ryan demands, without preamble.

"That's none of your business."

"Like hell it's not," my husband snaps. "When are you coming home?"

I suck in a sharp breath and close my eyes. "Why do you care? What, do you want to make sure Jenna is out of the house before I get there?"

There's a tense silence on the other line where Ryan doesn't answer. My stomach sinks with dread.

*Oh my God.*

I was being sarcastic, but that's exactly what's going on. Jenna is at my house right now with my husband, and instead of being worried about me, they're just worried about the scene I'll cause if I catch them again.

*Holy shit, my entire life is over.*

"Just tell me where you are," he says, his tone even, almost mocking. "This is ridiculous, baby. Just come home so we can talk."

"No!" Heat pricks my nose and the back of my eyes, and I swallow thickly. "I want a divorce."

Ryan chuckles. *Actually chuckles.* "That's not happening. We've been together too long to just throw it away. What will people think?"

"You're the one throwing it away, not me."

His voice hardens. "It was one mistake, Alix. You're so critical, you can't ever just let things go. And we both know you can't afford a divorce, anyway. How are you going to live on your own when I already pay all our bills?"

My chest tightens, and the first tear slips silently down my cheek.

I'm not even sad about splitting up. It's not him I want; it's everything else. One decision, and he's taking everything away from me. My marriage, my friend, my music—because there's no fucking way I can afford to keep playing violin for a living now that I'll be surviving on one income. He's snatching my financial security, my apartment, and my trust in men, all at the same time.

He's fucking me in a way he hasn't since he took my goddamn virginity.

"I can't do this right now," I say, unable to hold back the tears anymore. "I'll talk to you tomorrow."

"No," he snaps. "I want to talk now. I need to know where you are."

"We'll talk tomorrow," I grit out again, before hanging up the phone. Quickly, I turn off the phone and let out a shaky sigh.

I stare at the dark parking lot and the sign for Ted's, not really seeing them at all. Ryan is right—I can't afford to get a divorce, but I'm determined to figure it out even if I have to swallow my pride and beg my mom for money. After all, my marriage is already over. It was finished long before today, and now I just need to find a way to be okay with that.

My eyes sting with angry tears. I storm into the bar, intending to order an entire bottle of wine. I slam my phone on the bar so hard I wouldn't be surprised if the screen cracked.

"You alright, Peaches?" Daemon asks, tilting his head at me in concern.

I blink in surprise, having almost forgotten he was there.

My mind races. I don't even know this guy, but he's being nicer to me than Ryan has in years. I mean, I'm half-certain he's being so nice because he wants to get into my pants, but so what? He's crazy hot, and I hate the fact that Ryan is the only man I've ever been with.

My heart rate quickens, and I drag my tongue over my lips as a completely insane idea takes shape. A certifiably crazy idea.

Without a word, I lean toward Daemon and press my lips to his.

I hope he was serious about liking crazy girls.

# CHAPTER THREE

ALIX

*Oh. My. God.*

Oh my God, I can't believe I'm doing this. I've never had a one-night stand in my life. I've never even gotten close.

In my head, I'm a slut. But in reality, I just read a lot of spicy books. Until yesterday, I never would have pictured myself picking up a stranger in a bar. Apparently, I'm doing a lot of things differently than I was yesterday.

Daemon follows me back to the house on his motorcycle. *He drives a freaking motorcycle!* Like, of course he does, because he just had to go and get even hotter.

His headlight shines through my back window as we pull into the driveway of Nana's house. I take a moment before I turn off the car, staring at the bright yellow glow of my headlights shining against the house. I want to do this...I really want to, but my hands tremble with nerves and I have the worst feeling I'm going to make an idiot out of myself.

A shadow falls over me from outside the passenger window, and I look up to find Daemon standing outside waiting for me. Smiling, I turn off the engine before getting out.

"Nice place," he says, looking around at the big yellow farmhouse and the elaborate garden surrounding it. "Not really what I pictured when you said you were staying in Ironhill."

I laugh. "Did you think I was luring you back to my cave?"

His eyes flash with something—*surprise*, I think—then he grins. He steps closer and puts his hand against the car door, boxing me in against the driver's side window. "To be honest, even if you were, I would've followed you."

My heart does a stupid little pitter-patter, and suddenly I understand what the word "swoon" means. I smile and look up, meeting his impossibly green eyes. He really is absurdly handsome—almost unreal. Like if I couldn't reach out and touch him right now, he'd disappear, slipping back into whatever magical place he came from.

In the bar, both seated, it was hard to tell how tall he is, but now, he towers over me, nearly a foot taller than my 5'4" frame. I have to stand on my toes to wrap my arms around his neck, and my T-shirt rides up so high, my entire back presses against the cold car door, and I shiver.

Daemon moves his large hands to my sides, pressing his fingers into the bare skin of my waist. I suck in a breath. *God, he smells amazing.* Like the musky forest with maybe a hint of roses.

Then, he bends his head to kiss me.

His lips are soft and taste like some combination of cinnamon and spearmint. My stomach soars, and I open my mouth, letting him explore me.

He moves his hands down my side to cup my ass, and then without warning, grips the backs of my thighs lifting me off the ground. I gasp and twine my legs around his hips. I can feel him growing hard against my core, and I grind against him lightly, loving the friction of our jeans.

He pulls away, whispering against my lips, "Inside?"

"Yeah. I—"

Before I can finish, he lifts me more firmly into the air and walks toward the porch. I tighten my grip on his hips and move my head to the side to trail kisses along his neck and sharp jaw. The stubble scratches my cheeks and lips, but I don't care. I want to feel that roughness all over my body, on every inch of my sensitive skin.

Daemon carries me up the porch steps and toward the door.

"There's a key under—" I begin, but break off as he opens the door with one hand and we step inside. Huh. *Did I forget to lock it?* That's weird, I swear I did.

The confusion flies out of my head as he kicks the door closed behind us and murmurs against my hair, "Where to, Peaches?"

*Um...*

I look around the entryway of the house. The guest room I usually sleep in is upstairs, but I haven't even been up there myself, yet. For all I know, Nana has left art supplies all over the room or decided to use it as an indoor greenhouse or something. That would be hard to explain, and would definitely ruin the moment.

"Couch," I murmur, jerking my head toward the living room to our right.

The living room is probably the least cluttered room besides the kitchen. There's a long, red-velvet sofa pushed up against a large bay window, and a few eclectic armchairs all grouped around a spindle-legged coffee table.

Daemon carries me into the room, expertly navigating the maze of furniture, and lowers me down onto the red-velvet sofa.

I have to tilt my head all the way back to keep him in view as he towers over me. My heart is beating out of control, and I'm suddenly nervous again.

Forcing the anxiety away, I grip the lapels of his leather jacket and push it down his muscled arms. Underneath, he's wearing a simple white T-shirt, and my mouth waters when I spot the intricate tattoos covering both his arms from wrist to beneath the white cotton sleeves. They are covered in a continuous pattern of symbols. It looks like some cross between Norse runes and ancient Arabic characters.

"Nice ink," I blurt out.

He glances at his arm and smirks. "Thanks."

He drops to his knees in front of me, and I part my legs so he can kneel on the floor between them. Like this, we're almost eye to eye, and his smirk is sexy and arrogant as he runs his hands up my denim-covered thighs.

He traces his fingers over my waistband, fiddling with the silver metal button of my jeans. "Can I take these off?"

"Please."

He fumbles with the button and zipper for a moment, and I lift my hips to help him peel them down my legs. He tugs them off and tosses the jeans to the side, and the cool air makes goosebumps pebble on my bare skin. Fuck, I've never been so grateful in my life for laser hair removal, or to be wearing pretty underwear. My black thong doesn't match my bra, but at least I'm not wearing horrible laundry-day panties.

"Nice ink," he repeats my words, grinning. His fingers trace over the rose tattoo on my right thigh as he looks at me with a clear hunger in his eyes, and I writhe under his attention. Nobody has ever looked at me like that.

I pull my T-shirt over my head, but the fabric catches on my necklace. Daemon reaches out, untangling it with a careful touch. His gaze lingers on the gold pendant on my chest before flicking to the second tattoo on my upper arm—then lower, to my purple lace bra. Heat sparks in his gaze and he leans in, pressing his mouth against my collarbone.

*Good lord.*

I tilt my head back and moan when he drags his lips down, sucking lightly on my right nipple through the lace.

I yank off his T-shirt, revealing that the tattoos stretch from his arms, over both shoulders, and across his chest. He's corded with hard muscle as if he spends every waking hour in the gym. My eyes widen, lingering on his abs before I snap my gaze back up—as if I've only been admiring the tattoos and not his perfect body. "What do they mean?"

"They're a family thing," he replies distractedly.

"Like a motto?"

"Something like that," he mutters, then leans in to capture my mouth in another kiss.

I quickly forget my questions as the kiss turns heated again. He runs his hands up my bare legs and over my stomach to cup my breasts. Squeezing lightly, he runs his thumbs over my nipples, scraping with his thumbnails. A tingle travels through my entire body and lands in my core. I arch my back, pressing my chest more firmly against him.

He goes down my neck, across my chest again, and lower until he reaches my stomach, he presses an open-mouthed kiss to the skin just below my belly button. I suck in a sharp breath at the feeling of his chin scratching against my too sensitive skin.

He pushes my legs apart and plants a kiss against the triangle of lace. I moan, and he opens his mouth, dragging his tongue over the rough fabric until I'm soaking wet and writhing.

"Take them off," I demand.

He doesn't follow my direction, instead, simply hooking one finger under the lace and dragging my panties to the side, exposing me. I writhe as he lowers his mouth to my core again, this time sucking my clit hard between his lips.

"What do you know?" he murmurs. "You *are* delicious, Peaches."

*Oh my God.*

I've never felt this good. Not even when Ryan and I were newly married and all over each other, which was the last time I had anyone go down on me. Four years of only occasional, boring obligation sex, and I'd started to think I just didn't like sex with real people the same way the fictional characters in my romance novels seem to.

Wrong. Totally and completely wrong.

I do like sex, and even if I never see Daemon again after tonight, I'll be glad he taught me that.

Daemon sucks harder on my clit, scraping his teeth, and at the same time, he thrusts two fingers inside me. His fingers curl against my inner walls, and I scream. My entire body shudders, and I close my eyes, gasping for breath.

Without waiting for me to recover, he gets to his feet. He undoes his own belt much faster than he got my jeans off, and then he sits on the couch beside me. I only have a second to marvel at the size of his cock, standing straight up, before he's tugging me into his lap.

I let out a breathy moan when I feel his tip nudging against my soaking wet entrance. I press my hips forward and grind against him, sliding the head of his cock back and forth over my core. Fuck.

Somewhere in the back of my mind, I wonder if I should ask him to use a condom. Fuck it, I'll risk it. I'm on birth control, and even during the year that I wasn't, and Ryan and I tried to get pregnant, it never worked out. I'm not even sure I can have a baby.

Pushing that thought from my mind, I refocus on the man in front of me. Daemon's eyes are intense and seemingly lit from within. He makes a low sound of pleasure and reaches out to tear the cups of my bra down, sucking one nipple back into his mouth.

I sink down one inch and whimper, rocking harder against him, seeking friction against my clit.

"Stop fucking teasing," he growls against my skin, his fingers pinching my other nipple hard enough to sting. "I want to be inside you. I want you to sit your fucking ass down and bounce on my cock until you come so hard you can't see straight."

"Jesus," I breathe. "Where'd you learn to talk like that?"

"Prison," he deadpans.

He's joking, right? He must be. Do I even care right now?

Clearly tired of waiting for me to move, Daemon growls and grips my hips tightly. Spinning me around, he holds my back to his chest with one arm and presses my entire body down until I'm seated fully on his lap.

"Holy shit."

For a second, I don't move, adjusting to the fullness. He throbs and the pressure is so intense. I feel stretched to my limits. Impossibly full, and the sensation is almost overwhelming, but in the best way possible.

I spread my knees wider and rise slowly, sliding him out before sinking back down. His grip tightens, fingers digging into my skin, and I know I'll have bruises on my breasts and hips by morning. *I fucking love it.*

I rock faster and arch my spine, leaning my head back against his shoulder. He turns his head to press his mouth against the curve of my ear, and I shudder. He then reaches around to cup me, skillfully running his fingers over my sensitive clit as I ride him.

"Fuck, Peaches," he pants against my throat. "You feel so fucking good."

Still stroking my clit with his other hand, Daemon pushes my hair out of the way and sucks on the skin just below my ear. His tongue traces a languid path up the side of my neck, causing a shiver to ripple through me. Electric sparks dance along my skin, igniting and burning. My back arches, and I feel as if my entire body catches fire. My clit throbs, and my legs begin to shake both with pleasure and exertion.

"Are you going to come again for me?" Daemon murmurs in my ear.

I whimper, unable to form words as I roll my hips, taking him deeper with every stroke. Tiny lights dance at the edge of my vision. My body tenses and my hips buck as waves of pleasure wash over me. I feel boneless.

Without warning, Daemon lifts me and reverses our positions again.

He slams my back against the plush cushions of the couch, causing me to gasp in surprise. With a fluid grace that I almost envy, he positions himself above me and forcefully thrusts his cock inside, filling me with an intense pleasure that radiates through my body.

I scream as my orgasm crashes over me, tightening around him just as he fills me.

A surge of heat rushes through my body, causing me to instinctively squeeze my eyes shut. My muscles tense and my toes curl as I draw my knees up. Daemon holds them open, fucking me so hard my head bounces against the cushioned armrest.

His growl mingles with my moans. He grows harder inside me, before collapsing forward and pressing his face against my chest.

Despite our size difference, it's strangely not uncomfortable to feel his weight pressing against me. I'm completely enveloped in warm, tattooed muscles, and I lie there, growing a bit too comfortable as my breathing slows down and my heart rate returns to normal.

Finally, he pushes up on his hands to look at me. Our gazes lock, and just like that, the fragile, soap-bubble happiness of this moment bursts.

Now what?

Is he going to leave? What is proper one-night stand etiquette?

"Um..." I begin, having no idea where I'm going with this.

He grins, sliding out of me before standing. "Do you have anything to drink?"

I sit up. "Not really. I mean, there's water."

He gives me a cocky smile and drags his gaze over my naked body appreciatively before turning and walking naked across the room. Good lord, I want to sink my teeth into his ass.

"Water will do," he points out of the living room and down the hall. "This way?"

"Yeah," I mutter, pushing sweaty curls out of my face. "The kitchen is through the dining room."

"Good," he replies, already moving away. "I think you'll need to hydrate before round two."

My stomach leaps in excitement. "Round two?"

He grins over his shoulder at me. "Of course, Peaches. Did you think I could survive on only one taste of you?"

Fuck, I think I might *love* him. Like, not really, but I definitely love the way he fucks me. I can feel a real infatuation barreling toward me like a freight train.

I watch appreciatively as Daemon walks across the entryway and through the dining room toward the kitchen. He stops short in front of the stacks of books on the dining room table.

He picks up one of the books and looks closely at it, before turning around to face me with a grim expression. "What the hell is this?"

"Um..." It takes me a moment to process what he's asking. "Just books. Have you ever heard of Isabelle Reading?"

"Isabelle?" he says slowly, his voice slightly strangled.

The mood in the room has shifted dramatically. Shit. Maybe he is a fan of Nana's? If he wants to spend the rest of the evening talking about fairytales, I think I might die.

I sit up straighter, scrambling for my clothes. Instead, I find Daemon's T-shirt. I tug the shirt over my head like a dress and stand.

"What's wrong?" I ask, striding across the room.

Daemon remains focused on the books, his shoulders tense. Slowly, he turns to me, his eyes flicking from my face to my collarbone. He fixates on the lump of my necklace hidden beneath his T-shirt, a barrage of emotions flickering behind his eyes—horror, guilt, anger.

"Okay..." I let out a shaky laugh. "You're freaking me out. Have you read the books or something?"

"What's the name of the man on the cover?"

I furrow my brows. "That's King Thorne—he's in the book. Does it matter?"

He licks his lips nervously, and his handsome face crumples with resignation. "Fuck, Peaches. I'm so sorry about this."

"Sorry about what?"

He raises a hand in the air, and I don't get to hear his reply as everything goes black.

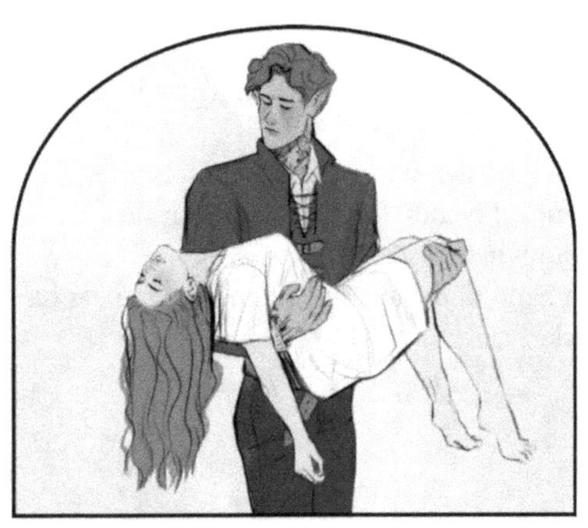

# CHAPTER FOUR

DAEMON

*What the fuck is happening?*

Alix slumps against the sofa, her head lolled to the side. I stare in abject horror and dazedly sink into one of the dining room chairs behind me. I look at the book in my hand and at Thorne's smug smirk flashing at me.

*What. The. Fuck.*

It's only been twelve hours since I crossed the barrier from Ellender and arrived in the mortal realm. I hadn't wanted to make the journey at all, but Thorne didn't leave me with many options.

Either I tried to find this Isabelle woman, or everyone I love would be tortured.

It was not a difficult choice.

I walked with my men, plus the old beggar, out of Dyaspora, thinking the entire time that Thorne might change his mind. He might turn around and murder all of us before I had a chance to react, or perhaps toss us into the frigid ocean to be drowned and eaten by the sirens.

But he didn't.

Thorne led us out of the snow-covered stone prison and out onto a frozen tundra. The area was brightly lit from dozens of torches and lanterns, and legions of red-jacketed soldiers stood around waiting for their king to return. An enormous ship, its billowing sails emblazoned with Thorne's coat of arms, bobbed in the water just beyond the shore.

This was really happening. We were going home.

Suddenly, Kastian gripped my forearm, and I turned to look at him. "What?"

His brown eyes widened. "Are you certain about this?"

"No," I said honestly. "What do you think?"

Kastian looked at the ship. "I think my father will shit himself if he ever finds out I managed to escape the Dyaspora with the King of Vernallis."

I laughed hollowly. I didn't doubt he was right.

Kastian had been my first friend while in exile. We'd met once as children, when the court of Hydratta had visited Vernallis. I never expected that the next time we would see each other would be in the cold, barren wasteland of Dyaspora, but it turned out to be the only thing that kept me going in those early years. Kastian was banished from his own court only two years after I arrived, and quickly became my confidant. To this day, no one but me knew the reason he was banished or who he'd been back in Hydratta.

"I don't think Thorne knows who you are," I mumbled.

He shook his head. "Nor do I. Your brother has never been very observant."

"Hard to observe anything with his nose so high in the air."

Suddenly nervous he might have heard me, I looked sharply at my brother's back several paces ahead of us. Thorne didn't so much as twitch, just kept walking toward the ship, ignoring the questions and comments of his soldiers as he passed.

"Listen," I muttered to Kastian, slowing my walk even more to give us an extra moment to speak alone. "I'm sure he'll expect me to go to the human realm the moment we set foot back on the mainland. I don't know what he'll do with the rest of you while I'm gone."

"I'm guessing he'll do nothing," Kas replied. "He really wants you to come back, so there's no point in harming us while you're gone. I assume we'll all be safe for the time being."

"But if I don't come back or can't find this woman..."

"I'll make sure we get out of Vernallis," he promised, without me even having to ask. "If you don't come back within the month, I'll take Jett and Fox to Hydratta. Your mother and sister too, if they agree."

I nodded once. I knew it was a true vow he was making, as returning to Hydratta would almost guarantee his own death. Even if I never returned, at least my family and most of my friends would survive.

· · ·

As so often happens, my prophecy soon proved correct.

We'd barely touched down on the soil of Ellender before Thorne demanded I find the nearest portal and begin my search for his bride.

Unfortunately, I had no idea where to look.

Isabelle came to Ellender sixty years ago. That would have been thirty years after I was sentenced to Dyaspora. I'd never met her, had no idea what she looked like, and didn't have a single fucking clue how she found Ellender in the first place. I didn't know why she left instead of marrying Thorne, and I didn't even know if she was still wearing the necklace that would keep her from aging. Perhaps she never wore it and I was searching for a woman in her eighties. Or perhaps she used to wear it but eventually stopped. In that case, she could be any age.

The entire task seemed hopeless. Like searching for a needle in a stack of other fucking needles.

The only clue I had was that Isabelle crossed over to Ellender in a town called Ironhill.

I knew every single portal location from my previous life ferrying people and goods back and forth between the realms. Centuries ago, there were countless doors, and we could move back and forth between worlds easily. Once, the Fae were everywhere, and mortals viewed us as gods or angels. Now, most of our gates have been destroyed, and there are only a few places left where one can accidentally fall into one of the four Fae kingdoms, or come across a creature not of this earth.

The Appalachian Mountains are one of those places.

When Thorne mentioned his missing bride was from Ironhill, it immediately clicked for me that she must have lived near the Appalachian gate.

But even that turned out to be a dead end.


As the sun began to set, I mounted one of Thorne's horses and set off, bracing myself for an uncomfortable journey.

The entrance to the gate was four hours away by horse, and I didn't dare waste any time. Not when I knew I needed to cross over to the other realm before nightfall. Once darkness covered Vernallis, the curse would descend on every member of Thorne's court, and by the time I was myself again, there was no way to know what might happen.

I rode as fast as I could toward the gate, barely taking notice of my surroundings. I didn't have time to stop and marvel at the lack of snow or appreciate the leaves on the trees—not if I wanted to reach the portal before nightfall.

Finally, I reached the gate.

I jumped off my horse and stood at the mouth of the cave. The darkness within seemed to stretch on forever, a never-ending abyss that sent shivers down my spine.

*There was no point in stalling.*

With the satchel of clothing slung over my shoulder, I stepped into the mouth of the ancient cave, and the oppressive darkness swallowed me whole. I trailed my hand along the rough stone walls, my pulse thrumming in my ears as I stumbled through winding tunnels for what felt like hours. Finally, the air shifted. A cool breeze brushed against my skin, signaling my arrival at the hidden barrier that separated Ellender from the human world.

As my foot crossed the invisible line dividing the two countries, a chill ran down my spine. The air suddenly felt heavy and a sense of uneasiness settled in my stomach.

Something was wrong.

The air was thick with smoke, its intense heat and sharp smell filling my lungs and making it hard to breathe. I struggled for air and my legs weakened.

As panic clawed at my chest, I felt a familiar pressure between my shoulder blades. Without conscious thought, my wings unfurled, displaying their striking combination of red and black feathers. Like most Fae, I kept them hidden, but in moments of intense emotion, they couldn't help but reveal themselves.

I gripped my worn satchel while shielding my eyes from the thick smoke swirling around me. Flapping my wings with all my strength, I lifted off the ground and soared toward the ceiling of the narrow cave passage. The intense heat and smoke made it difficult to see, but I managed to navigate over the flames and finally reached the exit, gasping for fresh air as I burst into the open sky.

A momentary sense of relief washed over me as I soared above the surrounding area, taking in the view. But as I surveyed the empty streets below, that feeling of relief quickly faded away.

It was a ghost town, deserted and in ruins. There wasn't a single soul, human or otherwise, to be seen anywhere.

Landing lightly on a hill, I paused to catch my breath.

My pulse slowed, and finally my wings disappeared, retreating back into the enchanted tattoos that covered my back.

*What the fuck is going on here?*

The gate was nearly destroyed, and this town looked like no one had lived here in generations. Was it possible that Thorne had sent me on a fool's errand, intending me to burn up in the passage?

It was possible, but why? He'd been torturing me for ninety years already.

No, Thorne couldn't have known. That must mean the fire was some natural disaster or borne of human error. I'd have to use another gate to return to Ellender. Assuming I found Isabelle, that was.

For now, I needed a plan.

Perhaps someone around here would know of Isabelle and could point me in the right direction. First, though, I'd need to find some humans.

I dressed quickly in my human clothing, leaving my prison rags on the ground. Then I cast a small glamor over myself. Nothing so strong as to make myself invisible, but now, any human I came across would see me as human instead of Fae. Perhaps I'd still look more attractive than the average human, but that really couldn't be helped.

I set off by foot in the direction of the town. Eventually, I found my way to the only business in the area that was open. A small rundown bar with dozens of motorcycles out front. At least not everything had changed, from what I remembered of the mortal world—the people still wore leather and denim, and I didn't stand out much in my disguise.

I took a seat at the bar and ordered a drink, before falling into contemplation.

There was only so long a human could hide the fact that they were immortal. Ten years? Maybe twenty, at most? After that, Isabelle would have had to take the necklace off, or else move on to avoid unwanted attention.

Should I look for her, anyway? Should I find some other mortal girl and hope that Thorne, with his impossibly short attention span and indifferent heart, might not notice the difference?

Over the next hour, I still hadn't made any decision about what to do, and my drink was now nothing but melted ice at the bottom of the glass. Just then the door opened, and I caught a glimpse of long, curly dark hair.

My breath hitched.

Before I'd been sentenced to the prison island, I'd had many lovers, but that was a long time ago. Women were rarely sent to Dyaspora and the few who were never lasted long. Subsequently, I hadn't been with anyone in over ninety years.

She was striking, with a pale, heart-shaped face and skin that was clear, almost incandescent. Her face was young, but her huge blue-gray eyes said she was no child. She'd seen enough of the world to be jaded by it. She wore tight, denim trousers and a short-sleeved pink shirt with some sort of painting on the front. As she grew closer, I realized it said: "Delicious like peaches and cream" across her chest. *Was that a promise or merely a suggestion?*

It was no coincidence that human myths frequently featured Fae males seducing fair maidens. We found humans just as beautiful and tempting as they found us. It was a match made in fairytale heaven. Or, hell, in this case.

*Damn it.*

"For fuck's sake," I muttered out loud, shaking my head vigorously. With a clenched jaw, I tore my gaze away from the woman in the suggestive T-shirt and downed the last dregs of my drink. I couldn't afford to be distracted right now—not for anything.

I made to stand up, but before I could leave, she dropped into the seat beside me.

Unable to look away, I remained in my seat, fixated on the woman as she flagged down the bartender and ordered a beer and a cheeseburger. Then, she leaned her head on her hand and stared off into space for a long moment. She looked...sad? Angry, perhaps?

"Oh my God, I'm losing my mind," she said.

"I doubt that, Peaches," I blurted before I could stop myself.

Those words had been the biggest mistake of my life.

Now, I stare across the room at Alix's unconscious body.

A moment ago, all I could see was her pretty face, flushed from her orgasm. Now, I wish I'd never walked into that bar; never met her. What are the odds that of all the women in the world, I'd find the one I was searching for immediately but not know it was her?

It seems incredible—un-fucking-believable, actually. But now that the pieces of the puzzle have started to fall into place, I can't help but notice all the signs I missed:

The book with a portrait of my brother on the cover, authored by Isabelle Reading.

Alix's gold and ruby necklace, which I ignored.

The fact that we're standing in the last fucking house in Ironhill.

So many questions fill my mind as I look from Alix to the book in my hand.

Even though I'm already certain, part of me still wants to prove myself wrong. I flick open the front cover of the book, hiding Thorne's self-satisfied smirk. Feverishly, I flip through the pages, reading a random sentence here and there. After a moment, the word "Ellender" jumps out, and a new wave of nausea hits me.

I shut the book with a loud snap, and it gives me a glimpse of the back cover. A monochromatic image of a woman looks at me. I quickly shift my gaze from the photo to the woman lying on the couch. There is no doubt in my mind that it is the same person. The resemblance is uncanny; from their hair to their eyes, and most notably, Alix is wearing the exact same necklace as in the photograph.

I try to remember what Thorne said about the necklace. It's a gold locket with his emblem embossed on the back, and it holds an enchanted mirror inside. My heart quickens as I stand and cross the room in two steps. I reach out for Alix's slender neck and softly tug on the chain hidden beneath the neckline of my borrowed T-shirt.

The gold pendant is warm to the touch when I flip it over. I knew what I would find, but I'm still disturbed at the sight of Thorne's rose insignia. I don't even have to open the locket to know for sure.

"I'm losing my fucking mind," I mutter aloud, echoing Alix's earlier words.

*Wait. What the fuck am I thinking?*

I'm echoing *Isabelle's* earlier words. Alix *is* Isabelle. There's no other explanation.

*This is a fucking mess.*

I came here to find Isabelle, and against all odds, I've managed to do it in under a day. I should be thrilled at my good fortune. Should be jumping at the opportunity to save my family and friends, restoring my old life all at the same time.

But I'm not.

My stomach still churns, and I am more conflicted than I should be. I just fucking met this woman. Yet, what kind of monster would sleep with a woman and then take her captive to force her into marriage with another man?

*This isn't about us.* It's about every citizen of Ellender. One mortal woman in exchange for the survival of an entire race can't be such a bad trade. And anyway, it's not as if we're going to kill her. Many women would kill for the opportunity to be queen.

I don't believe my own lies, but I push to my feet anyway, anger simmering just beneath the surface. I collect my clothing from the floor and dress quickly, leaving only the T-shirt that Isabelle is wearing.

I'm shoving a copy of Isabelle's book into the waistband of my jeans when something brushes against my leg. I jump and look down.

An enormous gray cat with gigantic green eyes looks at me, meowing loudly.

"Get off," I mumble, swatting at the cat to shoo it away. "For fuck's sake. Are you hungry? Is that it?"

"*Me-ow-ow.*"

I don't have fucking time for this.

I grab the cat and look around for something to carry him in. I suddenly wish I had thought to take Thorne's satchel with me instead of leaving it on the hill with my prison rags.

A cloth bag hangs from a hook by the door, and I shove the cat inside. He squirms, hissing angrily.

"Shut up," I growl. "At least I'm not leaving you here to starve."

Maybe Isabelle will be pleased to have her cat with her in Ellender. Pleased enough not to hate me for abducting her? Probably not, but it can't hurt.

Hoisting the struggling cat over my shoulder, I bend to pick up Isabelle's limp body. Her head lolls, falling against my shoulder.

Only then do I realize there's no chance I can take both of them anywhere without attracting notice, and I certainly can't perch them on the back of my stolen motorcycle.

Striding out into the yard, I take in a deep breath before unfurling my wings and launching into the sky.

I'm almost glad of the fact that I'll have to find a different gate from where I arrived. The next nearest gate is hours away, but I'm almost glad of it if only to prolong the moment that Isabelle finally wakes up and sees me for the beast that I am

# CHAPTER FIVE

ALIX

I t's an incredibly strange feeling to wake up with no memory of falling asleep.

I lie on my side, eyes still closed, semi-aware of the pounding in my skull. The scent of roses fills the air. I hear a rushing sound and the rhythmic tap of rain against glass—sharp and staccato, like 180 beats on a metronome.

I crack open one eye, and all at once, several realizations hit me. I'm not at home, or my hotel, or even at Nana's. I sit straight up in a panic, and my head swims.

*Oh my God.*

I'm lying on a plush, elegant bed in a room I don't recognize. The ceilings are towering, the walls a soft tan stone cut into geometric arched windows. It is indeed raining, because I can't see anything outside except the water and condensation on the glass. The bed beneath me is covered in a vermilion silk bedspread, miles away from the cheap red duvet at the Marriott.

Disoriented, I swing my legs over the side of the bed. Cold air brushes against my legs and I look down. I'm wearing nothing but a T-shirt. No shoes. No panties. Nothing. And worse, the T-shirt isn't even mine.

*What the absolute fuck is going on?*

"Easy, Peaches," a familiar voice says. "Crossing over can be disorienting."

I turn my head and jump. "Daemon?"

Daemon is lounging in a wooden chair in front of a heavy-looking door, his feet up on a white, spindle-legged vanity. He's back in his jeans, now wearing his leather jacket over his bare, tattooed chest. His expression is flat, almost bored—not the look of someone who has no idea where they are.

He saunters toward me, all cocky male self-assuredness. His expression is hard to read—not angry exactly, but not as friendly as last night, either. He shoves a mug of water into my hand. "Drink this."

Still dazed, I drink it without thinking twice. The room temperature liquid almost burns down my throat, and I cough. Somehow, that clears the remainder of my haze, and a spark of terror shoots through me.

*Oh my God, am I being kidnapped right now?*

"Where the fuck am I? What's going on?"

He reaches for a pitcher of water on the white vanity table and refills my mug. This time, I don't take it, and he sighs, putting it on the table. "Listen, I know you're confused but you need to calm down so we can talk."

I shove the mug away. "I need to calm down? Are you fucking insane? If anything, I'm not freaking out enough. Last thing I remember, I was on the couch in Nana's living room, and..." I trail off, a burning heat rising to my cheeks.

Daemon winces—the first hint of emotion I've seen from him since waking up. "I know. I'm sorry about that, but—"

"Sorry?" I stand. "I don't care if you're sorry. I'm really hoping I just passed out on the couch and this is some really vivid dream."

"It's not a dream," Daemon hisses, his eyes narrowing slightly. "Would you shut up and listen to me?"

"Afraid someone might hear me?" I open my mouth and scream as loud as I can. "Fire! There's a fire in here!"

"Alright, that's enough."

Daemon closes in and claps one hand over my mouth. He grabs me around the waist and lifts me off my feet, before dropping me back on the bed. He looms over me, and his height and muscles no longer make my mouth water. Now, they look like weapons. Like he could smother me without a second thought.

"I couldn't care less if anyone hears you, Peaches," he says, his hand still covering my mouth. "I'm trying to explain what happened, and we don't have a lot of time. Shut the fuck up and listen before I lose my patience."

I meet his gaze from over the top of his large palm.

In the bar, he'd been so nice, but maybe that was just an act to get me to lower my guard. It just figures that the first man to give me an orgasm that rivals my vibrator would be a kidnapping serial killer.

I nod slowly, and Daemon carefully moves his hand away from my mouth. When I don't scream, he relaxes.

"It wouldn't matter anyway." He drags a hand over his face. "No one in Ellender will blink an eye at a human screaming."

I go rigid. "Did you just say 'Ellender?'"

He nods, giving me a pointed look like I'm missing something obvious. "Of course. Don't act so surprised."

My heartbeat quickens, pounding in my ears. *Holy Fuck.*

Ellender is the kingdom from Nana's books. It's a magical fantasy world that every teenage girl would die to visit. Except, *it's not real.* Could Daemon be some kind of crazed fan?

Oh my God, no wonder he said he likes crazy girls. The man is literally delusional.

Daemon sits in his chair in front of the door while I sift through every true crime podcast I've ever heard, every episode of *Law & Order: SVU*, and the street smarts assembly from middle school. I need to force him to leave me alone—otherwise, I'll never get a chance to find a way to escape.

"Can I have some more water?"

He reaches for the mug that I refused to drink and holds it out to me. I lean forward to take it, but intentionally fumble my fingers. It crashes to the floor and rolls under the bed.

"Sorry!"

Daemon sighs, annoyed, and glances at his pitcher. "I need to refill this."

My heart leaps in excitement as he walks toward the door. I don't see him take out any key, but the lock clicks anyway. Swinging the door open, he stops, his bulk blocking anything outside from sight. "I'll be back in a second. Don't move."

I nod, my heart pounding so hard I'm almost surprised he can't hear it. "Sure."

He slips outside and shuts the door behind him with a snap. I wait with bated breath, hoping he'll forget to lock the door, but to my dismay, I hear a click, then the echo of his retreating footsteps.

A cold rush of adrenaline washes over me, making the hair on the back of my neck stand on end. I jump to my feet and turn in an awkward circle, searching for a phone or a clock or something. I can only assume we're in a hotel. It's not like any hotel I've ever seen, but the decor is so grand there's no chance this is his house.

I make my way over to the nearest window on wobbling legs. Clearing a patch of condensation, I press my nose to the cool glass and squint out at the rain-soaked surroundings. All I see are mountains and a patch of dark sky. That tells me nothing—the mountains could be anywhere in the Appalachians, and the dark sky could be a product of either the storm or the time of day. It could be noon for all I know.

Undeterred, I turn and dash to the door, trying the knob. I'm not surprised to find it locked, but disappointment washes over me all the same. I examine the door handle then. It's heavy and brass, with a keyhole large enough that I can see a sliver of light from out in the hall. I turn back to the room, and I scan for anything that will help me get the door open.

Aside from the enormous bed, there isn't all that much other furniture in the room. I throw open a large white and gold wardrobe and find it empty. Beside that, there is a small vanity table with nothing on it but a golden candelabra and an empty chipped teacup.

Frustration surges through me as I yank open the vanity drawer. I blindly reach toward the back, my fingers fumbling across the smooth wood until they brush against something small and thin. Relief floods through me as I pull out a vintage-looking bobby pin. *Hell yes.*

It only takes a few jiggles of the pin before I hear the lock click. I throw the door open and an involuntary scream falls from my lips. On the other side of the door, clearly trying to open it at the same time I was, is a...*creature.*

The creature is short, barely reaching my mid-chest, and dressed in a child-sized Renaissance faire costume—a long red skirt, a corset-style black cotton bodice, and a matching jacket. But it's not the clothes that have me screaming.

It's her face.

It's not...human.

There's no other way to describe it, and my brain is struggling to come up with an explanation. This thing isn't human, but neither does she look like an animal. Her scaly mauve-colored skin is stretched around an angular face that's sort of mouse-like in shape. Her eyes are beetle-black and pupilless like an insect.

"Lady Isabelle?" the creature asks in a high-pitched voice. "Are you well?"

She steps toward me, a white teapot in her long, bony hand. I scream louder, scrambling backward against the side of the bed.

The creature's face twists—in alarm, I think—before she cranes her neck over her shoulder. "Odessa! Come in here."

Before I can do anything more than flatten myself against the bed, another black-and-red-clothed figure appears in the doorway.

The second stranger is at least human in shape, though somehow that's hardly better. This woman has a face that is so ridiculously beautiful she doesn't look real. She tosses her long, strawberry blonde hair over one shoulder and wrinkles her nose at me. "What's going on?"

The first creature turns to the newcomer and cocks her head to the side in something like a shrug. "Something is wrong with our lady."

I look frantically between AI Barbie and the purplish alien. Looking at them fills me with an uncanny dread that makes me want to curl into a ball on the floor. Instead, I glance at the door. It's still wide open. Deciding to trust my instincts for once, I dive around the startled monsters and into the hall.

*Oh my God. Oh my God, oh my God!*

I sprint down the hall, and shouts echo behind me.

I barely notice my surroundings as I run, passing door after door. I don't know where the fuck I am, or what's going on, but I am not waiting around to get answers. I am getting the hell out of here, right now.

*I can do this.*

I run until I come to the top of an enormous flight of stone steps. The stairs descend into an entrance hall. I bolt downward, taking the steps two at a time, and reach the floor just in time to spot more alien creatures—some blue, some a reddish brown, and some so pale they look translucent.

The nearest creature steps toward me, cocking its large head to the side in a mimicry of concern. "My lady? Has something happened?"

*Holy shit. Never mind, I cannot do this.*

Like any self-respecting child of the 2000s, I've read my share of fantasy books. I've seen movies with aliens and monsters, with special effects so good they almost feel real. But there's a big difference between watching a CGI creature on a screen and staring into the enormous, bug-like eyes of a very real humanoid goblin.

This has to be a dream—some really fucked up, roofie-induced nightmare because there's no way I really fell straight into one of my fantasy books.

I lunge past the creature and toward the towering double doors. I throw myself against them, using all my strength to push through their weight until they finally give way and I tumble outside.

My brain comes to a screeching halt. I'd expected that if I could get outside, I'd have some idea of where I am, but somehow I'm more confused than ever.

The doors open onto a long, sweeping staircase that descends into what I can only describe as the grounds of a castle, with a wide lawn, enormous rose garden, and towering mountains in the distance.

To add insult to injury, it's *raining*.

I'd forgotten the downpour pelting against my window in my haste to escape, but now, it quickly saturates my hair and soaks through my thin T-shirt.

I look like I'm competing in the world's saddest wet T-shirt contest.

"Hey!" a loud male voice shouts from behind me. "What are you doing?"

The shout makes my back stiffen, and I instinctively straighten and look over my shoulder.

To my relief, it isn't Daemon.

A group of unfamiliar men jog after me across the entrance hall of the castle. I think it was the one in the lead who yelled. He's tall and just as handsome as Daemon, with deep bronze skin and medium-length wavy black hair, which falls into his narrowed dark eyes. He's dressed like something between a revolutionary war soldier and an extra in a pirate movie, with tight black pants tucked into knee-high boots and a cardinal-red military jacket.

For a long charged second, I stand on the steps, letting the rain soak me to the bone as I try to decide if I should ask for help or keep running. Then, I snap out of it.

*I choose the bear.*

I twirl on my heel and dash down the slippery stone steps.

"Shit," the strange man curses behind me. "Ashwater! Get down here, your damsel is in fucking distress."

My heart skyrockets as I run across the lawn and toward the dirt road, desperate to put as much distance between myself and the castle as possible.

I need to find help. A person with a phone or a gas station. *Anything.*

Unfortunately, I see nothing but trees and rose bushes all along the dirt road, and the horizon is obscured by the pouring rain.

I'm not much of a runner, and this is more exercise than I've probably done in a year. A stitch is burning in my side, and my breath feels sharp, like inhaling smoke. Tears begin to spill down my cheeks and I gasp for air.

I feel like I'm playing the worst game of *would-you-rather* in history.

Would you rather that your one night stand kidnapped you and took you to a castle full of monsters, or that you're really hallucinating in a mental hospital amidst a divorce-induced psychotic break?

Alongside the road, I spot a patch of thick trees and launch myself toward them. I fall to my knees behind the nearest tree and double over, dry heaving with both exhaustion and terror.

I want to cry, but I'm afraid if I start, I won't be able to stop. I don't know what could possibly be worse than this.

Then, as if summoned by my thoughts, things immediately get worse. Alanis Morissette would be losing her mind over the irony.

A deep growl echoes behind me and every muscle in my body goes tense. Slowly, I turn around and look up into a pair of piercing yellow eyes.

A blood-curdling scream bursts from me, and I scramble backward, trying to put as much distance between myself and the largest wolf I've ever seen.

Actually, what the fuck am I thinking? I've never seen a wolf in real life.

Still, somehow, I'm positive that this one is *far* bigger than it's supposed to be.

Its body is huge and covered in thick, matted hair. Its teeth are only a few shades lighter than its eyes and longer than my forearms. They glisten with drool in the faint light filtering through the trees.

My hands tremble as I frantically run them over the ground behind me, searching for a weapon. I need a rock or a stick or something—any kind of defense against the snarling beast in front of me. But I only come up with mud and rain-soaked leaves.

The wolf's hot breath brushes over me as its ears flatten against its head and it lets out a low, menacing growl. Its sharp teeth flash as it opens its jaws wide, ready to attack.

*I'm dead.* I know I'm dead, yet I can't seem to make my mind accept it.

I close my eyes tightly and raise my hands over my face. I'm about to fight this beast to the bitter end, even if it makes my death all the more painful.

Suddenly, a pair of strong arms wrap around me from behind and lift me off the ground. I suck in a startled breath as I rise into the air, higher, higher...*way too fucking high!*

My eyes fly open, and I find myself staring not at a wolf but at a familiar tattooed chest.

"I told you to stay in the damn castle!" Daemon's voice rumbles through his chest, as he holds me tightly, bursting out of the trees and flying over the castle grounds below.

I can't think of an answer. I'm too amazed by the fact that we're flying; *he's fucking flying.* I barely have a second to process it before he lands, setting me gently on the wet grass beside the towering castle wall.

Turning to face me, he grabs my shoulders, shaking me slightly as his intense gaze bores into mine. "Are you hurt?"

I try to speak, but no words come out. I can only stare in shock at the enormous wings protruding from his back. They're black and red and feathered—like a cross between a bird and a butterfly. They would be beautiful if they weren't so terrifying.

"Isabelle?" Daemon asks urgently, shaking me harder. "Are you hurt? Say something."

I barely even register him calling me by the wrong name. I yank myself out of his grip and double over, dry-heaving onto the ground.

I'm soaked, freezing, and about to throw up, which kind of rules out the possibility that this is a dream.

That means that I'm actually standing outside a castle filled with goblins. I *actually* almost got eaten by a wolf. And the guy I picked up at a bar can *actually* fly.

*I'm not in fucking Kansas anymore.*

My vision swims, a wave of dizziness descending over me like a dark cloak. My eyes roll up into my head, and I feel myself falling.

My last thought before I go crashing into Daemon's waiting arms is that this isn't just some dream.

Ellender isn't just a fantasy.

Nana's books are real, and somehow, I'm in one.

# CHAPTER SIX

ALIX



"*You were supposed to bring her straight to the king.*"

"*Yeah? What do you think Thorne would do if he saw his bride dressed like that?*"

"*So you decided to leave her alone to go running through the castle? Nice, Ashwater.*"

When I wake for the second time, it takes me less than a second to know where I am.

The scent of roses as well as the mattress beneath my cheek tells me I'm back in the ornate castle bedroom. Worse, the wet chill covering my body makes it clear that I'm still wearing Daemon's soaked and muddy T-shirt. *Gross.*

I want nothing more than to tear this thing off and crawl under the covers, but I resist. I keep my eyes closed, listening to three male voices arguing. I'm almost certain one of the voices is Daemon's. The other two are harder to place.

"I didn't have time to come up with a better plan," Daemon says. "How was I supposed to know she wouldn't recognize Odessa?"

"I don't understand why this happened in the first place," a lower, huskier voice replies.

"Yeah," says the third voice, with a smile in his tone. "We're not stupid, Ashwater. What the fuck were you thinking? No woman is worth going back to Dyaspora."

There's a loud bang, like the sound of a fist hitting the wall. "I was thinking I had no idea who she was."

Keeping my eyes closed, I tune out the voices. I need a plan.

Part of me still wants to believe that I'm dreaming or stuck in some perpetual renaissance faire, but I can't even sell that lie to myself. I just saw an entire castle full of magical creatures that not even *Disney World* could replicate. The only possibility is I am in Ellender.

Unfortunately, that doesn't make me feel the tiniest bit less crazy.

"Stop arguing," a fourth voice chimes in harshly, cutting off the background chatter. "She's awake."

I go stiff, feeling a room full of eyes on me. My closed eyes twitch, and I try not to move, feigning sleep.

A chair creaks, and I hear footsteps approaching, and sense the heat of a body leaning over me. "You're a bad actress, Peaches."

*Damn it.*

I open my eyes and look up into Daemon's brilliant green gaze. "Don't call me that."

Just as I thought, I'm back in the enormous bedroom with Daemon, but this time, we're not alone. In addition to Daemon, there are three strange men gathered around my bedside. All four of them are dressed identically in black pants tucked into shiny black boots, and bright-red military jackets.

Instantly, my gaze darts to Daemon's shoulders.

They're normal—aside from the golden tassels of his toy soldier costume. I'm 100% sure that if everything I've seen so far is real, then the wings were real too. But they're nowhere to be seen. I don't know whether that's a relief or more frightening.

"What's going on?" I ask, my voice shaking a little. "Who are you?"

Daemon's eyes narrow. "They're the ones who warned me you were outside in time to find you."

I narrow my own eyes in response. I'm the one who has the right to be angry here and *he's* giving *me* attitude?

The bronze-skinned man to Daemon's right looks between us and rolls his eyes. "Excuse him. I wish I could say the ninety years in prison are to blame for his manners but he was always like this. I'm Kastian."

Kastian holds out a hand for me to shake, and I grasp his fingers robotically, unable to think about anything besides *ninety years in prison*. Is that supposed to be a joke?

"That's Jett." Kastian points at a handsome east-Asian-looking man, who immediately flashes me a wide grin. He has close cropped black hair and impossibly straight, white teeth. He's shorter and thinner than Daemon or Kastian, but his muscles stand out even beneath the fabric of his own red jacket.

"And this"—Kastian claps a hand down on the fourth man's broad shoulder— "is Fox. He doesn't talk much, don't take it personally."

Fox's expression is flat, almost bored, and he barely looks at me as I sit up straighter. He's by far the largest of the group with muscles like a bodybuilder. His skin is pale, and his blond hair is tied back in a bun at the nape of his neck. He reminds me of a Viking.

"O-okay," I stammer. "Got it. Now tell me what the hell is going on. Why did you bring me here?"

Daemon falters, looking at a loss for what to say. Again, Kastian calmly takes over, leaning forward to look directly into my eyes. "No one is going to hurt you. You're safe here."

"Safe?" I scoff, inching further away from him. "Dude, there are *goblins* downstairs. I don't know about you, but that's not what I'd call fucking safe."

His soothing expression cracks. He raises an eyebrow and turns to Daemon. His eyes go wide, and he mouths *"Goblins?"* in a way that clearly translates to *What the fuck?*

*My thoughts exactly, dude; what the absolute fuck.*

Without warning, a bulky mass of ash-colored fur launches itself onto my lap. My heart jolts with fear, and I scramble backward, ready to defend myself from another terrifying creature.

Then the beast meows at me. "Sushi?"

Nana's enormous gray cat makes himself comfortable on my bed. My gaze flicks to Daemon. "Oh my fucking God. You didn't just kidnap me, you took my grandmother's cat too?"

"I thought you'd appreciate having your pet with you," Daemon drawls.

*Oh, so he's a thoughtful kidnapper now? Yeah right.*

Half furious, half terrified, I scramble out of bed.

The moment I stand, I realize that probably wasn't the best idea.

Daemon's wet shirt is stuck to my body which leaves absolutely nothing to the imagination. I might as well just take it off.

Shivering, I quickly cross my arms to cover myself. "Can I get something dry to wear? *Please?*"

Daemon stares at me for a long, charged second. Then, seeming to remember we're not alone, he tears his eyes off me and glowers at his friends. "Here." He rips the quilt off the bed and throws it at me. "Use that while we find you some clothes. Where's Odessa?"

"I'll get her," Jett says cheerfully, edging toward the door. "I saw her yesterday when we arrived, and Gods, she looks like she'd—"

"Stop!" Daemon and Kastian bark at precisely the same time.

Jett just grins wider. "I was just going to say she looks like she'd be really nice. I'll be right back."

"Yeah, I'll fucking bet that's what he was going to say," Daemon grumbles, running both hands through his burnt-honey hair. "Fox, go with him. He'll just end up bothering Dessa for the next hour, and Isabelle will freeze to death before Thorne ever knows she's here."

Fox nods and rises silently, following Jett out of the room. I barely notice him go, unable to split my attention as I stand with my arms crossed, dazedly watching Sushi make biscuits in the silk bedspread. There's a low buzzing in my ears and that's the third time someone has called me 'Isabelle.'

*What the fuck is going on?*

Daemon leans over to Kastian. "I don't know how long we can avoid Thorne. He's bound to know she's here after that shitshow downstairs."

Kastian rolls his eyes. "Actually, your luck continues to astound me, Ashwater. The king isn't here."

"What?" Daemon barks sharply. "Why? Where is he?"

"No one expected you back so soon. Last night the king dropped us here with the rest of the soldiers he doesn't want to keep close, then left for the Winter Palace."

Daemon lets out something between a laugh and a sigh of relief, then runs a hand through his already disheveled hair. "Damn. That's the first real stroke of luck I've had in the last century."

Kastian rolls his eyes again.

Just then, the door swings open again and Jett walks inside, followed by Fox. Now, they're accompanied by the same AI Barbie who was in my room before I tried to run. She's carrying an armful of fabric and laughing lightly at something Jett must have said in the hall.

My eyes widen and I take a wary step backward.

Everyone in the room is model-material, but this woman is a little creepy. She's curvy, like the Venus in the half-shell, with red-blonde hair that looks straight out of a shampoo commercial. Her face is way too symmetrical, her movements slightly too graceful to be real, and now that I'm looking more closely at her, I notice that her eyes aren't blue, they're *violet*. Like Harold and the purple fucking crayon.

"Oh hell," the woman says briskly, looking me up and down. "What have you all done to her?"

"We didn't do anything," Daemon mutters. "She did that to herself by running outside in the middle of a damn storm. She needs something else to wear."

"Clearly!" The woman laughs. "Don't worry, I'll fix her up before she goes to see the king."

I don't like how they're talking about me like I'm not here. Like I'm an object to be dragged around and dressed up for their own inscrutable purposes. The woman hurries toward me, and I shrink back toward the window.

At my obvious fear and disgust, the woman stops short, looking at me with concern. "Isabelle? What's wrong?"

"Oh my God!" I burst out. "Can you all stop calling me Isabelle? My name is Alix!"

I'm met with confused gazes, and there's a long pause before Daemon speaks. "You mean you were going by Alix to avoid suspicion, right?"

"No, genius, I mean my name *is* Alix. *Alixandria Knight.*"

Something weird is going on here—weirder even than being kidnapped by my one-night stand and ending up in a fantasy land. Somehow, they seem just as confused as I feel.

"Look," I continue, almost pleading. "I don't know what's going on here for *so* many reasons, but if you made a mistake or something, you can just bring me home now. I won't tell anyone, *I promise.* I wouldn't, anyway. I mean, claiming to have been to Ellender is a one-way ticket to a padded cell, so..." I trail off.

The men seem bewildered, but Odessa narrows her eyes, scrutinizing me. She walks around the side of the bed, coming close enough to look directly into my face.

"My Gods," Odessa breathes. "You're *not* Isabelle."

"What?" Daemon barks. "What the fuck are you talking about? Of course she is."

Odessa shakes her head. "She's not. It's been sixty years, but I remember my friend. Belle wasn't afraid of me. This isn't her."

"But she has the necklace," Daemon insists, hurrying around the side of the bed to stand in front of me. "And I found this!" He reaches into his back pocket and extracts a paperback copy of Nana's book. "Look," he says, pointing at the cover. "Her name is on it."

"That's not me." I almost laugh. "Isabelle is my grandmother."

Daemon and Odessa freeze, staring at me. After a long second, Daemon's face cracks into a smile. He looks like he's on the verge of laughing, like he thinks I'm fucking with him.

"Sure, Peaches." Daemon flips the book in his hand over to look at the back, then shoves it in front of my face, showing me the author photo beneath the blurb. "That's you. Isabelle Reading."

I look at the photo and wince. Why would the publisher choose this picture?

The photo is maybe forty years old, probably taken when *A Kingdom of Thorns* was first released. In the photo, Nana is in her late forties, but she looks at least two decades younger. She has the same long curly brown hair as me, our eyes are a similar shade of blue, and most incriminating of all, she's wearing the gold and ruby locket.

"That photo is old," I say. "It's not me. It's my Nana. Are you telling me that you know her? Like she's actually been to Ellender?

Daemon ignores my question. He glances at the photo, then back to me. "But you're identical."

"I guess?" I say weakly. "But it's not me, so whatever you were planning, I can't help you."

Daemon backs away from me and walks slowly around the bed again before sinking into his chair. He looks...broken. "That's it, then. We're all dead."

My brows furrow as I take in Daemon's shattered expression mirrored on every face in the room. "Um, that's a little dramatic, don't you think? How are you dead? Why did you want to bring my grandmother here?"

"Did Belle tell you anything about Ellender?" Odessa asks.

"Of course," I say, almost laughing. "She wrote that entire book about it."

As I speak, the full gravity of this situation finally dawns on me. If Nana's book wasn't fiction, and she actually came here at some point, maybe all of it was real. My gaze falls on Jett, who is the only one with short enough hair that I can clearly see the tips of his ears. Sure enough, they're pointed. "Oh my God," I blurt out. "You're Fae."

The four men just stare at me, but Odessa laughs. "Actually, I'm a siren, but I wouldn't have to be to see that you desperately need a bath.

Why don't you step into the bathing room with me, *Alix*. I'll help you get cleaned up and then we can all talk about how to fix this mess."

ODESSA LEADS ME INTO A LARGE ENSUITE BATHROOM, WHICH she calls the "*bathing*" room and closes the door behind us.

The bathroom is nearly half the size of the bedroom, with a white marble floor and towering ceilings lined entirely in arched windows. It's still raining heavily, letting almost no light in from outside. Instead, there are brightly lit oil lamps on the wall between the windows. In the center of the room, a round bathtub looks so inviting I could cry.

"I'm all set." I tell Odessa. "I don't need your help or anything. Just some dry clothes would be great."

To my chagrin, she walks over to the enormous porcelain tub and turns on the faucets. "Don't be silly. I don't mind helping."

"Respectfully, I'm not so sure I want to get naked in front of a stranger."

"*Respectfully,*" she mimics, raising an eyebrow and looking me up and down, "that ship has long sailed. You've been flashing the entire castle since the moment you got here."

My face flames and I silently cross my arms tightly over my chest, covering as much as possible of my wet T-shirt.

Odessa cracks a smile and sits on the edge of the tub. "Look, don't worry. I'm not going to stay, I'm just making sure you're settled and then I'm going to go find you some different clothes. I thought I was dressing you to go meet the king, but you don't need to wear a gown."

I huff. "Thanks."

I should probably be more grateful for her help but I'm really struggling to find it in myself to be grateful for anything at the moment. Anyway, Odessa still kind of freaks me out.

As if she read my mind, Odessa speaks up. "You'll get used to it—to me, that is."

I don't have to ask what she means and even though I'm beyond freaked out, I can't resist the urge to make sure I didn't offend her. "I'm sorry, I'm sure you're very nice, it's just..."

"You're frightened of me," she finishes, nodding. "Humans are so funny about that. You should be much more afraid of the Fae than the sirens. Outside the water, I'm no stronger than you are, but the Fae could kill you without blinking an eye."

I swallow thickly. She's wrong actually; I'm equally afraid of everyone at the moment, but it does help to know she's not any stronger than me. Anyway, if she really was friends with my Nana, she can't be all bad.

"So, you know my grandmother?"

Odessa trails her fingers in the rapidly rising bathwater. "Yes. Isabelle and I were fast friends. As I'm sure you and I will be."

*Yeah, no. No thank you.*

"I'm not sure I'll be here long enough to make any friends. I'm pretty much hoping that now Daemon has realized he fucked up, he'll take me home."

Odessa purses her lips, looking slightly disapproving. "Interesting."

I don't know what to make of her response and struggle to come up with anything to say. In the silence, a horrible idea occurs to me. "Oh my God. He's not your husband or something, is he? Please say no. That would be just fucking perfect. I'm trying to get over my own cheating asshole husband and end up being the other woman. Fuck, what is wrong with—"

"Hey, wait!" She holds up both hands, interrupting my diatribe. "Calm down."

I really wish people would stop telling me to calm down, but in this case, it might be warranted. I take a gasping breath and try to quell my panic. "I am so, so sorry. As soon as I can leave, believe me, I will."

"Alix, please stop. Daemon isn't my husband. He's my cousin. Kind of. Really more of a brother, actually."

"Oh." I blink at her, confused. "Okay...that's good, I guess."

She laughs. "You need to stop jumping to the worst possible conclusion."

"Yeah, well, rational thinking kind of abandoned me when I woke up in a castle full of goblins," I mumble. "So how can you be cousins if you're not Fae?"

She waves a hand in the air as if shooing away my question. "We're cousins by marriage, but were raised together like siblings. It's hardly anything you need to be worried about. All that matters is that for however long you're here, I'm happy to have you. Your grandmother was the last human to come here who I truly liked. I miss her."

"When did my Nana come here?" I ask quickly, glad for the change of subject.

"Nearly sixty years ago," she replies, standing abruptly.

"How long did she stay? What happened—"

Odessa cuts me off with another laugh as she walks toward the door.

"You have a lot more questions than she did. I think I'd better let Daemon answer them for you. This is his mess anyway."

"But wait!"

With her hand on the knob, she turns, her expression sympathetic. "Breathe, Alix. You don't need to hear the entire history of Ellender before you've even taken a bath. Just try to relax, and I'm just going to find you something else to wear. Do you have any requests?"

"Sweatpants?" I blurt out without thinking.

She laughs melodically. "Unfortunately, no. I wish. Human clothing is so interesting, I'd just die to be a part of your world."

On that enigmatic note, she closes the door, leaving me alone. For a long moment, I don't move. I stare blankly at the bathtub, still disbelieving that I'm really here.

*Nana, what the hell were you hiding?*

# CHAPTER SEVEN

DAEMON

"I don't know what you're up to, but I think we can safely say you've fucked it up."

I scowl as Odessa shuts the door behind her with a snap and strides into the bedroom.

We have hardly moved or spoken since Odessa had the good sense to get Alix out of the room. I'm grateful for her timing. The situation is bad enough as it is, but wasn't made any easier by the fact that I couldn't focus on anything except Alix's body in my wet shirt.

"You're not helping."

"I wasn't trying to help you," Odessa retorts, standing in front of me with her hands on her hips. "You've been back for all of a few hours, I don't even get a hello, and now you've kidnapped the wrong woman. That's quite an entrance."

My frown remains in place, but I stand begrudgingly to give my cousin a one-armed hug. It's been ninety years since I've seen Dessa, and I did miss her—even if at this precise moment, I can't recall why.

"How's my mother?" I ask, withdrawing from the hug.

"Fine, I believe," Dessa says a bit bitterly. "She's living at the Ashwater Estate."

I nod curtly. "You didn't go with her?"

She shakes her head. "You're lucky I didn't. How would you have recognized Alix without my help?"

I step back, my frown deepening, and sink into my chair. "This is a fucking nightmare. Did you find out what she knows?"

Dessa shrugs, leaning against the bedpost. "It's hard to tell. The book that Isabelle wrote will undoubtedly shed some light on things."

"I need to read this book," Jett pipes up, grinning.

"When have you ever read a book?" Kastian asks.

Jett shrugs. "There's a first time for everything."

I roll my eyes. "I doubt you'll have time. The second he finds out we don't have Isabelle, Thorne will send us all back to Dyaspora. We'll be lucky to be out for an entire day."

"I suspect you'll have at least a few days," Dessa says. "It will take that long for anyone to reach the king at the Winter Palace."

I pinch the bridge of my nose. "If that's the case, we should start running now. Maybe if we can avoid Thorne until the rose moon..." I trail off, realizing as I speak that there'll be no escape for me. The others might go free if they avoid the king until the curse becomes permanent, but if it's not broken in the next few weeks, I'll be lost to the curse forever just like everyone else.

"We could run," Kastian chimes in, "but what about Alix? What are you going to do with her?"

"Nothing," I growl. "I'll send her back home before Thorne ever knows she was here. I'll just tell him I found Isabelle, but she aged."

"But then there's no chance of breaking the curse," Odessa interrupts.

"There wasn't, anyway." My voice comes out rough and angry, but it's not Odessa or my friends that I'm mad at. "Thorne didn't leave enough time. He's fucked all of us. The curse isn't going to break, and telling him about Alix won't change that."

"Is Isabelle dead?" Kastian asks.

I shake my head. "I don't know. I don't think so from the way Alix talked about her, but wherever she is, she clearly didn't wear the necklace for the last sixty years."

"You should use her," Fox says flatly.

I'm startled by his suggestion. He's so silent, I had almost forgotten he was in the room. Judging by the way everyone turns to look at him, they had too.

"Aren't you listening? We can't use Isabelle."

Fox looks pained, like explaining himself is causing physical agony. "No, use Alix. You took that woman because you thought she was the king's bride. They're identical. Just take her to Thorne instead."

"That's fucking absurd," I say, laughing. "Thorne would notice that Alix isn't Isabelle."

"How do you know?" Jett says with a shrug.

"He's evil but he's not fucking stupid. It would be hard to miss that your betrothed was switched out with another person."

"No one else noticed, and they're not stupid either," Kastian says slowly. "And remember that the king didn't recognize me. He's not exactly observant."

"Why should he recognize you?" Jett scoffs. "You've never met him, have you?"

Kastian ignores Jett, still focusing on me. "Thorne hasn't seen the real Isabelle in sixty years. It could work."

I round on him. "You're not serious."

Kas puts both hands up as if in surrender. "I'm just making an observation. It's been a long time since they've seen each other and I doubt he ever paid much attention."

I shake my head angrily "Thorne might not notice that she's not her grandmother, but there's still the fact that Alix is not Isabelle. She can't break the curse."

"How do you break it?" Jett asks.

"It only breaks when the king finds his true love," Odessa explains.

"That's fucking stupid." Fox scoffs. "Why would anyone cast that curse?"

"Spite," I mutter bitterly. "Ninety-nine years ago, Thorne was betrothed to a woman the entire kingdom believed was his soul-bonded mate."

"She wasn't?" Jett asks.

I shake my head. "Apparently not, because the week before their wedding, he betrayed her with another woman. Unfortunately, the girl was a powerful sorceress. She was so heartbroken that she cast the curse on the entire kingdom, then flung herself off a tower."

Jett makes a startled noise, and Kastian's eyebrows raise so high they nearly disappear into his hair. Even Fox looks surprised.

I'm not shocked by their reaction.

Everyone knows that once mated, Fae males never stray from their partners. Ever. It's not exactly a choice, but a compulsion—a biological shift that only happens once in a lifetime. That's why it's so astonishing to hear the reason for Thorne's curse. I've only ever heard of two cases of infidelity in the history of the kingdom: my brother is one. The other is our shared father who betrayed the queen by taking my mother to his bed. Betrayal runs so deep in our family it's practically written on my bones.

"So you see, I don't think Thorne is capable of loving anyone."

"He must think there's a chance if he was so concerned about finding Isabelle," Odessa points out.

"True, but he doesn't love Alix and she certainly doesn't love him back."

"Does she have to?" Jett asks.

I frown. "What do you mean?"

"Is the curse broken if the king loves someone and they love him back? Or is it just that *he* has to love *her*?"

"That's an interesting question," Kastian muses. "If Thorne loves Isabelle and believes Alix *is* Isabelle, would it break the curse?"

My frown deepens, an uneasy feeling churning my stomach. "Wait a minute." I grit my teeth. "What are you suggesting?"

Kastian runs a hand over his jaw. "If it doesn't matter if she loves him back, maybe Fox is right. You could bring Alix to him instead. It might work."

"Exactly," Jett says, jumping on the chance to keep pushing his theory. "The worst that can happen if he notices is that we'll be thrown back in Dyaspora, just the same as if you don't bring her at all."

"Or he could kill us on the spot," I growl.

Kastian looks sideways at me. "Could he, though? That's a serious question—is he stronger than you?"

"We're evenly matched," I admit. "Or, we were, ninety years ago. All four of us together could beat him, but he has thousands of guards and I trained most of them myself so they wouldn't be easy targets..." I shake my head roughly. "But none of that matters because we're not doing this. As far as I'm concerned, you four should start running now. You're not cursed. Leave me here and go into hiding outside Vernallis until after the rose moon."

"While you just wait to die in a month?" Kastian asks angrily.

"Yes," I snap. "I've accepted it. I stopped expecting the curse to break years ago. What other choice is there except acceptance?"

Odessa flounces across the room to the dark window and peers outside, as if she can see anything beyond the rain. "If you ask me, you should try it, Daemon. At least ask Alix. If we leave you here, you'll die in a matter of weeks. If we bring Alix to Thorne, there's at least a small chance of saving everyone."

The uneasy feeling in my stomach churns harder, like excitement mixed with dread. "What about Alix?"

"What about her?" Fox rumbles.

"I can't force her to agree to marry a stranger."

"Maybe she'd be into it," Jett says, grinning widely. "Sure, Thorne is a first-class asshole, but he's a king! He's handsome and rich. What woman wouldn't be willing to overlook a few flaws if it meant she could be a queen."

I have no idea why but I have the strongest urge to punch Jett for saying that. I ball my hands into fists, forcing myself to stay calm.

Kastian shakes his head. "Don't worry about the details for a moment. The immediate problem is convincing Thorne that Alix is Isabelle. You could make a deal with her. Give her something she wants in exchange for playing along."

"Like what?" I ask through gritted teeth. "We don't have anything she would want. Maybe if this was before Dyaspora, but any money or land I had is gone."

"Then lie," Fox grumbles, shrugging.

"That's fucked," I snap.

"So is Dyaspora," he replies, his gaze hardening. "If it's a choice between lying to some human woman we don't know and all of us going back there, it's not even a question for me. It shouldn't be a question for you either. Who's more important? Your own life and all of ours, or the comfort of a woman you fucked once and have known for less than twelve hours?"

I hate that he's right.

I just met Alix last night, but I've been friends with them for decades. My loyalty should be to them and myself only. So why do I feel like shit about this?

I run a frustrated hand through my hair, and close my eyes in defeat. "Fine. You're right, I'll talk to her. But I can't force her to agree. It could still fall apart."

"Not a problem, Ashwater," Jett says cheerfully. "When have you ever had difficulty getting anyone to follow you? Especially women."

Again, I hate that he's right. I know I can convince Alix to help us; I just wish I didn't have to.

FIFTEEN MINUTES LATER, I STEEL MYSELF AND FIX A BORED expression on my face before knocking on the bathing room door.

"Come in!" Alix calls out.

She's wrapped in a large towel and stands with her back to me, squeezing water out of her hair with a second towel.

"Oh, hey, I'm just finishing up," Alix says, still not looking at me. "Did you end up finding any sweatpants?"

I shut the door behind me with a snap. "Afraid not, Peaches."

She jumps, her spine going straight, and whirls around to look at me. "What the fuck are you doing here?"

I raise an eyebrow. "You said to come in."

"I thought you were Odessa."

"Sorry to disappoint."

She wraps her towel more tightly around herself and looks down, unable to meet my eyes. "Get the fuck out, I'm not dressed."

The corner of my mouth twitches up in a smirk. "You can't exactly cry scandal. I've seen it all before."

Her cheeks flush pink. "Yeah, well, enjoy the memories because that's not ever happening again. Seriously, now get out!"

I ignore her protests and cross my arms over my chest, leaning against the wall. "Calm down, Peaches. I need to talk to you."

"Unless you want to talk about taking me home, then I don't want to hear it."

"Actually, that's exactly what it's about."

Her glare intensifies, and she mutters darkly under her breath before pulling the towel even tighter and sitting on the edge of the tub. She raises an expectant eyebrow at me. "Fine. Shoot."

I shake my head to clear it and blink a few times, casting my gaze at a point over her shoulder. I need to fucking focus.

I decided to have this conversation this way to put Alix at a disadvantage, but I'm starting to think I played myself. All I can think about is how easy it would be to yank her towel away and pick up right where we left off in the human realm.

"Well?" she says, annoyed at my silence.

I clear my throat. "I'm sorry. Despite how it probably looks to you, I don't typically kidnap women and I didn't plan to bring you here. I didn't know who you were."

"Right, so you were just planning to kidnap my grandmother?" Alix scoffs. "That's so much better."

"Look," I growl, frustrated, "I don't want to be involved in this any more than you do. I've never met Isabelle. If it were up to me, I wouldn't have brought her here either."

"So why were you looking for her?"

"It's complicated," I grind out. "Our king was put under a curse nearly a hundred years ago."

"I know about that," she says quickly. "It's in the book, but I thought the curse was broken."

*I need to read this damn book.*

"It wasn't broken, and unless it is by the end of the month, it will become permanent."

She lets out a breath. "I'm sorry. That sucks for you—seriously— but I don't know what you want me to say. I'm still processing that this is all real, okay? I definitely can't help you with anything, um, curse related..."

I stare at her, unsure where to go from here. "How is the curse broken in your book?"

"True love," she says, sounding a bit embarrassed.

"At least that part's right." *Sort of.*

"Wait, seriously? So you're telling me that the real King Thorne actually loves my grandmother?"

"I have no idea whether he does or not. All I know is that he came to me yesterday and asked me to find Isabelle."

"And you just jumped at the opportunity to kidnap a stranger? Who the hell does that?"

I take an involuntary step forward. "I didn't exactly have a choice," I bark. "Until yesterday, I hadn't been back in this palace in ninety years. I've spent decades longer than you've been alive in prison slowly freezing, working eighteen hours a day in the mines, then fighting to stay alive until morning."

Alix leans back, trying to put more distance between us. "So you escaped from prison to find my Nana?"

"No one has ever escaped Dyaspora. There's never been a pardon in the history of Ellender, until yesterday when Thorne offered me and my friends a chance to return to court in exchange for finding one human woman. That might seem selfish to you, Peaches, but after one day in the Dyaspora you wouldn't believe what men would do for a chance to escape. I used to have a life here—lands and money and people who depended on me. I could have all that restored. What would you do in my place?"

"Depends." She cocks her head. "What did you do to get sent to prison?"

I let out a defeated sigh. "It's a long story. Look, can you just understand that I didn't have a lot of good options. And I still don't. If I don't bring Isabelle to the king, he'll throw all of us back there without a fucking thought."

She shakes her head slowly, and conflict wars on her face. Finally, she lets out a defeated breath. "Okay fine, I get that, I guess...even though that doesn't really sound like something King Thorne would do."

I let out a harsh laugh. "Maybe not the fictional version you're familiar with. Trust me, Peaches, Thorne is no one's fantasy hero."

She scowls. "Fine, whatever. But why you? Why would he ask you to find my Nana if you didn't know her?"

I open my mouth to tell her that Thorne is my half-brother, then close it again. For some reason, I don't want her to know that. Maybe because soon, she'll meet him and realize what kind of man he is. I'd rather die than have anyone think we're the same.

So instead, I offer her a partial truth. "I used to travel to your world frequently. That's not unheard of here, but it's far from common. It requires more magic than most Fae have to spare."

"Why did you want to go to my world?"

Again, I falter. I don't really want to tell her about my time in the human realm or the reasons behind why Fae might want to escape to another world...not if she doesn't know already from her damn book. "I used to help people escape or find rare objects," I answer evasively.

"Is that why you were in prison?"

"Sort of," I grunt. "But that's not important right now. What matters is that there's only a month left before the curse becomes permanent. Thorne is desperate to break it, and he wants Isabelle. If I don't bring her to him, he'll make sure everyone I care about is tortured for centuries long after he's gone."

For a fraction of a second, pity flashes across her face before she quickly masks it. "I'm sorry. Truly. I wish there was something I could do to help."

"There is," I say, almost desperately. "You can pretend to be Isabelle."

I hold my breath as Alix just stares at me, then she lets out an incredulous laugh. "No. Absolutely not."

I let out the breath I was holding. I'm not sure if I'm relieved or disappointed. Alix gets to her feet and begins to pace around the room, her bare feet slipping slightly on the tiled floor.

My friends' faces swim in the back of my mind. Fuck, I need to pull myself together. I have to convince her.

"Why?" I take another involuntary step forward, reaching out as if to touch her. "It's perfect. You look so much like her even Odessa was initially fooled. You already know all about Ellender and Thorne from the book, and whatever you don't know we'll be there to explain to you."

Alix walks toward the windows. "You're telling me that the real Thorne is this evil guy who throws people into prison camps, but also that I should pretend to be in love with him? You're out of your mind."

"Probably. But you just said you wanted to help."

"Yeah, but I meant 'help' in a figurative sense. Look, where I come from, asking a friend for a stupid ride to the airport is a big deal and this is so, *so* much bigger than that. You might as well have asked me to donate both my kidneys. It's not going to happen."

I want to shake her, force her to understand. "You helping us is the only chance we have."

"No, it's the only chance *you* have," she corrects me. "I'm sorry, but I have nothing to do with this. I don't owe you shit. I just want to go home."

"I can arrange that," I tell her quickly. "You won't have to pretend forever, just for the next month."

"But I can't break it," she says, her eyes widening. "Even if it's true that my Nana could break the curse, I'm not her. I can't help and you'll stay cursed forever anyway, so what's the point of me being here?"

"Because we think there's a tiny chance it won't matter. If Thorne just believes you're Isabelle, it could be enough to break the curse." She scoffs, but I continue, "And even if that doesn't work, this would still help us because the curse doesn't affect any of them." I point toward the closed door to where Odessa and my men are waiting outside. "The curse only affects the Kingdom of Vernallis. None of them were born here, so as long as they don't get thrown back in prison in the next few weeks, they'll be safe."

"And what about you?" she asks, raising an eyebrow.

"What about me?" I scowl. "There's no saving me, Peaches. I already expected to be doomed. I have nothing to lose except for them and everything to gain if by some miracle the fucking curse does break."

"Look..." She turns to me with wide pleading eyes. "I'm probably suffering from some kind of Stockholm syndrome but I do kind of feel bad for you. I wish I could help, but I can't. I'm so not the right girl for this. I just want to go home."

I steel myself for what I have to say next. "The only way you're getting home is with my help."

"So if I don't agree to do this, you're just going to keep me here as a prisoner?"

I squeeze my eyes shut, feeling nauseous. "Think of it as a partnership. If you help us, I'll help you get home. The way I see it, Peaches, you don't have much of a choice."

"No?" she snaps, her eyes flaring with anger. "I'd say I do have a choice. I could tell King Thorne the truth and have him put you back in prison."

"He'd probably kill you," I say bluntly. "Or worse, send you to Dyaspora with us."

"Which means I'm fucked no matter what," she snaps back. "So the way *I* see it, you need me more than I need you. If I'm going down, I will gladly take you with me."

*This infuriating woman.* She's braver than I expected, or maybe she's just as crazy as she promised me she was. Unfortunately, she's also right. This plan is already almost certainly doomed to fail, but if Alix won't play along, we might as well give up now.

I wrack my brain, trying to remember anything she said about her life before everything went to shit. Suddenly, I remember her phone call —the one she probably doesn't realize I could hear every word of.

"You need money," I blurt out.

"Who doesn't?" she snaps. "Capitalism is the root of all evil."

I swallow thickly, suddenly realizing I'm about to do the exact same thing her husband is doing—use money to control her.

*It's not for me, it's for my family.*

"I know you need money more than anything else. I don't have any at the moment, but I will."

She narrows her eyes. "How?"

"I'm the Baron of Ashwater. That's a province north of here."

"So you're royalty?"

"No," I blurt, a little too quickly. "Just nobility. A regular member of the high court, but I lost all that when I was banished to Dyaspora. Thorne will return my title and land once I deliver his bride, and then I could give you enough gold to last you generations in the human realm."

"You're shitting me." She laughs harshly.

"Not at all. If you help us, I'll pay you every fucking coin I have and then take you home."

Her breath catches and she goes still. "How long would I need to stay here?"

"Just under a month. There's three and a half weeks until the solar eclipse that marks hundred years since the curse was cast. After that, the curse will be permanent and there's nothing more that Thorne can do to any of us."

"Nearly a month," she breathes. "That's a long time. My family will think I'm dead."

"But you'll return with enough money to restart."

She bites her bottom lip, obviously tempted. "Okay...I'm not agreeing to this but just like in theory, how would it work?"

"What do you mean? You just pretend to be Isabelle."

She widens her eyes. "Yeah, but my Nana is in her eighties."

I can't help the smirk that crosses my face. "So? I'm 121, and I think I still look pretty damn good."

She blinks at me, startled, then shakes her head roughly. "Sorry, I think I just had a mini stroke, but I'm good now. You're immortal. No big deal. I'm totally fine."

I raise an eyebrow. "Is there a question in there somewhere?"

"Yeah. Is your king so oblivious that he would think Nana didn't age?"

"That necklace you're wearing was a gift from King Thorne to Isabelle. He told me he enchanted it to keep her young until she returned to Ellender."

Alix reaches for the locket and holds it between two fingers. "Seriously?"

I nod. "I guess the real Isabelle didn't wear it, but it doesn't matter. Thorne is expecting that she did and will still be young."

I watch her carefully, trying to read what she's thinking.

"A month," she mutters again under her breath. "Alright. At least I can say I did something interesting with the last of my twenties."

My eyebrows raise in disbelief and I can hardly believe that I've managed to convince her. "Really?"

"Yes. I'll pretend to be my grandmother and in one month you'll send me home with more money than I could possibly spend in one lifetime."

She holds out her hand as if for me to shake, and I take her fingers immediately, my own hands feeling suddenly cold. The strangest sensation washes over me. It's relief mixed with anxiety. Satisfaction and dread.

Plastering a smirk, I squeeze her fingers lightly. "We have a deal."

Alix looks up and meets my eyes, her hand still clutched in mine. "God, this is fucking crazy," she mutters, more to herself than to me.

I answer anyway, "You've got that right, Peaches."

She pulls her hand back and tucks her fingers under her arm as if burned by my touch. "There's a lot of stories about how humans shouldn't bargain with fairies," she says, tilting her head in contemplation.

"I've heard them."

Her breath catches, and my gaze drops from her eyes to her mouth, watching as she drags her tongue over her bottom lip.

*For fuck's sake.*

Even through all the stress and worry swirling in my mind, I still can't stop thinking about how easy it would be to back her into the wall. How I could run my own tongue over her lip, then down her throat to every other part of her. But I can't. If by some miracle this plan works, Alix is about to become the most off-limits woman on the damn continent. I need to get used to feeling indifferent to her.

"Are those stories true?" she asks, a little breathlessly.

I smile grimly and take a step back, running both hands through my hair. "I don't know, Peaches. I guess you'll just have to find out."

# CHAPTER EIGHT

ALIX

The moment Daemon and I strike our bargain, I feel calmer. I've always appreciated having a plan, and knowing that there's at least a chance that in thirty days, I could put this whole thing behind me gives my adrenaline permission to chill out.

I get dressed in the pajama-like clothes that Odessa leaves for me and leave the bathroom, only to find myself alone. All the Fae have vanished, and if not for the castle and Sushi asleep on the bed, I might have wondered if I imagined them all.

*God, I fucking wish I imagined them.*

I'm pretty sure that meeting Daemon is the worst thing that's ever happened to me, which is really saying something. Apparently, falling into a literal fucking Fae trap was just the cherry on top of the sundae that was the shittiest week of my life.

I guess it's true what they say: things could be worse.

As in, it sucks that your husband is a prick, but it could be worse. You could get kidnapped by your one-night stand.

I'm *this* close to being the punchline in a sad standup routine.

Sighing, I climb into the enormous four poster bed beside Nana's cat. Someone has left a tray of food on the nightstand, and I lean over to inspect it. To my relief, almost all the food looks normal. There's roast turkey, crusty bread, salad, and some kind of stringy purple vegetable.

I'm so hungry I don't even care about all the folktales warning not to eat faerie food. I give Sushi some turkey, then eat everything except for the purple vegetables. When I'm done, I lie and stare at the golden canopy overhead.

I wouldn't have thought I'd be able to sleep in a situation like this, but I guess sleep deprivation can defeat even the craziest of circumstances, because the next thing I know, I'm being shaken awake.

"Alix?" a melodic female voice says in my ear. "You need to get up."

I blink my eyes open and immediately focus on Odessa leaning over me. She's dressed in the same red and maroon dress as yesterday, but her long strawberry-blonde hair is tied back in a tight braid. In her arms is another enormous tray of food, much like the one from last night.

I sit up, rubbing my eyes with the heels of my hands. I'm slightly startled that she doesn't look as scary this morning. She's still too beautiful to be entirely normal, but some of the uncanny valley seems to have worn off. I don't know if that's a good thing.

"What's going on?" I ask groggily.

"You need to get up," she repeats.

"Why?"

"We let you sleep as long as we could, but that means you don't have long to dress and eat before we need to leave." She places the breakfast tray in front of me and steps back. "I wasn't sure what you'd want to eat so I just brought a bit of everything."

She's not exaggerating. There's a plate piled with eggs, toast, and something I think must be fried sweet potatoes. Another plate is filled with sliced fruit, several of which I don't recognize. My stomach rumbles loudly. At least they obviously aren't planning on starving me.

"Oh, thank god, you have coffee," I exclaim, reaching for a teacup filled to the brim with a liquid far too dark to be tea.

Odessa smiles with satisfaction and walks over to the wardrobe in the corner. "Usually Shar would bring you your breakfast, but I thought that might be overwhelming for your first day here."

"Who's Shar?" I ask through a mouthful of toast.

"You met her yesterday."

*Oh, right, the goblin woman.* "Gotcha. So, where are we going?"

"We're going to escort you to the Winter Palace. If it were up to me, I'd give you a day to adjust but Daemon wants to make sure the king knows you're here as soon as possible. Or, that Isabelle is here, I guess."

I nod dazedly. That makes sense, given what they explained last night.

Biting my lip, I stay silent as Odessa throws open the wardrobe. It's stuffed to the brim with colorful gowns. I'm positive it was empty last night.

When would she have had time to fill it?

"Sorry, I don't have anything all that comfortable by your standards," she says apologetically. "Sometimes humans come here and influence our fashion, but there hasn't been a lot of shifts in trends since the curse was cast."

I laugh. "So you're telling me there's no polyester and I *have* to wear a gorgeous custom gown? How tragic."

She returns my grin. "In my opinion, it *is* tragic. I'd love to show off my legs more, but to each their own, I suppose." She pulls out a cap sleeve blue dress and holds it up, closing one eye as if picturing me wearing it. "How about this? It looks like something Belle would have worn."

"Sure," I say distractedly. "Honestly, pick whatever you want. It can't be worse than the T-shirt I arrived in."

Odessa's violet eyes flash with humor, and she looks like she's trying not to smile. "Actually, I'm glad you brought that up..."

She bends over and unearths some white stockings and a pair of brown leather shoes from the depths of the wardrobe. "Why?"

"Because I should have told you last night. You can't tell anyone what happened before you got here. No more announcing to strangers that you might have slept with their husband."

"Hey, I didn't mean—"

"I know," she soothes, "but really, it's best if you just act like Daemon is as much of a stranger as the rest of us."

"He is a stranger," I mumble. "And I really wasn't planning to say anything."

"Good. Because Fae males are more possessive than human men. I don't want to know what King Thorne would do if he found out you slept with his br—er, I mean, his captain—" She flushes, embarrassed at stumbling over her words.

"He does realize it's been sixty years since he saw Nana, right? What was he expecting her to do all this time?"

"I know it seems odd, but trust me. Males can be really jealous and irrational over their partners." Odessa grimaces. "Just be careful, that's all I'm trying to say."

*Alright then.* I guess I'll have to watch what I say. That shouldn't be difficult. It's not like I was a social butterfly back in Chicago, and I can't really see that changing here where I have even less in common with everyone else.

I finish my breakfast, then dress in the blue cap sleeve gown, a brown belt and matching shoes. Odessa helps me tame my curls into a low ponytail, then looks thoughtfully at the dark windows. "You'll need to wear a cloak since it's still raining. Here—" She pulls a long red cape out of the depths of the wardrobe. "That should do it."

I take the cloak, then follow her gaze toward the window. It looks like midnight. "What time is it, anyway?"

"Late morning," she sighs. "I know the rain seems gloomy, but we're actually very lucky. If the sun was out, we'd have to wait until nightfall to leave."

"Because of the curse?"

"Exactly."

In *A Kingdom of Thorns*, all the fairies turn into animals in the daytime and back into themselves at night. It's presented in the story as more of an inconvenience than something dangerous, but the way Daemon talked about the curse makes me think it's a bigger issue here than in the story.

I want to ask more questions about the curse, if only to check that Nana didn't leave any important details out of her book, but Odessa is clearly stressed about the time. She keeps tapping her foot and glancing at the door as if she's expecting someone to come bursting in at any second.

"Are you ready?" she asks briskly.

"Sure." I throw the cape over my shoulders, feeling a bit like I'm playing dress-up. "As ready as I'm going to be, I guess."

Odessa smiles at me a little wistfully. "It's actually incredible. If I didn't know better, I really would think you were Belle."

I snort a nervous laugh. "Let's hope you're not the only one."

She doesn't return my smile, her face falling slightly with worry. It does absolutely nothing to improve my confidence. I feel more optimistic about this plan than last night, but that isn't saying a lot.

Putting aside the very real possibility that this is some kind of Buffy season 6 fiasco and I'm really in a hospital somewhere, there are just so many ways the plan could go wrong. I was definitely paying attention when Daemon said that King Thorne will kill me if he finds out who I am. *No fucking pressure.*

No matter how much I need the money, I'm probably crazy for agreeing to this plan.

Odessa and I venture out of the bedroom and make our way down the long white marble hallway I sprinted down only last night. We pass several of those goblin-like creatures going about their own business and I manage not to stare or react.

"This place is huge," I muse as we reach the top of the sweeping stone staircase.

"I know. Would you believe the Winter Palace is even larger?"

I open my mouth to answer, but never get the chance. At that moment the sound of raised voices echoes toward us down the long stone hall. I recognize one of the voices immediately as Daemon's.

I glance at Odessa. "What's going on?"

"Probably nothing." Odessa blows out an annoyed breath through her nose. "Just Daemon being Daemon. He can't help but take charge of everything and everyone."

"So he's controlling?" I didn't really get that impression yesterday, but given that I also missed that he was literally a magical being from another world, my opinion should be taken with an entire ocean of salt.

"No, not controlling..." Odessa looks like she's trying to find the right words to explain. "He's just charismatic. He can't help but pick up followers. Like I can already tell those men he brought with him from Dyaspora worship him and will do anything he asks."

"Is that a bad thing?"

"Not exactly." Her worried tone doesn't match her words at all. "It's just complicated. The king doesn't like anyone in the court to get too popular, and he's always been wary of Daemon."

Huh. I guess that makes sense if this is an absolute monarchy, but the more tidbits I hear about the real King Thorne, the less I want to meet him.

We reach the top of the stairs and look into the wide entrance hall. My gaze flies to the group of red jacketed men waiting near the door, and I immediately pick up the gist of what they're saying.

"How fucking long does it take to get dressed?" Daemon complains.

He stands with his back to the staircase, speaking to Kastian, who leans against the wall, looking serious. He's not actually yelling as I'd thought—the echoes have simply amplified everything tenfold. Beside them, Fox stares into space, entirely unconcerned with whatever's happening around him. At their feet, Jett sits on the floor, his back against the wall. All four are dressed in uniform, heavy swords hanging from their belts.

"Calm down, we're here," Odessa calls down the stairs.

Daemon's back stiffens, and he turns to look up at me. Our gazes connect and my jaw goes slack.

I am such a fucking idiot.

I have no idea how I didn't realize that there was something weird about Daemon from the beginning. He's just so inhumanly handsome, even while glaring at me like I'm the cause of all his problems. It feels unreal. And worse, somehow he looks better today than I remember from last night. Maybe my brain superimposed an uglier face onto him so I could process the fact that I'd been abducted, coerced, and thrown into a possibly fatal bargain with a supposedly fictional character. Too bad my brain couldn't do me the solid of holding on to that delusion.

For a long second, our eyes lock. He leans forward, as if he's going to step toward me. Then, he shakes his head and his expression turns sour. "Finally," he barks.

"Oh, shut it." Odessa scowls, giving him a very sibling-like glare of annoyance.

In return, Daemon's scowl deepens. "If the rain stops before we get on the train, I'm blaming you."

"Train?" I blurt out before Odessa can respond. "You have trains here?"

They both turn to look at me and Daemon raises an eyebrow. "Of course."

"Hey, don't look at me like that," I grumble. "How should I know what technology you have? I'm honestly just grateful you have indoor plumbing."

His eyebrows furrow. "Why wouldn't we have indoor plumbing?"

I wave my hand vaguely in the air. "Because it's a castle? You're dressed like it's 1750...do you see where I'm going with this?"

He gives me a withering stare. "I know humans don't believe in magic anymore, but I would have thought that meant you'd improved your education."

I reel back. "Hey! I have over $200,000 in student loans that says otherwise, buddy. I am almost unnecessarily educated."

"In history?" he asks, a slight sneer appearing on his face.

"Well, no, in music, but—"

"That explains it. Even in your world, those things were invented long before you seem to believe, and many of the largest advancements of humanity came from Fae intervention."

I frown. He's probably right but he doesn't have to be an ass about it. "I liked you better when you were just some guy in a bar."

I mean it to be a throw away comment, and one that I expect him to have some quick retort for, but instead his face falls slightly. His eyes shutter, and he takes a step back. "So did I, Peaches."

There's a long awkward silence in which I remember we have an audience. My cheeks heat.

Odessa clears her throat. "Right, well, to answer your question, Alix, yes, we have trains. That's the fastest way to reach the Winter Palace, so unless you want to be on the road for a week or more, it's the only option."

"And here I was thinking we were just going to fly."

"Fly?" Kastian repeats, looking curiously at Daemon beside him. "Who said anything about flying?"

I raise an eyebrow at Daemon. "Yesterday, you—"

"Let's get moving," Daemon cuts me off sharply, clearing his throat pointedly and marching toward the door.

"Alright, then," I mutter under my breath. "I guess we're leaving."

Odessa looks apologetically at me. "I think he just really wants to get to the other palace to see King Thorne."

I huff a sigh. I mean, maybe, but I'm pretty sure it's just that the nice guy from the bar really was an act. I'm dealing with a first-class asshole, and I'm stuck with him for an entire month.

*It could always be worse.*

DAEMON

Alix practically skips down the rainy train station platform, her cloak streaming behind her and her head swinging back and forth every few seconds. Her mouth is open, and she seems unable to decide what to stare at first. It might be endearing, except that she's drawing so much fucking attention to herself.

"I don't know what she finds so interesting," I grumble.

Kas shrugs, as if to say he doesn't know but neither does he care. "Is there something I'm missing here?"

I glance sideways at him from under the hood of my rain-drenched cloak. "Like what?"

"Like why you're being a complete asshole to the one woman in Ellender standing between us and Dyaspora."

I press my lips together in frustration, my eyes instinctively finding the red-hooded figure several paces ahead of us. I watch Alix for a long moment, just to make sure she isn't listening, of course. "I wasn't trying to be an asshole to her."

Kas laughs. "Then I'd hate to see you try."

I scowl, knowing he's right.

Sometime between when I realized that Alix isn't Isabelle and when I saw her coming down the stairs, my mood darkened. I can't shake the bitterness simmering in the back of my mind.

Aside from the last ninety years in prison and the impossible situation Thorne has put me in, being back in Vernallis after all this time feels unsettling. For so long, this city was my home. Even after inheriting the lands and title of Baron Ashwater from the man who pretended to be my father, I spent most of my days here, leading Thorne's armies through peacetime drills. Now, I feel like I barely belong.

But none of that explains why I can't seem to stop myself from taking my mood out on Alix. I just find her...aggravating.

I feel Kastian's eyes on me and I glance over to find him scrutinizing me as if he can read my mind.

"What?" I bark.

He sighs, shaking his head slightly. "Nothing. I just hope you know what you're doing."

"I'm doing exactly what you all wanted me to do," I snap. "I'm doing what Thorne ordered me to do. What else do you expect?"

At that moment, Alix's voice rings out over the sounds of the platform and the pitter-patter of rain. "This is incredible! I can't believe it's all been real this whole time."

I take a deep breath, taking in the scent of rain and roses that always lingers in the air. "It's a train station," I grumble. "Take a fucking breath."

"It's a *magical* train station," she says pointedly.

"No, it's just a normal one," I correct. "It's no more magical here than our castles are. The only thing different from your world are the passengers."

Alix stops walking and pushes the hood of her red, rain-drenched cloak back. Raindrops splash against her cheeks and get caught in her eyelashes as she raises a brow at me. "Can you just let me have this one? *Hello*, it's a faerie *train*. This whole place is giving Hogwarts Express."

I have no idea what that means, and I shake my head, willing myself to be patient. In fairness to Alix, she might be drawing attention but she's not the only one.

Being large and imposing, our group is drawing enough stares all on our own. Alix walks in the lead, even though she clearly has no idea where she's going. Kastian and I trail behind her, taking it in turns to redirect her away from dangerous-looking strangers, open grates, and once the tracks themselves. Jett and Fox take up the rear, with Odessa walking between them, her face entirely hidden by the hood of her green cloak and carrying Alix's enormous gray cat in a picnic basket.

To our right, an enormous scarlet and black stream engine waits for passengers to board. I glance at the clock on the nearby ticket office. It's still early, but the rain is saving us from only being able to travel at night. Still, if the clouds clear...

I swallow angrily and raise my voice to be heard over the noise of the train. "We're boarding now. There's no fucking chance I'm letting us miss it."

My friends turn and file toward the open doors to the nearest train car, but of course Alix doesn't seem to hear me. I follow her gaze and realize she's staring at a group of trolls, clearly awestruck.

The trolls are gathered around a rickety market stall, using the shabby awning to shelter from the heavy rain. Their skin is mottled and scaly, their faces twisted into leering expressions as they converse in their guttural language.

"I take it you've never seen a troll before?" Jett asks her, hanging back from the others to talk to Alix.

She shakes her head. "Of course not. They're in Nana's book, though."

"What does it say about them?"

She swallows. "It says they attack humans and eat them."

"That's bullshit," I snap before I can stop myself. "There are many species of Fae, and most of them don't look like us. I'd try not to stare."

Alix turns around and scowls at me. "Why?"

"Because it's fucking rude, that's why."

A slight pink flush rises on her cheeks, but she doesn't drop her gaze from mine. "I guess you would know a lot about rudeness."

I open my mouth to retort, but Jett beats me to it. He throws one arm over Alix's shoulders. "Ignore Ashwater, Princess," he says, grinning at me over the top of her head. "I won't let anything eat you."

A hot spark of annoyance ripples in my chest, and I dig my nails into my palms beneath my cloak. I step forward and grab her roughly by the elbow, steering her away from Jett and the trolls, and toward the open door of the enormous red steam engine. I don't want him or anyone else touching her. *It looks bad, she's supposed to be here for Thorne.*

"Look," I mutter in Alix's ear, "I know this is the first time you're seeing any of this, but *Isabelle* has been to Ellender before. You have to stop being so obvious or this will never work."

Alix tries to pull her arm from my grip and fails, then tilts her chin up to glare more intently at me. "I never promised you I was a good actress."

"You could at least try."

"I will when we get to the other palace, or wherever we're going, but you're going to have to help me."

"With what?"

"You promised you'd explain everything I don't know, which is basically fucking everything, so you'd better get started."

I let go of her arm and drag a frustrated hand through my rain-soaked hair. She's right, of course, but being her personal Encyclopedia isn't exactly what I had in mind. I was hoping I would be able to avoid her as much as possible once we arrive at the palace. I envisioned pawning her off on Odessa to keep an eye on, and possibly retreating back to the Ashwater Estate as soon as Thorne returns it to me.

"Come on, let's just get inside," Odessa says, nudging Fox out of the way to step up behind Alix. "We can talk about this more once we're alone in a compartment."

Amenable as usual, Kastian jumps up onto the short steps of the train car, and turns to offer a hand to Odessa to help her up. She averts her gaze as if she doesn't see him and hauls herself up by the metal railing, stepping around him to disappear inside.

Kastian looks at me, nonplussed. "Did I do something?"

I shake my head, cursing under my breath. I can't believe I didn't realize this would be a problem. I step up onto the train steps and clap him on the shoulder, giving him a consolatory look. "Sorry, mate. I forgot to mention that Dessa is from Hydratta, and she's not as oblivious as Thorne."

He blanches and looks a bit green. "Fuck," he mutters, before disappearing into the train car after my cousin.

"Why does it matter what kingdom she's from?" Alix asks.

I hold out a hand to help her up. "Don't worry about it, Peaches."

Alix looks at my hand, weighing her options, before placing her fingers in mine. I pull her up onto the train and she stumbles, bringing us chest to chest. For a long second, I don't move.

"Excuse me," she says breathlessly.

I drop her hand and step back, wiping my fingers on my jacket as if to remove any trace of her. "Right, go on ahead."

Spotting our military uniforms, the conductor doesn't even bother to ask for tickets. We're directed to the nearest empty compartment near the front of the train.

Alix sits next to the window and immediately clears a patch of condensation with the back of her hand and presses her nose to the glass. Odessa and the cat sit next to her, and I take the spot across from Alix, leaving Kastian to squeeze in next to me facing Odessa. She glares at him, and he averts his gaze, pretending not to notice.

"We're going to find another compartment, Ashwater," Jett tells me, indicating Fox beside him. "The big guy here isn't going to fit."

I nod in agreement. "Don't go far. If something happens, I don't want to have to go looking for you."

"What could happen?" Jett says easily. "We're not in Dyaspora anymore, you can relax."

I grimace. I will never truly relax until my brother is dead and I've pissed on his fucking grave, but I know that's not what Jett means. He's noticed that I'm more on edge than usual, but until we see Thorne and know if he believes Alix is Isabelle, I can't calm down. There's too much at stake.

Jett shuts the compartment door with a snap, leaving only the four of us inside. An awkward silence fills the compartment, and I'm relieved when the whistle sounds and the train starts moving.

"Where is this palace?" Alix asks.

"North," I grunt.

Odessa rolls her eyes at me, scolding me with her gaze for being rude. "It's on the north-west corner of Vernallis," she explains. "It's much colder there, hence why it's called the Winter Palace. Before the curse, no one really went there because it's so cold, but now..." She breaks off awkwardly.

"Wait a second," Alix says, looking confused. "Where is Vernallis?"

Odessa blinks at her. "Um, here? We're in Vernallis."

"I thought this was Ellender?"

"In Isabelle's book, some of the city names are wrong," I blurt out, knowing exactly why Alix is so lost.

Alix raises her eyebrows. "Wait, you read it?"

I avert my gaze. "Yeah. Last night."

I wasn't able to sleep at all last night, my racing thoughts keeping me company well into the morning. I'd had hours to devote to understanding how Alix must view our land. It turns out that the book that the real Isabelle wrote was oddly compelling.

Unfortunately, it's mostly bullshit.

The magic seems correct, as are the descriptions of the Summer Palace and the servants, but the truth of the story ends there. Appearance aside, the characters are nothing like the real people who obviously inspired them, and worst of all, the details of the curse on Vernallis have been so sanitized that it's no wonder Alix was willing to bargain with her life to break it.

She thinks we're living in a fucking dreamland.

"In the book, there are four Fae kingdoms," I explain. "Ellender in the west, Hydratta in the south, Solistine in the east, and Thermia in the north. Ellender is the largest kingdom, and it's ruled by the Fae king, Thorne. In reality, Thorne's kingdom is called Vernallis, and Ellender is what we call the continent as a whole."

"Okay," she says slowly, her skeptical gaze falling on me. "So we're in Vernallis. Fine. But I still don't really understand how I got here."

"There are dozens of gates between our world and yours. There's a gate in the mine in Ironhill."

"Wait...seriously?" she asks. "But that mine has been burning for decades."

"So I discovered. I have to wonder if the fire was created by the gate itself, or started intentionally to prevent anyone from using it."

"So, did you kidnap Nana using that portal?"

I shake my head. "I have no idea how Isabelle made her way here. I was in Dyaspora."

"Belle found her way here on her own," Odessa interjects. "Her father was a miner, and accidentally traveled through the Ironhill gate where King Thorne took him prisoner. Belle followed, and agreed to be the king's prisoner in exchange for her father's freedom."

"God, I have so many questions to ask as soon as I get home," Alix muses.

"You know what I just thought of?" Kastian interrupts, evidently following his own train of thought.

I turn to look at him. "What?"

Kastian scrutinizes Alix as if he's seeing her for the first time. "Are we sure she's not related to King Thorne?"

I blanche. "What the fuck are you talking about?"

"I mean..." Kas tilts his head, his eyebrows raising. "The king is in love with her grandmother."

"*Possibly* in love," I correct, quickly. "We don't know that's why he wanted her."

"But we do know they knew each other," Odessa chimes in, looking as panicked as I feel.

I turn to look at Alix, horror washing over me like a chill wind. *No. No fucking way...* She can't be related to Thorne, because then she'd be my...great niece? Alix doesn't look anything like Thorne, but then again, neither does his other...

My stomach roils, and I'm positive I'm going to be sick.

"Woah..." Alix puts up both hands. "You guys really need to work on finishing your sentences. I never have any idea what you're talking about."

Kastian, the consistent voice of reason, leans toward her. "Is there any chance King Thorne is your grandfather?"

She chokes, coughing on what seems to be a giggle. After a moment, she can't hold it in and descends into laughter.

"This isn't fucking funny," I snap.

"It really is, though," she gasps. "First, Ellender is real, now you think I'm part Fae? What in the *Wattpad* is going on here?"

"It *is* possible," Odessa says.

"No, it's really not," she says, still trying to contain her laughter. "Look, even ignoring the fact that I am definitely not magical in like, *any* way, the math doesn't work. My mom wasn't born for almost ten years after you're saying my Nana came here."

"Who's her father?" I ask, needing to be completely sure.

"Not that it's your business, but he was just a regular guy from Iron-hill. He pursued my Nana for ages before she finally agreed to marry him, and then they were pretty miserable together. Nana likes books and gardening, but Grandpa was really into hunting and wasn't a super nice guy overall. It's not surprising, really. The women in my family have terrible taste in men."

"I'll say they do," Odessa agrees, shooting me a look.

I tip my head back against the seat, so relieved I don't even care that my cousin is insulting me. Alix doesn't know Thorne is my brother or how I just felt my entire life flash before my eyes, but everyone else here does. Kastian gives me a conciliatory clap on the shoulder.

"I need some air," I mutter, pushing to my feet.

The moment I stand, I can acutely feel the movement of the train. I sway on my feet and frown, suddenly aware of how fast we're traveling. Gazing back at the window, I spot a dark shadow whip past the glass.

"What are you looking at?" Kastian asks.

I shake my head, peering out into the darkness beyond the window. "Nothing..." I mutter. "But how fast do you think we're going?"

Kas frowns. "Hell if I know. Why?"

Alix frowns and presses her nose to the window again, peering outside. "Now that you point it out, it does seem like we're going really fast. I didn't notice because high speed trains are all like this, but aren't we on a steam engine?"

As if in answer, Alix's enormous cat begins clawing at the sides of his basket, letting out a sound more like a howl than a meow.

"I'm going to go ask the conductor," I declare, throwing the door to the compartment open. Suddenly, the train lurches dangerously. Stumbling, I throw an arm out to catch myself on the doorframe. "What the fuck—"

There's a loud screeching sound, like metal grinding against metal, and the train car jolts again.

Odessa shrieks, her voice mingling with other screams echoing down the corridor from other compartments.

Without thinking or taking a single moment to figure out what's going on, I throw myself at Alix, shielding her with my entire body.

# CHAPTER NINE

ALIX

“Ooph!”

I let out an involuntary cry as Daemon slams me against the metal wall of the train car.

I'd just stood from my seat seconds before, and now my back aches from the impact as he pins me against the window, his body pressed tightly against mine.

Is he protecting me, or trying to smother me?

I open my mouth to demand he let me go, but the words die in my throat. Without meaning to, I breathe in his deliciously masculine scent and my traitorous body reacts. Warm tingles erupt all over me and my heartbeat grows loud in my ears.

The train lurches again, jolting me out of my daze.

This time, the rattling is accompanied by a deafening screech of metal wheels against the tracks, and the ominous sound of cracking wood. I lose my balance and stumble, gripping Daemon's muscled shoulder for support.

"What the fuck is happening?" he growls.

"I was hoping you knew!"

Now that I'm paying attention, I can't believe how long it took me to realize that we're going fast. Like *really fucking fast*. It feels like I'm on the subway, not a leisurely vintage pleasure train, and we seem to be getting faster with every passing second.

What if we crash? The Fae will probably be fine, and Odessa can take care of herself. But me? I'm fucked. Forget magical creatures and faerie kings, I could easily bump my head too hard on the window and it would be lights out for me just as easily as if I were run over by the train. "What happens if we derail?"

Daemon grimaces, his face still mere inches from mine. "At this height? I wouldn't think about it if I were you."

*Height?*

I twist around and clear another patch of condensation on the window to look outside. The landscape is blurry by the dark, rainy sky, but it's clear we're traveling on raised tracks, built high on pillars, suspending the train over the rolling hills and thorny thickets of roses.

"How high are we?" I ask.

Daemon ignores me, but his mouth morphs into an even thinner line.

*Got it. That means we're really fucking high.*

Daemon pushes himself off me, and grabs my hand, enveloping it in his much larger fingers. "We need to see what's going on."

I don't bother to protest as he tugs me roughly out of the train car and into the narrow, dimly lit hallway.

Kastian and Odessa are already outside, and I'm grateful to see that Odessa is clutching Sushi tightly in both arms as he howls, screaming to be freed from his carrier. I glance to the right and spot Jett and Fox making their way toward us from down the corridor. Overhead, lanterns swing wildly back and forth like strobe lights. Other passengers poke their heads out of their compartments to yell their confusion at one another. Clearly, this isn't normal, even for the Fae.

"Who's driving this damn thing?" Jett yells.

"I don't think anyone is driving," Kastian mutters. "Where are we in relation to the locomotive?"

"We're only a few cars from the front," Daemon replies, his expression grim. "Come on. If the driver of this train isn't dead already, I'm going to kill him myself."

Daemon takes the lead and drags me along with him as he marches toward the small door connecting us to the next train car. He reaches for the door handle and tries to wrench it open, only to find it locked. My heart sinks, but then a split second later, the lock clicks and he shoves the door open.

"How did you do that?"

"Take a wild guess, Peaches."

Holy shit, he just used magic. Like actual magic. That's crazy and also somehow makes so many other things make sense. I knew I locked the door to Nana's house. This asshole used his weird Fae powers to break into my Nana's house!

I guess that's the least of my problems right now, but still. *The audacity of this man.*

Dragging me helplessly by the hand, Daemon practically runs down the corridor of the next car, which looks nearly identical to ours with a slim carpeted hallway and glass-walled compartments on either side. The ground shakes beneath us, the entire car rocking back and forth like it could tip over at any second.

At the end of the hall, we reach another door, connecting to the next car. I'm expecting to see a third long hallway, but instead, he tugs me through the door and into what must be the luggage car. It's dark except for the light coming from the open door, and I have to squint to make out the stacks of trunks and suitcases stretching all the way from floor to ceiling.

The train shakes again, and I shriek and duck as something comes flying toward my face. After a second, the impact doesn't come and I open my eyes to find Daemon holding a suitcase in one hand, inches from my face. "You're welcome." He smirks.

*Cocky asshole.*

Behind me, Kastian, Jett, and Fox force their way inside and immediately begin tossing luggage out into the hall behind us, clearing a path for all six of us to stand in.

Daemon drops my hand. "The locomotive is only one car ahead of us. Wait here."

I rub my fingers where he'd been holding them, suddenly feeling far more anxious than I was mere moments before.

Daemon pushes more luggage out of the way as he moves toward the door on the opposite side of the car. Trunks burst open as they get strewn around, and all manner of clothing, papers, and trinkets spill onto the floor. A glass vase wrapped tightly in tissue paper falls out of a carpetbag and smashes into a thousand pieces. My chest pangs with sympathy. It looks like people have packed their entire lives away into trunks, and now even if the train doesn't crash, their things will still be lost forever.

Daemon reaches the far door and presses his face to a round window in the center. Cursing under his breath, he glances back. "Brace yourselves."

"Wh—"

Before I can even ask what he means, Daemon yanks the door open. The train shudders violently as a powerful gust of wind and rain blasts inside, dousing us all with icy droplets. Behind me, Odessa lets out a little shriek and Sushi hisses angrily.

Apparently, the locomotive isn't connected to the rest of the train. It wasn't cold before we left, but with the speed we're going and the continued downpour, I wrap my arms around myself to keep from shivering.

My heart lurches as Daemon leans his head outside the speeding train, his hair whipping back from his face. "I'm going to see what's wrong with the engine."

Daemon disappears into the darkness outside. I want to protest, but then I remember that he can fly. I glance around, wondering if everyone else is hiding wings too. I hope so, because I'm starting to worry we'll have to jump.

I feel a hand on my shoulder and step aside as Kastian moves past me to stand in Daemon's vacant spot in the doorway. He doesn't seem bothered by the cold. In fact, none of the men do.

I hold my breath nervously, waiting for Daemon's shout, or better yet, the sound of breaks. After a second, Odessa makes her way toward me and stands at my shoulder in the middle of the car. She smiles. "It will be fine."

I grimace. "For you all, maybe. I can't fly."

"Don't worry, Daemon won't—"

Her words are abruptly cut off by another screech of metal.

For a split second, I think it's the brakes—that Daemon has managed to stop the train—but then it jerks again.

Odessa screams, scrambling to brace herself against the wall.

The deafening screech of metal fills the air, and I whip my head around, realizing the sound isn't coming from the locomotive—it's coming from the passenger cars.

Fox is standing just inside the luggage compartment, while Jett is still in the hallway of the passenger car. They'd been passing suitcase after suitcase out of our car, clearly trying to give us as much room as possible.

Suddenly, wood snaps, and I see the door to our compartment straining against its hinges. The bolts connecting the cars are clearly under too much strain, and in a moment, the passenger car is going to break off.

"Get in here," Fox barks at Jett.

Jett is already scrambling to reach the doorway, leaping over the suitcases that he himself just piled in his path. Fox leans between the cars, his hand stretched out to his friend.

There's another creaking and cracking of wood, and the train bucks like a roller coaster. The cars disconnect just as Fox grabs Jett's hand and pulls him inside.

Jett collapses in a heap on the ground, panting. "Shit," he breathes, somehow still smiling after all that. "That was close."

Before anyone can react or say anything, Daemon swings back into the car on the opposite side. "There's no conductor."

"How is that possible?" Odessa asks.

"I don't fucking know, but I'm not going to waste my time trying to figure it out."

"You couldn't just stop the train yourself? Or use magic?" I ask, a little desperately.

Daemon blows out an annoyed breath. "I have no fucking idea how a train works. I can't just command it to stop. The best I could do is blow up the engine. So unless anyone here can walk me through how this shit works..."

Everyone glances around, as if hoping that one of us has forgotten to mention they're an expert on train engines.

I turn back to the gaping hole where the door to the passenger car used to be. In the distance, the rest of the train shrinks, pulling farther away. An idea hits me then. "We have to disconnect from the front," I say. "Without the locomotive pulling our car, we can just coast until we slow down or can find a safe point to jump."

Daemon brightens immediately. "Good idea, Peaches." He turns to Kastian. "Want to help me?"

"I will," Fox rumbles, pushing his way toward the other end of the car.

Daemon glances at Fox, taking in his enormous muscles, before nodding. The two of them climb out onto the metal bars connecting the luggage car to the locomotive pulling it and begin trying to break it.

"Can't they just break it with magic?" I ask.

"It's made of iron," Odessa explains. "Iron is resistant to magic, which is why hardware like that is forged from it in the first place. It has to be resistant to tampering."

"Isn't that fucking convenient."

"Find us something heavy to break the tow!" Daemon yells.

Inside, Kastian, Jett, Odessa and I immediately rip open suitcases.

The contents of all the bags that haven't already burst open on their own get thrown around the car like the wreckage of a tornado. I paw through bag after bag of clothing, then throw open a large wooden trunk. Immediately, my heart leaps.

The trunk is packed tightly with what looks like the contents of someone's kitchen. I feel bad that whoever was leaving their home to start over somewhere new will have to do it without their things, but at least the train didn't crash and they're probably going to be fine.

I toss a couple of dishes, a feather duster, and an old-fashioned desk clock out of the trunk, before finding what I'm looking for. "Here!" I cry, brandishing a heavy iron skillet like a sword. "Use this."

I run over to the door and hand the skillet to Fox. He raises it like a mallet and begins hacking away at the metal bars. We hold our breath, waiting, until with a heavy clang, the toe connecting us to the runaway locomotive finally breaks.

Odessa cheers, but I just sigh in relief and move to the right of the door so Fox can leap inside. For a long second, I expect Daemon to follow, but he doesn't.

I crane my neck to see better, and my heart lurches into my throat when I finally see Daemon. He's perched precariously on a rain-slicked metal bar above the train tracks, his foot slipping dangerously close to the edge.

Acting on instinct, I grab his hand, pulling him inside, sending us both tumbling to the ground in a heap. I let out an "oomph" as he lands on top of me, knocking the breath from my lungs.

Daemon pushes himself on his hands until he's hovering over me in a push-up position. "What was that for?"

His hair flops into his eyes and drips water droplets all over my face. I suck in an involuntary breath, taking in his heady scent. "You were about to fall," I gasp. "You're welcome."

He scoffs, arrogance written in every line of his face. "I was fine. And even if I wasn't, I'm not thanking you, Peaches. Without you, I wouldn't be on this train."

"And without you, I wouldn't be in this world, so whose fault is it really?"

He grins, looking like he's almost enjoying himself despite our near-death experience. "Tell you what, if we all live through this, you can take all the credit you want."

I scowl and shove him off me with both hands. "Remind me never to save your life again. Next time, I'm just going to let you get run over."

"Hate to interrupt, but I don't think we're at the sexually charged banter portion of the show!" Jett yells.

Daemon and I turn to look at him in unison.

"What are you talking about?" Daemon asks.

Jett's eyes widen and he points over our heads. "Look!"

I squint through the rain ahead.

It seems my plan worked, because the locomotive is already nearly out of sight ahead of us and we're obviously slowing down. In the distance, the train is barreling toward a bridge that looks far too fragile to handle a train moving at that speed. Sure enough, we all watch as the wooden beams groan and snap, and the bridge crumbles under the weight of the speeding locomotive. So fast it almost doesn't seem real, the train falls, hurdling toward the ground with a sickening crash. Any relief I felt seconds before disappears, and terror washes over me.

"Fuck!" Daemon swears, jumping to his feet.

In the time it takes me to blink, his enormous feathery wings unfurl.

I gape at him, dazed. The wings are so large they're crushed by the walls of the train car, unable to fully extend. How the fuck does he keep those hidden? Are they magic? They must be, but—

My panicked questions are interrupted when Daemon grabs me, hauling me to my feet. He spins me around and pushes me toward the rear door of the train—or what used to be a door before it was literally torn from its hinges.

I blink in renewed shock when I see that everyone else has wings too. Kastian's wings are black like Daemon's but instead of red feathers, his are green like an oil slick. Fox's wings are entirely white, like an actual fucking angel, while Jett's are a dark purplish blue.

"Woah," I say. "If you can do that, why didn't you just fly out of here to begin with?"

I'm not entirely surprised that Daemon ignores my question, or that everyone else seems completely okay with this situation. Well, everyone except Odessa who also looks a bit alarmed to be suddenly stuck in a crowded car full of feathers.

"Kas, take Odessa!" Daemon barks.

Odessa shrieks, trying to scramble out of the way of Kastian's outstretched arm. "Do not touch me!"

Kastian grabs her and yanks the basket with a still screaming Sushi out of her arms. He shoves the cat at Jett, before throwing a struggling Odessa over his shoulder and leaping out of the train.

"Holy shit!" I blurt out as Jett jumps after them, followed by Fox.

"Let's go, Peaches," Daemon says, reaching for me.

"Are you crazy?" I yell over the wind. "I'd rather take my chances here."

"You'll have to if you don't fucking move," he growls, reaching for me.

"I have never wanted to try skydiving!" I scream. "I don't even like the high jump at the public pool!"

Daemon's face twists in frustration as he grabs me around the waist and launches both of us outside.

I scream for a long breathless second as we fall through the open air. My stomach swoops like I'm caught on an endless rollercoaster, and the wind rushes past my face, tangling my hair and making tears stream from my eyes.

Then, suddenly, it's like opening a parachute. Daemon's wings stretch out and we stop falling.

My heart thunders in my chest, and I struggle to catch my breath as we swoop in a circle over the train tracks. I look down just in time to see our train car plummet off the broken bridge and burst into a thousand splinters of wood.

"You're welcome," Daemon says in my ear, a hint of humor in his tone. "Looks like I get the credit, after all."

"I-I fucking hate you!" I gasp. "Don't you dare let me go."

He smiles against my ear. "Remind me never to save your life again."

# CHAPTER TEN

ALIX

Daemon finally lands on a grassy hill where the others are waiting, but we don't stay there for long. The rain is still pouring and has begun to turn to icy sleet. Fortunately, we're not far from a town and it takes only fifteen minutes to reach the lights in the distance.

"Couldn't we fly there?" I chatter, burrowing deeper into my cloak.

"I thought you hated flying," Daemon grumbles.

"I do, but I also hate walking, so whichever is faster…"

"We can't," Kastian says, when Daemon ignores me. "Fae wings only come out in particular circumstances. Life threatening situations being the most common."

"Like fish who change color when they're threatened," I blurt out.

Odessa laughs loudly and throws a mocking glance at Daemon. "How does it feel to be compared to a fish?"

"You tell me. I'm not the one with a tail," he snaps.

Her face falls, and she glances away. Clearly, he hurt her feelings.

"You know what I've been thinking about a lot?" I say, looking to distract Odessa.

"What?" she asks.

"You know when people say 'it could be worse?' Well, that's true. It could really always get worse, I mean, what's your husband cheating on you when you could be kidnapped? Who cares about kidnapping when you could nearly get eaten by a wolf or die in a train crash?"

"I think you're misunderstanding that saying," Daemon grumbles. "You're not supposed to expect things to get worse. It's supposed to mean that you should look on the bright side."

"Oh yeah? Tell me what the bright side of today is, because as far as I can see, it's pretty damn dark out."

Daemon glares at me, but Odessa interrupts before he can retort.

"Wait, did you say 'husband?'" Odessa asks, shooting me a surprised look. "Are you married?"

"Uh..." I falter, not having planned to have to explain this. "Kind of. Not really. It's complicated."

"All the best relationships are complicated," Jett says cheerfully, swinging poor Sushi's basket back and forth as he walks.

I stretch my hands out and make grabbing motions until he hands me the picnic basket. I peek inside to make sure the cat isn't too traumatized, then hold the basket carefully before finally answering. "I disagree. I like things to be really simple. Fall in love, happily ever after, the end. No traumatic epilogues."

Jett frowns in confusion. "Then why would you agree to—"

"There's an inn up ahead," Daemon interrupts. "We should stop there, at least to get dried off."

Kastian nods in quick agreement and the two of them speed up, forcing the rest of us to jog in their wake.

Soon enough we reach the town. There's only one long cobblestone street, and perhaps thirty buildings all built extremely close together. Any other time, I would be fascinated to be here—excited, maybe. But now, I barely notice anything around me as we make a beeline for the inn.

The inn looks no different from any of the other old-fashioned houses, except there are lights on inside and loud voices echoing out into the street.

"What time is it?" I ask, glancing at the sky.

"About noon," Odessa replies.

"And the whole town is sitting in the inn's tavern and drinking? Don't they have other things to do?"

Daemon grimaces as he pushes the door open and ushers me inside. "Since no one can go out when the sun is up, they've all gotten used to sleeping during the day. Think of this as midnight."

My brow furrows, but I keep my questions inside as we walk in. The tavern is a large room with a bar on one side and a rickety staircase on the other. It's filled with warm lighting and pipe smoke, and dozens of

Fae chatter loudly. In the corner, there's a tiny raised platform where a couple of musicians are seated, seemingly taking a break from playing. My heart aches with jealousy when I spot a man holding a violin.

"I want to drink my weight in ale," Jett says.

For once, Fox shows signs of paying attention and nods in enthusiastic agreement.

"No," Daemon barks. "We can't stay. We'll just get some rooms for a couple of hours to dry off and regroup."

"Are you fucking serious, Ashwater?" Jett asks, looking dismayed. "The first tavern you've set foot in in ninety years and you don't even want a drink?"

"It's not my first tavern," Daemon mutters, glancing sideways at me.

I feel my cheeks heat slightly. So, when we met at Ted's, it was the first time he'd been out of prison in ninety years? Jesus Christ. No wonder he seemed so interested in me. I hate that my ego is so bruised by this revelation, but at the same time, it kind of makes sense. Daemon is a magical Adonis with wings, and I'm just...me.

"Aren't you all forgetting something?" Odessa asks, interrupting my thoughts. "We don't have any money. Everything we brought with us is at the bottom of the lake in the train."

"We're in uniform," Daemon grumbles. "Who wouldn't serve the king's soldiers?"

As it turns out, this place doesn't give two fucks about the king's soldiers.

The bartender gives Daemon a withering look and tells him to come back with coins. For a moment, I think there's about to be a fight, but to my relief, he walks calmly back to our group.

I guess he's not an asshole to everyone, just to me.

"Now what?" Jett sighs dramatically. "Don't tell me we have to go back outside."

As if on cue, I shiver violently; the internal cold that has sunk into my bones not letting up. I am not the outdoorsy type, and trampling through the woods in the rain sounds like my own personal hell. "I'm with Jett on this one. If we have to walk the rest of the way in the rain, you may as well kill me now."

Daemon runs a frustrated hand through his hair. "I can't conjure coins out of thin air."

I frown, and my eyes dart over to the band in the corner. An idea occurs to me. "You can't conjure coins, but maybe I can. I'll be right back."

Daemon throws out an arm to stop me. "No! You need to stay close."

I roll my eyes. "Where are you expecting me to go? Just give me one second, I think I know a way we can stay."

Begrudgingly, he lets me go, and I stride over to the band. As I walk, I shrug off my cloak, thinking I might do better with them if I don't look like I just crawled out of a lake.

"Hi," I say awkwardly.

The band looks at me, unbothered. I'm not sure if it's because I'm human or because I'm soaking wet, but I decide to pretend I don't notice their judgmental stares.

"Listen. I see you're taking a break. Would you be willing to let me play a set?"

The nearest Fae male looks me up and down. "With what instrument, girly?"

I gnaw on my lip and laugh nervously. "Actually, I was hoping you'd lend me yours."

He bursts out laughing. "I'd sooner lend you my cock to piss with."

I sort of expected that response—if not in so many words—but this is the only idea I have to make some quick cash and I'm not giving up just yet.

"What if I give you something of mine to hold on to so I'll have to give you the violin back." I reach into the neck of my dress and pull out Nana's locket. "Here, how about you hold on to this. I think it's probably worth a lot."

The musicians lean forward to inspect the locket in my hand. One by one, their eyes widen, and their mouths fall open. Then, without a word, the musician hands me his instrument and bow.

"Thank you!" I gush as I take the violin. "But don't you want the necklace?"

He shakes his head. "Keep that thing hidden, girly."

"Okay...well, thank you."

I pluck the strings a few times and turn the pegs, tuning the strings before putting the instrument under my chin and drawing the bow in a couple of practice strokes. The instrument is a bit large for me, and it doesn't seem that they favor chin rests in Ellender, but any instrument is better than none at all.

Suddenly feeling more confident and at home than I have in days, I jump onto the small stage and turn to face the tavern. I'm shocked to find that I already have a captive audience. Apparently as my back was turned, nearly every person in here stopped to watch the soaking wet human try to bargain with the band.

I grin at the crowd. I feel like I should introduce myself but I don't know what to say, so instead I decide to treat this like playing on the street corner and just begin. I bring the bow to the strings and draw it back, letting the first notes of the theme song from *A Kingdom of Thorns* burst forth.

The tavern listens, swaying slightly, but the reaction to the song isn't nearly as enthusiastic as it would be back home. Unfortunately, I'm probably the only person in this entire world who understands how funny it is to play this particular song in this tavern. *Oh well.*

I skip the last verse and meander into another familiar tune, this one with a much livelier tempo. People clap along now, and by the time I've played for ten minutes, there's a small stack of coins at my feet.

Giddy, I close my eyes, letting the music take over. Each note is like a wave, carrying away any worries or negative thoughts and replacing them with pure joy. The room seems to come alive, the walls vibrating with the energy of the music.

I might not have any magic, but music is my magic, and it's casting a spell over every faerie in here.

Finally, when I sense I've been playing long enough, I begin my final song—the lullaby Nana sang for me as a baby.

As I draw over the strings playing the opening notes, a wave of recognition ripples through the crowd. A few cheers ring, some people even jumping out of their seats with excitement. Do they know this song? Why?

Searching for an explanation, my eyes travel over to the familiar group still standing by the door. They all watch me with clear awe. Odessa especially looks enchanted, like she might open her mouth and burst into song at any moment.

I falter when my gaze clashes with Daemon, nearly missing a note. He doesn't look happy at all. Instead, his eyes burn a hole through me, scalding me with alarming intensity. Is he mad at me? Why? Why do I care?

In less than an hour, I earn more than enough coins to pay for rooms at the inn, plus all the ale Jett can drink. I wish the crowds in Chicago were so generous, then maybe I wouldn't be in this mess.

Pleased with my performance, the innkeeper even offers up his son to drive us to the palace in his wagon. The only problem is, the wagon driver won't risk traveling during the day—even if it's raining. We agree to leave at midnight, which leaves us just over twelve hours to rest.

The innkeeper offers us six rooms on the second floor and hands me a pile of keys and gestures for us all to sit at the bar. Jett and Fox grin, and even Kastian looks pleased. Still, I can feel Daemon's eyes boring into the back of my head and it sends shivers down my spine.

I stay for only one drink and long enough to get some sliced chicken for Sushi. Then, even though I'm pretty sure it's only mid-afternoon, I decide to go to bed, leaving the others to their own devices in the tavern. After only a day, the backward sleep schedule and constant darkness is already disorienting. I feel jet-lagged; my body aches and the back of my eyes itch to close. When I get home, I'm taking some of my new money and checking myself into one of those fancy celebrity wellness spas.

"Want me to come upstairs with you and help with your dress?" Odessa asks.

I shake my head as I grab Sushi's carrier from the floor beside her feet. "No thanks. I've been dressing myself for twenty-nine years, I think I can figure it out."

She shrugs. "Suit yourself. Just yell if you need me."

I doubt she'd be able to hear me over the noise of the tavern and the loud voices of the men, already starting in on second and third tankards of ale. Still, I nod with gratitude.

I make my way up the rickety stairs and try my key in several locks before finding the right door. Poor Sushi is having a fit in his basket, and as soon as I close the door behind us, I let him out. He immediately leaps out onto the worn wooden floor, stretches, and hops on the bed.

"Well, Sush, at least there's bound to be some mice here for you to chase," I say, looking around the room with apprehension bordering on disgust.

It's a tiny, shabby room with a single bed and only one dusty window. There's a tiny desk and chair in the corner that look like they're meant for a child, and the quilt on the bed is fraying at every seam. If I were at home, I'd give this place -1000 stars on *TripAdvisor*, but I guess I should just be grateful that I have a bed.

I strip off my still damp dress and hang it on the back of the chair, then climb into the small bed in nothing but my underwear. The darkness and the silence of the room press down on me.

*This was a mistake.*

I should have stayed downstairs with all the noise and distraction. Now, with no phone to scroll aimlessly or audiobook to block out my thoughts, every thought I've suppressed in the last few days hits me all at once.

Holy fuck. I nearly died. *Twice.*

If I died today, my family would never know what happened to me. I'd never get to know what it feels like to be a real grownup, and I'd never get the happily ever after that part of me still thinks is out there somewhere.

In all those fantasy books I like to read, the main characters never seem to internalize all their near-death experiences, but that is so not me. I feel like I need an emergency therapy session and a prescription for horse tranquilizers—and that's just to deal with my impending divorce. How the fuck am I supposed to process all this when I can't even google near death experiences? Should I be crying?

Actually, I haven't cried at all about anything. I didn't cry when I walked in on Ryan and Jenna. I shed a single tear asking for a divorce, but that was hardly cathartic. Then I didn't cry when I thought I'd been kidnapped.

I roll onto my side and pull the thin quilt over my head. I blink a few times, making my eyes water, but no actual tears fall. My head feels fuzzy and too full, like I need to let out some of the pressure but for some reason the tears won't come.

I've never been much of a crier, not since I was a kid and I realized that tears don't change anything, but still...a normal person would cry right now, right?

What the hell is wrong with me?

I DON'T REALIZE I'VE FALLEN ASLEEP UNTIL MY BODY JOLTS awake and I bolt upright, my heart racing and sweat covering my skin. The ghost of my scream echoes through the dark room, reverberating off the walls.

I sit in the dark, panting and shaking. Unbridled anxiety tears through me, making it feel as if the entire room is trembling. I take a few deep breaths, trying to ground myself in reality.

*Just another nightmare.*

I've never been a sound sleeper. I remember hearing as a child that adults grow out of nightmares, but that's never been the case for me. I wake up screaming at least once a week, and every other night is a gamble. It used to drive Ryan insane, to the point that he insisted he'd rather sleep on the couch than be awoken by my terror every night.

Suddenly, the door bursts open and Daemon stands on the threshold, panting. "What happened?

I blink at him in shock. He's shirtless, his tattooed chest on full display in the dim light, and his hair sticking up at the back. Good lord, if I was looking for a distraction to snap me back to reality, this will do just fine.

"Alix, what happened?" Daemon demands again.

"Um, nothing," I stammer, pulling my blankets up to my chin.

"You screamed."

"I just had a nightmare," I mumble, my face heating. "It's not a big deal. Go back to your room."

Daemon's gaze lingers on me for a moment, as if he's trying to read my mind. I shrink back, waiting for him to berate me for acting like a child and waking the entire inn, but he doesn't. Instead, he takes another step into the room and lets the door swing closed behind him. "What did you dream about?"

"Nothing," I say quickly. "It was just the same dream I always have. I thought being in another world might mean I could escape it, but I guess not."

"Tell me what it was about," he says.

*Ugh, fine.* I don't feel like arguing with him about it; I just want this interaction to end as soon as possible. "My dad died in front of me when I was a kid, okay? I dream about it sometimes. A lot of times, actually."

His face twists into an expression I can't read. It's not pity...anger, maybe? But that doesn't make any sense.

"How did he die?"

"I don't want to talk about it. It was a long time ago. Sorry I woke you."

Daemon sucks in a frustrated breath. "I wasn't sleeping anyway."

"Why?"

He shrugs, and I snort a humorless laugh. I guess he likes to ask questions but doesn't like to answer them. *Hypocrite.*

For an awkward moment, we just stare at each other. Now that he's refused to answer my question, I expect him to leave. Instead, he reaches for the desk chair in the corner and sits. Compared with his large frame, the furniture looks even more comically tiny and I almost want to laugh.

"Um, what the hell are you doing?"

He reaches into the back pocket of his trousers and pulls out what looks to be a worn set of playing cards. He raises one eyebrow at me. "Want to play?"

I reel back. "Seriously?"

"It's better than nightmares."

I blink in surprise. "Do you just carry cards around with you at all times?"

"Pretty much. There's not much else to do in Dyaspora."

His mouth tips up in a smirk and my gaze catches on his mouth. "Fine. Move that desk closer. I'm not getting out of bed."

Huffing, he drags the desk and chair to the edge of the bed. I watch in fascination as he begins dealing two hands of cards. "Do you know how to play poker?"

"Do you?" I scoff. "That doesn't seem like a magical game."

"Who do you think taught the humans? Gambling is probably the second most popular Fae pastime."

"What's the first?"

"Seducing fair maidens."

I choke. I think he's joking, but with all his tattooed muscles right in front of me, I still hear his words as more of an invitation than anything else. *Kill me.*

"Is this normal poker?" I ask, taking a quick glance at my cards.

He smirks. "Except for the fact that we don't have any money. You shouldn't have let Jett order all that ale."

"Well, I'm not playing strip poker. It would be over in one turn."

He looks at me, his eyes flicking from my face down the length of my body and back. I think it's the first time he realizes I'm not wearing anything but underwear beneath the thin quilt. He blinks slowly, then shakes his head as if to clear it. "Fine. We'll just pretend, then."

I nod, flushing. Why am I always naked around this man?

Not only that, but I'd have to be blind not to notice the way he just looked at me. It was the same look he gave me yesterday in the Summer Palace, and the other night in my Nana's living room. Like he's on a diet and I'm a slice of chocolate cake. Off-limits but entirely too tempting.

An excited shiver travels down my spine, but a second later, I want to smack myself. I need to get a grip. The Daemon that I met in the bar the other night doesn't exist, and this guy in front of me right now is the magical soldier who kidnapped me and has been rude to me since the moment I woke up this morning. I mean, come on, I know my standards are a little low at the moment but I am not going to let myself obsess over a guy who can't stop rolling his eyes at me.

We're just going to play the game. Platonically. While he's shirtless and I'm practically naked. *Right.*

Daemon finishes dealing the cards, and I fidget nervously with my hand. I'm not entirely sure of the rules, but since we're not betting any real money, it doesn't really matter. We play a round, and to my own surprise and delight, I win. Grimacing, he deals another hand and we play for a few minutes.

"So, are we allowed to talk during this game, or is it a quiet thing?"

He looks at me and nods as if to say, *Go ahead.*

*Okay then.* "Why were you angry when I was playing the violin downstairs?" I ask, my gaze still focused on my cards.

"I wasn't. You're very talented," he says flatly, as if it's just a fact and not a compliment.

"But you were glaring at me."

He sighs, running a hand through his hair. "I was surprised you know that song. I haven't heard it in years."

"My Nana's lullaby?" I ask, confused. "Does it mean something?"

His brow furrows, then he glances away, refusing to meet my gaze. "It's just an old song. Isabelle probably heard it here."

"Huh. I guess I'll add that to the list of things to ask her about when I get back."

Daemon's brow furrows in what looks like worry, but he doesn't say anything.

"So if you didn't mean to glare, which is your real personality?"

"What?"

"It's just that you were pretty nice last night, then today, you'd think I kicked your puppy instead of literally risking my life to help you out... but now you're being nice again? Why?"

Daemon freezes, looking up at me for a split second before his face goes blank. "I wouldn't read too much into this, Peaches. I'm just glad to find someone else awake at this hour."

I think he's lying, but I also don't know why he'd bother. It's not like his behavior toward me gave any impression that he cares about my feelings.

I win a second hand, and he deals a third, then a fourth. "Rub some of that luck off on me," he jokes when I win my fifth hand.

I laugh and toss my cards back onto the table at the same moment as Daemon reaches for the deck. Our fingers brush and a jolt of electricity shoots up my arm, sending shivers down my neck. My breath catches, and I look up to meet his too-green eyes.

Just like that brief moment in the train, we stare at each other. Heat pulses between us, feeling almost tangible in the air. My pulse starts pounding hard in my chest, then lower.

I'm woman enough to admit that despite everything that's happened in the last couple of days, I'm still just as attracted to Daemon as I was sitting at the bar. Is that toxic? Maybe, but I'd hardly be the first girl to want a guy who was bad for her.

I part my lips to suck in a breath. Daemon's eyes dilate, and I'm sure he's thinking the same thing.

Ever so slowly, he shifts his fingers beneath mine, bushing back and forth over the edge of my thumb. Unbidden heat pools between my thighs as I recall the feel of those fingers stroking other more sensitive parts of me. I remember his mouth on my throat, his palms on my ass, fingers digging into my hips as I straddled his lap. I picture him now, throwing me onto the bed, and sinking into me again, filling me up. I lean forward and let go of the blanket so it pools around my waist.

Daemon's eyes flick over my body before landing back on my face. His eyes linger on my lips and heat flares in his gaze.

Before I know what's happening, his lips are on mine. My stomach flutters with a heady mix of excitement and desire as his hand cups my cheek, pulling me closer to him.

He kisses me feverishly, hungrily, and I eagerly respond, my fingers finding their way to the nape of his neck. I tug him toward me onto the bed, knocking the desk out of the way. He lands over me, hands braced on either side of my face. Then, he moves his lips away from mine and down the column of my neck.

I gasp, tingles erupting all over my body and heat pooling in my core. I drag my nails down his bare muscled chest and skate my fingers over his belt.

Without warning, he pulls away from me and jumps back. I blink, and he's standing nearly on the other side of the room. He drags a hand over his mouth, as if to wipe away any evidence of the kiss. "Fuck. Sorry."

The bubble of anticipation in my chest bursts, and a wave of cold washes over me. "What's wrong?"

He narrows his eyes at me. "You know what's wrong."

My eyes immediately fall to the thick outline of his cock straining against his pants. *Okay, so I'm not losing my mind, there is something here.* "Um, no, I don't, or I wouldn't have asked."

He blows out a frustrated breath. "The entire reason you're here is to try and make the king fall in love with you."

"No, I'm here because I'm broke as fuck and I want to be able to pay for my own house and a decent divorce lawyer. I'm not really my Nana and I don't even know King Thorne."

"Still. This" —he points between us— "can't happen. If I've been rude to you today, it's only because I am extremely aware of how dangerous it would be to act as if we've even met before today. For this to work, you have to mean nothing to me."

A sting of rejection shoots through me. I just want to feel...something. What's wrong with that? I rise on my knees on the bed. The blanket falls away entirely. "What about before?"

He winces and looks a bit guilty for a moment before his expression goes blank. "I fucked up before. I didn't know who you were, but that won't matter to Thorne. He's not the forgiving type."

I cross my arms over my chest, letting out a frustrated breath. "So you've said. You know, none of you are really selling why I should want to get anywhere near the king. I'm starting to think I understand why my grandmother ran away."

Daemon shrugs, like he has no good response to that. "I swear he won't hurt you. I won't let him."

"I don't know that. I don't know anything about your king except what you've said."

Daemon drinks me in with his gaze, then runs a hand through his hair, his expression one of actual pain. "You don't really know me either, and you shouldn't want to. I promise you, Peaches, you won't like what you find."

I suck in a shaking breath and blink a few times, willing myself not to say something pathetic. "Okay, I got it." I turn away. "Sorry things got weird. Let's pretend this conversation never happened."

"Wait, Alix—"

"I'm glad we got this cleared up before arriving at the palace. Now, get out. I want to catch another hour of sleep before we have to leave."

I roll over, giving him my back. I can feel his eyes on me for a long second before the floorboards creak, and I know he's leaving.

# CHAPTER
# ELEVEN

ALIX

I don't get a wink of sleep after Daemon leaves my room, but it hardly matters. Before long, it's time to meet the others downstairs and set off for the palace.

The innkeeper's son is waiting outside with a large wagon hitched to two white horses. The back of the wagon is piled with hay and cozy blankets, and it's surprisingly warm and comfortable as we set off through the woods.

There's something about the wagon ride that feels nostalgic, even though I've never experienced anything like it before. There's a heavy scent of rain-soaked pine and roses in the cool air, and before long, the rain turns to fluffy snowflakes. I put my tongue out to catch one and smile.

I feel eyes on me and glance up to find Jett watching me with curious dark eyes. "It's childish, I know."

"No, it's not." He shakes his head, smiling as always. "I've just never seen anyone enjoy snow."

"Really?"

"Until Dyaspora, I'd never even seen snow."

I cock my head in question. "Where are you from?"

"Solistine," he answers with a lopsided grin. "But I suppose you don't know what that is."

"I do," I say quickly. "It's the kingdom to the east of here, right?"

"Yes! Practically, the entire place is one big desert, and what isn't covered in sand is mountains. It's always hot, even in the rainy season."

"Do you miss it?"

He nods slowly and almost looks like his smile might slip for a moment, but it doesn't. "I can't really complain though, can I? This place is far better than Dyaspora even if it is still cold."

My eyebrows furrow. Of all the things I have to worry about, the criminal history of Daemon and his friends isn't exactly at the top of my list. Still, maybe I should at least know who I'm traveling with. "Why did you get sent to prison?"

"Theft," he says, matter-of-factly.

I grimace. "I hope you at least stole something worth taking."

For the first time, his smile falters and anger flashes behind his black eyes. "It was worth it," he growls, sounding a bit like Daemon.

Jett's words hang heavy in the air for a second. Then, he quickly hides his reaction, his grin returning even brighter than before. He throws an arm out to the side, catching Fox around the neck and drawing him closer to us. "But enough about me. Fox here is the only one who's used to the cold. Make him tell you about Thermia."

"Is that where you're from?" I ask, turning to Fox.

Fox's arctic blue eyes narrow on me for a moment, as if he's trying to decide if it's worth wasting his breath by answering. "Yes."

I wait, but he doesn't elaborate.

I remember what Kastian said yesterday: *Fox doesn't talk much— don't take it personally.* God, he really wasn't joking, and as someone who takes everything personally and seeks regular validation, this is like some hellish immersion therapy.

Soon, we spot lights through the trees up ahead. They look magical, like we're approaching the north pole at Christmas. At the edge of the woods, the wagon stops, just as the dirt road is transitioning into frost-covered cobblestones.

"Can you make it from here?" the driver asks, twisting around in his seat to look at us.

"Yes," Daemon says roughly. Then, as if it's an afterthought, he adds, "Thanks."

I crawl across the hay and blankets, following the others out of the wagon. Gripping the railing, I hold the edge of my skirt and stretch my leg to reach the ground.

Suddenly, one of the horses lets out a snort and paws at the ground.

I jerk in surprise, and my foot slips.

"Woah." Jett steadies me. "You alright?"

"Yes." I flush again as I take his hand and scramble the rest of the way out of the wagon. "I'm just not a fan of horses, actually. As long as they stay over there, they're fine, but if one gets near me..."

He furrows his brow. "Why are you afraid of horses?"

"I—"

"Are you two done chatting?" Daemon barks, interrupting us. "Or did you want to waste the rest of the night standing out here in the fucking snow?"

I turn to realize that Daemon, Kastian, and Odessa—carrying Sushi in his basket—are already thirty yards ahead, making their way toward the castle looming over the city. Only Jett, Fox, and I are still lingering by the wagon.

"Yup," I sigh. "Coming. Sorry..."

Daemon grumbles something under his breath and turns his back on us.

"What crawled up his ass?" Jett mutters under his breath.

"What, is he not normally like that?"

He shakes his head. "Nope. Ashwater is intense, but he's not usually an ass. Ever since going to the human realm, something has been off. I wonder—"

Fox bumps him hard with his shoulder. "Don't wonder," he says under his breath. "You might strain a muscle."

Jett seems to take Fox's suggestion to heart and doesn't continue. Still, my mind immediately flies to his explanation last night. *"For this to work, you have to mean nothing to me."*

Now, I'm the one wondering.

Is something about my presence making him act cold to not just me but everyone? If Daemon isn't usually so moody and the only new person here is me, am I the problem?

UNLIKE THE SUMMER PALACE, WHICH IS SURROUNDED BY rose gardens and what looked to be miles and miles of forest, the Winter Palace stands in the heart of a small city.

The city is alive with activity despite the late hour, and we pass dozens of Fae as we wind down the cobblestone street. Many stop to stare, especially at Daemon, but he ignores all of them.

When we reach the town center, my eyes land on a set of long marble stairs. They rise from the middle of the square—where I'd expect a fountain or statue to stand—and stretch nearly out of sight. At the top, the front door of the rose-covered palace looms over the city below. The white stone walls and spindly red-roofed towers are veiled in thorny vines, and even from this distance, I can see red roses improbably blooming despite the snow. At the base of the stairs, two red-jacketed soldiers watch us openly, their expressions unreadable.

I stop walking to gape at the palace, entirely lost in the awe of such a place being real. It's just like I pictured it a thousand times over how many readings of Nana's books. Goosebumps erupt on my arms and my skin begins to tingle with dark anticipation. "I don't know if I can do this."

Everyone stops walking as one and turns to stare at me. Kastian and Odessa look at Daemon, as if expecting him to be the one in charge of my panic attacks.

*Kill me now.*

"What's wrong?" Daemon asks roughly.

*Do I really have to explain this?*

"Um, everything? This is all just hitting me all over again. Assuming the king doesn't recognize me right away, how am I supposed to know what to say? What if he asks me a question I don't know the answer to? Am I supposed to be excited to see him, or angry to be back? What if—"

"Calm down," Odessa says soothingly.

"Okay, the next person who tells me to calm down is getting punched in the face."

She rolls her eyes. "Okay, how about 'take a breath?' It's going to be fine."

"How can you know that? I mean, how am I supposed to act when I meet him?"

"Thorne is a blatant narcissist," Daemon says bluntly. "If you act like you're glad to see him, he won't question why. Even if you had every reason in the world to hate him and years of pent-up bitterness, he'll expect you to be overjoyed to be in his regal presence."

*Sounds like he's speaking from experience.*

"What if he brings up something from when Nana was here before and I don't understand."

Again, Odessa jumps in. "Belle and the king didn't spend a lot of time together when she was here before, so it's not as if there can be a lot of moments you're expected to remember, and anything you don't know, you can blame on the sixty-year difference. Just say you forgot."

*Okay...maybe that could work, but that's a pretty strong maybe.*

"What did she do while she was here?" I ask.

"Mostly she was in her room with Shar and me, or in the library. Well, except for the dinners."

"What dinners?" Daemon asks, whipping his head around to look at his cousin.

"King Thorne always wanted Belle to eat supper with him."

"And you weren't there?" I ask, trying not to let my own panic and frustration sound in my voice.

Odessa shakes her head. "No one was."

Daemon grimaces. "So in other words, we have no idea what they talked about."

*Oh my God, I'm going to crash the fuck out.*

I spin in a circle, looking around anxiously for somewhere to sit down until large hands clamp down on my shoulders, stopping my movement. I look up, and find myself staring into Daemon's too-green eyes.

"Stop it, Peaches," he says, not entirely unkindly. "Let's just hope he doesn't recognize you. If the court is still like it was before, there will be hundreds of people in the room when we go to see him. He might not have time to ask you a lot of questions."

My eyes widen. I don't know why he thinks having an audience of *hundreds* will make me less anxious.

He moves closer, and something pangs in my chest. He reaches for my chin and forces my eyes back up to his, literally holding my attention.

"I told you, I'm not going to let anything happen to you. As long as I'm breathing, no one will touch you."

I blink, sure for a second I must have misheard. *God! Who says things like that?*

I suck in a deep breath and my hands fall loosely to my sides. I have no reason to take him at his word, especially when every other thing out of his mouth is slightly insulting.

But for some reason, I do.

DAEMON

Alix's cheeks flush as she pulls her chin out of my grasp and steps back.

I blink, suddenly aware that we've been staring at each other for several seconds longer than is normal. I shake my head as if to clear it.

*What the fuck is wrong with me?*

I've already fucked this situation up enough as it is—first by allowing myself to be distracted by Alix. Then by letting my frustration with my brother spill into every conversation with her. And worst of all, by going to her room last night.

Once I realized that her scream wasn't caused by some attack, I should have left. There was no reason for me to linger there with her, and even less of a reason for me to be thinking about it now...

*Except that I wanted to.*

*I wanted her.*

I still want her, which is way too fucking dangerous. I could justify to myself anything that happened before I knew who Alix was, but now? I can't let anything happen again. Even when she looks at me like she did last night, and I know without a doubt she'd let me fuck her again in a heartbeat.

I need to ignore her.

*I need to get a fucking grip.*

I turn back to my friends and find them all watching us. Fox looks annoyed, Jett amused, and Kastian seems worried. I make the mistake of catching Odessa's eye, and find her smiling smugly.

I blow out a frustrated breath and blink repeatedly, determined to stay focused on anything but Alix. I straighten my shoulders and force my expression back to neutral as we approach the palace. "Let's go!"

"Stop!" the nearest guard barks when I'm only a few feet away.

Sneering, I keep walking, brushing past the nearer of the two guards. "Move back, kid. You see the uniforms, right? The king is expecting us."

"Wait!" The other guard moves from his position, jumping out in front of me as if he intends to physically bar me from entering. "I've never seen you before. You'll have to speak with our commander."

I look at the guard, bemused. The idea that he could stop me is laughable; I'm twice his size. Still, I can appreciate the effort.

Technically, *I'm* their commander—or I will be in a matter of minutes. Thorne wasn't at the Summer Palace to make the transfer of power clear among the guards, but he promised to reinstate all my positions the moment I brought him Isabelle. Thorne is almost entirely made of flaws, but he doesn't tend to promise things he can't deliver.

Still, I suppose I'd like to know who's been leading the army in my absence, and this is as good a time as any to find out. "Fine," I bark. "Bring us to him."

The guard looks startled, but motions for us to follow up the stone stairs. I nudge Alix forward to walk in front behind the guard. Jett throws me a shit-eating grin and darts after her, forcing me to walk behind him. *Fucking idiot.*

"Who puts a castle at the top of all these stairs?" Alix pants as we climb. "You guys couldn't use some of your magic to make escalators?"

"We're almost there!" Odessa calls bracingly from the back of the group.

"Bullshit, we are *not*," Alix hisses, then stops and turns to Jett directly behind her. She holds both arms out, like she wants him to pick her up. "Okay, I changed my mind, the wings aren't scary. Let's go, fly boy. Beam me up or whatever."

"Uh..." Jett stammers, for once at a loss for words. He freezes and glances over his shoulder at me, obviously waiting for instructions.

*For the love of fucking God.*

Part of me realizes that Alix is probably only gravitating toward Jett because he's *nice*, the same way she's already warming up to Odessa. Still, I find myself grinding my teeth.

I make sure Alix isn't watching me before growling under my breath so only Jett can hear. "Don't you fucking dare."

"Sorry, Princess," he says jovially. "There are no shortcuts here. Keep walking."

Alix groans and keeps climbing, clutching a stitch in her side. I grind my teeth even harder. I don't like watching her discomfort. *I could always carry her myself, but how would I explain that to the others?*

"You have to tell her not to bring up flying," Kastian mutters under his breath.

"I don't have to do anything," I growl, still watching Alix out of the corner of my eye. "Just because I found her doesn't make her my pet. You tell her. You're the one who convinced her we're like goddamn fish."

I can't see him behind me, but I can tell just from his tone that he's shaking his head. "You're being a fucking idiot. Just say something before she brings it up around Thorne and ruins everything."

I know he has a point, but there's no time to argue. I just hope I'm right—that the throne room will be crowded enough to keep Thorne from questioning Alix—Isabelle, that is—too closely.

Before I decide if I should offer to carry Alix, we finally reach the top of the steps and the guard leads us through the front doors and into an entrance hall. "Wait here, I'm going to get the commander."

I nod and cross my arms, leaning against the wall near the door. The Winter Palace is larger than the summer one, but the architecture is mostly the same, with towering ceilings carved from golden marble, ornate pillars in every corner, and red tapestries hanging on every available wall.

We stand around for a few minutes in the entrance hall while the guard searches for their commander. I watch Alix out of the corner of my eye, noticing that she's wringing her hands in her skirt and seems to get more anxious by the second. That guard better come back quickly, or I'm going to take matters into my own hands and burst into the throne room whether I've been invited or not.

I'm relieved when finally I hear footsteps descending down the huge stone steps.

"Ashwater!" the figure in the distance raises a hand in greeting.

"Oh, fuck me," I growl under my breath. "I should have known."

"What's wrong?" Kas asks.

I don't have time to answer before the commander is only a few feet away. I raise my hand unenthusiastically. "Hello, Foulo. It's been too long."

Foulo barks out a laugh as he stands in front of me. He nudges my shoulder with his as if we're friends. "You could say that, but I'd say ninety years is a light sentence compared with most who enter the Dyaspora. I called a dozen men liars before breakfast when they told me you were back on Vernal soil. What happened? Did the king find it in himself to grant you mercy?"

I keep my mouth shut. There's no answer that I can give that wouldn't somehow come back to bite me in the ass.

Foulo is a lesser nobleman, older than me by several decades. He's short for a Fae male, barely reaching my shoulder, and so muscular he looks a bit like a troll. His usually close-cropped blonde hair and beard are in need of a trim, and as he grows closer, I notice that his crimson military jacket seems slightly too small in the neck and shoulders while too long in the arms.

Foulo and I didn't grow up together, but we still entered the army around the same time as I started far younger than anyone should. He's fanatically loyal to my brother, and I'm not surprised that he replaced me as commander.

"I'm here to see the king," I bite out. "He's expecting us."

"Oh really?" Foulo's eyes dart over to my friends behind me. They linger for a fraction of a second on Kastian, then far longer on Alix.

*Fuck.*

My fingers curl into a fist, and I shove them in my pocket, trying to remain calm even as I've just realized a potentially deadly mistake.

Thorne might be oblivious, but the entire castle isn't. There are hundreds of people who may have crossed paths with the original Isabelle and could notice that Alix is an imposter. I've thought at length about what to say if Thorne seems suspicious, but I've never thought about what to do if someone else immediately sees through us.

As if he can hear my thoughts, Foulo glances at me, then back to Alix. His eyes narrow slightly. "Lady Isabelle. I admit, I almost didn't recognize you."

I hold my breath.

Fuck, this is it. We're going to get caught before we even enter the palace.

This is my fault. I should have prepared Alix better.

In a split second, I make a decision. If Foulo recognizes Alix, I'm going to kill him right here, right now. I hope it doesn't come to that, but I'm prepared to react if it does. I'll play nice as long as possible, pretending to be the perfect loyal soldier, but if anyone tries to hurt Alix or any of my friends, I won't be caught off guard the way I was ninety years ago.

This time, I'll fucking kill them all—even Thorne.

"Hello Foulo," Alix says in a clear tone, neither too friendly nor unfamiliar. "It's a pleasure to see you again."

I nearly laugh with relief. I can only assume she's been listening and picked up his name from my conversation, but she makes it sound like she's known him for years.

Foulo puffs his chest, looking pleased. He steps forward, reaching around me to grab Alix's hand. "Come. The king is in the throne room. I'll walk you there."

"Oh—" Alix blurts out as Foulo tugs her roughly forward. "I'm fine on my own."

"Nonsense," Foulo says, too enthusiastically. He grips her too tightly, dragging her like a limp rag doll away from me and further into the palace.

Spontaneous rage erupts inside me. Before I can stop myself, my hand shoots out, gripping the back of Foulo's jacket. "Let her go. Now."

ALIX

OH MY GOD.

Foulo chokes and splutters as Daemon pulls him backward, strangling him by the collar. His fingers slide off my arm, his hands flying to his throat.

*Oh. My. God.*

I gape at Daemon, half horrified and half pleased that he clearly isn't playing around. Then again, he's probably just thinking about the optics. Soldiers probably aren't supposed to grab the king's girlfriend... or whatever I'm supposed to be.

I could swear Foulo looked suspicious when Daemon introduced me, but he seems to have gotten over it quickly enough. I guess now he has other things to worry about...like breathing.

Looking a bit too smug with himself, Daemon lets go of Foulo's jacket collar. The soldier gasps for breath, then whirls to glare reproachfully at Daemon and then me. "I thought you said the king was expecting you." He sneers. "I was only trying to help."

Daemon gnashes his teeth. "She can walk on her own."

Still looking angry—and worse, suspicious—Foulo doesn't reach for me again. Instead, he gestures for us to follow him across the high-ceilinged grand entryway and down a short hallway that ends at a set of intricately carved golden double doors. Beyond them, I hear the muffled voices of what sounds like hundreds of people, mingling with the delicate notes of live music.

Immediately, my anxiety spikes. My hands turn cold and clammy while every other part of me seems too hot. The "practical" blue dress that Odessa chose for me is clinging to my skin, and I'm pretty sure the best thing to do would be to turn around and sprint down the hall.

Daemon immediately stops and turns around as if he can sense my panic. The anger he showed Foulo is still on his face, but it dissolves into concern as he looks at me. He stays further back than he did outside—probably afraid that getting too close will make Foulo suspicious—but still, his gaze is just as intense as his bright green eyes pierce mine.

"Nothing is going to happen," he breathes. "It's going to be fine."

I suck in a deep breath trying to calm down, but my gaze finds Foulo's suspicious dark eyes. I can't think of anything to say that won't give us away...which really feels like a sign this was a bad idea. If I can't even pretend to be Nana in front of a random soldier, how am I going to convince King Thorne—*The* King Thorne, who I wrote fanfic about in middle school and secretly kind of liked in the terrible movie adaptations.

"Is something wrong, Lady Isabelle?" Foulo says, his tone syrupy with false concern.

"She's fine," Daemon snaps. "Just nervous."

Foulo nods to me. "Of course. Do you need a moment? Or perhaps to freshen up?"

I shake my head robotically. "No. I'm fine."

I am so *not* fine, but if I "take a moment to freshen up," I'm pretty sure I'm never coming back. And since my alternate option is wandering alone around a magical kingdom with giant wolves and who knows what else...yeah, I'm kind of stuck here.

Foulo turns his back on us to push the double doors open wide. To my surprise, Daemon reaches out and grips my fingers for the briefest half a second before he turns his attention back to the doors. It's like he's saying "Thank you" or maybe "You'll be fine."

My heartbeat speeds up a little, and the tips of my fingers tingle with heat. Against all reason, I feel a little better. Braver.

Finally, Foulo pushes open the golden double doors. Beyond, I see a long throne room with towering cathedral ceilings and gilded arches over every window. Dozens of lords and ladies, dukes and duchesses litter both sides of the room, like something out of a renaissance painting.

When my gaze finally lands on King Thorne, I nearly choke.

The king lounges on his throne, watching us as we approach. He's absurdly handsome, with flowing dark blond hair and light eyes, which he turns on me the moment we enter the room. He looks *exactly* like the character I've always pictured. No wonder Daemon realized something was up—that cover artist must be some kind of psychic.

Daemon takes a long step toward the door, followed closely by

Kastian and the others, but Foulo throws out an arm, blocking them from entering the throne room. "I'm sure the king has better things to do than entertain criminals and servants."

"You two go," Kastian mutters to Daemon. "We'll all stay here. We don't mind waiting outside."

Daemon nods, then once again tries to walk into the room, only for Foulo to stop him a second time. Foulo's eyes narrow, any pretense that they're friends has vanished and now he just looks bitter and angry. "Only Lady Isabelle can enter."

I step back. *Um, is he kidding? I'm not going in there alone. No fucking way!*

Clearly, Daemon and I are on the same page for once. He growls low, throwing Foulo's arm off with enough force that he stumbles. "That's not fucking happening. I'm going with her."

"No!" Foulo snaps. "I'm the commander of the guard now, and I say you're not welcome."

Clearly trying and failing to keep his anger under control, Daemon turns his back on Foulo and stands in the still open doorway. He looks up over the heads of the court and raises his voice to a near shout. "Thorne! I don't know how you expect me to bring you your woman if I can't even enter the palace. Call off your dog or I'll take Isabelle back where I found her."

For a long second, the entire crowd falls silent. Foulo splutters, and even I draw back, nearly choking once more on my own surprise.

Across the enormous hall, the king's eyes lock on Daemon, then slide to me. I hold my breath.

Then, the king smiles and raises a lazy hand to beckon us both inside.

Daemon and I walk side by side down the long aisle in the center of the throne room. Hundreds of eyes track us, and I feel my brain start to shut down from nervousness.

Daemon stops about ten feet from the base of the raised dais where the king sits on his throne. I halt beside him and look up. For a moment, I forget everything—why I'm here, the danger pressing in from all sides, even the warnings Daemon and the others have given me about the kind of man Thorne truly is.

Because right now, it's an out-of-body experience.

I'm staring at the exact character I've read about for years, brought to life in vivid, impossible detail. The face I've imagined a thousand times in the pages of *A Kingdom of Thorns* is here, flesh and blood, watching me.

"Ashwater," Thorne drawls in a tone that sounds like a greeting and a judgment all at once.

"Your Highness," Daemon replies, a hint of sarcasm in his tone.

He makes a funny jerking movement with his head, like he knows he should bow, but is physically rebelling against it. Perhaps his arrogance is too much at odds with that level of royal respect.

I guess the king thinks so too because he laughs coldly. "'Your Highness,' is it? Wasn't it just yesterday that you were telling me to go fuck myself?"

There's a sharp intake of shocked breath from around the room, but Daemon doesn't seem rattled. "When you save a man from the Dyaspora, you earn yourself eternal loyalty."

Thorne smiles.

I can't help but remember what Daemon said outside. That King Thorne is so self-centered he will believe anyone is overjoyed to see him, regardless of what reason they might have not to be. Am I witnessing that in action, or is Daemon honestly grateful to the king?

I don't have long to think about it as at that moment, the king turns his attention to me. He steps off the dais and walks toward me, arms slightly outstretched as if he expects me to run to him, but I freeze.

*Should I hug him, or am I supposed to bow?*

*Should I say something?*

*If he realizes I'm not my Nana, what will he do? Will he kill me right here? Would Daemon let him?*

I try to smile but can't as Thorne reaches me, standing just inches away. His eyes skim over me, sharp and assessing, before settling on the necklace resting against my collarbone. A flicker of something—recognition? Satisfaction? —flares in his gaze. Before I can react, his arm snakes around my waist, pulling me flush against him. My breath catches in shock, but I don't have time to process it before his lips crash onto mine.

The force of it steals the air from my lungs. His mouth is hot, demanding, his tongue gliding over my parted lips like he has every right to be here.

A jolt of something electric shoots through me—whether from shock or something more terrifying, I don't know.

*Oh my God, I'm kissing a fairytale.*

As King Thorne holds me to him, a tingling sensation that has nothing to do with the kiss spreads through my body, sending shivers down my spine. I can almost feel Daemon's piercing gaze burning into the back of my head.

Finally, King Thorne lets me go.

"Belle," he breathes, his lilting accent drawing out the word like a caress. "Forgive me. I never thought I'd see you again."

I stumble back, dazed. My lips part, but I'm at a loss for what to say. I can't even begin to guess what Nana might say in this situation. My mind goes blank, and before I know what I'm saying, I steal a melodramatic line from Rose, the protagonist. "I've counted every moon since we were last together and thought the sun might never rise."

*Ugh, kill me.*

I feel my cheeks heat. I can't believe I said that out loud. But then again, maybe it was a good thing because King Thorne beams at me. "Perhaps it would be better for us to speak in private. I want to know all that has happened to you since you left, and why you've agreed to return now."

"Y-yes," I stammer. "I'd like that."

Thorne turns away from me and smiles at all the courtiers watching us. "Lady Isabelle has returned to us. Though the rose moon is fast approaching, I have no doubt that now that she is here, our plight will soon end."

Cheers erupt, and I turn to look at them as well and am startled to see them looking at me with excitement...perhaps hope?

I glance behind me, my gaze searching out Daemon's for reassurance, but can't catch his eye. His jaw is clenched tight, and his hands are curled into fists at his sides.

What the fuck is he so upset about? His plan worked; he should be happy.

"Your Majesty, if I might ask a question..." Foulo's smug voice rings out over the crowd of watching courtiers.

King Thorne glances imperiously at the man and nods for him to continue.

Foulo clears his throat. "Not only the uh, former Baron Ashwater, but several other unknown soldiers arrived with Lady Isabelle. As the commander of your army, I think—"

Thorne raises an eyebrow. "Thank you for bringing this to all of our attention, Foulo."

Foulo's broad chest puffs out in pride. "Of course, Your Majesty, I—"

King Thorne cuts him off, continuing as if there was no interruption. "This is an ideal time to make the entire court aware that in recognition of finding Lady Isabelle and returning her to me, I have promised to return all lands and titles to Commander Ashwater."

"W-what?" Foulo splutters. "But...Your Majesty..."

King Thorne just waits as Foulo launches into complaints.

I glance over at Daemon, wondering how he views all of this. Is he enjoying the king putting Foulo in his place? I would think any normal person would be. He's getting public recognition, plus all his stuff back after years in prison. Except, his expression doesn't reflect that. He looks pissed. No, *furious.*

"What's wrong?" I whisper, under the cover of Foulo's loud protests.

Daemon doesn't seem to hear me.

"Foulo, enough," King Thorne says loudly. "Why don't you make yourself useful and escort Lady Isabelle to her chambers before dinner."

Foulo scowls. For a moment, he doesn't move. Then, clearly realizing he has no choice but to obey, he stalks toward me.

*Oh God. Here we go again.*

I'm not sure if he is over eager to follow orders or just controlling, but this time, I expect the large fingers reaching for my upper arm and dodge out of the way. Instead, Foulo's fingers close around the ends of my long curly hair.

"Ow!" I blurt out.

In a split second, several things happen at once.

Beside me, the king goes stiff. His hand flies out, but not as if he's going to grab for me. The hand in my hair disappears, and before I can process what's happening, Foulo is flying across the room and landing spread-eagled in the middle of the carpeted aisle.

*I gape at the king. Did he do that? Is it magic, or—*

My thoughts stutter to a halt as I realize it's far from over. Daemon launches himself after Foulo, his outstretched fingers closing around Foulo's throat.

"Keep your filthy fucking hands off her," Daemon roars, his voice echoing all around the now silent room.

Foulo turns beet-red, but it's unclear if that's from embarrassment or because Daemon is cutting off his windpipe. He jerks backward, freeing himself from Daemon's hold, and sneers. "Or what, Ashwater?"

"Or I'll make sure you never touch anything again. Enjoy jerking your tiny cock while you can, because the next time you touch her will be the last time you have fingers."

*Holy shit.*

He sounds unhinged, and...hot? I don't like when guys have too much alpha male energy, and I definitely don't go for roided-out psychopaths. So why am I suddenly warm all over?

"Stop!" Thorne raises his voice in a deafening command.

Instantly, the room goes silent. Daemon freezes, and even Foulo stops struggling and goes still and quiet. Even I find myself rooted to the spot, and I'm not sure I could open my mouth to speak even if I wanted to.

After a long second, Daemon is the first to move. He turns slowly, looking over his shoulder at Thorne. For the briefest second, I think I see him pale. His eyes dart all around, as if he's only just now realized where he is and what words just came out of his mouth. "Thorne—"

The king strides forward. His face is twisted in anger, but as he approaches Daemon and Foulo on the floor, the anger melts and is replaced with...amusement? He stops and gestures for Daemon to stand. "I didn't know you cared so much about protecting what's mine. Should I take that as a sign that against all odds, the Dyaspora has reha-bilitated you?"

Daemon straightens his posture and smirks. His expression is arro-gantly pleased, yet the smile reaches every part of his face except his eyes. "As I was saying before, when you free a man from the Dyaspora, you earn yourself eternal loyalty."

Thorne grins back, looking satisfied. "That settles it, then."

"Settles what?" Daemon asks sharply.

"You'll guard Isabelle for me until the rose moon." He shoots a mutinous look at Foulo on the floor. "I can't have anything happening to her before then."

"What happens at the rose moon?" I ask, but no one seems to hear me.

"But—" Daemon chokes, looking horrified. "I can't guard her."

"Why not?" The corner of the king's mouth tips up. "I thought you wanted to return to the court."

"What about during the day," Daemon demands, a bit more rudely than I would expect anyone to speak to a king.

Thorne seems to take it in stride. "She'll have to adopt our habits eventually. Sleeping when the sun is high is no hardship if one remains in the dark."

"But you just said I would have all my positions reinstated." He sounds a little desperate. "The commander cannot spend all his time guarding one woman. Who will run the army?"

"I cannot think of a more important role for the commander of my army than making sure my rose is kept safe until the moon."

Daemon looks equal parts angry and horrified. "But—"

"Be quiet!" Thorne rumbles, using the same commanding tone that silenced the room only minutes ago. "Do not test me, Ashwater. You've gotten everything you've ever wanted just as I promised. You should be kissing the fucking ground in gratitude. Do not give me a reason to change my mind."

Daemon grits his teeth, but finally steps back. He nods once. "Fine."

"*Yes, Your Majesty*," King Thorne corrects, his tone mocking.

The muscles in Daemon's neck strain. His hands curl into fists, and he looks as if he's physically holding himself back from attacking the king like he just attacked Foulo. I suck in a breath.

Seeming to hear my gasp, Daemon glances over at me. Our eyes connect and I see a hundred thoughts pass behind his eyes. Then, just like that, he relaxes. His face turns blank and he tips his head toward Thorne in something resembling a bow. "Yes, Your Majesty."

Thorne claps his hands and smiles. "Good."

Movement and sound seem to return to the room, and the king's anger vanishes just as fast as it came. Still, my ears are ringing. I feel shocked—exhausted, even. I don't know what I just witnessed, but the tension in the room and between Daemon and the king feels so thick it's hard to breathe.

"Take Isabelle back to her room to prepare for dinner. I want to see her every evening until the rose moon," Thorne says to Daemon, speaking about me as if I'm not present.

"What happens at the moon?" I ask again, louder.

They both turn to look at me. Thorne's eyes narrow, somewhere between confusion and anger. "Our wedding, of course."

*Holy shit.*

A stone drops into my stomach and for a moment I think I'm going to be sick. Or maybe even pass out again. I've never fainted in my life until this week, but I swear I can't get enough air into my lungs. I put a hand to my forehead.

At the same moment, both Daemon and the king step forward, hands outstretched as if to catch me if I fall.

My heart thunders in my chest, and I glance between them.

Daemon's eyes are wide with panic, while the king's narrow with something like annoyance.

For the briefest moment, I feel trapped. Caught in the center of two forces I'm not sure I really understand.

Then I suck in a breath and steady myself.

No one has to catch me, I did it myself...but there's a little voice in the back of my mind that tells me this won't be the last time I feel stuck in the middle.

# CHAPTER
# TWELVE

ALIX

"A wedding?" I whisper loudly as I speed-walk down a long hallway beside Odessa, who is carrying Sushi in his basket. "A goddamn wedding? No, *no*, abso-fuckin-luely not."

"Would you shut up," she hisses. "We can't talk about this here."

I glare at her. I'm confused, frustrated, and worst and most embarrassing of all, I feel a strange sense of betrayal. Like Daemon owed it to me to tell me about this. "I just want to know what the fuck is going on!"

"Shhh," Dessa says, almost desperately. "Belle doesn't swear."

I raise an eyebrow, momentarily distracted from what I'm upset about. "Um, yes, she does. Whose fault do you think it was when I called my kindergarten teacher a cun—"

"Shh!" she interrupts again, glancing over her shoulder. "We're almost there, just wait a minute!"

I didn't faint in the throne room, but it was a near thing. I was quickly ushered outside into the entrance hall, where suddenly I could breathe normally again. Daemon didn't say a word to me or even look at me once we were outside. He merely demanded that Odessa take me to my room.

I didn't point out that the king had told him to escort me himself, but now I wish I had. I need answers *now*, and Dessa isn't giving them to me fast enough for my panicked brain to understand.

She finally stops outside an unremarkable looking door and throws it open, practically shoving me into a bedroom.

It's similar to the one at the Summer Palace, except instead of white and gold décor, this room is decorated in moody shades of red and purple. There are arched stained-glass windows on every wall which I'd imagine would be beautiful in the sunlight, but are now dark and hard to make out.

Odessa shuts the door and quickly darts around the room, opening the wardrobe and checking the bathroom and under the bed, like she's expecting to find someone hiding. When she's satisfied we're alone, she lets out a long breath. "Alright. Say whatever the fuck you want."

I almost smile, but then I remember that she's undoubtedly part of this and the humor leaves me in a whoosh. "Did you know I'm expected to get married?"

"Yes."

"Why didn't anyone tell me?"

"I thought you knew."

"No! I would never have agreed to this if I did."

She grimaces. "Many women would be thrilled for a chance to marry a king."

"Yeah, and many women haven't been married before," I snap. "I don't want to go through that again so soon. Maybe ever! And anyway, if my grandmother didn't want your king, then I have to assume she had a good reason. It's not like my grandfather was such a prize."

"Ca—"

"Do not tell me to calm down!"

I flush, feeling slightly bad for snapping at her the moment the words leave my mouth.

To cover my discomfort, I pick up Sushi's basket from beside the door and stride over to the red velvet covered bed where I let him out. The cat looks at me reproachfully and I give him an apologetic scratch on the head. Then, I sit on the end of the bed and face Dessa, taking a deep calming breath. "Explain."

She wrings her hands in her skirt. "I just don't understand the miscommunication. How did you think the curse was broken? The king has to find true love."

"Yeah...but I didn't realize that meant marrying him."

Odessa grimaces, looking apologetic and nervous at once. "I'm sorry. I really thought you knew."

"I can't do this, I—" I start to say I'm already married, but that doesn't even feel like the point here. I don't think the Fae would care about my human marriage certificate from another world. "I don't even know him."

"Neither did the others."

My eyes widen. "Excuse me? What others?"

Odessa purses her lips and crosses the room and sits beside me on the bed. "You know...I mean, did you think the king let the curse go on for a hundred years without trying to do anything about it?"

"I hadn't really thought about it."

"He's tried six other times to find the right woman to break the curse. Belle was the only one who left before they could be married. I assumed that's why he wanted her back—perhaps she was the one who would have broken the curse, after all."

"So what happened to the other wives?"

"He let them go back to their homes once it was clear the curse hadn't broken."

I blink at her. "If he was just fine letting them leave, wouldn't that mean he didn't love any of them in the first place?"

Odessa frowns. "That's what I always thought too. Which is why it seemed to make sense that Belle is the right one, you know? She was the one who got away and obviously the king wanted her to come back. He gave her the necklace to stay young and everything."

I pull the necklace out of my collar and inspect it. Even though I heard and accepted what Daemon said about it the other day, it still hasn't fully sunk in that Nana could have stayed completely immortal if she'd wanted to.

"Oh God," I blurt out, eyes wide. "If I wear this, will I stop aging? Wait, don't answer that...I already know. I just hadn't thought about it."

We fall silent, Odessa watching me as I think.

In the book, Thorne and Rose get married, but I didn't realize it was a requirement to break the curse. In a weird way, I feel bad for the king. It was hard to tell from only a few short minutes in front of a large audience, but the king didn't seem like that bad of a guy. Maybe a little cold? But from the way Daemon and Odessa were talking about him, I was expecting a vicious beast, but King Thorne seemed no different than the character I grew up crushing on.

"Well, I'm not getting married," I insist. "I promised Daemon I would stay for one month and at the end, he'd pay me and take me home. Nowhere in that conversation was marriage mentioned."

Odessa bites her lip. "Maybe Daemon has a plan?"

"Oh yeah," I blurt out. "That's another thing. What the hell was Daemon doing in the throne room? He literally attacked that other soldier."

"Yeah...we could hear it outside. I don't know what he was thinking, but he's always hated Foulo. Maybe that was all it was about."

"Why would King Thorne want Daemon to be the one to keep Isabelle safe? He just got out of fucking *prison*."

"Maybe because he owes Thorne for letting him out of Dyaspora and if the curse doesn't break he'll never get to enjoy his freedom. And I wouldn't judge him for being sent to Dyaspora. You don't understand."

"Yeah, because no one has told me what happened. Why was he exiled?"

"You should really ask him about it. It's not my story."

I sigh, thinking back to my conversation with Daemon when I agreed to pretend to be Nana, and a sense of unease settles over me. He never said anything about saving the kingdom, just about his friends...

"Even if I was willing to get married, would it even matter? I know you guys think there's a chance I can break the curse even if I'm not really my Nana, but I'm not sure that will work."

"Neither are we, but there's not a lot of good choices left. There's only a month before all of Vernallis is lost forever. It won't affect me, but everyone I know will just be gone." Her voice turns sad, and her expression grows stricken as she talks.

"Explain to me again why it doesn't affect you?" I ask, gnawing on my own lip.

"Because I was born in Hydratta," she answers quickly. "That's the kingdom to the south of Vernallis. Even though I spent nearly my entire life here, I'm technically not a Vernal citizen."

"And that's the same with Jett, Fox and Kastian?"

She nods. "I think so. I don't know them any better than you do, but Kastian is definitely from Hydratta."

"Do you know him or something?"

She shakes her head, her expression darkening. "Not really. We've met before, but clearly it wasn't memorable since he didn't even remember me. I mostly just know of his family. He's—" She breaks off at the sound of a sudden loud knock on the door.

The door opens and another maid walks in, dressed in the same red and black uniform as Odessa and carrying an enormous purple box. She curtsies stiffly. "Afternoon, my lady. I was asked to bring you this."

She holds up the box like she's presenting a prize on a gameshow before setting it down on the dresser near the door.

"What is it?" I ask.

The maid just shakes her head. "I didn't ask, ma'am."

The maid retreats without another word and Odessa jumps off the bed, striding across the room. She opens the box and gasps.

"What is it?" I ask again, more urgently.

My mind is jumping to the worst possible options. *Maggots...fruitcake...someone's head.*

"This is gorgeous," Odessa exclaims, pulling out a glittering silver gown and holding it up to herself. "And there's a note. It says, *Supper is at 3.*"

I raise an eyebrow. "At three? Isn't that a bit early."

"3 in the morning," Odessa clarifies. "You'll get used to living in the dark. It's not really that bad after a while..."

I grimace and bury my face in my hands. *I highly fucking doubt that.*

In a matter of hours, Odessa has cajoled me into taking a bath and putting on the silver gown. She does my hair and makeup, and by the time she's finished, I barely recognize myself.

"Reason number 1075 why I would never go through with this wedding." I glance at myself in the full-length mirror in the corner. "Once in a while is nice, but I could never dress like this every day."

"But you look amazing," Odessa squeals.

The gown is strapless with a corset-style bodice and a floor-length A-line skirt. The fabric is slightly metallic and shimmers every time I move. The whole look is giving prom more so than Met gala, but I have to admit I do look good.

Comfortable on the other hand? Not at all.

"Are you going to walk to dinner with me?" I ask. "I don't know where I'm going, and I'm guessing 'Belle' would know."

My perception of Belle and Nana is getting wider by the minute. I feel less like I'm pretending to be my grandmother and more like I'm cosplaying as Rose from *A Kingdom of Thorns.* Maybe that's not so bad. If Nana based Rose on herself, my impression of her will hopefully be believable.

"Daemon will walk you to dinner," Odessa says, interrupting my thoughts. Her brow wrinkles. "I'm surprised he's not here already. The king said to guard you, and if he doesn't, he'll be in serious trouble."

"What is he supposed to guard me from? Isn't the castle safe?"

She shrugs. "The rest of the court, I assume. We all like to pretend the curse isn't an issue, but it could be really dangerous for you."

As if we summoned him, the door opens and Daemon walks in. He didn't bother to knock, and I cross my arms over my chest. What if I'd been changing?

Actually, that probably wouldn't have mattered at all—keeping up with the tradition of my never wearing clothes in his presence.

Daemon walks in with his head down, lost in thought. His expression is unreadable, his brow furrowed as if he's turning something over in his mind. Then, after a moment, he looks up.

The second his eyes land on me, he freezes. His mouth parts slightly, and something flickers across his face—shock? Recognition? Hunger?

His gaze drags over me, slow and thorough, like he's committing every detail to memory. It's not just a glance; it's an inspection, an unraveling. My skin prickles, heat blooming under his scrutiny, as though he's stripping me bare without laying a single hand on me.

When his eyes finally meet mine again, I swallow hard, feeling trapped—pinned beneath the weight of something I don't fully understand.

"That bad, huh?" I joke, trying to cover my anxiety.

He swallows and shakes his head roughly. "Are you ready?"

"I guess," I mutter. "I'm assuming I don't have a choice?"

He shakes his head again. "Better to get it over with now. If you can convince him you're definitely Isabelle during this dinner, then he's not likely to bring it up again."

"Is he already suspicious?" I ask, panicked.

"No...I don't think so."

The way he says that doesn't fill me with confidence, but there's not really anything to do except follow him out into the hall. Daemon gestures for me to walk ahead of him and I pick up the hem of my dress so I don't trip, like a princess in a movie.

"If he's not suspicious, then why did you have to stay behind and talk to him? What did he want?"

"That's not why I stayed behind," he says shortly.

"Oh...then why?"

He keeps his eyes fixed firmly in front of him, as if he doesn't want to look at me. "Maybe I just needed a minute to myself before committing to spending literally every second of the day with you for the next month? It looks like we're about to get really familiar with each other, Peaches."

"That sucks," I blurt out.

He looks sideways at me and raises an eyebrow.

"I just mean that sucks for you. You probably weren't expecting to ever have to see me again, then you think I'm Isabelle, and now you have to follow me around all the time. *Woof.*"

He stares at me for a shocked second, then turns away. "I guess you could put it like that."

"I hope you realize this sucks for me too," I continue, seeming unable to stop the nonsense spewing out of my mouth. "I don't know much about one-night stand etiquette, but I'm positive this isn't how it's supposed to go."

"Sorry," he growls.

"You could make it up to me with some honesty."

Daemon sets his jaw. "What is that supposed to mean?"

"Were you going to tell me about the wedding?"

Daemon looks so uncomfortable you would think he was in pain. "Eventually."

"So you intentionally didn't mention it," I accuse. "I was going to give you the benefit of the doubt that you just thought I knew, but please, feel free to share any other information you've kept from me."

He keeps his eyes fixed on the long hall, seeming completely unwilling to so much as glance my way. "Nothing has changed in our agreement."

"I don't see how that's possible."

He huffs a sigh. "It's not like a wedding to Thorne will be legally binding for you. You get married and then the curse becomes permanent anyway. Thorne won't care if you leave once he's consumed with the curse, believe me. I'll tell Kastian to take you home."

It's not lost on me that he's stopped pretending he'll be the one to take me home. Now, he's planning for Kastian to do it. Because he knows the curse will take over or is it something else?

"What if the curse breaks?"

He shakes his head. "Honestly, I doubt it will, but if it does, then I'll think of something. We'll fake your death, or you could just disappear."

My head spins. He truly doesn't seem to understand why this would matter to me. Or maybe he's just not thinking it through? The actual wedding hardly matters. I'm mostly thinking about after. Is he expecting me to sleep with the king to keep up appearances?

Actually, forget after the wedding—are they expecting me to sleep with him over the next month? *Yeah, no...that's not what I signed up for.*

Before I can voice that very disturbing thought, I nearly trip on my gown and Daemon finally looks sideways at me. I hold my gown above my ankles and practically jog to keep up with him. As if he just noticed he's walking far too fast, he stops short in the middle of the hall.

I don't expect him to stop, and my momentum carries me forward another step. I trip and nearly fall flat on my face, before a large hand snaps out and wraps around my upper arm, steadying me.

I look up at him, startled, then down at his fingers on my arm. It's the most basic touch ever, and yet my heart speeds up in a way it definitely didn't when King Thorne kissed me. My mouth goes dry, and my stomach flutters. *Oh god, that can't be good.*

Daemon doesn't drop his hand, instead stepping forward slightly into my personal space. "Look," he says quietly. His tongue darts out, tracing over his bottom lip nervously. "I'm making this shit up as I go along just the same as you are. Nothing has changed."

"What *exactly* happens at the end of the month if I don't marry the king or the curse doesn't break?" I say, very aware that while we're alone in this hallway, someone could come upon us at any second. "You turn into animals, right?"

He drags a hand through his hair, looking slightly conflicted. "No, not exactly. Your book changed some things, and that was one of them."

"Tell me the truth, then."

"Let's put it this way: the curse causes us to act like animals even if we keep our own faces."

*Act like animals?* "Is that what's supposedly so dangerous that I need a full-time bodyguard?"

As if just realizing he's holding on to me, he drops his hand and steps back. He clears his throat. "Yes. And before you ask for details, just know that I'm hoping you never have to see what the curse really does to us."

"Because you think I can really break the curse?"

"No, Peaches. Because you won't be anywhere near us when it takes hold. Even if it's the last thing I ever do—and it probably will be—I'll make sure no one hurts you."

My heart starts pounding again. "Why do you keep saying things like that?"

He blinks, obviously confused. "Assuring you that you'll be safe?"

"No..."

I don't know how to explain that the way he's making these promises don't exactly feel platonic. If a normal human guy said something like that to me, I'd assume a proposal was forthcoming or that he was a lunatic stalker, but that's kind of a separate issue altogether. I guess, it's just that his tone isn't giving reluctant babysitter and bodyguard. It sounds like he cares.

I swallow thickly, already embarrassed before I even speak. "You keep saying things that sound like you...I don't know...care about me?"

"I do," he says flatly.

My heart picks up a beat, pounding against my chest.

"Without you, there's no way to save my friends from Dyaspora. There's not even a shred of a chance of breaking the curse. Of course I fucking care what happens to you." He swallows thickly and takes another large step back. "You're going to be late for dinner."

My heart seems to stop, and when it starts again, it's no longer thrumming with tension.

Again, I'm such an idiot. He's made it clear what his agenda is, and I can't seem to get it through my head that the guy from the bar and the Faerie soldier in front of me are two very different people. Everything changed when he realized who I was, and this isn't building into some fairytale romance. I'm here to play fake fiancée to the king, and I need to stay focused on that, or the consequences could be deadly.

"I've just gotten word of the unfortunate accident on the train," King Thorne says. "I'm sorry that your return to Ellender has already been so difficult."

"Oh...that's fine," I say, even though it's anything but fine.

The king and I are sitting on either end of a very long dining table in the center of an ornately decorated dining room. It looks as if the table is usually set for twelve people, if not more, but tonight, there are only two chairs on either end. The only other person in the room is Daemon, who leans against the wall, looking equal parts bored and annoyed to be stuck here watching us eat.

It's the stupidest seating arrangement I've ever seen, but I don't comment on it not wanting to blow my cover.

"How did you survive the crash?" the king asks.

"Oh...well..."

"Our car slowed down enough to jump off," Daemon interrupts.

The King looks over at him, obviously annoyed. "I didn't ask you. Be quiet."

Daemon just shrugs, looking unapologetic.

"So tell me." Thorne turns to me. "What have you been doing all this time we've been apart?"

I've actually prepared my answer.

There's a part toward the end of *A Kingdom of Thorns* where Rose leaves Ellender because her father is dying. Granted, in the book, she returns and marries King Thorne. I'm hoping that this part is at least mostly true.

Maybe Nana left, but wanted to return, just like Rose.

Maybe the mining fire is the reason she could never go back, so she wrote the book about what might have happened?

If so, that's incredibly sad and my heart pangs with guilt and sympathy thinking of Nana staying in Ironhill all these years, wishing she could return to Ellender.

"Well—" I begin.

"Does it matter what she was doing if she's back now?" Daemon interrupts again.

Thorne looks furious and drops his fork with a loud clang. "The next time you interrupt, I'll put your head through the fucking table."

Daemon's expression clearly says *I'd like to see you try*, but he just says, "I'm only answering your questions."

"Don't," King Thorne snaps. "You are making it impossible to forget that you're here."

"If you don't want me here, then why order me to be?" Daemon snaps back. "I'd happily be anywhere else. You're the one insisting I watch her every fucking minute."

My eyes go wide. How the hell is he getting away with talking like that to a king? Everyone else has implied that it's important to be careful around the king. What is Daemon thinking?

To my shocked relief, King Thorne ignores Daemon and turns back to me. "Please continue."

My mouth falls open, and I struggle for a moment to remember what I was saying.

"I couldn't return," I say when I've found my breath again. "The gate was blocked by a mine fire. I would have come back; I wanted to, of course, but I couldn't. I stayed in the same town for sixty years, even after the fire drove everyone else away, hoping one day I could return."

King Thorne's eyes widen for a moment, then his expression turns blank. "And you wore the necklace the entire time?"

"Uh—" I think back to Nana wearing this locket throughout my childhood. At some point, she stopped wearing it, but I can't recall when. "Yes, of course."

He smiles broadly. "It must have been painful for you to be alone all these years with no family."

I smile weakly. Even though Nana wasn't alone all these years, and I'm living proof of that—the way he's smiling thinking about it feels a little gross.

The smile he had for me in the throne room is gone. He's looking at me like he's admiring a very expensive car, and it's uncomfortable. Not at all the look of a man in love. Then again, what the hell do I know about what a man looks like in love? I've certainly never been able to identify that look before.

*I'm overthinking this.*

But then again, he was married six fucking times since Nana left. I almost want to bring that up, if only to hear what he has to say, but I don't want to get Odessa in trouble for telling me.

I'm trying to think of a way to point out his hypocrisy without blowing my cover when King Thorne changes the subject. "There's not long before the wedding, but I think we should remind the court who you are before then. We'll have a ball to celebrate your return and our renewed engagement."

He says this like it's already decided so once again I just nod. "Of course."

"Perhaps two weeks from tonight," he muses.

Again, I just nod. Maybe a ball will be fun? Like the thirtieth birthday party I would have had if money weren't a problem and I had more than two friends who would go.

Hang on. What date is it? Is it possible that the ball will fall on my actual birthday?

I open my mouth to ask, but I'm startled by the sound of Thorne's chair scraping across the stone. He drops his fork with a clang and stands abruptly.

"Oh—Are you finished?" I ask, startled.

"The sun is rising," he says sharply, pointing toward the window.

I turn, and sure enough, it finally stopped raining. There's the slightest hint of pink on the dark horizon.

Thorne turns to Daemon. "Take Isabelle back to her room."

For once, he doesn't argue. His face is tense as he quickly grabs my hand and ushers me out of the dining room, practically dragging me up the stairs.

"Did that go well?" I ask as we hurry along. "He's a hard guy to read. I felt like I was in a never-ending job interview."

"It went fine," Daemon says sharply. His grip is tight on my hand and he keeps glancing behind us toward the windows.

"Are you sure?" I fret. "Because he didn't seem all that..." *Interested? Engaged? Excited to see the woman he apparently wants to marry after sixty years apart.* "...happy."

"Thorne is never happy. The only time he pretends to be is when he has an audience. But I don't think he noticed anything. You did fine."

"But..." I try again. "I mean, if it really went well wouldn't he be like...I don't know."

Daemon stops in the middle of the hall and turns to me. "Spit it out, Peaches, we don't have much time before the sun rises."

I sigh with exasperation. "Okay, I'm just wondering why he's making you be with me all the time instead of doing it himself?"

"Because he's a king and he doesn't do anything himself."

"Yeah, but why are we in separate rooms?"

The corner of Daemon's mouth turns down and his eyes narrow at me. "Are you trying to ask why he didn't kick me out so he could fuck you?"

I feel my cheeks redden, but I don't back down. "Yeah, pretty much."

His fingers flex, like he wants to reach out and grab me. "Did you want that?"

"No! But you guys are telling me that I'm supposed to be marrying this guy and that we already know each other well. Isn't it weird that he didn't want to spend more time with his fiancée?"

Daemon curls his flexing fingers into a fist and stuffs it in his pocket as he turns away from me and continues walking down the corridor. His strides are forceful and somehow angrier than before. "The court is old-fashioned. He's probably just trying to be respectful. I've never known Thorne to turn down a woman, though, so if you want to get fucked, you could probably just ask him."

"Um, no. That's not what I meant. I don't want it, I just—"

"You seemed fine with him kissing you," he grumbles.

"Okay, fine. I can see you're determined to be dense about this."

Daemon's jaw tightens, but he doesn't answer. Maybe he agrees with me and just refuses to admit that there might be a problem. Or maybe he's just being an idiot. Either way, I'm sure this issue will come back up, and I'll need to be ready to handle it when it does.

We reach my door, and Daemon stops, gesturing for me to go inside.

"What am I supposed to do now, just wait in my room?"

Again, his answer is clipped. "Yes."

"But I'm not tired. I'd like to see the city in daylight, I—"

"No!" he hisses, turning sharply to me as we arrive in front of my door. "You cannot leave your room for any reason until the sun sets again. Promise me."

I reel back, alarmed by the urgency in his tone. "I promise?"

"Good. Lock your door and don't open it for anyone. Not even me."

I raise an eyebrow. "Are you planning on trying to come in?"

He shakes his head and steps back. "No, but I never truly know what the curse will make me do."

A shiver travels up my spine. "Daemon, what does—"

"There's no time for talking. Go inside," he snaps, nodding pointedly toward my door.

A tiny prickle of fear travels over me. Is that why the king thinks I need a constant bodyguard? But how is Daemon supposed to keep me safe if the curse affects him too?

Who's supposed to protect me from him?

# CHAPTER
# THIRTEEN

ALIX

I blink and several days go by.

I get used to the backward schedule and end up sleeping when it's light out—the consequence of which is I never encounter the cursed court, but I also start to feel a little depressed. I thought seasonal depression was bad in Chicago, but here, it's like a thousand times worse.

When it's dark out, I can leave my room and do whatever I want—the problem is there's nothing to fucking do. I have no phone, no Kindle, no TV, and no podcasts. I've never been more aware of how addicted to technology I am, until suddenly I'm living in basically 1750 and housework is starting to look like a fun and exciting alternative to staring at the walls.

Whenever I want to leave my room, Daemon accompanies me. Usually, he brings one of his friends under the pretense of making sure I'm watched at all times. When he brings Kastian or Jett, he spends all his time talking to them and acting as if I'm not there. Today, however, he brings Fox, so the silence between us is more palpable than ever.

I wander aimlessly down the winding path that leads through the castle garden. The snow from the other day is still covering the ground, and most of the plants are dormant or covered in frost. The only flowers that seem to be able to stand the weather are the roses, which look almost unreal with their red and pink petals dusted in ice.

It's as cold as February in Chicago, and though I'm bundled in a fur-trimmed red cape and matching gloves, I really miss my North Face jacket and beat up Uggs.

"Do the Fae not get cold?" I ask, glancing at Fox and Daemon over my shoulder.

"We do," Daemon responds. "Why?"

"Cause your winter clothing doesn't seem all that warm. I wondered if you never had a reason to make warm clothes."

"If you're cold, we can go inside," he grumbles.

"So I can sit and stare at the wall until dinner? Oh goodie."

I walk a few steps further along the path, absently trailing my hand over the bushes and pushing the snow off the leaves. I stop at one of the still blooming roses and reach over to dust the ice from its petals. A long thorn stabs through my glove and into my finger, making pain shoot up my arm. "Ow!"

I pull off my glove and stick my finger in my mouth, sucking on the wound.

There's a prolonged silence where Daemon and Fox just watch me, and I'm nearly bowled over with shock when Fox is the one to break it. "In Thermia, it's always winter and our clothing is warm."

"It's always winter?" I ask, popping my finger back out of my mouth. "Do you mean it's just a cold climate or—"

"It's always winter," he repeats. "The seasons never change anymore."

Okay...weird distinction, but I'm willing to go with it. At least we're talking about something.

"Did they used to change?" I ask.

Fox looks uncomfortable, not because of my question, I suspect, but because he just doesn't like to talk. "Yes."

"Are they cursed too?" I ask, directing my question more to Daemon than to Fox, who seems relieved that he doesn't have to keep talking to me.

Daemon shakes his head. "Not exactly, but Vernallis isn't the only kingdom with issues, Peaches."

"I suppose you're not going to elaborate on that?"

He shrugs. "I don't know that much about it. You can pester Fox if you want, but good luck with that."

My eyes dart to the huge blond man, and I shake my head. "Never mind. Let's just go inside."

They escort me back to my room.

"Can I have that copy of *A Kingdom of Thorns*?" I ask Daemon.

"I left it at the Summer Palace. I didn't think it was worth risking anyone here seeing it."

"Oh."

"Why? Haven't you read it before?"

"Dozens of times, but I'm so bored I'd think reading the back of a shampoo bottle was exciting."

Daemon looks a little guilty, his eyes shifting to the side rather than looking directly at me. "If you want to read, there are hundreds of books here."

"Really?" I perk up slightly. "Where?"

He starts to answer, but he's cut off by a shrill scream from the end of the corridor. "Daemon!"

I turn around to find three blonde women coming around the corner toward us. They're all absurdly beautiful just like all the rest of the Fae, dressed in identical silk gowns in different colors—one red, one gold, and one green.

The woman in the green gown breaks away from the group and runs toward us, evident excitement on her face. She throws herself at Daemon. "I heard you were back," she cries, "but I hardly believed it."

His eyes widen in surprise and he puts his arms out to catch her, as if on instinct. "Hello, Claudette."

She pulls back and slaps him playfully on the arm. "That's all I get? Hello? It's been ninety years!"

I roll my eyes. I wish I could say this was the first time someone had thrown themselves at Daemon, but it's not. In only the couple of days since I've been here, I've noticed he's very popular. The entire court seems thrilled to see him and we're often stopped so he can catch up with acquaintances. Still...none of them have been quite as pretty as this woman.

Daemon lets go of Claudette and steps back, smiling slightly. "How are you?"

"Oh, the same." She sighs.

She begins chattering away, telling him about her sister, who has evidently gotten married recently and whatever else has gone on since they last saw each other. I don't want to assume anything, but it seems like this is an ex-girlfriend, or at the very least, a former hookup.

*Which is totally fine.*

I don't care at all—really. It's just that I feel awkward, trapped in a conversation I'm clearly not part of. I shift from foot to foot, and out of sheer discomfort, I fixate on trying to place the origin of her accent instead of actually listening to what she's saying.

Daemon has always sounded slightly Irish to me, while Kastian, Odessa, and Jett sound British. Fox doesn't talk enough to be completely sure of where he's from, but he doesn't sound anything like this woman. She's French, I decide finally—or at least, something like it.

"I couldn't believe it when I heard about what happened in the throne room." Claudette says so loudly that I'm forced to tune back into their conversation.

"You weren't there?" Daemon asks, sounding more relaxed than I've heard him since before I knew who he really was.

She shakes her head and laughs merrily. "To think, the one time I decide to take a long bath, I miss the only interesting thing to happen in decades."

Daemon grins. "It wasn't that exciting."

She laughs and smacks his arm again. "Tell that to Foulo."

*Okay. That's enough for me.*

We're not far from my room and I can walk by myself. I don't have to stand here feeling uncomfortable. Actually, the best possible thing I could do is leave and give them privacy. Daemon doesn't owe me anything. I hardly even know him.

*I don't care.*

I back away from them and take several long strides down the hall. I glance back. Daemon hasn't noticed that I'm moving, but Fox clearly does. He looks at me and shrugs. I take that to mean he doesn't care if I walk away. Perfect.

I take a page out of Fox's book and don't say anything as I slip away down the hall alone. The halls are so echoey that I can still hear Daemon's distant voice even after I've turned the corner.

I walk on autopilot, my eyes fixed loosely on the floor in front of me. Then, I jump when I hear a shout behind me. "Where the fuck is she?"

*Oh shit.*

I hear Daemon yelling something, then the muffled low response of Fox answering. Claudette's high-pitched voice chimes in, and then loud footsteps echo as clearly Daemon starts running after me.

*Oh shit, shit, shit! This is so not good.*

My pulse picks up, and I lift up my skirt and start running too.

I don't even know why I'm running. I'm not doing anything wrong walking down a hall by myself. But also, I really don't want Daemon to catch me right now. I don't want to have to explain myself, and I especially don't want to look jealous when I am *not. At. All.*

I just wanted to go back to my room because I'm tired. Being jealous is actually fucking crazy. I need to be more evolved than this.

I hammer that idea into my head as I jog down the hall, fully aware of the irony and hypocrisy in what I'm doing. Admitting you have a problem is the first step to recovery, and I will certainly be recovering... after I find somewhere to hide.

This castle feels like an endless maze of hallways and stairs, but I've kind of got the hang of the layout...*kind of.*

Daemon's voice echoes as loudly as his footsteps, and the cacophony makes it sound as if he's everywhere at once.

At the end of the hall, there's a closed wooden door. I throw it open and keep moving. After a second, the door swings shut behind me with a snap and abruptly all sound cuts off. I stop walking and turn back to the door, startled by the sudden silence. Huh, they've got really heavy doors here.

Now that I can't hear Daemon anymore, my pulse slows a fraction. I slow to a brisk walk.

"Isabelle!"

I freeze and glance up. Striding toward me is King Thorne. He's wearing a green silk waistcoat today and a cloak over it, as if he just came from outside. His expression is dark—somewhere between angry and suspicious.

"Oh, hello!" I say brightly, raising a hand in greeting.

"What the fuck are you doing here?" King Thorne demands, anger heavy in his tone.

"Uh..." I falter. "Sorry...is something wrong?"

He stops in front of me, practically seething. I step back, startled.

He's clearly mad, but I have no idea why. I've seen the king at dinner several nights in a row now, but he still feels like a complete stranger. I can't tell him I ran away from Daemon because I'm crazy and I don't like watching him talk to a pretty woman.

"I'm sorry. I was just exploring," I say finally. "You know...reacquainting myself with the palace."

Thorne reaches me and stops right in front of me, forcing me to tilt my head back to maintain eye contact. His expression is dark. *Livid.* "You're free to do whatever you like, but you know you are not allowed in my private wing without my permission!"

I glance around. Is that where we are? His private wing? I don't remember anyone saying I couldn't go there, but maybe it's supposed to be obvious? "I'm so s-sorry," I splutter. "I honestly didn't realize that's where we were. It's been a long time since I've been here and I guess I forgot."

Thorne glowers. "You are not to enter this tower. Ever. And for that matter, why are you alone?"

"I'm sorry," I repeat, just hoping he'll drop it.

I've learned from years of living with my mother, and later from living with my husband, that the fastest path to peace is to apologize. Profusely. Even if I have no idea what I'm supposed to be sorry for.

It seems that this strategy is universal, because King Thorne deflates slightly. His anger recedes a fraction and his lip curls in a sneer. "Where is Ashwater? Shouldn't he be keeping you from forgetting where you're supposed to be?"

"Oh...I'm not sure where he is, actually."

His eyes narrow to slits and immediately I realize I've said the wrong thing. I should have lied and said there was something serious Daemon had to deal with. Simply not knowing where he is actually makes things worse.

"What I mean is, I don't know precisely," I quickly add. "He had to go deal with something important, and I don't know where that would be happening..."

*Oh my God. I am the worst liar on the planet.*

"What was so important to ignore my orders to guard you at all times?"

"Um, I don't know. You have to ask—" I search frantically for the name in the back of my head. "—Frowno!"

"Foulo?"

"Yes, that's it. Sorry. *Foulo* needed Daemon's help with something."

I'm pretty sure I've managed to fit so many apologies into this inter-action that the word "sorry" has started to lose its meaning. I hate feeling like I have to take the blame for things that aren't my fault, but at least it worked. Thorne now looks less angry and more perplexed. I'm not sure if that's better but anything I say seems to make it worse so I don't continue.

"Would you care to walk down to dinner together?" Thorne asks after a long second.

I blink, startled by his sudden change in tone. "Oh...sorry, what?"

"Would you like to walk to dinner together?" he repeats.

"But I'm not dressed."

He glances over me with absolutely zero heat in his gaze. "You look fine. Come, we'll go now."

"Oh. Um, okay."

King Thorne takes my elbow and guides me back down the hall and through the door I now realize was the entrance to his private wing.

*Whatever that means.*

The silence stretches endlessly, but not in a companionable way like it did with Fox. It's awkward and leaves me feeling obligated to fill the silence.

"I've been happy to be back in the castle," I say.

Thorne nods. "Not exploring too much, I hope?"

"Uh, no. Not really."

"Good."

I try several more versions of inane chitchat, none of which seem to have the slightest effect on him. From the way he greeted me in the entrance hall, I thought he would have much more enthusiasm about these dinners, but I guess one kiss was enough to last him until the wedding?

We enter the dining room and sit on opposite sides of the absurdly long table.

"Do you usually have guests?" I ask.

"Yes. Courtiers often join me for dinner."

I let out a relieved breath. At least he answered me. "They could still join us. I mean, I'd like to meet your friends."

*And I'd like to have someone to help me carry the conversation.*

"No," Thorne says flatly. "I want to spend this time getting reacquainted."

"Right..."

I'm more than a little relieved when our food is served because at least it gives me something else to talk about.

"This is good," I indicate my plate with my fork.

King thorn looks down at his own plate and nods once, but doesn't continue the conversation.

I sigh. *Here we go again.*

"Where did you go today?" I try again.

He frowns at me. "Why?"

"No reason. Just looking for something to talk about."

His shoulders relax ever so slightly. "Hunting."

"Wolves?" I ask hopefully. "I had a run-in with one when I arrived."

"Really? Tell me about that."

I open my mouth, then pause. I probably can't tell him anything about that, because the question would be why I was so afraid to find myself in Ellender? Why wasn't I wearing clothes? Why was I so cozy with my guard?

*Shit.*

Just then, the doors fly open and Daemon bursts into the room, looking frantic. The king and I look up from our dinner in benign silence. Daemon sucks in a sharp breath, panting as he looks back and forth between us.

"Nice of you to finally remember your job," Thorne snaps. His words are casual, but I can hear a cold bite in his voice.

Daemon straightens and strides across the room in total silence. He leans against the wall in his usual place while the king and I return to our dinner.

But I can't eat.

I can feel Daemon's cold, furious gaze on me all through the rest of dinner. He's seething, and I know that the moment we're dismissed to walk back to my room, he's going to unleash all that fury on me.

Strangely, I'm almost looking forward to it.

SURE ENOUGH, THE VERY MOMENT DAEMON AND I EXIT THE dining room, he rounds on me. His voice is a dangerous whisper. "What the fuck, Alix."

"Isabelle," I correct, looking pointedly around at the public entrance hall.

"I don't give a single fuck what your name is. What were you thinking?"

I raise an eyebrow. "Um, I was thinking that King Thorne asked me to walk to dinner with him and it would have been really weird and suspicious to say no."

"Bullshit. You left before that."

"Whoops," I reply sarcastically. "I forgot that I'm a child and can't walk down a fucking hallway on my own without my daddy or my babysitter."

His eyes flash, his chest rising and falling with each breath as he takes another step closer, breaching the last of my personal space. He inhales sharply, nostrils flaring, then flicks his tongue across his lips— like he's tasting something in the air. "I thought you left," he growls. "And then I thought maybe Thorne wanted to have dinner with you alone because he knows who you are. Anything could have fucking happened, Alix."

"That's stupid." I shove at his arm and brush past him, striding purposefully down the hall toward my room. Or at least, what I think is the direction of my room.

Daemon chases after me, his emerald eyes narrowed on me and me alone. "What was I supposed to think?"

"Maybe that the king wanted to spend time with Isabelle because they're—we're—engaged?"

"You should have told me where you were."

"How was I supposed to tell you where I was when you weren't there?"

"You should have waited for me. I looked up and you were just gone."

I stop short and spin to face him again. He skids to a halt and nearly runs into me, leaving us mere inches apart.

"You were busy," I say. "I'm not going to wait around for any man. My time and attention belong to people who are thinking about no one but me."

Without warning, his hand shoots out and lands on the wall behind my head, boxing me in. He leans down so his mouth is mere inches from mine and bares his teeth. "Then I should get every single minute of your fucking attention."

I suck in a startled breath. I meet his eyes and my pulse pounds in my throat and...lower.

It is definitely not lost on me that Daemon is just as angry now as Thorne was when he found me, yet I haven't apologized to Daemon once. I don't really feel any need to shrink myself around him, or just say whatever will end the argument fastest.

Meanwhile, I'm supposed to be acting like I'm in love with the king, but he and I can't even seem to manage a polite conversation. When Thorne looks at me, there's absolutely no heat, but when Daemon and I snap at each other, there is enough heat to light the damn building on fire.

In an instant, my eyes flick to his pulse visibly pounding in his throat and I imagine how easy it would be to stretch up on my toes and lick that spot.

"Back up. You can't be so close to me when anyone could walk by."

His gaze darts to my lips for a fraction of a second. "You're suddenly really interested in telling me what I can't do."

My heartbeat speeds up again. Fuck, I don't even know what we're talking about anymore. Is this about Claudette or the king or Daemon and me? What am I even mad about again?

Daemon looms over me, breathing heavily. There's a raw energy, a power, rolling off him in waves. I'm pretty sure I'm supposed to be trembling, cowered by his dominance. And if I know myself, if he were any other man, I would be. I'd be terrified.

But instead, I'm defiant. Exhilarated. Turned on.

My pulse pounds in my core, and my breathing is labored. My skin feels too sensitive, and I could swear there's an electricity sparking between us. Since the moment he first opened his mouth, this has felt less like fighting and more like foreplay.

Somewhere in the echoing halls of the castle, I hear distant voices, and the sound is like a bucket of cold water over my head.

Daemon glances to the sound, but doesn't seem as bothered as I am. He doesn't step back from me. Rather, he moves ever so slightly closer, until I can feel the warmth of his body everywhere.

I glance around the empty hallway. We can't keep standing like this. And more, we can't keep arguing because the tension is so high that it's about to break right here.

I close my eyes, already half regretting this. "Look…" I run a hand through my hair. "I'm sorry if this became a bigger issue than it needed to be."

"You're what?" he blurts out, the heat in his eyes cooling with confusion.

"I'm sorry," I repeat, knowing that word is exactly the one that will defuse the situation. "Everything is fine. The king was mad that I went into his private wing, or whatever—"

A growl rumbles through his chest. "You went *where*?"

"His private wing. I got lost, but he didn't seem to notice anything weird about me so I think it's all going to be okay. You should probably find Foulo and pretend something serious happened in case the king asks about it."

"Alix, what the—"

"Anyway," I barrel on, talking over his protests. "Going forward, if you're busy, you can just send Fox, Jett or Kastian to watch me."

Daemon glowers down at me, still standing so close that it would be all too easy to close the distance between us. Something dark flashes in his gaze. "Would you prefer they watch you instead of me?"

"I don't really care. I want to get through the next month in one piece. I'm sure your friends can handle keeping me from dying for a few hours while you're busy."

"Busy with what?" he snaps. "Why do you keep saying that? The only thing I'm busy with is you."

"You know, with Lynette." *Ugh, that was petty. I know her name.*

Somehow, this has become about my issues—my marriage, my standards for how I want to be treated, and the trauma that bubbled up the second I lost his attention in favor of another woman. Which isn't really fair.

"I mean, Claudette," I correct myself.

*I am calm. Healed. Not at all toxic.*

Daemon looks confused, bordering on frustrated. "Claudette and her sisters are just old acquaintances. It's a small court, and there's an even smaller group of us under the age of two hundred. She was just saying hello."

The petty side of me wants to ask if that hello had a happy ending, but I restrain myself. "It's totally fine. You don't need to explain yourself to me."

"Evidently I do because you're not letting me do my job."

"Which is what exactly?"

"To protect you."

"Protect me from what?" I snap. "As far as I can tell, the only times I've nearly died have had to do with you, so I don't need you constantly hovering. Send your friends to watch me or don't, but don't act like I owe you anything."

With that, I shove past him for the final time and march to my room alone.

*Definitely not calm, healed, or rational.*

# CHAPTER FOURTEEN

DAEMON

"You don't need to attend dinner with Thorne tonight."

Alix looks up from her breakfast and cocks her head, her brow furrowing. "Why?"

"He's leaving the palace for a few nights. It looks as if it's going to snow, so he's clearly taking advantage of that to travel during the daytime."

"Oh." She shrugs. "Okay, whatever."

Alix and I are sitting in one of the parlor rooms that is somewhere between a dining room and a lounge. I'm watching her eat breakfast and trying not to stare too much at her mouth every time she licks strawberry juice off her full bottom lip.

It's been two nights since the argument in the hall and we're both pretending it never happened. I still don't have any fucking idea how things got so heated. I barely remember what was said, but I do remember Alix complaining that she's bored.

I know I shouldn't feel guilty about it. I don't need to keep her entertained, I need to keep her alive. Still, I find myself trying to think of things to do with her, and justifying why Alix should be able to mingle with the court—at least, in a controlled setting.

Which is how I ended up bringing her to the parlor for breakfast. Many of the courtiers take their meals in the parlor, and we're drawing stares from other tables as Alix eats. I'm already wondering if I made a mistake.

"So where's the king going?" Alix asks, swallowing a gulp of coffee.

"That's a good question. I don't know."

"Really? Shouldn't you know as the captain of his guards?"

I shrug. She's probably right, but I can't pretend I really care where Thorne is going or why. I can't seem to make myself care about anything lately; my head is too full of Alix.

She said something the other day about only caring for men who think about no one but her.

I don't think she knows what she's asking for.

I don't understand what's happening to me or how it started. I can only assume that it's a proximity issue—I'm forced to spend all my time guarding Alix, and therefore I can't focus on anything else.

Except that doesn't explain the insane rage that came over me when Foulo grabbed her, or how I'm jealous of my own friends for watching her when I was the one who asked for their help. It doesn't explain the all-consuming terror of realizing I couldn't find her the other day, or how I can't stop fixating on the memory of burying myself inside her tight little—

"Good morning, Lady Isabelle!"

Alix drops her fork against her plate with a loud clang, and I jump, abruptly coming to attention. "Fuck!"

Alix barely spares me a glance, before looking up at the woman running across the parlor toward our table. Claudette darts toward us, holding her mint green dress off the ground. Behind her, I see her sisters hovering near the door. I nod once to them before turning my attention back to Alix.

"Good morning," Alix says stiffly.

Claudette stops beside the table and dips into something resembling a half-curtsey before straightening. "I'm so glad to see you this morning. I wanted to apologize for the other day."

Alix's expression stays neutral. "Why?"

"I should have immediately greeted you and introduced myself, of course." Claudette smiles, and I feel her look sideways at me. "I was just so excited, it's been years since we've seen each other."

There's a long silence. I know this is my cue to say something, but I don't want to. I don't care about being polite to Claudette, and I'm not about to do something that will start another argument with Alix. Especially not here, with so many eyes on us.

"It's fine," Alix says, filling the silence. "You were busy."

There's that word again. *Busy.*

"Have you finished with your breakfast?" Claudette asks, turning her body slightly so it's clear she's addressing both of us. "My sisters and I were just going to sit down. We'd love if you joined us."

"We can't," I snap.

"Oh?" Claudette pouts. "Why not?"

"Yeah," Alix says suspiciously. "Why not? It's not like I have anything else to do except sit alone in my room."

"Oh, that's horrible!" Claudette cries dramatically. "You should be socializing with the court. Here, let me—"

"No!" I snap, and all chatter in the room stops.

*Fuck.*

"Everything okay, *Baron Ashwater*?" Alix says, her eyes wide with feigned innocence.

I grind my teeth. No, everything is not alright and I'm not even sure why. I have no fucking idea what's wrong with me except that the woman sitting across from me is clearly sapping me of whatever shreds of sanity I didn't lose in Dyaspora.

I turn to Claudette. "Lady Isabelle has things to attend to this morning. Er, wedding preparations..."

"Oh, alright," Claudette says, looking wounded. "Well, if either of you change your mind, we'll be over by the window."

I don't react as she turns and walks back over to her sisters. Alix waits all of two seconds for Claudette to be out of earshot before leaning across the table toward me. "Why don't you want to talk to her?"

"Because I'm talking to you."

She rolls her eyes. "What about yesterday? You had a lot to talk about then."

"No, I didn't. I spent two minutes being polite to someone I haven't seen in years, and you were gone. I spent nearly an hour running all over the fucking castle because you decided to storm off without telling me where you were going."

The apples of her cheeks flush slightly. "Oh."

My scowl deepens. Yeah, *oh*.

I'm not completely oblivious. Clearly, Alix thinks I ignored her the other day in favor of Claudette, but not only is that wrong, I'm having a hard time believing that Alix is actually jealous.

*Actually, that's not it at all.*

I can easily imagine how Alix might feel because I've never been jealous of anyone in my damn life until this week. Suddenly, I want to tear my hair out every time I have to watch her eat dinner with Thorne or smile at one of my friends, and that's far fucking crazier than her being bothered by Claudette.

Except, I can't let myself think about that.

Because if Alix is jealous too, then I'm not alone in this. And once I start thinking about that, I'll remember how she looked at me in the hallway the other night, or how I could smell her arousal in that inn... and that's a dangerous damn path to go down.

I can't touch Alix; I can't even look at her.

Even if I want to.

Even if *she* wants me to.

"I think she wants you to follow her," Alix mutters under her breath.

I look up. "What? Who?"

She jerks her head to the left, and I follow the movement. Across the room to the left, Claudette is hovering in the doorway. She's walking so hilariously slowly that it will probably take her ten minutes to walk five yards.

I chuckle under my breath and look down at the table in front of me. Fuck, this whole thing is so twisted. If anyone is fixating on Claudette, it's not me; it's Alix.

"Well?"

"Well what?" I press.

"She clearly wants you to follow her and say you're sorry that you can't spend time with her this morning."

"So?"

"So...are you going to?"

"No. Why would I? You're not done eating."

She harrumphs and takes another bite of her eggs.

I meet Alix's gaze. She looks...nervous, and suddenly I feel bad for not being more clear with her. I keep forgetting that her marriage just fell apart due to infidelity. Maybe this isn't even about me. Maybe she's not jealous at all and I'm just projecting what I want to see onto her.

*I shouldn't be thinking about this.*

"Are you finished?" I ask her shortly. "We should go."

Alix puts her half-eaten toast down and rolls her eyes. "Oh goodie, can't wait to get back to my gilded cage."

I make a split second decision without thinking it through. "We're not going back to your room. I have work to do this morning, and you'll join me."

"What kind of work?"

"Does it matter? I thought you were bored."

She raises a surprised eyebrow. "I didn't realize you cared."

I shake my head. "There's a lot of things you don't seem to realize, Peaches. And I don't know whether I should be thanking the fucking gods for that or shaking you until you understand."

## ALIX

As soon as I'm finished eating, Daemon ushers me out of the parlor and down a seemingly endless flight of stairs.

"So what work do you have to do?" I ask.

"Nothing," he grumbles. "Normally, I'd have to go back to the barracks and keep the soldiers in line, but my only job lately is watching you."

I don't know what to say to that.

"We're going into the city," Daemon says after a few moments.

"Why?"

He looks sideways at me, his expression somewhere between bored and smug. "You'll see, Peaches."

I shiver slightly at his use of the nickname I hate.

*Sort of hate.*

*Okay, I don't really hate it at all.*

"I don't like surprises," I warn him.

"It's not a surprise, I'm just making shit up as I go along," he says flatly.

I furrow my brow. I'm not sure if that's true, because Daemon seems pretty sure of himself as he leads me through the entrance hall and outside onto the top of the long stone steps that I haven't seen since we arrived. Then again, he always seems sure of himself. *Must be fucking nice.*

Outside, the wind is bitterly cold, but at least it's not snowing. The twinkling lights of the city are beautiful, and as I glance up, I'm startled to see thousands of stars twinkling at me.

I point up at the sky as we begin our descent down the long stairs. "I wonder if these are the same stars that are on Earth or different ones."

Daemon tilts his head back and pushes his hair out of his eyes to better see what I'm talking about. After a second, he lets out a harsh breath. "I never thought about it."

"Maybe they're the same, but in a different timeline."

"What?"

"You know, like a string theory thing. What if all the worlds are next to each other. Or maybe this world is inside the other one. Ooh, if I walk through a bookcase, do you think I'll see Matthew McConaughey?"

Daemon is fully laughing now. "I don't understand half of what you say, Peaches."

I grin. "Likewise."

*Yet weirdly, I don't feel like it's hard to communicate. If anything, it's too easy.*

"I thought it was supposed to be snowing," I say quickly, glancing up at the sky again.

Daemon shrugs and looks up too, following my gaze. "I guess not. Thorne won't be able to travel during the day. That probably means he'll be gone an extra night...What a shame."

I look sideways at Daemon and find him grinning widely. "Why do you hate him so much?"

He looks affronted. "Have you met him?"

"Yes...and that's just it. He's not exactly my favorite person in the world, but he doesn't seem like a monster."

His smile slips. "You don't understand."

"Obviously!" I almost laugh. "So explain it to me."

"No. Not now. We're almost at the bottom, look." He points ahead of us, where indeed there are only a dozen or so steps left. Beyond the stairs, the town is just as busy as the night we arrived, with pedestrians, merchants and even some soldiers flooding the streets.

Daemon grips my elbow tightly and pulls me closer as we merge with the teeming crowd.

"Stay close to me. I don't want you getting lost."

I roll my eyes. "Yes, Daddy."

His eyes flash with something like interest and he grips my arm tighter. "Say that again."

I flush and stumble over my words. "I-I just mean I'm not a toddler. I don't need to hold your hand in the crowd, and I can walk perfectly fine on my own."

"Right. Fair enough." He lets go of my arm, but leans closer to whisper in my ear. "But be careful what you call me, Peaches. Next time you say something like that, I'm going to take it as an invitation to spank you."

*Um, yes please? Fucking go for it. I would have zero objections to anything Daemon wanted to do to my ass.*

...But of course I don't say that. Because we're in the middle of the street and apparently the logical side of my brain hates me.

Daemon steps back as if nothing unusual happened and strides off in the direction of the shops. He doesn't reach for me again, and as I hurry to keep pace with him, part of me wishes I hadn't said anything. Which is stupid because like I just said, I'm a goddamn adult. I don't need to be getting butterflies over holding hands. *Jesus Christ.*

Unlike the first time we walked through the city, I'm not quaking with anxiety and I actually have time to stop and look around. It seriously looks like Santa's elf village, with dozens of gray brick buildings with thatched roofs and merrily smoking chimneys. Outside every house is a flickering oil lantern, and even more lanterns line the sidewalks warding off the oppressive winter darkness.

As we walk, various people shout greetings at Daemon. Especially the other soldiers are eager to wave hello.

"It's like walking the red carpet with a celebrity," I mumble under my breath.

Daemon looks at me. "What?"

"Everyone knows you. I thought you'd been gone for decades."

As if on cue, he raises a hand to wave at some grinning merchants, before focusing back on me. "I have been, but it's not as if there's been a lot of change in the population since I've been gone."

I want to ask about that. The entire town is seriously exactly the same as it was 90 years ago? And even if that's true, why is he so damn popular? But I don't get the chance because at that moment Daemon stops in front of a stone house on the corner with a bright green front door and stands back for me to enter in front of him. I open my mouth to ask where we are, but close it again as my eyes go wide and my question is answered for me.

"Oh my God. Is this a magic craft store?"

"You have to stop assuming everything is magical," he says without any real bite to his tone. "It's just a regular craft store."

I reach out and grab a ball of yarn from the display table to my right. The yarn is actively changing color, and as I hold it, the fibers blend from blue to purple to pink right before my eyes. "What do you call this, if not magic?"

Daemon presses his lips together and just shakes his head. I grin. I take it that I won that round.

"Good evening!" an elderly female voice calls from the back of the shop. "Let me know if there's anything you need help with."

"Thank you," Daemon replies, raising a hand to wave at the shop owner.

"What are we doing here?" I ask excitedly, still looking around at everything. I feel like a kid walking into Wonka's chocolate factory.

"You said you were bored," Daemon says flatly, looking almost embarrassed. "Is there something you might want to do here? Do you paint or something?"

"Um, no I don't paint, but I would definitely be into magical rainbow crochet. I don't have any money, though."

He rolls his eyes at me. "Just pick out whatever you want."

I beam. If he thinks I'm going to argue with him about that just to be polite, he's crazy. I'm about to have such a Veruca Salt moment. *Daddy, buy me the magic craft store.*

FIFTEEN MINUTES LATER, WE LEAVE THE SHOP WITH SEVERAL bags of color changing yarn and various crochet hooks and knitting needles.

"I'm going to make a scarf first, just to remember how to do this. It's been years since I crocheted."

Daemon looks down at the paper bag in his hand. "You could make twenty scarves with all this."

"Maybe I will. I'll make one for everyone. It's not like I have much else to do."

He presses his lips together, looking like he's fighting a smile. "If I'd realized you were so easy to please, I would have done this days ago. It would have saved everyone a headache."

I glare at him, but can't quite work up the energy to be actually mad. Not when I'm in such a good mood after so long. "I am genuinely excited about this, thank you."

"You're welcome."

"The only thing that would make me happier is if there's a music store around here. If you could get me a new violin, I wouldn't just let you spank me, I'd marry you in a heartbeat."

He stiffens, and I falter, realizing what just came out of my mouth.

*Oh God. What is wrong with me? I don't say things like that, especially not out loud!*

*Kill me.*

*Actually, please, let a meteor fall out of the sky and squish me right here because I cannot handle the level of cringe I feel right now.*

Daemon stops walking in the middle of the street and turns to me, ignoring the fact that there are dozens of people all around us. He looks me over, his too intense gaze seeming to see more than what's in front of him, stripping me bare and scorching me from the inside out. His fist tightens around the handle of the shopping bag. I have no idea what he's thinking, but I've never wanted to know anything more in my entire life.

"There's no music store," Daemon says flatly.

I gnaw on my lip. "Bummer."

My mind races, grasping for something—anything—to say that might bring back the easy mood from mere seconds ago. For once, Daemon had been normal. Nice. Like he was when we first met at Ted's. And for my part, I was almost... happy. Not just because I got presents —though that didn't hurt—but because, for a fleeting moment, I forgot about all the terrifying and downright shitty things that had happened to me this week. I forgot to pretend to be Nana or Rose. I was just having fun. But then I had to go and ruin it.

I'm seriously considering flinging myself into the nearest lake, when somehow the mood gets worse.

"Ashwater," a snide voice calls from somewhere behind me. "What are you doing with Lady Isabelle?"

Daemon stiffens once more, his hand flying to the hilt of the sword in his belt. I turn around nervously.

Foulo is pushing his way through the crowd to reach us, his red military jacket and bulging muscles immediately recognizable.

I glance nervously between the two men. I'm not sure if this is the first time they're seeing each other since whatever the hell went on in the throne room, but I really don't want a fight to break out in the middle of the street. Once was kind of hot, but again? No thanks.

To my relief, Daemon's posture relaxes and his voice is even when he finally reacts. "Foulo. I thought you went with the king."

His expression sours. "And likewise, I assumed you would be traveling with him. You're the captain now, after all."

Daemon jerks his head toward me. "I have other priorities."

Foulo turns his gaze on me, and his sneer remains firmly in place. "Doing some shopping, my lady?"

I nod. "Is that a crime or something?"

He shakes his head. "I just seem to recall that you valued frugality."

I shrug. "People can change in sixty years."

He purses his lips. "Clearly."

A shiver travels up my spine. I don't like the way he's looking at me. The friendly eagerness of the other day is completely gone, and now he just seems suspicious. Maybe getting his ass kicked in front of the entire court turned him against me as well as Daemon. Shame.

"Well, if that's all," Daemon says in a clipped tone. He reaches out and grips me by the elbow.

Foulo's eyes immediately fall on Daemon's fingers on my arm and his scowl deepens. I get the feeling Daemon is doing it on purpose to fuck with Foulo, and I'm totally on board with that sort of non-violent pettiness. I smile sweetly and let Daemon turn me around to head back toward the castle steps.

"Actually, that wasn't all I had to say," Foulo calls after us.

Daemon looks over his shoulder. "What?"

"I just got word of a pack of wolves running far too close to the city limits. Someone needs to go out there and deal with them before they get bold enough to start attacking people."

I grimace, thinking of the enormous wolf in the woods of the Summer Palace. An entire pack of those things in the crowded city? Yeah, that sounds like it's going to quickly turn into *"My grandma, what big teeth you have."*

"So," Daemon says. "Are you going to go deal with it?"

"Shouldn't you be the one to go, Commander?" Foulo replies snidely.

Unconsciously, Daemon's fingers tighten on my arm. "I'm busy, and anyway, any first-year recruit could take care of a few wolves."

Foulo shoves his hands into his pockets and rocks back and forth on his heels. "Suit yourself. Obviously, you can order anyone to go, but if it were me, I'd do it myself. You've been gone a long time, and those first year recruits you just mentioned don't trust you yet. It will only get worse if they think you're not willing to put yourself in danger. Just some friendly advice."

Daemon scowls, but when I catch his eye, I know he's considering it.

"I have to take Al—Isabelle back to the palace first."

"I can take her," Foulo offers.

"No!" Daemon and I snap in unison.

I look up at him, flushing slightly. "Sorry, I mean, I can go back on my own. It's a ten-minute walk."

Daemon grinds his teeth. "No, I'll take you and then go deal with this."

"Splendid," Foulo says, gleefully. "Good to have you back, Commander."

"I'm assuming Foulo is right? About the soldiers, I mean."

Daemon holds the front door of the castle open for me, his jaw tight and eyes narrowed with frustration. "Yes," he grumbles, as I duck under his arm and cross the threshold into the entrance hall. "Foulo is a fucking prick, but he's not a bad soldier...usually. And he's right about this. A commander shouldn't send anyone to do a job they're not willing to do themselves."

I gnaw on my lip, thinking. "Not to sound paranoid, but I think he has an ulterior motive."

"So do I, Peaches."

My eyes flick excitedly up to his. "What do you think it is?"

"No idea. It could be as simple as he was expecting me to say no and then he could turn the barracks against me."

"But everyone seems to love you." I bite my lip. "I mean, do you really think the soldiers will care about such a small thing?"

He shrugs. "Honestly, I'm not sure it matters. There's only two weeks left of having an army anyway, and even if there were no curse, I doubt Thorne will let me stay in the palace long enough to really fall back into my role. But it's still the right thing to do. I can kill those wolves in minutes, while newer soldiers could get hurt."

"Pretty sure of yourself, aren't you?" I ask, trying to lighten the mood.

"Yes," he says, clearly missing my attempt at humor.

"Your humility is inspiring."

"It's not arrogance, it's just fact. The curse has sapped a lot of magic from the kingdom, making the army far weaker than it once was. I had more magic than the rest of them to begin with, so I'm still twice as strong as anyone else...except Thorne, maybe."

We reach the top of the steps and walk through the front doors and across the entrance hall. It's empty, and we don't encounter anyone on the familiar path to my room.

"I won't be gone for long," Daemon says when we reach my door. "It's only a few hours until daylight, and I'll have to be back before then. Still, I'll send Kastian to sit outside until I get back, but you should lock your door anyway."

I take the bags of yarn from him and open the door to my room, lingering for a moment on the threshold. It's stupid, but I almost feel like he's dropping me off after a date...

I turn around and tilt my chin up to meet his gaze. "Well, thanks for the first not terrible day since I've been here. Even if it was cut short."

He looks down at me with that intense look I've seen a few times now. I feel my skin heat under the weight of his gaze, and goosebumps erupt across my neck and arms. My tongue darts out to lick my lips, and his eyes track the movement closely, his attention fixed on my mouth.

He leans closer, and his scent envelopes me.

My lips part.

I close my eyes...

Daemon steps back sharply, running a hand through his hair. The spell breaks. "Lock your door," he repeats, then turns to walk away without another word.

With a sigh, I step into my room. *Jesus Christ...*

Sushi is sleeping on the end of my bed, and at the sound of the door closing behind me, he lifts his fluffy gray head and gives me an imperious yellow stare.

"Well, Sush, I think I'm fucked," I mumble as I put the bag of rainbow yarn down on the floor beside the door.

Only a few days ago, I had no idea what Daemon was thinking and barely believed him when he said he would protect me. Now, I have no doubt in my mind that he's serious.

As long as he's around, I don't need to be afraid of the curse or the Fae or even creeps like Foulo. Daemon won't let anyone hurt me—physically, anyway.

But emotionally is another story.

I'm pretty sure I'm already doomed to get hurt—destroyed, even. My feelings are bound to crash and burn like our train car, and this time, there's no jumping off.

# CHAPTER
# FIFTEEN



I wake up abruptly and sit straight up in bed.

For a long moment, I have no idea where I am or what's going on. I immediately assume I've had a nightmare, except, this time, I'm not shaking. There's no anxiety coursing through me—and actually, I can't remember my dreams at all.

I shake my head, confused and look around to ground myself.

I remember now—Daemon walking me back to my room and then leaving. Me getting ready for bed early and falling asleep on top of my newly started crochet project. That can't have been that long ago. Now, I'm alone in the moody purple bedroom at the Winter Palace, except... I have to blink a few times to make sure I'm seeing correctly.

There's bright light streaming through the stained-glass windows, lighting up the scene and creating magical patterns against the floor. I gasp. It's the first time I've seen the windows in the light, but that means it's actually daytime. More concerning, I can hear raised voices and the distant clanging of a bell.

*What the fuck?*

I swing my legs over the side of the bed and rub my eyes. The distant voices seem louder now that I'm paying attention. There's shouts of laughter, screams and chatter. It sounds like some kind of party is going on outside...but it's daytime. How is that possible?

I stand up from bed and cross the room to the double doors leading out onto the balcony. I've barely used this balcony since arriving here—

it's not much fun to sit outside when it's pitch dark and cold enough to snow. Now though, I throw the doors open and step outside.

I'm standing on a small curved stone balcony, barely five feet wide. Roses climb up the railings and stone walls of the castle, and sun streams down from a nearly cloudless sky. I immediately let out an involuntary sigh as the sun hits my face and beats down on the top of my head.

*Oh, Vitamin D, how I've missed you.*

I wish I could stop and just soak it in for a moment, but I can't. The fact that anyone is awake when the sun is out is definitely cause for concern. Possibly panic. In the distance I can hear the loud clanging of a church bell, ringing continuously. I put my hands on the railing and lean over the balcony to see what's going on below.

There are dozens of people out on the lawn, screaming, laughing. They don't look cursed.

Someone is rolling in the snow, while another man chases a redheaded woman like they're playing tag. I spot another group out of the corner of my eye. Three men are standing together, their voices raised in some kind of argument. As I watch, one of the men punches another across the face. *Oh shit.*

The man who was hit reels back, then spins on his attacker…Wait, is that a knife? A split second later, the redheaded woman's laughs turn to screams as the man chasing her tackles her to the ground.

I stumble back a few steps toward the doors to my room.

*Okay, what the fuck is happening?*

Obviously, there's violence going on in broad daylight on the lawn, but no one looks like they turned into an animal or monster or anything like that.

Before I can dwell on it too long, a banging sounds against my door.

"Alix!" I jump at the sound of Daemon's deep voice screaming my name. "Alix! Let me in!"

Um, what the fuck? When did he get back from dealing with the wolves? And more importantly, why is he screaming my real name where anyone could hear him?

I scurry to the door and flick the lock, throwing it open without thinking. "What's happening?" I blurt out. "It's daytime!"

The words dry up in my mouth as I look at Daemon standing on the threshold.

Immediately, I know I've fucked up.

A sense of uncanny dread drops into my stomach when my gaze meets his. It feels like the first time I saw Odessa and her too symmetrical face filled me with a primordial knowing that she was dangerous. I've never gotten that feeling from looking at Daemon...until now.

"Shit!" I curse, trying to close the door again, just as the warning Daemon gave me on the first night comes flooding back. *Don't unlock the door for anyone, not even me.*

How could I be stupid enough to forget that?

I try to shove the door closed, but he puts a hand out and easily holds it open. I give up, and instead scramble backward.

*The Fae can kill you without blinking an eye.*

*The curse causes us to act like animals, even if we keep our own faces.*

Daemon lets the door fall closed behind him and looks at me for a long second. There's definitely something off about his eyes. They're tracking me.

"Uh, hey," I mutter. "I think something is going on. Maybe we should go grab Odessa, or any of the guys..."

He ignores me, just stepping further into the room, never taking his eyes off me.

Because apparently my brain is broken, I don't immediately collapse in terror. Instead, my stupid, traitorous mind jumps to how inhumanly handsome he is, even when he's looking at me with that strange predatory glint in his gaze. He looks hungry—but not like I've seen him look at me before. This isn't lust; he's looking at me like I'm food.

I stumble back a few more steps, glancing down to avoid his eyes. "I don't know what's going on," I stammer at the floor. "But whenever you go back to normal, you're going to be really pissed that you killed me. You need me, remember?"

He stops moving, his footsteps coming to an abrupt halt. "You think I'm planning on killing you?"

His voice sounds normal, which seems like a good sign, but still, something is very weird here.

"I'm honestly not sure what you're thinking right now."

Daemon moves so fast that I barely blink before he's closed the rest of the distance between us and he's standing right in front of me. "I'd never hurt you."

"Okay, good. Then let's talk about this tonight when you're feeling back to normal."

He doesn't react or move a single inch. Instead, he lifts his hand and pushes my hair back from my face, then trails his fingers down the length of my cheek. A jolt of electricity shoots through me, sending little sparks all over my body.

"Look at me," he demands.

*Oh God.* There is something seriously wrong with me because my brain is at war with itself. One part of me is terrified and another steadily growing part is excited as the tension in the air practically crackles with heat.

His gentle fingers turn demanding, and he grips my chin in one hand, forcing my face up to his. His eyes dart all over my face. "You're so fucking beautiful, Alix."

I suck in a sharp breath, and my pulse begins to thrum even faster beneath his fingers. "What?"

"You're so damn perfect, it makes me fucking angry."

"Angry?"

He doesn't answer immediately, leaving the question hanging in the air as his fingers tighten on my face and he walks me backward toward the edge of the bed. I think he's going to push me onto the mattress, but instead, he snakes one arm around my waist and pulls me flush against him.

Every time we touch it's like I forgot how fucking good it felt the last time. How the hard ridges of his muscles feel beneath my fingers, and how my pulse thrums between my legs, ready and begging for more.

"I can't stop thinking about you," he growls. "You're in my head every fucking second reminding me exactly why I shouldn't be looking at you. It's infuriating. *You're* infuriating."

*Jesus Christ.*

He's got to be drunk. Or could it be drugs? Maybe the entire court is high and that explains why everything is so weird.

"Daemon..." I begin as the hand on my chin trails down my throat.

His fingers stop tracing my skin and settle loosely around my neck. He's barely touching me but I'm all too aware that if he wanted, he could close his fingers and choke the breath from me. That should scare me, but as I feel him grow hard against me, I can barely suppress the moan that wants to escape my lips.

He dips his head so his mouth is pressed against my tangled hair, and his hot breath tickles my ear. "Did you know that Fae senses are much stronger than humans? I can always smell how much you want me to fuck you. I can taste it, and it's driving me fucking insane."

I suck in a gasp. He can smell me getting wet for him? Um okay, that's so fucking embarrassing. Please let me just drop dead now.

My internal panic attack immediately goes silent when his hands dart down and cups me between the legs through the fabric of my nightgown. He scrapes his fingers over the thick fabric, and a jolt of pleasure shoots through me. I whimper.

His lips crash down on mine, swallowing the sound.

I melt against him. He kisses me hungrily, his lips hot and demanding, as if he's lost all inhibition or control. I part my lips, matching his intensity, and heat floods me, pooling in my core.

He pulls his hand out from between my legs and replaces it with his thigh pressing firmly between my legs. I gasp into his mouth and shift my hips, grinding against him. My clit pulses with need, and all I want is for him to touch me. Take me. Break the painful tension that has been building between us ever since he promised me a round two back in Ironhill.

His fingers dig into my hips, pressing me down hard against his thigh. My pussy throbs, and I roll my hips, desperate. Needy. Unrestrained.

He pulls his head back, breaking our kiss, and instead presses his face against my throat. He inhales sharply and nuzzles his face back and forth against my skin. "Alix..."

The door bangs open, and I jump in surprise just as Daemon drops me on the bed. I blink in confusion at Kastian in the doorway. Behind him, I can see the outlines of Fox and Jett in the hallway, and that's when I suddenly remember that mere moments ago, I was terrified of whatever was going wrong in the castle.

Kastian glances at me for a fraction of a second before focusing on Daemon. He runs a hand over the back of his neck and sighs, looking resigned. "I guess it could be fucking worse."

I wince. I wish he hadn't said that.

## DAEMON

When I wake up, I know exactly where I am.

The curse doesn't steal memory, but sometimes, like now, I fucking wish it did.

I groan and sit up on the thin mattress in the soldier's barracks and swing my legs over the side of the bed. My skull throbs, and I rub the spot on the back of my head where I think Kastian must have hit me.

"Kas!" I bark into the empty dormitory style room.

As I expected, Kastian pokes his head into the room, clearly having been waiting directly outside the door. He doesn't smile, just watches me warily. "You're up."

"Yeah," I growl, shaking my head. "Unfortunately. What the fuck happened?"

He steps into the room and leans against the doorframe, crossing his arms. "I hit you."

"I figured…" I shake my head. "That's not what I meant. What happened before then? What went wrong?"

He shakes his head too, but more in bewilderment. "Someone started ringing all the church bells, and it woke the entire court."

"What?" I growl, jumping to my feet. "Who the fuck would be so stupid?"

"Dunno," he says. "There were at least a dozen casualties, and they've only just started to look for people."

Gods. "Anyone we know?"

He shakes his head again. "No, but it easily could have been."

"Fuck, I need to go talk to Alix. Explain, or something…" I trail off. What the hell am I supposed to say to her? "I could have fucking killed her."

Kas shrugs. "I don't think so."

I laugh hollowly. "What do you mean? She's human, of course I could have hurt her."

"I don't know, mate. You didn't seem that interested in killing her. And before you try to tell me that's worse, she seemed pretty willing to me."

I glare at him, but it's half-hearted. Kas did all he could in that situation, and he's right—I remember all too clearly the sounds she made and how fucking wet and ready she was, and just thinking about that makes heat burn in my chest.

But that doesn't change the fact that I could have hurt her.

And it doesn't change the fact that it's incredibly clear to me what really happened here.

Someone did this on purpose—there's no doubt about it. Everyone in Ellender knows that waking the Vernal Court during the day is deadly. What's more suspicious is that I almost wasn't here when it happened. If I'd been delayed in the forest dealing with the wolves, or worse, injured, then what? Alix would have been alone. *Not that she was all that much safer with me here…*

It doesn't feel like only hours ago that I brought Alix back to her room with her bags of yarn and left to deal with the wolves, but it was. I brought Jett and Fox with me, leaving Kas here in case anything happened to Alix.

Except, when we arrived in the forest, there weren't any wolves.

Another soldier might have wasted time looking for them, but not me. I returned to the palace just before dawn and found nothing amiss, and chalked it up to coincidence and paranoia.

But now, I'm not so sure.

"I'm going to find Foulo," I state, more to myself than to Kastian.

"Foulo?"

"He sent me out of the castle. This must have something to do with him. The slimy, evil, pri—"

"I doubt it," Kas interrupts. Foulo is cursed just like you. "He couldn't have had the presence of mind to ring the bells; it must have been someone from outside."

I blink at him. He's right. *Fuck.*

I turn on my heel and storm toward the door.

Kastian sighs with exasperation. "Wait, where are you going now?"

"I'm going to find Thorne and make him do something about this."

"He isn't here, remember? He went somewhere with a handful of guards."

"Then I'm going to fucking fly to wherever he is and drag him back by his hair. He's the damn king, he should be here."

It's a testament to how angry I am and how well Kas knows me that he doesn't bother to ask how I'm going to fly to wherever Thorne is when my life isn't in immediate danger. My adrenaline is so goddamn high right now it's a struggle to keep the wings hidden. Flying across the continent would be no trouble at all.

I reach the door and stride halfway down the hall before Kastian runs after me. "Daemon! Wait, before you go rampaging all over the damn castle, you should check on Alix."

"Why?"

"I know you probably don't want to hear this, but if your instinct wasn't to kill Alix but claim her—"

"You're right," I bark. "I don't want to hear that because it's bull-shit. It doesn't mean anything. I was out of my fucking mind."

Kastian's eyes narrow. "Maybe, but from what I've seen over the years, the curse doesn't make you do anything you wouldn't do other-wise. It doesn't turn you into a different person; it intensifies who you already are."

"Tell that to all the people I've killed."

"Yeah...but that's my point. If your instinct was to kill Alix, you would have. You've killed guards and assholes trying to start shit. People we all secretly wanted to kill anyway. You've never tried to hurt me or Fox or Jett."

"I haven't tried to hurt you *yet*," I grumble darkly. "Once would be all it would take."

And that's exactly why a tiny part of me is grateful that this will all end in a matter of weeks. Once the curse takes over fully, I'm sure the other three kingdoms of Ellender will band together to wipe Vernallis off the map.

Then at least, I won't have to worry about hurting anyone I care about ever again.

I MARCH THROUGH THE CASTLE IN THE DIRECTION OF Thorne's tower. All around me is chaos.

Furniture and windows are smashed, the floor is bloody, and several people are weeping in the halls. Gods, this brings back dark memories.

In the early days after the curse was cast, it was always like this— every day was a new opportunity for destruction, every daylight hour, anyone could be the next to be attacked, or become the attacker themselves.

I march angrily up the grand staircase, stepping over what looks like the charred remains of burned books and perhaps someone's jacket.

"Ashwater!"

I turn on my heel toward the sound of my name. Thorne strides toward me, paying no mind to the destruction around him.

I don't bother to greet him. "I was just coming to find you. When did you get back?"

He grimaces. "An hour ago. What the fuck happened?"

"Shouldn't you be answering that question," I hiss. "You're the king, after all. You need to find out who started this. It would have had to be someone from another kingdom to be able to ring the bells when it was already light out. Or maybe someone with enough magic to make them ring themselves..."

His lip curls. "Interesting theory."

"Why don't you seem angry?" I demand. "This is your fucking king-dom. An attack on Vernallis is an attack on you, and—"

He cuts me off. "Is Isabelle alive?"

"Alive?" I blurt out, blinking in confusion. I shake my head to clear it. "Yes, she's fine."

"Are you sure? You were outside her room when this started, weren't you?"

"I—Yes. I was asleep in the hallway when the bells must have woken me up along with the rest of the court."

"No one broke into her room?" Thorne asks. "She didn't leave to see what was happening?"

I shake my head. "She's fine."

He sighs. "Good. I feel terrible that she's had yet another near-death experience so soon after returning to Vernallis."

"Yeah, you sound really broken up about it."

He narrows his eyes at me. "Just make sure you stay with her at all times. If Isabelle gets hurt before the rose moon, I'll know exactly who to blame."

I open my mouth to tell him about the supposed wolves and how I nearly wasn't here for the attack but stop. I don't know what's going on here, but being honest with Thorne has never worked out well for me in the past.

"I'm not going to let anything happen to her," I growl instead.

Thorne looks down his nose at me, the corner of his mouth pulling up in a sneer. "Then you'd better go find her before something else goes wrong. Humans are so fragile, it only takes the blink of an eye to snuff them out."

Despite knowing she's fine, I'm still relieved when I find Alix safe in her room. Fox is sitting outside, and he just looks up at me when I approach.

"Is she in there?"

He nods and gets to his feet, walking down the hall without a word. I've never been so fucking grateful that he doesn't talk.

I suck in a breath and knock.

"Yeah?" Alix calls.

I take that as her version of "come in" and open the door.

Alix is lying on her bed, staring at the ceiling. She's wearing a high-necked purple dress today with her hair pulled up and off her face.

I mean to say "hello" but what comes out instead is, "What are you doing?"

"The same thing I do every night," she grumbles, not looking at me. "There's nothing to do here."

"Where's your yarn?" I demand, completely distracted from why I came in here in the first place.

In answer, Alix raises a hand in the air and points toward the corner of the room.

Her gigantic gray cat is sticking halfway out of the shopping bag and I can see strands of tangled yarn sticking to his fur. I shake my head and turn back to Alix. "Listen…"

She sits up and looks directly at me, her pale blue eyes so steady I feel the urge to step out of the way of her piercing gaze. "So the curse makes you act like animals, huh? You couldn't have been a little more clear about how that works?"

I close my eyes for a moment. I start to say "I'm sorry" but realize mid-word that I'm not sorry. Not exactly.

I'm fucking furious that she could have been hurt and that Thorne doesn't seem to care about the court anymore now that it's so close to the rose moon.

I'm relieved that I didn't physically harm Alix, and that nothing worse happened.

I'm consumed with the memory of how it felt to touch her again and pissed as hell that we were interrupted before I could taste her.

But I'm not sorry; not when she so clearly wanted it too.

But I can't say any of that.

I clear my throat. "I wasn't myself last night. It won't happen again."

Alix scoots to the end of the bed and swings her legs over the side, her bare toes skimming the floor. She folds her hands in her lap and looks at me through her lashes. "What won't happen again? Me finally seeing you all cursed, or you kissing me?"

I clear my dry throat again. "Both. If anyone aside from my friends found out, I'm not sure Thorne would bother with Dyaspora. He'd just order me executed."

*And unfortunately, the threat of hurting my friends or Alix would probably mean I wouldn't fight, I'd just let him do it.*

She narrows her eyes at me. It's infuriating to have no idea what she's thinking, and I hold my breath…waiting.

"I'm fine pretending it never happened as long as you're willing to explain exactly what happened last night. No leaving out important details or letting me draw the wrong conclusions on my own. I'm sick of not knowing what's going on."

I suck in air through my teeth. Among all the other things I've gone out of my way to keep from her, I haven't wanted to explain the curse. I don't want her to be afraid of the court...or more especially of me. But now I don't have a choice.

I run a frustrated hand through my hair, trying to think of the right words to explain. "I wasn't lying before. The curse causes us to revert to our most basic instincts, like animals."

She looks sideways at me, her eyebrow raising. "Explain."

"It strips us of anything that makes us Fae. Magic, reasoning, logic. We don't turn into another form, but in a way that's worse because you might think you're looking at someone you know but it's not them at all."

I shudder, remembering the early days of the curse before we'd all collectively agreed to sleep during daylight hours. And almost worse, the hour a day in Dyaspora when I lost all sense of myself. I wasn't the only one from Vernallis in the prison, and that hour of sunlight each day was always nerve wracking—for me in the hours leading up to it, and for my friends while they had to ensure I didn't kill anyone by mistake. They weren't always successful, and there were many nights we were forced to bury the dead.

"So it removes inhibitions," Alix says, like she's thinking out loud rather than asking a question. "Like being drunk."

"No," I say sharply. "Nothing like that. Drunk people are still people, but the curse strips away anything but animal instinct. It's impossible to form a coherent thought. Everything just becomes need-driven. Food, sleep, sex, territory—those are the only things that matter."

"You seemed pretty coherent last night for someone with supposedly the same reasoning capabilities as Sushi."

I turn to look at her cat again, who is now batting a ball of yarn across the rug and darting after it, his sharp claws outstretched. He looks harmless, but in reality, all he's doing is showing his instinct for hunting. If the cat were six and a half feet tall and 250 pounds, he wouldn't look so cute. I need Alix to understand that.

"At least twelve people died last night. And that's just the actual deaths, there were countless other attacks. The castle is nearly destroyed."

She reels back. "Seriously? From what I saw, everyone looked like they were having fun?"

I close my eyes. "Sometimes they are. It's hard to explain instinct. One moment it's like you're high, and the next a brawl will break out with no warning. Not everyone is inherently good and some people's base desires are perverse, deranged and violent. When the curse was first cast, we lost a third of the citizens of Vernallis in the first six months, and another third in the hundred years since."

"Jesus."

"Those of us who are left try to sleep through most of it. Sleep is also a base instinct, so while it doesn't lift the curse, it makes it more manageable."

She bites her lip. "Wait, then when do you sleep?"

My brow furrows. "What do you mean?"

She looks confused. "I mean...since you're always with me when you're not, you know, cursed...when do you sleep?"

"Worried about me, Peaches?" I blurt out before I can stop myself.

"Oh, never mind," she huffs, a flush rising to her cheeks.

"I sleep when you do," I say finally, jerking my head toward the door. "Out there."

For a long second, she just stares at me. "Are you serious? You're sleeping outside my room."

I give her a pointed look. What the hell did she think Thorne meant by watch her every moment of the damn day? "You didn't notice?"

"No!" she screeches. "That's so fucking creepy."

I laugh, but not necessarily because it's funny. If she thinks that's disturbing, she'd hate to be inside my head.

I know I told her last night how I can't stop thinking about her. I hope she assumes that was just a product of the curse, but it's more true than even I'd like to admit.

In a very short span of time, my entire existence has shifted to revolve around Alix. I wake up when she does, walk her to and from meals, and stand against the wall always watching her. Even when she doesn't come out of her room all day, I sit there, watching the door. She's the only damn thing I can think about anymore to the point that I can't keep track of why I'm doing this. Am I here because Thorne ordered me to be or because I promised to keep her safe?

I cross my arms and lean back against the wall. "If you don't like it, tell Thorne. Maybe he'll let me leave."

She looks up at me, her eyes narrowing. "Why do you bother?"

I blink at her. "Are we speaking the same fucking language right now? I just said Thorne won't let me leave."

"Yeah, but you ignore all the other orders the king gives you."

"No, I don't."

It's her turn to laugh. "Yes, you do, I've seen you."

"Thorne is just—"

"And that!" she interrupts. "You call the king by his first name, even to his face. I haven't heard anyone else do that. Why doesn't he correct you?"

I pause. *Shit.*

I guess she was bound to figure this out eventually. I don't even know why I've bothered to keep it from her. The rest of the damn court knows, and now that Alix knows about the curse, I suppose she can know about me too. "I call Thorne by his first name and treat him differently than everyone else because I've known him my entire life. He's my older brother."

ALIX

I WALK OVER TO THE BED AND SINK ONTO THE EDGE, if only to give myself a moment to think. "Um, what? But you never said—"

"Half-brother," Daemon amends. "And no, I've never mentioned it because it's not something I like to think about. I'm not exactly proud of where I came from."

"You're just full of secret family members. First, a siren for a cousin, and now a royal half-brother. Any illegitimate children you'd like to mention?"

*Please say no.*

"No, no children and not that many other family members either. Other than Thorne, I'm an only child. My father—both the real one and the one who raised me—are dead. My mother is still alive and living nearby, but I haven't seen her in about a century." He chuckles. "If we're getting technical, I suppose I'd call Kas, Jett and Fox my brothers too, but that's everyone. When you grow up like I did, you have to make your own family."

My family was kind of a mess too and I always wanted to find the kind of group of friends you see on TV who do everything together and always have each other's backs. It just never really happened for me.

"So you're a prince, then?" I ask, eager to keep him talking.

He lets out a harsh bark of laughter. "No, I'm not a fucking prince."

I feel myself leaning forward with interest, but it's like a bucket of cold water over my head when he stops talking. "Getting information from you is like pulling teeth," I complain. "What do you want?"

"What do I *want*?" He looks genuinely confused and it makes me smile. It's nice not to be the one in the dark for once.

"I mean, Fae like bargains, right? There must be something I trade you for the information."

I hadn't exactly meant that to sound like a proposition, but our eyes lock and I know we're both remembering last night. Even if it was just the curse making him act like that, it still felt real. And I have no excuse. I just...wanted to.

"Fuck," Daemon curses and runs a hand through his hair. "Don't say shit like that, Peaches."

"Why? There must be something I have that you want."

He closes his eyes, looking like he's fighting with himself not to look at me. He backs up a few steps. "Alright, fine, you want a story? I'll give you one."

I sit up straighter on the bed, unable to hide my excitement as I settle in to listen.

"My parents—the ones who raised me, that is—were members of the court. The Baron and Baroness of Ashwater. It was a badly kept secret that King Florian took mistresses among the women of the court, but he usually stayed away from married women—until my mother."

"She was the king's mistress?" I ask, hardly able to believe that he's actually explaining this.

"Yes, at least for long enough to get pregnant. I think her husband—my adopted father—must have known I wasn't really his son because he always hated me and wasn't subtle about it." He barks a harsh, humorless laugh that I'm positive is hiding some real trauma. "Poor bastard must have been livid that he never had any other children so he died knowing I'd inherit his title and lands."

"When did he die?" I ask breathlessly.

Daemon rolls his eyes as if searching for the answer in the back of his head. "A little over a hundred years ago? I was young and in school with all the other noble children, including my half-brother, Prince Thorne."

My mouth falls open, and I forcibly shut it again, swallowing thickly before I can string two thoughts together into a question. "So, when did you find out?"

Daemon leans against the wall beside the door, then slowly sinks down until he's sitting on the floor. He looks resigned, like he knows that now that he's started, I won't leave him alone until he finishes explaining.

"Pretty much from the moment I first saw the king," he admits. "I never looked like the Eleventh Baron Ashwater, but I didn't think much of it—until the first time I met King Florian. Turns out, I do look like my father."

I swallow. Shit, that's intense.

"So, I assume other people noticed? That you look like him, I mean."

"Yes."

It's hard not to notice that Daemon and King Thorne look nothing alike, even now knowing that they should. They're the same height and built similarly, with strong lean muscles, but their features are worlds apart. The king must resemble his mother. I wince. That couldn't have made the situation any easier.

"That doesn't explain why you're familiar with King Thorne, though," I point out. "Did he know you were his brother?"

"Yes, eventually," Daemon replies. "As I said, we were schooled together, but I wouldn't say we were friends—the opposite actually. I hated him, and believe me, it was mutual. And then he had to go and do the worst fucking thing imaginable."

"What?"

"He saved my life."

I cock my head to the side. I can't say I know the king well—or at all, really—but from what little I've seen, he doesn't seem like the self-sacrificing type. "How did he do that?"

Daemon shifts around again, seeming to stall for time as he readjusts his seat. "Schooling in Ellender is nothing like it is in your world. We focused a lot on honing magic, and being young, it didn't occur to me how dangerous it might be to draw attention to myself."

"Dangerous how?"

"I was...unusually talented. As is Thorne—or at least, he was prior to the curse—but what with looking so much like the king and rivaling the crown prince in magic, I began to attract rumors. By the time I was seventeen, those rumors had reached the queen, and she ordered that I be killed."

"Killed? Just like that?"

"Yes. There's no room for questions when it comes to the royal line. The queen knew she had to make sure her son's path to power was clear of challengers."

"But he saved you?"

"Yes, Thorne suggested that instead of being killed, I was merely banished."

"So that's how you ended up in prison?"

"No, not yet. That came later. Initially I was banished to the human world."

"You're shitting me," I say, in complete disbelief.

He laughs for real this time, and against my will, my heartbeat quickens.

"How do you think I learned to travel back and forth through the gates?"

I shrug. "I don't know. But how did that work—living in the human realm?"

"It probably wouldn't have worked except that I got lucky. This was just over a hundred years ago by your timeline, and I arrived in Britain just after the First World War. With so many people displaced, it wasn't hard to claim I was a foreign orphan looking for work. A little magic, and no one questioned me." He exhales heavily. "After a few years, though, I couldn't take it anymore. Magic is far easier to use here than in the human realm. Or at least it was prior to the curse. What little I can do now is nothing compared to the power I once had, and I grew restless without it."

I think about how I would feel if I lost access to music. Like my arm had been cut off. Even after just a few days without my violin, I feel like I'm going through withdrawal. I imagine it's the same for him with magic.

"So you came back?"

"I did. The banishment was intended to be permanent, but I'd gotten wind that the king and queen had both died, and that Thorne would be ascending the throne."

"They died?" I ask, taken aback. "How?"

"That is the question, isn't it?" he says bitterly. "It was blamed on an accident, but no one was ever really clear what happened. At the time, I didn't care. I was excited that Thorne would be taking the throne. We hadn't gotten along as children, but he'd saved me and I assumed he'd allow me to return."

"And he sent you to prison?"

He lets out a humorless laugh. "If you want to tell the story, by all means, go ahead—"

"Sorry."

"I returned and went straight to see Thorne. As I'd expected, he welcomed me back. I was appointed captain of his guards almost immediately, and everything was fine for a while."

"That was nice of him."

Daemon scoffs. "Nice isn't what I would call it. His decision was strategic. Thorne is self-absorbed and unobservant, but he's not actually stupid. He realized that keeping me close and in debt to him would be far less dangerous than letting me walk around freely."

A chill runs down my spine. It's impossible not to notice that perhaps the same thing is happening now. From what I've gathered, King Thorne broke Daemon out of prison, let him bring his friends, and gave him his old job back...but if this has happened before, then where is that all leading?

"Then what?"

"Then Thorne decided it was time to take a wife."

I blink, caught off guard. That's not where I thought this was going. My mind races. Is this whole thing a fight over a woman? Who? It couldn't be Claudette...

Daemon continues, unaware of my internal monologue. "He met with dozens of noble women from all over the continent, and even some from the neighboring continents. He even met with one of Kastian's—" He stops short.

"One of Kastian's what?" I urge.

"A woman from Kastian's city," he corrects.

I frown. That's not what he was going to say, but I don't interrupt. Not when he's talking more than he ever has before. "So, did he pick someone?"

"Yes. Even though he met with princesses from all over Ellender, he chose a commoner with no important connections whatsoever."

"Why?" I ask, wrinkling my nose.

"At the time, everyone assumed it was love. Now, I think it was because the was a sorceress and came from a long line of powerful magic. I think he believed his children would have strong magic. They got engaged and the wedding was planned for the upcoming rose moon."

"I'm assuming it didn't work out?"

"No," he says bitterly. "Before the wedding, Thorne had already lost interest. He abandoned his fiancée for another woman and she disappeared. In revenge, she cast the curse on the kingdom."

My head spins. "I'm the first person to defend reacting however you want to betrayal, but it seems a little unfair to curse the entire kingdom along with him."

"I doubt she was thinking rationally. The betrayal was fresh and extremely unexpected." He pauses. "This might be difficult for you to understand, but infidelity among the Fae is incredibly rare."

"But your father—"

"Was the only male I'd ever heard of who betrayed his partner. Until Thorne became the second. It simply doesn't happen."

I scoff. "How is that possible?"

He sounds uncomfortable. "We're not human, no matter how much we might appear to be. Our biology is different."

"From what I recall, your biology was just fine," I blurt out without thinking.

He snorts a laugh. "That's not what I meant. We live far longer than humans and Fae children are rare. The average couple has one child roughly every 250 years."

"So?"

"So once committed, Fae males don't leave their partners. Ever. There's a kind of...shift that takes place once you meet the right person. Once that instinct kicks in, we become entirely loyal for the rest of our lives. It's not a choice, it's—"

"An instinct," I finish for him, thinking of the curse.

He grimaces, and I wonder if he's also thinking about the curse. "Exactly."

"And this is only the men, not the women?"

"No, it happens to the women too, but usually later—after the mating has taken place." He coughs. "This isn't exactly the point of the story."

Maybe not, but it's pretty much all I can think about now.

I suddenly remember what Odessa said about Fae males being possessive. Is this what she meant? Not just a cultural tendency toward aggression but an actual physical compulsion? I'll have to ask her about it tomorrow because I'd die of embarrassment asking Daemon to elaborate...even though I really want to.

"Is that why the curse is broken by true love? Because Thorne didn't love the sorceress?"

"I suppose."

I ponder that for a moment. "So how did that send you to prison?"

Daemon runs a hand through his hair—something I've come to recognize as a nervous habit. "Once the curse was cast, thousands of people tried to leave Vernallis. They went to other kingdoms first, but discovered that the curse was not on the land but the people themselves. The only way to escape it was to go somewhere where magic couldn't be used. There was suddenly a rush of people trying to go to the human world, and since I'd been there before and returned, I was primed to be the one to ferry them through the gate."

"Is that not allowed?" I ask.

"It is. Not even the monarch can force anyone to stay here, but with such a large number of Fae leaving, the kingdom was in jeopardy. All the previously loyal citizens were leaving, and those who remained were starting to whisper that Thorne was not fit to be king and a new king would help end all the suffering. There hadn't been a war in Ellender in centuries, but if one had broken out then, he didn't have enough soldiers left to defend his throne."

My eyes widen. I think I finally see where this is going, and how it all comes full circle. I remember again something Odessa said, *Daemon can't help but gather followers, even without meaning to.*

"Were they looking to you to replace Thorne?"

There's a pause, then he answers, "Exactly. I look like my father, who for all his faults was a popular ruler, and I'd been the head of the guard for some time. I already had more Fae loyal to me than I ever intended."

"Were you going to do it? Be the king?"

He pauses. "Maybe. I never wanted the job—I still don't—but I could see what the people were saying. Thorne had run the country into the ground and was digging deeper. I didn't believe it was possible for him to love anyone but himself, and so yes, I was considering it, but before I could decide what to do, Thorne ambushed me."

"There is a continent called Dyaspora just north of Thermia. It's a barren, ice-covered rock that never thaws all year round. Nothing grows there, and the sun only rises for an hour or so each day, resulting in a never-ending winter. The only creatures who can live there for any length of time are monsters you couldn't even imagine."

"That doesn't sound much better than death."

"Worse."

"But you survived for ninety years?"

"Yeah."

"How?"

"A combination of things. I allied myself with Kastian. We knew each other informally before prison so it wasn't difficult to become friends. Later, we met Fox and Jett and the four of us watched each other's backs." He clears his throat. "And even cursed, I have a lot of magic left."

I hum, raising an eyebrow.

I believe him—but I also suspect the real reason he survived so long wasn't just magic. It was loyalty. And leadership.

And now, knowing who his father was... I can see why Thorne was threatened by him.

# CHAPTER
# SIXTEEN

ALIX

Following the debacle that revealed the curse and the conversation in my room, Daemon loosens the reins on his guard duties. He gives no explanation or warning, but starts disappearing for long stretches of time and sending his friends in his place. I'm not sure if I should be hurt or relieved.

The craziest thing is, I can always tell when he's outside versus when one of the guys is. Even with the door closed, it's like I can feel his presence like a prickle on the back of my neck. Once I think I sense him leaving, and I rush to the door to find Kastian sitting outside in his place.

"Where's Daemon?" I blurt out.

Kastian looks up at me from beneath startlingly long eyelashes. "Had to go talk to Thorne about something. Why? Do you need anything?"

"Nope, I'm fine!" I flush with embarrassment and retreat back inside.

I close the door and shake my head, internally berating myself for my stupidity. It was just a coincidence. I obviously can't really feel Daemon's presence...I'm clearly starting to lose it.

Three days go by with relatively little incident. I rescue my yarn from Sushi and knit two and a half scarves and spend my time getting to know Daemon's friends. Each of them is so different, and I quickly learn more about them just by nature of proximity.

Kastian is clearly Daemon's best friend. That much is obvious to me

—not just from the way they talk to each other but also because he's the most frequent of my substitute bodyguards. He doesn't talk to me much, and always looks a little sad when I poke my head out into the hallway to check who's on duty. I only try talking to him once before I discover that he doesn't want to talk about his past, why he was sent to prison, or basically anything more substantial than the weather. Still, his presence is calming. Steady. Like the anchor of a ship on stormy waters.

When Jett guards me, he usually comes inside my room to chat with me which makes the time pass far faster. I learn that he's younger than the others by several decades, which I suppose accounts for why he seems more human to me, even though he's clearly not. Jett explains that he grew up on the streets in Solistine with a pack of other homeless kids. The "theft" that got him sent to Dyaspora was just a single loaf of bread that he stole to feed a group of young children.

"And you got sent to prison just for that?" I ask, horrified. I'm sitting on my bed knitting yet another scarf, but I stop and look up at Jett, waiting with bated breath for his reply.

Jett sits on the floor, dragging a bit of yarn across the rug for Sushi to chase. He doesn't look up at me. "Yeah. Being poor is just as bad as being a murderer in most parts of Ellender. Worse, actually, because most murderers have enough money to cover up their crimes."

I purse my lips. "Ellender isn't the only place where that problem exists.

"Too bad Fox didn't have more money when he was caught."

I raise an eyebrow. "He killed someone?"

Nodding, he kicks his feet out, putting his head back against the wall. "He was in the army in Thermia, kind of like what Ashwater does here except that Vernallis never fights any real wars. Thorne's army is mostly used for keeping order in the villages and guarding the king. Thermia is at the very top of the continent, close to Dyaspora. Their army is constantly fighting with monsters crawling down from the mountains or up out of the ocean."

"So Fox killed someone while in the army?" I cock my head. "I mean...isn't that the point? I'm not saying I'm pro-violence or anything but there's got to be some nuance there."

Jett shakes his head, and for once, his grin slips. "No, he killed a superior officer. Slaughtered him, as far as I understand."

Jett doesn't sound all that broken up about it.

"Why?"

"I guess this officer had raped a woman Fox knew. I'd tell you to ask him about it, but you know how he is."

I nod. At this point, I know exactly how Fox is.

When he's on guard duty, sometimes, I amuse myself by trying to say things he'll feel the need to reply to. Once, I just ask why he's so quiet. I'm not really expecting an answer, but he says, "Most conversations are just to fill silence. Silence has never really bothered me."

"That's so Zen of you. Very Yoda."

Unsurprisingly, Fox said nothing.

THE GUYS ARE FINE, BUT MY FAVORITE SUBSTITUTE GUARD IS Odessa, who never sits outside and always comes into my room to hang out or takes me on walks to explore the castle. She's the only one who seems to care if I'm not just physically alive, but also not scratching tally marks in the walls and muttering nonsense to myself from the lack of entertainment or social interaction. She never guards me on her own, and always turns up with either Jett or Fox, but never Kastian.

On one such occasion, Odessa walks down to the breakfast parlor with me while Fox trails silently behind us, providing our scary dog privilege.

I can't exactly say I love the parlor, but I dislike eating alone in my room more, and there aren't many options for hangout spots where I can also fill the never-ending void in my stomach.

We walk into the parlor, and of course, my gaze immediately finds Claudette and her sisters sitting in their usual spot by the window. This feels like fucking high school, with established groups at regular tables.

I hated high school, and I like this even less.

Odessa watches me as I raise an unenthusiastic hand to wave at the three identical blondes.

"What's the deal?" she asks under her breath.

"What do you mean?"

"Do we hate them? I mean, I've known the triplets for nearly a century, but if you hate them, I am totally on your side."

I appreciate the blind loyalty, but I can't accept the offer. I'm not in high school, I need to be a grownup...even though I really don't want to.

"We don't hate them," I mutter. "I don't even know the red dress and the yellow dress."

"Paulette and Laurette," Odessa supplies.

I raise an eyebrow. "Are you fucking serious? Their names are...actually never mind. It doesn't matter. I'm not going to be petty."

*Even if they are identical triplets with basically the same damn name. Did their parents hate them or something?*

"I've never heard of her," Fox says, startling Odessa and I.

I glance up at him. "Excuse me?"

He shuffles on his feet uncomfortably. "That woman. I've never heard her name."

"So?"

His arctic blue eyes widen, and he blows another frustrated breath out—which I've come to understand means that he's exhausted by having to explain what he thinks should already be obvious.

"I wasn't in Dyaspora as long as Ashwater. I came forty years ago, but forty years is still a long enough time to hear every story worth telling. I don't like to share, but I listen. I know all their families' names, every friend, every relationship. I don't know of Claudette."

"Why are you telling me this?"

He raises an eyebrow at me. "I told you. I listen."

"Uh...okay. Thanks."

"See!" Odessa says bracingly. "He's never heard of her. We can absolutely hate her."

"Oh my God," I groan, pushing the heels of my hands against my eyes. "No, I really don't. I'm not sixteen I don't hate other women for no reason, and I don't even know her. She didn't do anything wrong. She's actually been nice."

"But...?" Dessa prompts.

"But," I lean forward and lower my voice, "I don't know. She just reminds me of a former friend, that's all. But it's a me thing. I'm being weird and I need to get over it."

Odessa looks at me sympathetically. "The friend who slept with your husband?"

I raise an eyebrow. "Did I tell you that? I don't remember ever explaining—"

"You didn't," she says quickly. "But I'm not an idiot, and you drop a lot of not-so-subtle hints."

My cheeks heat. "Oh. I didn't realize."

This is so goddamn embarrassing. Fox and Dessa clearly think I'm jealous, which means they think there's something going on with Daemon and I. They're wrong. Maybe there was something between us at one point, kind of, but not now. Now, it's just a lot of residual energy with no outlet

*And sometimes that energy comes out in the form of heated arguments and intense instinctual kisses.*

*Yup. That's it. Makes total sense...*

Odessa waves a hand in the air. "It's fine. At least you had a husband to lose in the first place. I'm still looking for anyone I can stand long enough to lie in bed with for five minutes post-sex."

Fox looks sideways at her, as if he's considering her before his gaze flicks away. Odessa doesn't notice, but it's all I can do to stop myself from pointing out that someone who doesn't talk probably wouldn't be annoying to lie next to.

But then again, she probably needs to be with someone who balances her out. She's all spontaneous emotions and endless energy. She needs someone calm, and while Fox might seem calm because he's so quiet, what Jett told me about how the big guy got in prison makes me think there's some simmering rage under his blank expression.

Yeah, no. They'd be a terrible match. She needs someone more steady.

"Well, don't look at me," I say, sighing. "I'm hardly the expert in that area. Maybe you'll meet someone at the ball."

She rolls her eyes. "Doubtful. It's not exactly the most festive environment for a party when everyone knows they might die in two weeks."

I sit up straighter, alarmed. "Die? I didn't think they were going to die, just be cursed."

"It's kind of the same thing. I mean, you saw what they were all like during the day." She waves a hand in front of her face. "The lights are on, but no one is home. You know?"

"Honestly, Daemon didn't seem that different to me. I thought he might be drunk, but not that he was a different person."

Odessa shakes her head. "That just means you got lucky—or maybe that his gut instinct is somehow in your favor. Trust me, you don't want to see what it looks like when someone's instinctive desire is violence."

I shiver. Yeah, I don't want to see that. I don't really have a frame of reference for how it must feel to be cursed, but I keep picturing that old news story about the guy who ate someone's face while tripping on bath salts. I bet it's kind of like that.

I put my chin in my hand, sighing. "You know, sometimes I have no idea what I'm doing here."

"You're keeping us all out of prison."

"Yeah, I know that. That's not what I mean. I mean, what is Isabelle doing here? Everyone who has uttered two words to me doesn't seem all that confident that I'm going to break the curse, and I don't blame them. Even if I really was Nana, King Thorne has shown *zero* interest in me. None. I'm actually starting to wonder if there's something wrong with me."

"There's nothing wrong with you," she says automatically. "You're beautiful."

I look down. "That's not what I meant, but thanks, I guess. I meant, I'm afraid he knows. But if he does, then why is he stringing us all along?"

She inspects her nails for a long second, then bites off the tip of her pointer finger nail and inspects them again. Finally, she shrugs and looks up at me. "Yeah...I see what you're saying, but I have no idea what to do about it. There's not really anything you can do. Maybe Daemon—"

"I've hardly seen Daemon for days. I don't think he wants to talk to me after what happened the other night."

Odessa scoffs. "He's so moody. He'll get over it, you'll see."

"I shouldn't even be worried about that." I feel a slight heat rise in my cheeks. "What I should really be worried about is how the king barely talks to me. Even during dinner, he just doesn't seem interested."

"Maybe the king will finally show some interest at the ball. You're going to look stunning. I've already picked out a dress for you."

Instead of making me feel better, this just raises my anxiety higher. "Should I be worried about the ball?"

"Why?"

"I don't know...it's a ball. Social anxiety?"

"You don't need to be anxious. All anyone will care about is how you look."

"Oh, that's perfect then," I say sarcastically. "It definitely helps my anxiety to know everyone is going to actually be staring at me and it's not in my head."

"You have nothing to worry about. You could wear an old sack and still be the most exciting thing in the room."

I purse my lips. "You're on fire with compliments today, but you don't need to lie."

She cocks her head. "I'm not. Look, just think of it like this: humans find Fae to be exceptionally attractive, but that goes both ways. A human queen would be the most beautiful woman in all of Ellender, and a queen is what you're going to look like at the ball."

I gape at her. "Seriously? I didn't know that."

She nods and glances back at Fox. "Back me up. Tell her how all you guys act like virgins in a brothel the second you see a human."

Fox's eyebrows raise and he just stares at her, before giving me a single, curt nod.

"See?" Odessa gushes. "It's definitely a thing. Sirens like humans too, but not as much as Fae do. I think because you drown so much faster."

I blanche. Okay, so brushing aside that extremely disturbing comment, can what she's suggesting be right? It would certainly explain a lot. Does that mean Daemon wasn't just bored when we met in the bar?

"I guess that makes me feel a little better," I say. "Good thing, because I didn't want to spend my birthday feeling self-conscious."

She looks at me sharply. "Your birthday?"

"Yeah, didn't I mention that? It's kind of hard to keep track of the date here but I think tomorrow is my thirtieth birthday. I was thinking of using the ball to celebrate in my head, since it's the next day and everything."

"You definitely didn't tell me that!" Her eyes widen, and she jumps up. "I need to tell the kitchen. I'm sure they'll want to make you a cake for tomorrow and maybe another one for the ball. Oh Gods, I have so much to do..."

"That's really not necessary," I say automatically.

"Yes, it is!" Odessa insists. "In Ellender, we all live so long that you're not even really considered an adult until your thirties. It's an important day."

I open my mouth to protest again. The socially acceptable and polite thing to do is to insist I don't need or want anything, except...I kind of do. Before I came here, I really wanted just one person to make a big deal out of my birthday and then I felt guilty for even hoping for that. Why shouldn't I indulge just a little?

"I'll be right back!" Odessa exclaims, leaving me and Fox sitting alone.

## DAEMON

"Congratulations, asshole. You've ruined everything!"

I pause, lowering my cards, and glance toward the door. "Hello to you too."

Odessa sweeps into the room, barely sparing me a glance as she wafts around the edge of the table and drops into the only open seat between Jett and Kastian. She puts her elbows on the table, her long copper hair falling in a sheet over the pile of cards strewn across the wood. She lets out an exasperated breath. "You've ruined everything."

"I don't know what the fuck you're talking about," I growl, raising my cards again.

"Alix. Who else would I be talking about? She's miserable, and now we almost missed her birthday. You spend all day with her, how could you not tell me?"

I scowl, trying to ignore her as I toss my cards down on the table. "I fold."

I'm sitting in the barracks with the guys playing poker just like we did every night in Dyaspora. It's been weeks since we've been able to play, or even talk openly since I'm always guarding Alix or dealing with other soldiers who are somehow still loyal to Thorne. I'd been glad for a moment to relax, but I'm not relaxed at all since I keep losing.

Jett lets out a whoop of laughter and reaches out to drag the pile of coins at the center of the table toward him. "Another round, another handful of Ashwater's gold in my pocket." He leans over Odessa, pretending to whisper to Kas. "I think he likes losing. That's the only explanation."

"Fuck off," I growl without conviction.

"Daemon, are you listening to me?" Dessa demands.

I spare her another glance. "Not really."

Kastian begins dealing another hand, and Dessa huffs angrily even as she nods over to him to deal her in. "You should care. Alix is wilting. She'll never make it to the end of the month like this. I'm surprised she hasn't tried to find her way home already."

"Did she say something to you?" I ask, forcing myself to remain detached.

"No, but I can tell. She's bored and lonely."

I glance at my new hand—a pair of tens—and toss two coins at the center of the table, before answering, "Go, hang out with her then."

"I have been, but it's not enough!" she whines.

I close my eyes. Odessa is the sister I never needed or wanted, and right now, I can't recall exactly why I care about her in the first place.

"What do you expect me to do? I showed her where the parlor is, I brought her into the city to get something to keep her entertained. What else is there? I'm not going to encourage her to socialize more. The less time she spends with anyone who knew the real Isabelle, the better."

"She can be around us, though. You could be playing cards in her room instead of hiding in here."

Yeah, no. That's not going to happen.

The only way to keep myself from ruining everything is by staying as far away from Alix as possible. Since the incident the other day in her room, I've been trying to keep my distance. Or, at least, more distance than I got this past week, spending every second, day and night, mere feet away from her.

I'm positive that it's just the constant proximity that's making it impossible for me to stop thinking about her. I just need some time away to get my shit together.

For the last few days, I've swallowed my inexplicable jealousy and allowed my friends to take shifts guarding Alix instead. And when I do have to be around her, I try not to talk too much. I don't want to know anything more about her because every new thing I learn is fascinating and makes it harder to think of her as Isabelle.

Nothing has helped yet, but it will. I'm sure of it.

I toss two more coins into the center of the table, raising the bet. "Alix is fine. It's already been almost two weeks and no one suspects anything. Thorne has dinner with her every night and he still has no idea she isn't Isabelle. There's only two weeks left."

Her eyes widen. "Yeah, two weeks until you're all cursed forever? That sounds just perfect."

"Hmmm."

The truth is that I can't think about the curse because whenever I do, new plans start forming in my head.

If I went back to the human realm permanently, I wouldn't be cursed. Of course, I could never see my friends or family again, and I'd be leaving the entire kingdom to its own destruction, but that would happen anyway. And, if Alix is going back to the human realm...maybe it wouldn't be so bad?

I shake my head roughly. These are the sorts of thoughts I can't allow myself to have.

There's still a chance Thorne could love Alix—even if he thinks she's Isabelle, maybe it won't matter. Maybe somehow everything will work out for everyone.

*Everyone except me.*

"You're the one who brought Alix here and promised to take care of her," Odessa continues. "You have to do something."

"I promised to keep her safe, not to keep her happy."

"If you ask me, happy and safe are the same thing," Kastian says, offhandedly.

"No one asked you," Odessa snaps. "But yes, she's not really safe if she's unhappy."

I groan loudly. Despite my protest, a pang of guilt and worry shoots through me. I know Dessa has a point. It's my fault that Alix is here at all, and even without Thorne's order, that would make her my responsibility.

"Wait," I ask Odessa, suddenly thinking of something. "What are you doing here?"

She gives me an odd look. "Well, you see, I came here as a child and—"

"Oh, shut up," I snap, a bit more aggressively than I intended. "I meant if you're here, who's watching Alix?"

"Fox," she replies airily. "But even if he wasn't, she's a nearly thirty-year-old woman, she can take care of herself for half an hour."

"Yeah, that's what I'm fucking afraid of," I hiss angrily, scooting my chair back from the table and tossing my cards down. "I fold. I need to go find Alix."

Jett reaches over and flips my cards over, a grin passing across his face. "Aww, tough luck, mate. The one time you have decent cards, and I'm still going to take your money."

I roll my eyes as I stride toward the door. "And you'll spend it buying us all drinks, so it's really more charity on my part than anything."

"Wait, weren't you listening to me?" Odessa jumps up. "Fox is with her."

I heard her, but I still yank the door open angrily and march down the hall.

I'm being irrational, I know.

As long as I don't think about Alix being alone with my friends, there are no problems, but as soon as I remember, I find myself storming back upstairs or pacing the barracks, unable to calm down until I'm near her again.

These are my men, and I'm the one who keeps asking them to guard Alix for me. I don't have a problem with Fox guarding Alix or doubt that he could protect her.

Still, I feel an overwhelming compulsion to get her because she's *mine*.

I don't understand it.

Being jealous is not only insane, I don't know where it's coming from. But when it comes to that woman, I can't think straight. I feel like an addict; I have to abstain completely from thinking about her or I'll overdose on memories of the taste of her.

"Wait!"

I stop when a shout echoes down the hallway and I turn to find Odessa hurrying after me. I run a hand through my hair. "What?"

"Do you realize that tomorrow is her birthday?"

"So?"

"So we should do something. She mentioned celebrating at the ball, but I'm not so sure that's a good idea because then Thorne might start to wonder about her age."

I groan internally. That's not a bad point, and I hate that I agree. "What are you suggesting?"

Dessa's violet eyes flash with satisfaction, and I know she thinks she's already won.

"We'll take her down to the village tavern."

I shake my head. "Too dangerous. Anyone could recognize her, and if she's drinking, she could forget—"

"Okay fine," Dessa cuts me off. "What if we take her to the Ashwater Estate?"

That's not the worst idea. I've been meaning to go there anyway, but I can't because I'm always watching Alix. But if I brought her with me...

I pull a pocket watch out of my trousers and glance at it. "There's no time. She has to eat with Thorne in less than an hour."

"Tomorrow, then," Dessa insists. "That's better anyway because it's her actual birthday."

I grimace, sure I'll regret this immediately. "Fine."

Dessa squeals in excitement and gives me a quick hug which I don't return.

"Thank you! I promise everything will be perfect."

I highly fucking doubt that, but it's too late. It looks like Alix is getting a birthday party, and I'm getting yet another fucking opportunity to pretend I'm not growing obsessed with her.

"WHAT DID YOU DO TODAY?" ALIX ASKS.

Thorne looks at her from across the table. "Nothing you would understand," he replies dismissively.

"Try me."

He puts his fork down and smiles at her. Well, the corners of his mouth turn up at the very least, but it's more of a sneer than a smile.

I resist the urge to bash my skull against the wall behind me.

These dinners would be boring enough if I was actually allowed to be a part of them, but standing against the wall watching it unfold is nothing short of torture.

Which, of course, is why Thorne is making me do it.

I'd been suspicious of how easily he accepted my return. Sure, he'd promised to do so, and I'd expected that he would, but I thought I'd have to work harder for it. Thorne likes to remind everyone around him that he's the one with the power, especially me. It was diabolical, really. He reinstated my position and power, but immediately ordered me to watch Alix so that I can't use any of it.

The only mistake he made is that he thinks I hate guarding Alix.

Which I do...kind of. Not really.

*Fuck me.*

"I've been preparing for the rose moon celebration," Thorne tells Alix.

"Is that a lot of work?"

"It shouldn't be, yet the incompetence of the court continues to astound me."

"What exactly is a rose moon?" she asks.

"It's a lunar event that happens every twelve years. The sun is blocked for an entire twenty-four hours and total darkness falls upon the land."

"That must be convenient, what with...everything." She shrugs awkwardly, clearly not sure if he'll be offended by her mentioning the curse.

He nods. "Exactly. There have been many rose moons in the last century, but only one that falls on the final day of the curse."

She leans forward curiously. "Does that mean something?"

"That is what I have been attempting to discover. With only one final chance to end my suffering, I want to ensure everything goes smoothly."

She frowns, looking worried. I curl my fingers into a fist, spread them out again, and repeat.

Thorne is being nice to Alix—or at least as nice as I've ever seen him. It seems like he wants her—or Isabelle, rather—to see him as kinder and gentler than he really is. That might be a good thing, except I fucking know better. He hasn't changed; his acting has simply improved.

Not that I should care. Fuck, if Alix does fall for this, then all the better, right? I should want nothing more than for her to somehow fall in love with him and break the curse.

I make a fist again and this time I don't let it go.

"I have wanted to ask you something as well," Thorne says.

Alix swallows a sip of her wine. "Yes?"

"Why have you stopped reading?"

*Shit.*

Alix freezes and glances seemingly unconsciously over at me. Her eyes dart to mine and I'm positive that Thorne notices from the way his posture goes rigid.

"Stopped reading?" Alix says, clearly hoping he'll elaborate.

"Yes. You used to bring books to the table every evening, but you have not done so since you've returned. Why?"

"Oh, well, I suppose I just haven't felt like it..."

I suddenly remember that Alix asked about books earlier this week. I'd completely forgotten that I was going to take her to the library, since she's barely been out of her room since. Fuck, could I have avoided this if I'd remembered?

Seeming to realize that her excuse wasn't very believable, Alix glances at me for a second time. I don't think she realizes she's doing it, but this time I'm sure Thorne sees her.

"It's my fault," I blurt out, no idea what I'm going to say next.

Thorne's eyes narrow at me. "Your fault? Explain."

*Shit. Fuck. Cocksucking mother...* "I don't like Isabelle to wander, it makes my job so much more tedious."

His expression turns dangerous. "Do you really think your comfort matters?"

"Always." I flash him a grin, knowing it will annoy him, perhaps enough to forget what he was suspicious about.

Thorne scowls and picks up his fork again, resuming his dinner. "Take her to the library from now on."

I nearly laugh with relief. "Of course. Whatever you say."

To my enormous relief and surprise, the rest of the dinner is uneventful. Alix seems bored, and Thorn, annoyed, but at least the suspicious look has disappeared from his gaze.

When Alix is finished with her dessert, I finally push off the wall and walk over to stand beside her chair. She stands, says goodnight to Thorne, and I walk stiffly beside her to the door.

"Ashwater," Thorne calls after me. "One moment."

I turn to Alix beside me. "Just wait outside for a moment."

She shrugs and leaves the dining room, closing the door behind her. I turn around and give my brother a bored look. "Thorne. What can I do for you?"

My brother grimaces, but doesn't say anything.

He calls me by my last name for nearly the same reason that I use his first—he wants a constant reminder that while we're related, I'm never going to be in line for the throne, and I like to remind him that no matter what he does, he'll never be able to escape my existence. I'm sure that the reason he never corrects me for using his name is because he doesn't want to draw attention to the issue. That's also almost certainly why he didn't want me killed all those years ago—because my execution would legitimize the threat I pose to him and his court.

All of that baggage hangs in the air between us as he approaches.

"Are you enjoying yourself?" he asks.

"What do you mean?"

"Are you enjoying being back at court?"

I have to refrain from a sneering retort, reminding myself that he thinks I've grown more loyal to him since leaving Dyaspora. Still, I can't manage to sound enthusiastic. I shrug. "There's nearly as much snow here as Dyaspora, but at least the food is better."

He looks annoyed but doesn't push it. "I wanted to ask you about Isabelle."

My ears prick up. "What about her?"

"Has she seemed strange to you since she returned?"

My heartbeat speeds up. What does he mean? Did Foulo finally crawl out of the hole he slunk off to and tell Thorne of his suspicions?

"Strange how? I didn't know her before, so I have nothing to compare with."

His brow furrows in a scowl and he glances over his shoulder, clearly looking for Alix. "Has she seemed afraid?"

"Afraid?" I draw back with genuine surprise. "No."

He makes a sound somewhere between a growl and a hum.

"Why?" I ask, hoping my eagerness for his answer doesn't show in my voice.

"I'm concerned she might have seen something she shouldn't have before she left all those years ago. She hasn't been exploring when you've been watching her?"

I shake my head. "She hardly leaves her room."

"Good," he says, sounding distracted. "There's another thing. I need to get her a wedding gift, something that could be presented at the ball in front of the court. Can you think of anything she would like?"

"I really don't know her as well as you do."

"How is that possible when you're with her all the time?"

I narrow my eyes in confusion. He is talking about Isabelle, right? The woman he wanted returned to him after decades apart? The woman he got an enchanted necklace for to keep her immortal? The woman he freed me to go find? How the fuck can he not know what to get her as a gift? Unless he knows there's something different about her.

"You must know something," he says, exasperated.

"A violin," I blurt out.

He narrows his eyes at me. "Does she play?"

*Oh fuck.*

"She mentioned taking up playing in the last few years," I lie. "I don't know if she has any talent."

He frowns, still looking suspicious. "Alright then."

I remember Alix commenting that Thorne didn't seem interested in her, and at the time, I wasn't able to process anything she was saying beyond the irrational rage at the idea of her potentially wanting to fuck my brother. Now, I see what she meant. He's blatantly not interested in her—it's clear from the way he doesn't want to be around her, and doesn't even seem to be aware of her presence. I can barely stop myself from watching her long enough to have this conversation, but Thorne is very clearly not suffering from the same obsession.

But does that mean there's something wrong with him?

Or is there something wrong with me?

# CHAPTER
# SEVENTEEN

ALIX

"Alix, get up!"

I open my eyes to the strongest sense of déjà vu and Odessa's face looming over me. "Hey," I yawn. "What time is it?"

"About 5 in the evening."

For a second, my sleepy brain can't process what she means and I have to take a second before I remember that 5PM is like 5AM here. Ugh, I might be used to the hours now, but the terminology will never fully compute. "Right..." I stifle another yawn. "Are we going somewhere?"

"Yes, but it's a surprise. Happy birthday!"

In spite of myself, a smile crosses my face.

Odessa dances over to the wardrobe, bouncing with every step. She pulls out a teal wool coat with white fur trim and holds it out to me. "This is a good color for you."

It hasn't taken long for me to learn that it's easiest not to argue with her about things like this and just go with it. I dress quickly in a sage green dress and the heavy teal coat, then accompany her downstairs.

It's early—or rather, late—so there aren't many courtiers in the hall or milling around outside the throne room. The castle feels still, and even more imposing that's usual for all its echoing emptiness.

Odessa leads me through the maze of corridors to the first floor entrance hall. The only people we pass are one of the red-jacketed guards, standing in an alcove and talking in hushed tones to a dark-haired woman. The guard is blonde and on the thin side with large copper-colored wings.

"That's so sad." Odessa sighs under her breath.

I frown. "What is?"

"His wings are out and he's not under direct threat. I guess unless she's holding a knife to his gut." She glances back over her shoulder at the whispering couple. "Nope. No knife, so it's definitely just sad."

"I don't understand. Explain it to me like I'm five."

The corners of her mouth tip up for just a second, before her expression turns serious again. "Thousands of years ago, Fae had wings all the time, but they evolved past it. Now the wings only come out in moments of intense emotion."

"Like near death experiences," I chime in, remembering what Kastian explained.

"Exactly. Fighting is the most common time wings are seen, but that's not all. Males tend to show their wings around their soul-bonds, even before the bond has fully formed. Casually seeing the wings of someone you're dating is like"—she waves her hand in the air— "this whole important thing."

"Huh. Okay, I guess that makes sense."

We reach the front doors of the castle and Odessa pushes them wide. The cold night air spills inside, bringing in the scent of snow and roses, and making goosebumps rise on the exposed skin of my face and neck.

"So that's why whatever was going on with them back there is so depressing." Odessa continues as we step out onto the icy steps. "They're clearly new bonds, but there's only a few weeks left until the rose moon. It just doesn't seem fair to find your bonded and then lose them so fast. I'd rather never find them."

A gnawing dread rises in my stomach. I press my gloved fingers to my abdomen, willing the churning to stop. "So you don't think the curse will break?"

She looks at me sharply and has to throw her hand out to the railing and catch herself before she trips down the endless steps. "No, sorry...I didn't mean it like that."

There's an awkward silence, because clearly, she did mean it like that. I guess I'm not the only one with doubts about this plan. Maybe if I really was Nana, it would work...but maybe not even then, because the king is so disinterested. It really doesn't look or feel like fated love.

Odessa exhales sharply. "Look, sirens are really superstitious. Culturally, we believe a lot in fate, and I don't think things like this just happen. When Belle wandered into Ellender all those years ago we all thought she was the one who'd finally save all of us. Now her granddaughter is here when there's only weeks left to break the curse? That feels like fate to me. I don't know what's going to happen, but I believe there's a reason you're here."

The sick feeling in my gut intensifies. I personally don't believe in fate, but for once, I hope I'm wrong. The longer I spend here, the more real all of this seems, and the more I can't imagine that in two weeks the entire court will just be gone. *And Daemon will be gone along with them.*

"I hope you're right," I flash her a weak smile, then cast my mind wildly around for anything to change the subject. "For a siren, you seem to know a lot about Fae..."

She gives me a sideways look. "Well, yeah, I was raised at court."

"But you're not Fae, even though you and Daemon are cousins?" I prod.

I'm intensely curious about this world and how everything works, but no one seems inclined to explain it. I get the feeling that Odessa and the others aren't hiding anything from me on purpose. They just don't think to explain things that feel obvious to them.

"King Thorne is Daemon's half-brother through his biological father, and I'm his cousin through his mother, Lady Ashwater."

I frown, trying to keep it all straight in my head. "Oh, okay then."

"My mother was a siren and my father was Lady Ashwater's brother. That would make me half-Fae, except that all female children of sirens are also sirens."

I nod. I note as someone whose father also died that she's saying "was." Her father *was* Daemon's uncle, but he isn't now. A rush of empathy that can only come from also losing a parent floods me, and I instantly feel closer to Odessa without her having to do anything at all.

I don't want to make her go into detail if she doesn't want to, but there's still a question that I can't help asking. "So...sorry if this is rude, but why do you have legs?"

In my head, Gretchen Weiner's voice screams, *Oh my God, Alix. You can't just ask people why they have legs!*

"It's a long story," Odessa says evasively. "And we're almost there, anyway."

I duck my head, feeling a little awkward for prying. Maybe siren tales are like the Fae's wings and only appear sometimes? Or maybe Odessa isn't like the fairytale mermaids I've been picturing and she's something else?

Odessa hooks her arm through mine and jogs down the remaining steps. We turn left at the bottom, and she leads me a short way to a low wooden-walled building. Immediately the scent of hay and barnyard hits me.

I freeze. "What is this?"

"The stables," Odessa says.

Um, no. No thank you. Get me out of here right fucking now.

We're standing in a long room, larger than it appeared from the outside. On both sides, there are rows and rows of horse stalls with a walkway down the middle. At the end of the row, I can see four familiar red jacketed figures fixing saddles onto several enormous black and chestnut horses.

I barely notice the men, as I'm completely fixated on the horses. I take a large step back, lingering just inside the doorway.

"What's wrong?" Odessa asks.

Before I can answer, Kastian, who is nearest, looks up at the sound of her voice. His sudden movement startles the horses, because the stallion next to him paws the ground nervously and he pats its neck to calm it down.

Odessa grabs my hand again and tries to tug me further inside. "Come on, this will be fun!"

I dig my heels in, trying not to let her drag me. "What are we doing here?"

"We're going on a little day trip," Odessa says happily. "Or, a night trip, I guess would be more appropriate."

"And we're taking those?" I ask nervously, looking up at the nearest horse.

"Yes," Daemon replies, stepping out from behind one of the beasts.

I glance up and meet his eyes. We've barely spoken in days, but of course my traitorous body doesn't know that. My heart beat speeds up at just the sight of him, and I feel a strange swooping in my stomach.

*God, get a grip!*

"Um, okay." I tear my eyes from Daemon and look down, biting my lip. "But just to clarify, you mean we're taking a wagon pulled by the horses, right? Like when we came from the inn?"

*Please, please say yes.*

"No," Daemon replies. "We're riding. The train still hasn't been repaired, and it doesn't go to where we're headed anyway."

"Uh, no. No, thank you," I blurt out, yanking my arm away from Odessa and backing up a few steps. "You can do whatever you want, but I'm not getting on a horse."

"Have you never ridden before?" Kastian asks, sounding surprised.

"Once?"

"What happened?"

"I don't want to talk about it. It doesn't matter. I'm just not comfortable with horses. They're fine at a distance, but I'm not riding one."

Perplexed, Daemon turns to the others. "We can't bring a wagon. It's too slow."

"She can ride with you," Jett says.

*As if it's so easy.*

I put both hands up. "No way. That doesn't make it less horrifying, just less comfortable."

Daemon grimaces. "Then I guess we're not going."

I glance around. Odessa looks crestfallen, and even the others look disappointed. Immediately, I feel terrible. They're trying to do something nice for me, and my stupid fear is ruining it. I sigh and pinch the skin between my eyes.

*I hate disappointing people.*

I agree to at least try the horse, and everyone watches with bated breath as Daemon lifts me up into the saddle. I'm holding my breath too, but for completely different reasons. I'm afraid to move a muscle and scare the horse.

"Take the reins," Daemon says.

"Nope, I'm good right here," I say stiffly, my fingers curling tightly around the edge of the saddle.

He closes his eyes and tips his head back, evidently praying for patience. "I take it you don't know how to ride?"

I move enough to glare at him. "I told you I don't go near horses. The closest I've ever come to regular contact with farm animals is when my Barbies rode the My Little Ponies. Why the hell would you assume I know how to ride?"

Jett leans back against one of the stalls, crossing his arms. "I'm telling you Ashwater, all this would be solved if you just have her ride with you."

Daemon lifts a brow at me in question.

At first I say no, but after another ten minutes of back and forth, somehow, I find myself agreeing to riding with Daemon. I really need to work on standing my ground, or at least explaining myself better when I'm uncomfortable, but I guess today isn't that day. Anyway, I do want to celebrate my birthday, even if that just means new scenery.

I expect to sit on the back of the horse, like we're on a motorcycle. Instead, Daemon positions me in front of where he will ultimately sit. I'm perched on the edge of the saddle, the hard leather ridge digging into my ass.

It only gets worse when Daemon climbs on behind me.

It's very clear he knows his way around a horse because he climbed up into the saddle with the sort of confident muscle memory that belies years of practice. Unfortunately, the moment he sits, I feel him tense. "You have to slide back."

"Uh, no, I'm okay." This is already horrifying enough—I don't think pressing my ass against his crotch is going to improve the situation.

"You can't sit on the edge of the saddle like that," Daemon grinds out.

"Why not?"

"Because the second we start moving, your pretty little cunt won't be so pretty anymore. You'll be so sore you won't be able to walk tomorrow."

My mouth falls open, heat rushing to my face. "Excuse me?"

He doesn't respond. Instead, his hands clamp around my waist, dragging me backward until my spine is flush against his chest.

I shift slightly, readjusting, and just as I'd feared, my ass presses firmly against him. "Are you happy now?"

"Fucking perfect."

It takes me a second to process that his response is in no way an answer to my question. A shiver travels up my spine, and I have to bite my lip to keep from saying something stupid as we finally start moving.

It doesn't take me long to realize that I've been right to be afraid of horses. Riding is terrifying, and made all the worse because the only thing to distract me is the musky rose and pine scent of whatever soap Daemon recently used, and how my ass bounces against him with every movement.

Soon, we get to the dirt road through the forest and everyone fans out, riding in groups of two or three. Clearly, they've all been riding horses for years—probably as long as I've been riding in cars, I suppose.

"Why are you afraid of horses?" Daemon asks.

I grit my teeth. "I don't want to talk about it. And anyway, this is probably the worst possible time to remind me that I'm afraid."

He sucks in a breath like he's going to say something else, but he doesn't.

We ride for fifteen minutes in silence with Daemon sitting perfectly straight and still behind me. Finally, he adjusts slightly, his chin landing just over the top of my head. Without intending, I relax enough to stop sitting at such a tension, leaning my back more firmly against his chest.

He doesn't comment on it, and I'm glad because I don't know if I could explain myself. Half of me wants nothing to do with him, while the other half wants to crawl into his lap and see if he kisses as well as I remember.

We crest a small hill, and my mouth falls open at the sight of dozens of glittering lights in the distance. As we draw closer, a small village comes into view. I know Nana never saw this place because if she did, it would have absolutely made it into the book.

The village is picturesque, with brightly painted cottages, flowers in every window, and sparkling lanterns hanging from every rooftop illuminating the street so that even though the sky is dark, everything feels warm and inviting.

As we pass, people come running out of their houses to see us and wave or cry out greetings.

"Why are they cheering?"

"Because no one has been here to watch over them for ninety years."

I wrinkle my nose in confusion. "So you're like their king."

"No, I'm a Baron. It's a lesser noble title, like..." He thinks for a moment, clearly trying to find the right word. "Like a governor."

"And no one became the new governor while you were gone?"

He shakes his head, and I feel the movement against my back. "It's an inherited title. Unless I die or have children, these people are on their own."

I frown. That doesn't seem right. But then again, I am way too modern to deal with Fae politics. I've seen Le Mis like twenty times and if I were the one dealing with an absolute monarchy day-to-day I'd totally be singing the song of angry men.

"What's the village called?" I ask, changing the subject.

Daemon clears his throat. "Storia."

I want to stop and explore, but we keep riding and eventually come to a sudden halt in front of the extravagant mansion. The weathered stone walls are adorned with climbing roses and ivy, giving the home a rustic yet elegant feel. The shadow of a small tower rises up behind the peak of the roof, and to the side of the house, I spot a large rose garden. Out front is a courtyard where all our horses stop.

"Don't tell me this is your house?" I say, awed.

Daemon doesn't answer, just swings down from the saddle and lands lightly on the cobblestone. "Let me help you down."

I swallow. I don't want to seem helpless, but at the same time I have no clue how to get off this thing. Somehow, I get my leg over the horse's neck, then Daemon reaches up and wraps his strong arms around my waist, lifting me down gracefully. A surge of electricity courses through my body at the touch of his fingers against my skin, sending shivers down my spine.

"Thanks," I breathe.

He opens his mouth to say something, but never gets a chance.

There's a loud cry and suddenly a blur of movement overtakes us.

A woman comes running out of the house and completely ignores me as she launches herself straight at Daemon. She says something, but I can't understand her over her sobs. Daemon seems to understand though, because he says, "I'm so sorry."

The woman is lightly plump and shorter than my 5'4" frame by several inches. Her raven black hair is twisted into a bun at the nape of her neck and she's wearing a frilly purple and gold apron over a cream-colored dress. My stomach twists. How many exes am I going to have to meet?

And as usual, why the fuck do I care?

I back away toward Odessa and the others, but don't make it there before Daemon disentangles himself from the crying woman and steps back. She takes a handkerchief out of her pocket and blows her nose loudly.

Looking a bit lost, Daemon turns in a circle, seemingly looking for me. "Al—Isabelle," he says, stumbling over my name. "Come meet Lady Ashwater, my mother."

Oh. *Oh.*

Now I feel like a fucking lunatic because that was clearly a parental sort of hug and I'm obviously on edge for no reason.

In fairness, Lady Ashwater does look *really* young to have an adult son. This must be what happens when no one ages—it's hard to tell the parents from the grown children. Still, I'm clearly dealing with some weird jealousy issues that I've never experienced before. Ever. Not about Ryan, or anyone else. *What the hell is going on with me?*

"It's nice to meet you, Lady Ashwater," I say, sure I'm blushing.

"Oh please." Lady Ashwater blows her nose loudly, then smacks her son on the arm with the same handkerchief. "No one calls me a lady anymore. You can call me Beatrix."

"Okay. Hi," I repeat, slightly dazed by the whole exchange.

I don't know why it didn't occur to me that going to Daemon's family estate might mean meeting his family. I don't have a great track record with meeting families—Ryan's mother hated me from the moment she laid eyes on me and I was never really able to pinpoint why. *I wonder if she'll like Jenna any better.*

"What's your name, dear?" Beatrix asks. "I didn't catch it."

"This is Isabelle," Daemon says pointedly.

Beatrix frowns and leans closer, the way Odessa did when we first met. Her eyes dart shrewdly over my face for a long moment. "Isabelle... what?"

"*Reading*," I fill in quickly.

"Interesting." Her eyes narrow for the slightest moment before she pulls back and smiles. "Well, come inside. You'll want tea, I'm sure, and dessert?" She gestures to the door. "Be my guest!"

THE ASHWATER ESTATE IS JUST THAT—AN ESTATE.

I never really knew what that meant before and always associated the word with gated communities and private golf courses, but Daemon's house is nothing like that. Every inch of the entrance hall sparkles— from the glittering mosaic on the floor to the grand staircase leading up to the other levels.

Beatrix leads us past the grand staircase and through a set of intricately carved double doors, into a formal dining room. Beyond the dining room is an expansive kitchen, fit for a gourmet chef despite the lack of modern appliances. Despite the enormous size, the room is warm and homey. The scent of freshly baked bread wafts from the oven, filling the room with nostalgic comfort.

As promised, Beatrix makes tea and biscuits. Given that she's a lady, no matter what she likes to be called, I was expecting her to have an army of servants, but Beatrix surprises me by preparing everything herself. She bustles around the kitchen with a very "mom" type energy that I've never really experienced before.

While she boils water, Beatrix monologues about everything that's happened while Daemon has been gone. The village hasn't grown much, but they've lost less people to the curse than other villages in the area. Someone started a new bakery and the traveling book merchant decided to settle here last year and has opened a permanent bookstore. Beatrix has been working in the garden often, and someone named Aurelia is doing well, except that lately she's been asking to travel outside of Storia.

"Where is she?" Daemon asks at the mention of Aurelia.

"Oh, around here somewhere," Beatrix says airily, as she carries a plate of biscuits over to the table. "I'm sure she'll come out at dinner time."

She takes a seat at the head of the large wooden breakfast table and fixes her son with a stern gaze, her previously teary eyes now unyielding. "Well, are you going to explain what you're doing here, or shall I guess?"

I glance over at Daemon, suddenly very interested to see how this goes. I've heard the best way to see what a man is really like is to pay attention to how they treat their mothers. I only wish I'd heard that before marrying Ryan. He was always rude to his mother, while she acted like he shat roses and rainbows.

I shake my head.

I am not evaluating Daemon for anything, and I shouldn't care one way or another how he treats his mother. In fact, I should probably excuse myself before I do something stupid...like get too comfortable here or melt into a pile of emotional goo for no reason.

I stand abruptly. Everyone turns to look at me.

My gaze travels around the kitchen and falls on a back door. Beyond, I can see rows and rows of rosebushes. "Does anyone mind if I explore outside? It's so pretty, and I've heard this story anyway."

Six sets of eyes swivel off me and onto Daemon, clearly waiting for his orders. His jaw clenches, like he's fighting some internal battle. I'm about to argue that it's my birthday, when he says, "Fine. One of you go with her."

As one, Fox, Jett and Kastian all stand. They look at each other, shrug, and the four of us file toward the door.

"I'll go too!" Odessa says, quickly standing up.

"Sit," Beatrix says sternly. "Don't think you're getting away without explaining to me why you haven't visited in years. You weren't in prison; you have no excuse."

Odessa sits with a huff and blows her bangs out of her face. Under the table, I see Daemon kick her chair and throw her a look like "At least I'm not the only one in for a lecture." Dessa makes a face at him, then reaches for a fork on the table and twirls it between her fingers, scowling with evident boredom.

I almost laugh. For a fraction of a second, they seem like teenagers and for the first time ever I can envision how this mismatched little family used to operate.

A spark of jealousy and longing hits me straight in the chest.

Yup, I need to get out of here.

I do not want to think about that because some stupid part of me is dying to be a part of some perfect little family unit, and the last thing I need is to forget that I don't belong here.

THE GARDEN FEELS LIKE ANOTHER WORLD ENTIRELY.

There are rows and rows of rosebushes stretching down a hill and out of sight. Some are so tall, they might as well be trees, and weaving between them feels like being stuck in a fragrant hedge maze. The velvety darkness is illuminated by a sea of twinkling fireflies.

"Shit, this place is enormous," Jett says in awe, turning in a circle to see every inch of the garden. "I don't feel bad about taking Ashwater's money in poker anymore. He's obviously good for it."

I grimace, remembering Daemon's promise to pay me more gold than I could possibly imagine. At the time, I'd sort of thought he was exaggerating, but I'm so broke I wasn't in a position to negotiate. After seeing this house, though, I'm wondering if he was being literal. I don't even want to know what a place like this would cost back home. $10,000,000? $100,000,000? It's hard to say.

"Didn't you all know about this house?" I ask.

"Hell no!" Jett grins, striding across the garden wearing an expression like a kid visiting Disney World for the first time. "We knew he had a title before Dyaspora, but I've never even seen an estate like this that wasn't a royal palace."

"I knew," Kastian says without inflection.

I glance at him. "You did? Why?"

He shrugs, looking like he wishes he hadn't spoken. "I know what a Baron is. This isn't unusual for that kind of title."

"Did you grow up in a place like this too, then?"

He shifts uncomfortably. "Where I grew up is nowhere worth remembering."

*Huh. Okay...*

Feeling slightly awkward, like I accidentally brought up something that upset Kastian, I quickly trot after Jett who has disappeared into the wild rose garden.

Except, Jett has completely disappeared.

Several paces into the wild roses and I already feel completely cut off from the estate and the village beyond. It's silent except for the sound of my feet against the frosty ground and the air is thick with the scent of blooming roses and jasmine, creating an intoxicating aroma that pulls me further in. I wander further into the darkness pressing in around me, until I'm not paying attention to where I'm going at all.

My foot catches, and I stumble, jumping back as I nearly collide with a figure kneeling in the middle of the path. "Ah!"

The woman on the ground looks at me with enormous startled eyes, like a deer in the headlights. She scrambles back across the snowy path and just manages to avoid my foot as it comes down hard right where she was sitting.

I jump back, trying to steady myself and my hand flies to my now rapidly beating heart. "Oh my God, shit, I'm sorry!"

"Oh...that's alright." The woman blinks up at me, seeming slightly dazed.

"Here, let me help you." I hold out my hand to help her up.

She looks at my hand for a long second, and my chest constricts with guilt and embarrassment until she finally grasps my fingers.

"Thanks," she breathes, straightening and dusting herself off.

The woman is lovely in a delicate sort of way. Petite, thin, and wearing a bright magenta cloak over her shoulders. Her skin is tan, almost as dark as Kastian's, and she has enormous brown eyes nearly the same color as her dark hair. Her hair is cut short, just above her chin, and pushed behind pointed ears. Being Fae, it's hard to know exactly how old she is, but her expressions make me think she's on the younger side.

"Sorry," I say again, my overactive heartbeat slowly returning to normal. "I was just exploring."

"Really, it's fine." She flashes a shy smile. "I shouldn't be in the middle of the path like this, but I spotted this patch of rapunzel and I couldn't stop myself from stopping to collect it."

"Patch of what?"

The woman points. I follow her gaze toward a patch of tiny bell-shaped blue flowers growing at the base of the nearest rose bush. Beside the plant, sits a little pile of plucked leaves.

"Oh," I say, though I don't entirely understand. "Well, I didn't mean to bother you."

"That's alright." Her voice is small and delicate, just like her appearance. "Are you visiting the manor?"

"Yes. I'm Isabelle," I say, the name feeling foreign on my tongue.

She holds out a hand to shake mine. "Aurelia."

"Oh!" I grin. "Beatrix mentioned you. Do you live here, or..."

"Yes!" She nods, her demeanor quickly changing as she recovers from her shock. "I do, and we never get visitors, so—"

"Alix!"

Aurelia breaks off and we both turn to find Jett crashing through the roses behind us. The thorny branches get stuck to his bright red jacket and in his hair and he throws them off roughly, taking out his long sword to better hack his way toward me. "Alix! Where—" He spots me and his eyes light up. "Oh, thank fucking Gods, I thought Ashwater was going to skin me alive for losing you. Don't tell him, okay?"

I smile, bemused, but Aurelia looks up at me curiously. "I thought your name was Isabelle?"

"Uh...long story." Jett finally reaches us and I turn to him, seeking a distraction from fumbling my name. "Aurelia, this is Jett. He's—" I struggle for a moment to find the right word to describe Jett. "—a friend."

I expect him to respond with an enthusiastic greeting, but he doesn't. I glance at him, and find that he's not smiling at all anymore, just staring at Aurelia with obvious shock. You'd think he'd never seen a pretty girl before, but I've seen him flirt shamelessly with Odessa and even me sometimes. "Um, do you already know each other?"

Jett shakes his head, then refocuses on me. "Come back to the house. These gardens are weird, I swear I only walked a few feet and got lost."

"Oh yeah, that happens," Aurelia says with a tinkling laugh. "Come on, I'll show you the way out. Careful of the thorns. One of these days, I swear they're going to poke someone's eyes out."

She grabs her basket of herbs and walks confidently down the path, clearly having recovered from my startling her. Uncharacteristically, Jett is still silent and unsmiling as we follow her.

"Are you going to join us for dinner?" I ask.

She shakes her head, stopping at the edge of the garden where the lights of the house are visible once more, and the top of the little tower stands out against the dark sky. "No...I don't think so. But it was nice to meet you, *Alix*." She gives me a mischievous smile and glances once at Jett before retreating into the house.

Daemon and Odessa finally emerge from Beatrix's lecture, and for the rest of the afternoon, the six of us explore the estate and the little town of Storia. The town is magical—even more of a fairy-tale wonderland than the city outside the Winter Palace, and I spend hours pursuing the little shops. The new bookstore that Beatrix mentions is especially exciting: dusty and haphazard in the way that the best kind of bookstores should be.

"I have a book here written in English," the shopkeeper tells me excitedly. "Look!"

I take the book, flipping through the thin pages in confusion. The book itself is beautiful—a gilded copy of an old classic, but I frown. I lean over to Fox, who is standing the closest. "I thought all these books were in English."

Fox looks down at me and raises an eyebrow. "No. We don't speak that."

I laugh. "Um...yes you do. We're speaking English now."

Only as the words leave my mouth do I realize how bizarre that is. Not only do they speak English, but there's hardly been one moment when I didn't understand what any of them was saying as if we grew up using exactly the same vocabulary.

Fox shakes his head. "To my ear, we're speaking Thermian. The continent of Ellender is enchanted with universal language."

*Oh. Huh.*

I'm bursting with questions, but I'll probably have to ask Odessa about it if I want more details, since Fox might have an aneurism if he has to string three sentences together at once.

"What did you find?" Daemon asks, coming up behind me.

I jump, startled as much by his voice as the feel of his breath on the back of my neck. I wonder what language he's really speaking. How do I sound to him? Am I as awkward as I always feel like I am, or is it smoothed out by the magical language filter?

I shiver, and hold up the book to show him. "It's a first edition. Do you know how much this would go for back home?"

He stares at the book for a second, then looks up at the shopkeeper. "Can you wrap that up for her?"

"Oh...no, I didn't mean," I start to protest.

"Do you want it?"

"Well, yeah, but you don't have to get it for me." I feel a flush rising to my cheeks. I have no idea how the money works here, but I have to imagine this book is way more expensive than my yarn and that makes me feel a little weird.

Daemon reaches over my shoulder and takes the book out of my hand, passing it to the shopkeeper. "It's your birthday, right? Think of it as a gift."

I swallow but just nod. "Thank you."

He looks like he wants to say something else but he doesn't. He pays the shopkeeper, who looks pleased enough that I know it must have been a lot and leads me back outside into the village.

It's somewhere around midnight and it's started snowing lightly, so we all duck into a tavern for a drink. By the time we leave, it's time to return to the estate for dinner and everyone is a little tipsy. Jett and Odessa are talking so loudly that their voices echo all down the street, and even Daemon looks a little less serious than usual—more like the guy I first met in Ironhill.

He seems to feel me looking and glances over at me, meeting my gaze head-on. My stomach does an excited flip and I promptly look down, focusing instead on the shopping bag in my hand. Looking at the bag doesn't help one bit with the butterflies dancing in my stomach.

DINNER IS SERVED IN THE GARDEN.

Beatrix claims that the formal dining room is too stuffy and the kitchen table isn't big enough for all of us and we'll be more comfortable outside. I'm certainly not complaining.

There are two long tables set up on the rose-covered patio, large enough to comfortably seat all six of us, plus Beatrix.

We carry plates of roast meat, vegetables and huge bottles of wine out to the table family style.

Daemon takes one end of the table and Beatrix takes the other, leaving us to all fill in the seats on the sides. I sit next to Daemon and across from Kastian. Poor Odessa sits next to Beatrix and I can hear her being scolded all the way down the table.

"Was it your idea to come here?" I ask Daemon.

He shakes his head, swallowing the bite in his mouth and washing it down with wine. "Dessa's."

"That was nice of her." I try to catch her eye but can't.

"We don't really celebrate birthdays after the first few decades," Kastian says. "It's nice to have something to celebrate."

I flush and glance over and tune into Fox and Jett having a loud argument—or rather, Jett is having an argument and Fox is nodding or shaking his head at the appropriate times. Odessa looks like she's escaped her scolding and cuts in now and then, filling in Fox's side of the argument with more colorful insults.

I take a large sip of wine.

This is...nice. It's strange, but nice.

We finish eating and Odessa jumps up from the table, dashing inside to get something. She returns carrying an enormous pie. "I wanted to get you a cake," she says. "But there wasn't time. I hope you like snow-berries."

"I don't know what those are." I laugh. "But I'm sure they're great. Thank you."

She puts the pie down, and I glance around. "Don't you guys sing?"

"Sing?" Daemon asks, sounding revolted.

"Yeah...like happy birthday?" I hum the first few notes of the song. They stare at me blankly, and I sigh. "I guess that's a human thing."

"If you want music, I'm sure we can get some," Odessa says quickly.

"No, that's okay! I didn't mean it like that, everything is great."

But she's already gone, dashing back inside.

I cut the pie into large slices and pass them down the table before cutting one for myself. Dessa was right, it's amazing.

Speaking of which, she returns at that moment carrying a huge instrument, somewhere between a guitar and a banjo. I vaguely recall that one of the musicians at the inn had one.

"What is that?" I ask.

Jett holds his hand out. "I don't know what you would call it, but we play them in Solistine. Give it to me."

He takes the instrument and I'm surprised that he actually does know how to play. I was half expecting him to play *Wonderwall*, but I'm pleasantly surprised when he strums the strings a few times, before starting up a jaunty tune.

Odessa starts to clap along. "Ooh, let's dance."

"No," Daemon says darkly at the same time as I'm nodding in excited agreement.

Maybe it's the wine, but dancing sounds like the most fun I'll ever have. I jump to my feet.

Daemon looks at me with an expression akin to being told he has to have a tooth pulled.

Across the table, Kastian stands and holds out a hand to me. "Shall we?"

I grin and put my fingers in his palm, letting him lead me in a circle around the table and then into some approximation of a swing dance.

"I have no idea how to do this," I say. "I never took dance."

"I wish I could say the same," he replies, smoothly spinning me around. "I've spent more days in dance classes than you've probably been alive."

"Why?"

He shrugs stiffly. "Just something my parents thought was necessary. Good thing too, because otherwise I'd look like that." He jerks his head to the left.

I look to where he's indicating and find that Odessa has somehow convinced Fox to dance with her, but neither of them seem to know how to do it so she's just twirling around him in a circle while he stands there looking bemused.

"They look like they're having fun," I say. "Or, she does, I guess."

He glances over again and watches Odessa spinning for a long second. I'm about to suggest he abandon me as a lost cause and ask her to dance, when Jett finishes his song and begins a slower one.

Kastian blinks a couple of times and seems to try and compensate for his inattention by spinning me into a low dip.

I stumble and flail my arms, losing my balance and feeling the sharp sting of fear in my chest. Before I can even process what is happening, strong arms wrap around me, steadying my fall.

I know Daemon is behind me before I look. He holds on to me for a moment, his steady heartbeat against my back, before gently guiding me back to my feet.

"That's enough," he says roughly.

He's clearly speaking to Kastian, not to me, but I answer anyway. "Excuse you? It's not your job to tell me when to be done."

"I thought you didn't want to dance," Kastian says, sounding almost smug.

Daemon glowers at him before turning his back on his friend and holding out his hand to me.

I look stupidly at his palm, not entirely sure what's going on before I finally snap out of it and place my hand in his.

My stomach swoops like I'm on a roller coaster when he pulls me closer and his other hand lands on my lower back. Unlike Kastian who was all sweeping bows and twirls, Daemon leads me firmly into the steps of something like a waltz. It feels different—not fancy, but somehow secure.

"I thought you didn't know how to dance," I say, desperate to fill the silence.

"I don't like to dance, I didn't say I didn't know how," he grumbles.

"If you don't like it, then why cut in?"

He doesn't answer me.

I tilt my head all the way back to catch his gaze and he looks down at me, our eyes locking. For a second, I forget anyone else is there—I lose track of the sound of Jett's strumming and Odessa's giggles, and just sway, letting him guide me.

My skin begins to heat. I feel tingles in the places where our skin touches, and I can't help but think of how it felt before, when so much more than our palms were touching. How he kissed me, and how he's seemed much more relaxed any time we're alone.

I like this. *I like him.*

Just as that thought crosses my mind, he drops my hand abruptly and steps back.

"What's wrong?"

He stares at me, then without a word, turns on his heel and marches back toward the house.

I blink in surprise, and it seems like the volume has been turned back up in the garden. I can hear the music again and the talk and laughter from around the table. I stared dazedly at Daemon's retreating back.

"Uh, I'll be right back," I stammer, only to look around and realize no one is paying attention to me. They're all drinking, chattering to each other as if Daemon and I aren't even there.

I dash after him.

It takes me a long few seconds to find Daemon.

As usual in Vernallis, it's dark and I'm not familiar enough with the manner or the yard beyond to know exactly where he went. I dash through the garden and back through the doors into the kitchen, turning in every direction. The kitchen is dark and quiet, but somehow the air hums with awareness. I know he just came through here.

"Daemon!" I call.

There's no reply. But again, I can almost feel his presence. I can picture in the back of my mind, like I'm remembering a scene out of a movie. Storming through the garden and through the kitchen, angrily throwing a door open and marching down the hall. Then, stopping short at the sound of my voice...

Acting on instinct—and perhaps insanity—I fling open the door and dart down the unfamiliar hallway. I turn the corner and skid to a halt. "Daemon?"

At the end of the hall, Daemon stands frozen with his back to me. "You shouldn't be here, Alix. Go back outside."

"I'm sorry," I blurt out automatically, even though I don't have any idea what I'm supposed to be sorry for.

He doesn't bother turning to meet my gaze, but his posture stiffens and his hands clench into tight fists at his sides. "Stop apologizing. You didn't fucking do anything."

"Okay...then why did you leave?"

He doesn't answer, but instead makes a low sound in the back of his throat almost like a growl. I suck in a sharp breath as I'm suddenly viscerally reminded of what he said last night: *We're not human, no matter how much we might appear to be.*

I should probably take his warning and go back outside with the others, but I can't.

I move closer, and with each step, my heart beats faster and my palms turn sweaty. I'm full of nerves and trembling with the sort of terrified excitement that sinks in my belly at the top of a roller coaster.

I stretch my fingers out and brush the back of his arm, so lightly it's barely a touch at all. Still, he whirls on me like I slapped him. His eyes are blazing green fire and almost seem to glow in the low lighting. "Don't."

"Don't what?" I ask, even though I'm fairly sure I already know the answer.

"I can't—I'm not allowed to touch you."

"You're not touching me..." I steel myself—pushing back the embarrassment of being vulnerable long enough to voice what I want. "...unless you mean that you want to."

Daemon doesn't move. He barely breathes. Then, I see the exact moment his resolve breaks.

His hand whips out and his fingers wrap around the back of my neck, hauling me toward him at the same time as he steps forward, crowding me against the wall. My back hits hard stone, but I hardly notice as his free palm slams flat into the wall beside my ear. Then, before I can even take a breath, his mouth crashes down on mine.

Holy fuck.

A whimper escapes me as my eyes flutter closed and I instinctively open my mouth against the onslaught of his lips. His tongue sweeps over my lips and into my mouth and I respond in kind—exploring, tasting. His hand travels up my neck and into my hair where he wraps my entire long ponytail around his fist.

We've kissed before, but not like this. Not this desperate, needy, starving. My heart is pounding in my ears and then my pulse drops lower, throbbing between my legs.

I press closer, standing up on my tiptoes to try and bring our faces even closer together. I drag my body against his, my hardened nipples tingling as they scrape against his chest. He groans into my mouth, pressing his cock more firmly against me.

I moan and dig my fingernails into his shoulders, trying to pull him closer.

I didn't know kissing could feel like this—not like an obligation as a prelude to sex, but so intense I think it might leave me permanently burned from the inside out.

There's something here between us—I know there is. Something that goes beyond just physical attraction. It's small and unsteady, flickering in and out like the flame of a new candle, but it's there. It's not just me.

The sound of cracking air, like a flag in the wind has me opening my eyes again, even as I tilt my head to deepen the kiss.

"Wings..." I murmur against his lips, apparently unable to form an entire sentence.

He blinks and pulls back from me by a few inches looking dazed. His mouth starts to form a word, but he stops, seemingly also realizing in that moment that his enormous red and black wings have reappeared, taking up the majority of the hallway and cocooning us against the wall.

I stare open-mouthed at the gleaming iridescent feathers, my already thundering heartbeat strumming even faster.

I've seen the wings before, but never so close and never when I wasn't sure I was about to die. They're remarkable—nothing like the faerie wings in stories, but exactly as I would have pictured a fallen angel.

I wonder if this is where ancient painters and scholars got the idea. Did they see the Fae, with their too beautiful faces and magnificent bird's wings, and assume they were divine?

Without thinking, I reach out a hand to touch the nearest feathers, stroking them like I might run my fingers through someone's hair. "Incredible."

He shivers. "Sorry, Peaches. I can't ever seem to hold on to control around you."

"No..." I mutter softly, my face flaming. "Don't be sorry. I like it."

*I like you.*

"Alix!" Odessa's slightly shrill voice rings through the quiet house. "Al—I mean, Isabelle! Are you in here?" There's a loud creaking as a door opens and we both turn to see Odessa standing in the doorway at the other end of the hall. Her eyes widen and she jumps back in surprise. "Oh! Shit, sorry."

I shimmy under Daemon's arm and move away from the wall, my pulse still pounding. "Hey. What's up?"

Her eyes dart back and forth between us and I can't read her expression at all. Finally, she says, "We need to leave if we're going to make it back to the palace before it's light out."

"Sure," Daemon says flatly, his tone almost bored. "Tell the guys to get the horses ready, we'll be right there."

She bites her lip, looking like she wants to say something, but then just nods. "Okay."

She lets the door close behind her with a heavy click. I let out a breath and glance back at Daemon.

The wings are gone.

# CHAPTER EIGHTEEN

DAEMON

F*uck.*

This is bad. So incredibly bad I'm not sure there's any coming back from it.

Alix isn't for me. I can't have her. I shouldn't even be spending so much time around her, let alone *touching* her.

More than likely, she's going to return to her world in a matter of weeks and forget all about me and this nightmare charade I've forced her into. The only alternative is that she'll somehow be the one to break the curse and marry Thorne, and then probably hate me for the rest of eternity for tricking her into it.

There is no world in which she's mine.

Yet, I can still feel her everywhere. My skin hums where hers touched mine, I can still taste her on my tongue, and I can remember all too clearly how it felt to be inside her, owning her entirely, as if she really was mine.

I practically shove Alix back outside with the others, but I hang back for a moment. I'm so painfully hard I need a second to recover before I have to ride a horse for an hour, with Alix's ass bouncing against me the entire fucking time.

I lean my forehead against the cold stone and take a deep breath, closing my eyes and willing the memory of her hot little body against mine to disappear. It doesn't work at all.

I need to fuck someone—that's all there is to it. Before I was banished, there was hardly an evening where I slept alone, but after so many years in Dyaspora, I'd gotten almost used to being alone. But Alix had to go and remind me what I was missing.

I bang my fist on the wall in frustration before stalking down the hall in the opposite direction of the kitchen. Maybe when I get back, I'll take one of the court women up on their not-so-subtle offers. I can't have Alix, but there are dozens of women at court who would be more than willing.

I try to picture it—riding back to the palace, walking straight to the noble apartments to find Claudette or one of the other ladies. My stomach roils. No, that won't fucking work. I know exactly who and what I want and she has pale skin and long dark curls, expressive eyes and an occasionally sharp tongue that I want to feel all over my body.

Fuck—my nausea is completely banished by the picture of Alix kneeling before me, dragging her tongue down my stomach and over my cock.

I throw open the first door on my right, a storage pantry, and duck inside, closing the door behind me. It's dark, the air thick with the scent of dust and dried herbs, but I hardly notice as I lean against the shelf, unbuckle my belt, and pull out my cock.

I wrap my fist around it, and it swells, growing even harder in my palm. I stroke once down the length, hating myself even as it feels far too good to stop.

Fuck, I can still feel Alix's hands on me, and for a moment, I imagine it without berating myself for thinking of her like this.

*I see her in her pink peaches T-shirt and nothing else, kneeling before me on the stone floor of this closet. Her small hand wraps around the base of my cock and she smiles up at me. "This is crazy."*

*"I like crazy," I tell her.*

*"Mmm, I can tell." She leans forward, brushing the head of my cock over her closed lips.*

*"Open," I demand.*

*She smiles wider before he lips part and she wraps her mouth around me, sucking my entire length into the back of her throat.*

The tattoos on my back ache, bringing me back to the present. I can't let the wings come out here. For one thing, they won't fit in this tiny cupboard, but more importantly, I need to get a handle on my control again.

The wings are triggered by adrenaline. They're a defensive mutation, created by thousands of years of faerie wars.

Lately, my heart has been pounding so fast I'm surprised they're not a permanent symbol of my crumbling self-control.

In the back of my mind, I conjure up Alix's expression of awe when she saw the wings. I feel her fingers tracing down the feathers, sending shivers up my spine.

My fantasy changes, and now I imagine that no one had interrupted us in the hall. That I'd turned Alix around, pressing her palms flat against the wall.

*She arches her back and looks over her shoulder at me. "What are you waiting for?"*

*I lift her skirt up and cup her between the legs. She's not wearing anything under her dress, and I find her pussy, wet and ready for me. I drag my fingers through her and she whimpers, pushing her ass more firmly against me.*

*I stroke my hands over her bare thighs, her ass, tracing out everything I intend to do to her until she's whimpering with anticipation.*

*"Please," she whines.*

*"Do you want this?" I ask her, enjoying the idea of hearing her beg for my cock. "Tell me how much you want it, Peaches."*

*"Please," she breathes again. "Fuck me."*

*"But I shouldn't," I remind her. "I can't."*

*"You can. I need you to."*

*My cock is pulsing now, just on the edge of release. I can feel a warmth building at the base of my spine and black spots appear at the edges of my vision.*

*"Tell me who you belong to," I tell her.*

*"You," she replies obediently, almost crying with need.*

*"That's right," I tell her as I line myself up with her hot, tight entrance.*

*"You're mine."*

Pleasure surges through me as I come hard, spilling over my hand. My own voice echoes in the silence of the storeroom.

*You're mine. You're mine. You're mine.*

By the time I emerge, the horses are already saddled. Nearly everyone is mounted, ready to leave.

Even Alix. She's already in my saddle.

For a second, I wonder who the fuck *helped* her up. A possessive growl bubbles in my throat, but I shove it down.

I shake my head to clear it. I'm being fucking insane—irrational—and it has to end now.

My friends' eyes dart over to me, but no one asks where I've been. I hope they assume I've just been reacquainting myself with my old home.

I stride around the back of the house to say goodbye to my mother, then return to the group. Odessa marches up beside me.

"What the fuck was that?" she mutters under her breath.

For one horrifying second, I think she knows where I've just been. Then I realize she means the kiss she interrupted in the hallway. "Nothing," I lie. "Don't worry about it."

"I am worried," she mutters.

"Don't be. Alix is fine."

She cocks her head at me. "I wasn't talking about Alix. I know she'll be fine. I'm worried about you."

I scoff, feigning indifference. "How much wine did you drink?"

She rolls her eyes. "I'm serious, Daemon. This is a bad idea."

I press my lips in a tight line. She doesn't need to tell me that. Getting even more involved with Alix than I already am is possibly the worst idea I've ever had for so many goddamn reasons. "I know it's a bad fucking idea," I growl. "But out of curiosity, why do you think so?"

Odessa looks at me with something too close to pity. "Because she doesn't belong here."

"You were the one who thought she was brought here by *fate*."

"Yeah, but not for you," she hisses. "Alix will never be meant for you, but you'll fall in love with her anyway."

"You don't know th—"

"I do!" She meets my eyes, unflinching. "I know you. You'll risk everything to keep her, and I don't know if she'll love you enough to stay."

Odessa's warning plays over and over in the back of my head all the way back to the palace. In a way, that's good, because it keeps me from focusing on Alix sitting in front of me. The ride to my estate felt like fucking torture, but the ride back is painful in an entirely different way.

I'm silent as I walk Alix back to her room. She looks at me sideways, and it's not difficult to know what she's thinking. I'm ignoring her, *again*. Fuck, I must be giving her whiplash, blowing so hot and cold. If only she knew the turmoil roiling in the back of my head.

I can't touch her, but I want to.

I need to stay in control of myself, but I can't.

I'm afraid I'm becoming obsessed with her, but Odessa is right. Alix doesn't belong here and there's no scenario in which I get to spend more than a few more days with her.

I practically shove Alix into her room and slam the door. Guilt and frustration wash over me as I unbuckle my sword belt and place the blade on the floor, before sinking down beside it facing her door.

The last thing I want to do is sleep, but I know I can't stay awake much longer or God fucking knows what my instincts will make me do to try and keep her here.

THE FOLLOWING EVENING, I WAKE UP ON THE FLOOR outside Alix's room determined to do better.

Yesterday was nothing. A small lapse in control, but it's behind me now. There's nothing to keep me from treating Alix exactly how I was before—like she barely exists.

*I can do this.*

Her door opens sharply, and I jump, startled.

Alix steps out of her room wearing a simple blue and yellow dress. The dress itself isn't anything special, but the way it hugs her body, dipping low at the neck, I—

*I can't fucking do this.*

Unaware of the mental battle I'm fighting, Alix looks down at me on the floor and the corner of her mouth tips up. "Caught you."

I grab my sword and scramble to my feet, scowling. "Caught me doing what?"

"I know you said you'd been sleeping out here but I had to see it for myself."

My scowl deepens. "I hope you're amused. Now what are you doing out of your room?"

"I wanted to eat early today," she says simply, starting off down the hallway in the direction of the parlor where she eats every meal that isn't with Thorne. I automatically follow.

"You could come in my room, you know," Alix says.

I blink at her, my mind taking far too long to ascribe meaning to her words. "No. Nothing could be more dangerous for you."

She wrinkles her brow and I know she's remembering the day I proved just how instinctual it was for me to seek her out. Does she realize how dangerous that could have been if it had been allowed to continue?

"If it's so dangerous for me to be around anyone cursed, why is the king making you sleep outside my room?"

"Ask him," I grumble. "Maybe he'll take you more seriously, because he doesn't fucking listen to me when I bring it up."

"Hmmm. Maybe I will."

My stomach drops unpleasantly. If she does ask Thorne, will he assign someone else to guard her? Maybe he'll do it himself? How the fuck am I going to survive knowing she's spending all day with anyone else?

"Can we go to the library after breakfast?" Alix asks.

I blink. That's all she has to say? Doesn't she realize I'm fucking dying, and she's thinking about the library? "If that's what you want."

"It is."

My hands curl into fists at my sides. "Sure. Gods fucking knows I can't deny you anything."

She shoots me a playful grin. "Oh, that's right. The king told you to bring me so you can't say no. Perfect!"

I dig my nails into my palms so hard I feel them penetrate the skin. I wasn't talking about the king's orders; I just can't say no to her anymore, and nothing scares me more than the inevitable moment she realizes that and asks me to let her go.

## ALIX

The moment we step into the library, a sense of exhilaration washes over me.

Quickly followed by rage.

I whirl on Daemon, narrowing my eyes. "What the hell is this?"

He frowns. "The library?"

"Exactly," I bite out. "It's the biggest, most beautiful library I've ever seen. I could have kept myself entertained here for months, and instead, you've been letting me stare at the walls!"

Daemon looks down, avoiding my gaze. I can't tell if he's feeling guilty, but I fucking hope he does.

I stride toward the nearest row of shelves. It really is the most magical library I've ever seen, with row upon rows of books, some towering all the way to the arched ceiling. There are twinkling chandeliers hanging from the ceiling and winding staircases and ladders to reach the top most shelves. Even the dark windows look more ethereal rather than oppressive when surrounded by all this beauty.

I lose myself in the stacks, wandering deeper into the labyrinth of shelves. The collection here is vast—history books on subjects I can't even begin to understand, strange texts filled with symbols I don't recognize, and...fiction. Not just Fae fiction, either. My jaw drops when I recognize human titles. *A Midsummer Night's Dream?* Okay, that makes sense. But... *dark romance?* How the hell did *that* get here? Shrugging, I grab something that promises to be smutty and return to the front of the library.

Daemon is stretched out on a green velvet couch under a massive stained glass window. It's the kind of spot that would be incredibly cozy if the midafternoon sun was streaming through the windows, but as usual, the sky outside is pitch black. Still, the twinkling lanterns and candles fixed to the wall make the couch look inviting.

Daemon clearly found a book as well, but looks as if it didn't take him nearly as long to choose one, and he's already settled into reading. He looks up at the sound of my footsteps and his eyes dart to the book in my hand. "What the hell is that?"

I hold it up. "*Thieves' Honor.* It's a mafia romance."

He raises a skeptical eyebrow. "I'm not sure what's worse—that the library has that book or that you want to read it."

"Hey!" I say indignantly as I flop onto the other side of the couch. "Reading is reading. I love books like this."

He shrugs. "Whatever, Peaches."

"You know, men should be more open to smut. I've learned so much from books like this."

I feel his eyes on me, and heat creeps up my neck.

"You've learned a lot, huh?"

"Um...yeah." I lick my lips. Maybe that wasn't a thought I should have said out loud.

He smirks. "By all means, share with the class."

I roll my eyes and sit down to read my book. But of course now I can't focus. Of course. All I can think about is the other night. Neither of us have brought it up. Should I? Am I brave enough to hear what he's thinking? Or worse, maybe he's not thinking about it at all?

The silence between us thrums with something unspoken and my skin buzzes like a live-wire as we sit side-by-side reading in silence.

Daemon shifts, stretching his legs out and throwing one arm over the back of the couch. His arms are so long, his fingers nearly brush the ends of my ponytail.

I nudge his knee with my foot. "You're taking up way more than your share of this couch."

"You're smaller. You don't need as much space."

"That's not fair," I grumble.

He grips the end of my hair and tugs it lightly, half teasing, half punishing. "What's not fair is I was here first. You could have sat anywhere else. If you want more space, move."

I glare at him, indignant. "Did you just pull my hair? What are we, five?"

He tugs on my hair again while looking pointedly at the book in his lap. The corner of his mouth ticks up like he's trying not to smile. I scoff and pull my feet up so we're not touching anywhere. Then I try to return to my book.

Except I can't focus. Ugh.

I read the same sentence five times, all while I'm hyperaware that he has not removed his hand from my hair. Seemingly without conscious thought, he begins wrapping the end of my ponytail around his fist.

*Oh...my God!*

I jump up, and Daemon's hand slips from my hair along with the blue ribbon that was holding my ponytail in place.

"Um, I think this is book two," I blurt out. "I'm going to go look for the first one."

He glances at the hair ribbon in his hand, then back down at his book. "Don't disappear."

"It's one goddamn room," I mutter under my breath. "What the hell could happen?"

I speed walk away from the couch and back into the stacks, making my way to the other side of the enormous room as if I'm being chased.

I just need a second to think.

I'm probably being stupid.

Actually, no, I'm definitely being stupid.

It's just that attraction and explosive chemistry is one thing, but casual displays of affection are my kryptonite. If I didn't kind of like him before, I definitely would now, and somehow that realization is so much more alarming now than it was the other night under the influence of too much wine and birthday pie.

I drop to the floor and start inspecting one of the lower shelves at random, even as my mind is still racing.

So I care a little about Daemon.

*Just a little.*

But not in a true love, real feelings kind of way. More like a good sex, mind-blowing orgasms, magical fairytale soldier, kind of way.

I'm just bored and lonely. He's hot and he's always around saying weird shit about how he's going to die to protect me. Plus, the only other man I have to think about is Ryan, which is a can of worms I don't care to open.

*This is not a big deal.*

I've developed a situational crush, and it will go away the second I don't have to see him all the time. I need a break from him to get over it. Like a sexual juice cleanse.

"I thought I'd find you here."

I jump and drop the book in my hand, standing up and whirling around to see a short Fae soldier behind me. I recognize him immediately, but it takes me a moment to remember his name. "Hello...Foulo. You scared me."

Foulo gives me an apologetic smile that looks almost genuine. "Apologies. I'm simply glad to find you following the king's advice."

I furrow my brow. "His advice?"

"You're reading again."

"Oh...right."

Foulo is a good example of how being good-looking doesn't necessarily make you appealing. Like all the Fae, his face is unlined and more symmetrical than any human could ever hope to be. He's shorter than the other men I've seen in Vernallis, but he's still got to be nearly six feet tall and extremely muscular, like he spends every day lifting weights. If I saw him on the street, I would definitely look twice. Here, though, he's unremarkable and most importantly, his vibe is all wrong. He seems overeager to please and bitter at being upstaged. He also clearly has some rivalry with Daemon, and it's not hard for me to choose a side.

"I was just looking for a book and I think I'm in the wrong stack," I say quickly. "Excuse me."

"Wait!" Foulo throws out an arm to stop me, and I reel back, affronted.

I don't like feeling trapped. I especially don't like feeling trapped by sad, angry little men with grabby fingers. I glance over my shoulder, searching for Daemon.

"I was just thinking the other day about the last time you were here," Foulo says, still keeping his arm outstretched and preventing me from passing.

I back up a few steps. "Oh yeah..."

"I was down in the stables and I saw you leave the palace with that band of criminals Ashwater brought from Dyaspora."

I raise an eyebrow. "Did you follow us there?"

"No!" he says quickly. "I happened to be checking on the horses and I saw you refuse to ride on your own."

I narrow my eyes. *Yeah right.* "So what?"

"So, remind me what the name of the horse you used to ride was?" he asks smugly. "It's been so many years I can't recall, but I remember you were so fond of the beast. Peter, was it? Phillip?"

My heartbeat picks up, pounding against my chest. Oh my God—he knows I'm not Nana. Or at least, he suspects I'm not, and he's clearly trying to catch me in a lie before going straight to the king. What will Thorne do to me if he believes Foulo? What will he do to Daemon and the others?

I crane my neck, searching for Daemon again and raise my voice as I answer. Surely he'll hear me talking to someone and come to investigate. Right?

"That was sixty years ago," I say shortly. "If you can't recall the horse's name, I don't know why you'd think I can."

"Shame," he says. "What about where you used to go riding together before you developed this mysterious aversion to horses."

I keep backing up, but my heart jumps into my throat when my back hits solid wall. He's literally backed me into a corner, and there's nowhere to escape.

I jut my chin out, hoping I look braver than I feel. "Unfortunately, I don't have time to reminisce at the moment. I need to get ready for my dinner with the king and you're in my way."

I shove at his arm, but he doesn't budge. Gritting my teeth, I stare him straight in the eye. "Move."

His lip curls. "I don't think so. I don't know who you are or what scheme you and Ashwater cooked up, but you're not Lady Isabelle."

"Prove it," I snap.

He leers at me, and I cringe as he reaches out and plucks a lock of my hair between two fingers. "Oh, I will. But if you want, I'll keep the information to myself. All you have to do is make it worth my while."

I knock his hand back. "You're disgusting. Don't touch me."

His face contorts in anger. "You'll regret that when I tell the king who you really are, bitch. How are you making yourself look so much like the Lady Isabelle? Is it this?"

His hand shoots out, and for a terrifying second, I think he's going to wrap his fingers around my throat. But instead, his grip snags on the chain around my neck. He yanks—hard—clearly expecting the necklace to snap. It doesn't.

Panicked, I let out a strangled scream.

# CHAPTER
# NINETEEN

ALIX

The next ten seconds in the library unfold in slow motion, so much so that later, when I think back, I won't be able to remember how it actually happened.

One second, Foulo has me pinned against the wall, strangling me by the chain of my necklace. I can't get enough air to even scream, and black dots start creeping into my vision. I know I'm fucked. This is my third near-death experience since I arrived, and it seems like my luck has run out.

Then, a split second later, I hear the swoosh of a blade through the air. The pressure against my throat disappears, and I cough, sucking in a gasping breath at the same moment as something warm and gelatinous splatters my face. Something lands on the floor at my feet with a sickening wet thump, and I raise a confused hand to my cheek.

Then, Foulo lets out a bloodcurdling scream unlike anything I've ever heard before and stumbles back against the ground.

"I told you the next time you touched her, I'd make sure it was the fucking last!" Daemon roars, his face contorted with rage.

I don't even know when he got here, and I don't have the space in my head to think about it as I look down in horror at the severed arm lying on the floor at my feet, and the writhing, screaming man lying in a pool of his own blood, clutching the stump that has been severed just below the elbow.

Daemon leaps over Foulo and rushes toward me. His hands find my cheeks, smearing the spattered blood. "Are you okay? Did he hurt you? Alix!"

I open my mouth but nothing comes out. There is blood all over my face and a fucking arm on the floor.

There is an *arm. On. The. Floor.*

I open my mouth again and this time my scream joins Foulo's. I stumble over the severed arm and sprint as fast as I can down the rows of shelves.

"Alix!" Daemon screams after me, evidently uncaring that Foulo will hear him call me by another name.

Still, I don't stop.

I rush out of the library and make a quick right, rushing down the hall toward what I hope is the entrance hall. I haven't spent nearly enough time exploring this castle, and what little I have seen, I've always been with a chaperone. It's like being familiar with a route via GPS but getting lost when your phone dies. Without a guide, all these damn hallways look the same.

Finally, I find a set of stairs. I look behind me, expecting Daemon to be on my heels. He isn't, but I still dash down the steps two at a time.

My breath heaves as I run.

*Holy shit.*

That wasn't a normal reaction. I heard him threaten Foulo before, but I assumed he was being hyperbolic. Now my heart is pounding with fear, my skin is coated with blood, and all I keep wondering is if this is normal behavior for the Fae, or if Daemon is actually fucking insane.

Unlike him, I don't like crazy.

I reach the bottom of the stairs and again I have no idea where I am —still, I don't stop. I sprint down another unfamiliar hallway and thankfully find a door outside. I throw it open and find myself on the backside of the castle.

I stare out at a snow-covered lawn. In the distance is a line of trees and before thinking it through, I dash toward it.

I'm not dressed for the outdoors and cold nips at my skin as I sprint through the snow. My gown trails behind me and my feet push easily through the hard crust of the snow, until suddenly my foot hits against something hard and solid. I slip and slide forward a few feet, my arms spinning to regain my balance.

I somehow stay on my feet. I look down, all too aware that I'm standing on solid ice.

I stop, both to catch my breath and because I'm not sure where to go next.

Now, the completely flat lawn just behind the palace makes more sense. It's not a lawn—it's a lake, currently frozen underneath a layer of ice and frost.

I know I need to get off here. I don't know how frozen the water is, but I can't imagine it's solid since it takes less than an hour by horse to reach a far warmer climate.

Worse, the blood splatter is mingling with my sweat and dripping down my face. It lands in the bright white snow like dozens of vicious rubies.

I heave in and out, trying to calm my breath. But then, before I've decided what to do, the door to the castle bursts open behind me.

I don't need to look to know who's behind me.

And I don't look—I swallow my heaving breath and start running again as far away from the castle and the Fae as I can manage.

"Alix, stop!" Daemon commands.

I don't stop.

The sky is dark as always, but the moon casts a bright indigo glow over the ice. I dart across the frozen pond, my gown fanning out behind me, praying with every step the ice doesn't crack.

Quick footsteps pound through the snow behind me.

I look back. I should have known better than to think I could outrun one of the Fae. He runs so fast it's like he's flying.

Then, just as suddenly, he is. His wings unfurl and he smoothly goes from sprinting to gliding in one swift movement. His hand reaches out to grab for me.

My feet slip out from under me, and in slow motion, I fall back, my head cracking against the ice. An explosion of pain radiates through my skull, and an involuntary cry escapes my lips, echoing in the cold, empty air.

Daemon looks furious as he lands over me, his blood-covered hands crashing into the ice on either side of me and making crimson stamps against the white. His eyes dart to mine like he's searching for something in my eyes. "Are you hurt? Did he fucking touch you?"

My lip trembles and I shake my head. "No." The pain in my skull is throbbing, but that's the last thing I want to tell him.

"Then why are you running? I handled it, he's—" He breaks off, clearly seeing the answer to his question in my eyes. His gaze turns dark, his pupils dilating to the point that the green is nearly eclipsed by black. "Tell me, Peaches. Are you afraid of me?"

*Yes.*

*No...*

*I'm not sure.*

I shake my head again, but he must read the conflict in my eyes because his angry expression doesn't change. He leans even closer so we're sharing the same air. "I told you, I will always protect you. I warned him that the next time he touched you would be the last. You should have always known this is who I am."

"Which is what—a psychopath?" I blurt out, finding my voice again.

Daemon's eyes snap to my mouth for half a second, before he looks me straight in the eye. "Maybe. But only when it comes to you."

A spark of excitement shoots through me, and I let out a gasp.

*There is something seriously fucking wrong with me.*

Clearly, he's unhinged. A moment ago, I was running for my life, but now all I can think about is how close we are. The entire length of his body presses into mine, and the sensation is intense—freezing cold on one side and pulsing heat on the other.

My entire body begins to tremble, and my pulse pounds in my throat and...lower. Without really meaning to, I shift my hips against him. I feel him growing hard against me and heat floods my core in response.

"Are you afraid of me?" he repeats.

"Yes."

I'm fucking terrified of him, but not because I think he'll hurt me. I'm scared because I'm starting to believe he won't.

To my surprise, he grins. "Good. If you knew half the things I've thought about doing to any male who looks at you, you should be afraid. As long as I'm breathing, no one will fucking touch you, because I'll kill them and fuck you in their blood."

*Jesus Christ.*

A tiny whimper escapes my lips and I'm not sure if it's fear or desire...or both. There's no room for questions or doubt in my mind anymore after a statement like that. He wants me, but...

"What about the king?" I ask, barely more than a whisper.

"What about him?" he growls, pressing himself even more firmly against me.

"You brought me here for him. What do you think is going to happen if we stay engaged?"

His expression twists in rage once more, and his wings unfurl behind him. His hand shifts to hold on to my hair as he brings our faces even closer together. "You're fucking mine, Alix, and no one but me will ever touch you again."

At that exact moment, a deafening crack sounds through the air, making sleeping birds take flight in the nearby trees. The ice breaks beneath me, and I scream as the ground literally falls out from under me and I drop into dark icy water.

## DAEMON

IN A SPLIT SECOND, THE HAZE OF LUST and rage that had been warring inside my head clears. Ever since I heard Alix scream in the library, I haven't been able to think straight, but all of that disappears the moment I see her fall below the surface of the water.

My hand is still in her hair, and it begins to slip through my fingers so fast I just barely have a moment to hold on.

I plunge my arms into the frigid water, grabbing on to whatever I can reach. Fuck, it's colder than Dyaspora, and the bitter frost sinks into my skin, seeming to freeze my bones. If it's doing that to me, I can't imagine what it's done to Alix.

My fingers close around the neck of her gown and I haul her toward me. She's not moving or thrashing, and fear shoots through me.

"Alix!" I drag her out of the water with a huge splash and lay her on the ice.

She coughs and blinks at me and I've never been so relieved in my life.

But only a moment later, the relief disappears.

Her lips are blue, her skin too pale, and within seconds, she's shaking violently.

My heart pounding against my ribs, I gather her up in my arms and launch into the sky.

Alix's room has a balcony overlooking the city, and it's far faster to fly there than to run back through the castle.

I land and cross the balcony in two strides. I can't move my fingers to unlock the double doors with magic, so I just shoulder them open, uncaring about the splintering glass and wood.

We drip water onto the floor as I stride across the room to the bathing chamber.

"I'm going to put you down," I tell her. "I have to start the bath."

For a moment, she doesn't say anything, but then as I lower her to the ground and turn away, she extends a hand to stop me. "Wait. No." Her teeth chatter with every word. "Just help me get this dress off."

I glance at the laces of her dress for less than a second before deciding it's not worth the effort. Grabbing the fabric with both hands, I tear it directly down the center.

The heavy gown slides off her shoulders, and Alix shrugs it off, letting the fabric pool on the floor.

Underneath, she's wearing a thin slip over a corset, stockings and lacy pink bloomers. Immediately she begins shucking those off as well, her hands shaking as she struggles to unlace her shoes and peel off her stockings.

Unsure how to help, I watch her, wide-eyed. All her clothes are now piled on the floor and she's walking toward her room, entirely naked. I dash after her. "Where are you going? You could die if you don't get warm."

"I know," she snaps.

She climbs into bed and pulls the blankets up over her head. The lump of blankets that is Alix shakes violently, her words coming out in chattering gasps. "If I get warm too quickly, I could have a heart attack. This is the best thing to do for hypothermia."

"And you just know that off the top of your head?" I growl.

"Y-yes," she chatters. "It's just one of those things you learn as a kid. If you fall through ice, take all your clothes off and get warm slowly."

I want to know what kind of childhood she had where that would be common knowledge. I feel completely helpless and it isn't a feeling I'm familiar with.

"What do you need me to do?" I ask, almost desperately.

There's a long pause, where she's evidently thinking—or steeling herself for something. "Take your shirt off and get in here with me," she says finally. "I need the body heat."

I don't even stop to question it. I peel off my shirt and kick my boots off before beginning to undo my belt. "Trousers too?" I ask the lump of shivering blankets.

Alix doesn't answer, which I take to mean that she's leaving the choice up to me. I take the belt off but leave the trousers on—hopefully they'll serve as a reminder to myself that this isn't an invitation to fuck her senseless.

I reach for the corner of her blanket. Alix lets go of the fabric, allowing me to draw it back and climb in beside her.

"Just put the blanket back over us and lie there," she says.

I nod, but I already know it will be impossible to just lie here in silence. Instead, I gather her in my arms and place her shaking body over my chest. Alix barely protests as I replace the blanket.

It's impossible not to be aware that she's lying on top of me completely naked, the hard press of her nipples against my chest and her breath fluttering against my neck. If she weren't shaking with cold, it would be impossible to keep my hands off her like this, but instead I just wrap both arms around her back and hold her tightly to me.

"Don't let me fall asleep," she mutters against my throat.

A shiver travels up my spine, but I force myself to ignore it. "How?"

I can already feel her body shivering less violently and her breathing evening out. She yawns. "I don't know. Talk about something."

I can't think of anything to talk about except for how relieved I am that she's alright—how I'm worried I might be becoming obsessed with her. I clear my throat. "Maybe you should do the talking if you're the one who needs to stay awake."

She doesn't answer, and after a moment, I shake her violently. "Alix!" I say loudly in her ear. "Come on, talk to me. Tell me how you know what to do if you fall through ice."

She yawns again, but I see her eyelids flutter. "Where I grew up, it wasn't cold all year but the winters could be really bad. I liked ice skating."

I nod. I remember seeing children ice skating from my years living in the human realm. "Did you fall in?"

She shakes her head. "No, but my dad used to take me down to a pond near our house and he was really paranoid that the ice might break. Before I could go skating, he'd always jump around to check for thin spots, then he'd remind me what to do if I ever fell in." She laughs softly. "I guess he was right to worry about it."

I let out a long breath. I'm grateful to this man I don't even know and never will for teaching Alix to take care of herself. Then, my stomach lurches and I abruptly remember her words back at the inn when she woke up screaming from a nightmare. *I watched my dad die. I dream about it sometimes—a lot of times, actually.*

*Fuck.*

"How did your father die?" I ask, unable to hold in my curiosity.

For a long moment, she says nothing, then finally, "Horseback riding accident."

I blanche. "How the hell did that happen?"

She sighs, and I can feel her tense. Clearly, she doesn't like talking about this. "Whenever I say I saw my dad die, people always assume it was suicide or a car accident or something, and then I say how it happened and I end up having to explain that horses actually kill way more people than you'd think." She stops to draw in a shaking breath, her teeth chattering. "There's thousands of deaths every year. On average, you'd be far better off swimming with sharks or skydiving than getting too close to a horse."

She doesn't have to explain this to me. I've been riding since before I could walk, and if I was as fragile as a human, I probably wouldn't be lying here now. Still, I feel her getting agitated and without really meaning to, I lift a hand and run it through her wet hair, dragging my nails over her scalp. She freezes and goes quiet, like she's holding her breath, then finally exhales, relaxing. With another rattling breath she continues, speaking against my chest.

"For my sixth birthday, I wanted pony rides, but my mother is a chronic over-achiever, so instead, my parents took me on one of those trail rides for tourists where they strap a bunch of people who have never even seen a farm onto the backs of two-thousand-pound animals and send them off into the woods barely supervised.

"Long story short, I was six and I didn't know you can't walk close behind the horses or you could get kicked. I was standing close enough to get my skull bashed in when someone pointed it out to my dad. He tried to grab me and ended up getting kicked in the chest. He probably would have been fine but it triggered a heart attack from some dormant valve defect he didn't know he had and he died in like ten seconds flat. It's the only time I've ever seen my mother really upset about something that wasn't herself."

She falls silent and I'm frozen, my hand caught in her hair.

"I don't know what to say," I admit finally.

"That's okay. No one really knows what to say to something like that, which is why I hate explaining it."

"I'm sorry."

"It's fine," she tries to brush it off.

My hand tightens in her hair and I force her to look up at me. "No, really. I'm really fucking sorry." I shake my head. "And I'm especially sorry I made you get on a horse on your birthday. Fucking hell..."

She laughs, startling me. "Honestly, that was my fault. I didn't want to disappoint anyone or explain—"

"You wouldn't have."

"I know," she says with a half-smile. "I'm working on not always assuming I'm the disappointment. Apparently, it's a lifelong process or at least a thirty-one-year process because I'm not quite there yet."

My head spins. How does she think she's disappointing anyone? Especially now when she's here risking her life to help a bunch of strangers, but even before that. I don't understand how someone like Alix could ever feel that way.

"Do you still go skating?" I ask, just to break the silence.

She shakes her head again, her face brushing back and forth over my collarbone. "No. It's just one of those things you do as a kid that you don't have time for anymore when you grow up. I always thought if I had my own kids I'd do that sort of thing again, but that never happened so..."

"You don't want kids?" I ask, just trying to keep her talking.

She laughs bitterly. "Sure, I do. Or, I did, but I'm thirty and I'm getting divorced."

"So?"

She shifts around, repositioning her body over mine and crossing her arms under her head like a pillow. "It'll probably take years to get all that finalized and before I want to start dating again. Then I'd have to be with someone for a few years before even considering getting remarried. And that's all assuming I even make it back to my world at all. So, yeah... children are probably not an option for me."

I know what she's trying to say, but still an irrational feeling of jealousy shoots through me. I don't want to imagine her returning to her world and finding some human to date and have children with.

Which I know is the stupidest fucking thing I've ever thought. I'm the one who promised to help her go back home. Am I expecting her to never move on with her life? To never have a future just because I never will?

"You don't need to worry about that," I finally say, dully.

"Why?"

"Because you don't have to age. You can just wear that necklace," I say through my teeth. "If you wanted to, you could live forever just as you are now."

She freezes.

"What's wrong?"

"Nothing...I just remembered how we even got here in the first place."

Fuck. I shouldn't have brought up the necklace. Now she's back to thinking about fucking Foulo.

My eyes flick to the faint red line on her throat just below the golden chain of her locket. Rage bubbles up in my throat. "If you're waiting for an apology, don't."

"I wasn't."

"Good, because I'm not going to be fucking sorry for saving your life."

She rises up slightly and looks at me, her arms coming to rest on my chest. Her hair is still dripping, but at least her lips are no longer blue and her shaking has gone from rocking tremors to the occasional shiver. When she glares at me, her gaze is steady and alert. "Thank you for doing that, but it was still crazy. I mean, you can't just...kill people."

"Like Foulo would have killed you?" I snap. "Make no mistake, Alix, he would have killed you."

"I think he just wanted the necklace. I don't know why, but he said something about proving I'm not Isabelle and then he grabbed the locket."

"Don't be naive. Even if that's all he wanted, he wouldn't have hesitated to kill you in the process. You're so incredibly fragile compared to us. He could and would have strangled you by accident and wouldn't have felt a shred of remorse over it."

She looks conflicted. "Yeah, but you..."

"Handled it," I growl. "And I didn't even kill him, so I don't know why we're arguing about it."

She looks confused. "You cut off his arm and left him there to bleed out."

"I don't know how to make you understand that we're not like you. I can't die from cold and Foulo isn't going to die from blood loss. He lost his arm, but I'm quite sure he's still alive and it's only because I'm here with you that I haven't gone back to finish him."

She gasps. "So not only are you not sorry, but now you're planning murder."

I narrow my eyes. "Of course. Do you really think it's just going to end there? He's licking his wounds right now but he knows there's something off about you. I have to get rid of him."

She shakes her head. "No. That can't be how things are done here, that's…"

"Crazy?" I finish for her, using her favorite description.

"Exactly."

"Why do you think I'm here?" I ask her.

"Right now?" She falters and glances at her bare chest pressed against mine. A flush rises to her cheeks. "I don't know, I—"

"Not right now," I interrupt. "Why do you think I'm always with you? Because Thorne knows that Isabelle could be in danger and wants me to stop anyone who tries to hurt her."

"Stop, okay, but—"

I let out a frustrated breath. "Again, what do you think '*stop*' means? You can use endless euphemisms, but the reality is that it's my job to kill anyone who even thinks about hurting you. We don't usually arrest people in Ellender, we kill them. It's far quicker and easier than sending someone to Dyaspora. That's all there is to it."

Her brow furrows, and I can feel her pulse pick up, drumming against my chest. "So that's why you did what you did? Because it's your job?"

I freeze. Fuck, we're back here again.

Why am I doing this? What do I want from her? Is all this because I need her to keep being Isabelle, or is it because the thought of anyone putting a hand on her makes me so fucking crazy I can't think straight. I don't know how to answer her, and I'm afraid if I try, I'll say too much.

Except, that hardly matters anymore. Because I've already said it, haven't I? I've already told her how obsessed I am with her, and all I can do now is hope she thinks it's nothing more than lust.

"Please don't murder Foulo," Alix says. "I don't want that on my conscience."

"But—"

"Unless he attacks you first," she adds. "Then, I guess it's self-defense. Just don't hunt him down."

"But he knows you're not Isabelle."

"No, he suspects I'm not, but there's got to be an easier way to deal with that than literal fucking murder. I'll just tell Thorne I developed a fear of horses. That's true, anyway."

I hum, considering her request. Tentatively, silently, I let my hand trail over her back and brush over the base of her spine, inches from her round ass. "Fine, Peaches. You win. I won't hunt him down, but if he or anyone else ever touches you again I won't just kill them, I'll burn down the fucking kingdom."

Her breath catches, and her eyes dart to my mouth. She draws her tongue nervously over her own bottom lip and suddenly I can't think of anything else besides how badly I want to sink my own teeth into that lip.

I can hear her heart beat, nearly as loud as my own pounding in my ears.

And I'm lost.

My already precarious self-control shatters, and all I can do is pray that I'm not about to damn the entire kingdom in exchange for a few moments of ecstasy.

I don't know who starts it.

Alix leans down at the same moment as I'm rising up to kiss her. I love tasting her, feeling her lips against mine and drawing every little sound I can from the back of her throat.

She whimpers softly, and it's like a spark of adrenaline to my system. I reach up and grip the back of her neck, holding her to me as I roll, flipping her onto her back.

Holy fuck.

I've been trying to compartmentalize my thoughts the entire time she's laid on top of me, not allowing myself to dwell on the feel of her bare skin on mine or how goddamn perfect every inch of her body is, but now, she's spread out in front of me, ready and all fucking mine.

"Are you warm enough?" I ask roughly.

She shakes her head. "Not yet, but I'm sure you can *handle* that."

*Fuck me.*

I lean back on my heels, looking at her as I throw the blankets off us. My eyes trace down her body slowly, imagining the path I'm going to follow with my tongue. She squirms under my gaze, her face and chest flushing.

"You're so fucking perfect," I say under my breath.

He blush deepens, turning her pale skin scarlet, like the blood on the ice.

My cock is painfully hard, straining against my trousers. I've never been more grateful for the forethought of keeping them on, because otherwise this would be over far too quickly.

I put two fingers into my mouth and suck for a moment, before reaching down and drawing them through her folds. Fuck me, I didn't need to bother sucking my fingers—she's so goddamn wet already. Wet and ready and waiting for me.

I draw my fingers over her a few more times, and she whimpers louder and shifts her hips, chasing my touch. "More."

I oblige and watch her face carefully as I rub lightly, cataloging her reactions and searching for the spot she likes best. I get the impression that the asshole she was married to never took the time to figure out what she likes, and maybe because of that she doesn't know what she likes either. I want to try everything I can think of with her, and spend eternity figuring out how best to make her scream my name.

I press my fingers into her entrance and she moans. I smile with satisfaction and push my fingers in deeper—just two, then a third. She rocks her hips against my hand, trying to force me to move faster and deeper. It gives me an idea.

I stop moving. "Fuck yourself."

She blinks. "Excuse me? Fuck you too."

I laugh, but the humor doesn't last long as I look down at her. She's so goddamn beautiful it pisses me off. I hold my fingers still, just barely grazing her entrance. "No, I want you to fuck yourself on my fingers. I want to watch you come before I've barely even touched you."

She gasps and blinks at me. I watch the calculation take place behind her eyes. She's wondering if I'm serious, and probably if she's willing to let go of her broken self-image long enough to find out if she likes this.

I half expect her to shrink away, but instead she keeps her eyes on mine as she rolls her hips and slides an inch lower on my hand. She rolls her hips again, rising back up, then sinks even deeper.

Holy fucking shit.

My fingers disappear inside her and my cock throbs painfully, growing somehow even harder. I didn't think this would turn me on as much as her, but there's something so charged about seeing her use me to get herself off.

I drag my tongue over my teeth and watch, memorizing every inch of her. My gaze locks on her clit, right in front of me, practically begging to be stroked. I can't stop myself from reaching over with my free hand and grazing the pad of my thumb over it, rubbing lightly.

A shiver travels through her entire body and she stops rolling her hips. "Oh my god."

"Don't stop," I command.

"I can't take this," she whimpers. "I need you inside me."

I close my eyes for a moment. Holy fuck, when she says things like that...

"Not yet," I tell her. "I want you begging for my cock."

"I am," she replies flatly. "Seriously. I don't even care how that sounds. I need you to fuck me."

"Earn it. Show me how you come apart pretending you're riding my cock."

When she doesn't move, I flick her clit hard. She lets out a hiss and starts rolling her hips again, fucking my fingers like she's picturing riding me.

I smile and lean over her, grazing my mouth over her throat and down to her breasts before sucking one tight nipple into my mouth. I roll it back and forth with my tongue for a moment, but it's not enough. I want to taste her and see if it's as fucking sweet as I remember.

I duck my head and give her no warning before pressing my mouth to her clit.

She gasps, arching her back and letting her eyes flutter close. "Yes, more."

I suck hard, swirling my tongue and getting high on every tiny sound I can wrench from her. She moves her hips faster, rolling against my mouth and my hand, as her breath comes faster.

"Are you imagining me fucking you?" I ask between licks.

"Yes," she pants.

"How does it feel?"

"So good—Oh my God! Please, fuck me. I want to come with you inside me."

God, I want that too, and I'll have it, but first, I want to taste her orgasm.

I give up on not moving my hands, and fuck her faster, lapping hard, while she rolls her hips completely out of control.

I curl my fingers inside her, stroking over her inner walls, and she screams. Her hips rise, her back arches off the bed, and her taste floods my month. I feel her squeezing my fingers and shaking, tremors rocking through her for several long seconds after she finally flops back down, exhausted.

I wait for a long moment, staring down in satisfaction at her limp body. Then her eyes flutter open again, and she's looking up at me.

She sits up and scrambles over to me, her hands falling to my shoulders as she climbs into my lap. She straddles my waist and I don't bother to keep my hard cock from pressing into her center.

"Jesus fucking Christ, you're better than a rose toy," she mutters, bringing her lips a mere hairsbreadth from my mouth.

"A what?"

She laughs. "Never mind. I guess you wouldn't have to invent vibrators if all Fae are as good at sex."

A possessive anger flares to life in the back of my mind. "I don't want you even thinking about other Fae."

She grazes her mouth lightly against mine. "I'm not."

I grip her ass and jerk her closer, pressing her body down until I'm sure she can feel how hard I am. "You're mine," I growl in her ear. "No one else will ever touch you or feel you come. Every part of your pleasure belongs to me."

She moans and grinds down against me. "Whatever you want."

She fastens her mouth to my throat and trails kisses up to the point of my ear, but I can't focus. I should feel calmer, hearing her agree not to let anyone else touch her, but I don't. I don't recognize this feeling, like I don't just want to possess her, but I need her to know. To say it. To swear on her life that she belongs to me, and I belong to her.

I have no idea where this is coming from. I've never felt any sense of ownership or responsibility over any of my partners, and I don't have any right to claim possession of this woman especially.

Alix grinds down on me again and I try to push the thoughts away, to focus on slipping back inside her and making her come once more on my cock.

I reach down between us to undo my pants, but out of the corner of my eye, something makes me stop. I turn just my head and look at the window.

*Fuck.*

There's a tiny pink haze illuminating the tree line in the distance and turning the black sky indigo.

"Alix," I breathe. Then when she doesn't seem to hear me, I repeat louder, "Alix!"

She pulls back, her hands still around my neck. Her lips are swollen from kissing, her face flushed and eyes bright. "What's wrong?"

My stomach twists painfully and my mind races just from looking at her, but I force myself to keep my voice steady. "The sun is coming up."

Her eyes widen in shock and panic, and she whips her head around to the window. "Oh shit."

Oh shit is right.

I nudge her back and she climbs off my lap. I run a hand through my hair, glancing from Alix to the window and back.

Could I risk it just to stay here with her?

No, of course not—what am I thinking? I don't know what I might do under the influence of the sun, when there will be nothing in my mind except pure instinct. I could hurt her somehow, I could—

But a larger part of me knows that I'd never hurt Alix; I might do something worse. I might claim her, take her as mine for real, forever. I'm sure that if I was ever to be with her when my own thoughts weren't getting in the way and there was nothing stopping me from doing exactly what I'm meant to do, all I would care about was protecting her and keeping her forever.

Which is why I have to leave.

I leap up from the bed, reaching for my trousers, murmuring curses under my breath. Alix sits up, but doesn't say anything to stop me. She's not an idiot, she knows that I can't stay here, but she doesn't understand why.

I glance toward the door to her room and run my fingers through my hair again. "Fuck, I can't sleep out there."

"Uh, you could go back to your room..." she says. "I'm sure I'd be fine."

I look at her wildly. She doesn't understand. There's not a chance in the world I'll be able to fall asleep right now, and short of chaining myself to the wall I know I'll find my way back to her.

"I'll—" I start to say something but clamp my mouth shut. Whatever is about to come out of my mouth right now can't be said.

I turn on my heel and march out of her room, slamming the door behind me so loudly that I'm surprised the hinges don't break.

I stride down the hall at double the speed I'd normally walk, buttoning my trousers as I go. I left my shirt and shoes in Alix's room, but I don't care—not even when I pass several courtiers rushing back to their quarters before dawn. All of them stop, clearly forgetting what they're doing as they stare at me in shock.

I drag my hand through my hair in frustration and break into a jog, then a sprint. In seconds, I reach the door to the barracks and I burst inside, eyes wild. "Kas!"

Every bed is full, as all the soldiers have returned from their posts before dawn, but I ignore everyone as I march down the row of beds in search of Kastian.

At the end of the row, he sits up abruptly in bed. His dark eyes dart over me, taking everything in at once. "Daemon, what the fuck?"

"I need you to guard Alix."

"Of course." He rises from his bed, looking confused. "But what—"

"And I need you to lock me in here before you go."

He glances around the barracks. "In here? Are you sure that's a good idea?"

I don't have time to talk when I've already thought through the end of the conversation. I'm already striding down the length of the barracks again and marching into the attached bathing chamber.

Kastian darts after me. "Are you out of your mind?"

"Yes. Probably." I step into the bathing room. "Lock me in here. Then guard Alix."

"Why?" he demands.

"Just trust me," I beg, glancing again at the window where the pink tinge to the sky is getting steadily brighter. "*Please.*"

Kas nods. "Fine."

I let out a relieved sigh as he steps back and closes the bathing room door behind him. I wait a long second, then finally I hear a key turn in the lock and the sound of wood against the floor as Kas pushes something in front of the door. Hopefully that will be enough.

With an angry sigh, I sink onto the floor and try to lean against the wall.

Only then, do I realize my wings are out. I don't remember releasing them, but that explains the strange looks I got in the hall and from Kastian. I know immediately what they're all thinking—what I'd be thinking if this were happening to anyone else. But it's impossible. No matter how I feel, Alix isn't really mine. She's not my bond—she doesn't even belong here.

Shaking my head, I fold the wings around myself and lean against the wall, watching the sunrise outside the windows.

When it finally does, I've never been so grateful for the moment that the curse takes over and my mind shuts off.

# CHAPTER TWENTY



I can't sleep.

With Daemon gone, I drifted off for what felt like only five minutes before I woke up again, gasping and shaking. I curled my fingers around the blanket and waited for the tremors to subside, sucking in deep breaths.

After that, I stay awake all night, pacing my room and thinking.

It's hard not to notice that this is my first nightmare since that night at the inn. Usually, it happens nearly every night, but here, I've gone several weeks without panicking or waking up screaming. Is that something to do with the backward schedule, maybe? Or could it be what I'm starting to suspect...that this is the first night I can feel that Daemon isn't outside guarding me. Even before I realized he was sleeping out there, I think I felt...calmer. Safer.

Ugh, I don't want to go there.

Because once I start picking at that thread, it unravels fast. If I think about the nightmares, I'll have to think about the wings and the intense promises and how my stupid heart squeezes every time he looks at me.

But if I think about that, I get depressed, because this isn't going to work out. There is no happy ending here. The best-case scenario is that I marry his brother, somehow trick him into ending a decades long curse, struggle my way through a wedding night with a guy who clearly detests me, and then fake my death. Frankly, even the Grimm brothers' versions of fairytales sound better than that.

I'm jittery and I don't know what to do with my body so I decide to take a bath. It's been long enough since I fell through the ice that I think it's safe to sit in the hot water.

I step into the bathroom and see the light shining through the windows for the first time ever. The arched stained glass creates colorful patterns against the tile, and I smile as I take it in. My smile slides off my face when I see the wet pile of clothing on the floor.

*Ugh.*

I cross the room and start the bath, sitting on the edge until it's nearly full. I turn off the faucet and slowly lower myself into the water. For a long second, I wait, nervous that all my muscles will atrophy at once or my heart will give out, but nothing happens.

All I can think about is what I'm going to say to Daemon when the sun sets again. He can't possibly want to pretend nothing happened, right? I get that things are complicated, but that would be so high school...we at least have to talk about it.

Except, I don't know what I want to say.

I mean, a large part of me says fuck the complications, we can worry about that after we hook up again...maybe a few times. How many times until I want to stop and talk about feelings? Eight? Ten? Never?

The situational crush I was trying to justify in the library suddenly feels way bigger and more important than it was ever supposed to.

I lean my head back against the edge of the tub, closing my eyes. When I open them again, the room is dark, and there's a sharp knock sounding on my door.

"Shit!" I stand and lukewarm water splashes everywhere. "Just a second."

Clearly, it's nighttime, and I've been in the bath for hours. I fumble my way out of the tub and across the slipper floor, trying not to fall and crack my skull open in the dark. That would happen to me.

I turn in a disoriented circle, searching for a towel, then I make it to the doorway and then a few feet into my room where I can switch on the bedside lamp.

The knock on the door sounds again, more urgently.

"One minute," I repeat, louder.

Despite the annoyance in my voice, I feel a tiny shred of excitement knowing that Daemon is awake.

I dry off quickly and grab the first item of dry clothing I can find off the floor and throw it on, before marching to the door.

It's dark out, so I don't bother to ask who it is before opening the door. This turns out to be a mistake.

I throw the door open and look up into icy blue eyes. "Oh my God!" I blurt out, jumping back.

"Isabelle?" King Thorne says, a slight question in his tone.

My eyes widen as I take in the entire hallway. King Thorne is standing there with an enormous box in his arms. Behind him are two soldiers I don't recognize—presumably his guards, and to the left, Kastian is standing against the wall looking equal parts amused and horrified.

"Good morning," I blurt out. "I mean, evening. Sorry, I, uh...just woke up."

The king's eyes dart over my wet hair and down my body. I look down as well and my heart sinks when I realize I'm wearing Daemon's shirt. I must have grabbed it off the ground...holy shit.

I cross my arms over my chest. "Was there something you wanted?"

The king's expression is completely flat and unreadable when he meets my eyes again. "I brought you this." He shoves the box at me. "For tonight."

"Oh okay, thank you..." I mumble. I have no idea what "tonight" is but I'm not about to make things worse by asking.

There's a long awkward silence.

"Did you finally return to the library?" the king asks stiffly.

"Yes! It's even more beautiful than I remembered."

Rather than looking pleased, the king frowns. "It was an uneventful trip, I hope?"

"Uh, yes," I mumble.

He can't possibly know what happened with Foulo, right? If he did, wouldn't he just ask about it? But what else about a library would be "eventful?"

King Thorne doesn't explain himself.

He steps back from the doorway, his gaze tracing over me again and lingering on the shirt I'm wearing. I brace myself, half expecting him to reach for my throat like Foulo did.

"I'll see you in a few hours," he says shortly. "Make sure you're ready on time."

Without another word or so much as a smile, he turns on his heel and departs.

I realize I'm shaking with anxiety as I look up at Kastian. "What the fuck was that?"

"*Lucky* is what that was." Kas lets out a breath and glances at the T-shirt I'm wearing instead of a dress. "You should change."

I flush, but nod and retreat inside.

Kastian might think the king ignoring Daemon's shirt was lucky, but I'm not sure. I don't even think he noticed. He doesn't care.

God, in what universe would it be normal for an engaged couple to act like this? If I didn't know better, I would say King Thorne doesn't even like me—Nana, that is. If I was really in love with Thorne, or cared at all what he thinks about me, this behavior would send me spiraling.

Fuck, I don't even care what he thinks, and it's still kind of bothering me.

The clear contempt when he talks to me wars with what I understand about the curse. He has to at least believe he loves Isabelle, right? *Right?*

WITHIN THE HOUR, EVERYTHING MAKES MORE SENSE.

Well, not *everything*.

I still don't know what the fuck is going on with the king and thinking about Daemon sends me into waves of uncertainty, but I at least learn what "tonight" is.

I'd completely forgotten about the ball to reintroduce Isabelle to the court until Odessa turns up at my door to help me get ready.

"Do we really have to begin so early?" I ask, glancing at the windows. "The ball won't start for hours."

Dessa flounces across the room and takes a seat in front of my vanity mirror, pausing to assess her own reflection before answering. "Trust me. We need as much time as possible. You're lucky I didn't break down your door while it was still light out."

Over the next several hours, I'm washed, brushed, shined, polished and waxed in ways I didn't even know were possible. I'm wearing a red dress to the ball, so Odessa spends over an hour weaving actual roses into my hair, then another hour and a half on a pink eyeshadow look.

"I thought you said I could wear a sack and it wouldn't matter," I complain as she pushes my cuticles back with what looks like a fork. "And I'm wearing closed toed shoes, no one will even see my feet. Who cares what my nails look like?"

"I do," she insists. "You were lucky enough to be born with legs, you might as well take care of them."

I sigh. I was lucky enough to be born with a finite lifespan as well, but she doesn't seem very concerned about making the most of my time.

Finally, *finally*, Odessa declares that I'm ready.

I cross the room to look in the mirror and my eyes go wide. That doesn't look like me. I mean, it does, but the person in the mirror is better than me in every conceivable way.

The gown Dessa chose is a deep pinkish red, like the color of a pomegranate or—appropriately—a rose. The bodice is fitted, resembling an exterior corset, while the skirt is full and iridescent. The sleeves are voluminous and off the shoulder, and there's a high slit on the right side of the skirt which shows off just a hint of my tattoo. To complement the dress, Odessa used the exact same color roses in my hair, all fixed to my curls in tiny individual braids.

I spin around, grinning.

"Told you," Dessa says smugly. "Now, don't you see how all that time was worth it?"

"You are definitely allowed to say I told you so. Thank you so much!"

She waves me off. "It was nothing. I like doing this sort of thing."

"Now what?" I ask, glancing at the window. "What time do I need to go downstairs?"

"You'll only have to wait a few more minutes," she replies, gathering all the makeup on the vanity back into the drawer.

"Is Daemon coming to get me?"

Odessa shakes her head. "No, the king is. It's your ball together, after all."

"Oh...right. Of course." I bite my lip. "Do you think the king really loves Isabelle?"

"I'd like to think so. Why?"

"He barely even speaks to me," I say, sinking onto the bed. "Not that I'm complaining, but if I was really Nana, I think it would bother me. Like what does he even do all day?"

"He's been preparing for the rose moon."

"Yeah, but how much preparation does he really need to do? He has all these servants, and isn't that supposed to be our wedding? Shouldn't I be included?"

"Do you want to be?"

I sigh. "No, not at all, but again...it just seems weird. Why is he always leaving me alone all day, and with his brother? I thought you said Fae males were possessive."

"They are." She frowns, and her brow wrinkles.

My mind immediately replays Daemon's words from the other day. *"You're mine. No one else will ever touch you or feel you come. Every part of your pleasure belongs to me."*

I flush.

*Possessive is an understatement.*

Except he's not the one I'm supposed to be marrying. I'm sure there's something off about this and I don't think the problem is that I'm not really Nana. With the way King Thorne ignores her—um, me— I'm not sure it would have mattered if I really was her.

"Maybe it's because of the other wives?" I muse.

"What do you mean?"

"Well...I don't know. What if one of them was his fated mate or whatever."

"That's not a real thing." She laughs.

"Okay, I don't know what to call it. His imprint buddy. Twin flame. Whatever you guys call it when you lock on to one person."

"Soul-bond."

I let out a breath through my nose. "Exactly. What if one of the other wives was his soul-bond and so he can't love Isabelle. I mean, me."

Odessa looks sideways at me. "Daemon told you about soul-bonds? Gods. What the hell else do you two talk about?"

"I don't know..." I flush. "Not much. But do you think I'm right? Could that be the problem?"

Odessa shakes her head. "I doubt it. I met the other wives, remember? As far as I recall, he spent even less time with them than with you. Look, I'd try not to worry about it. You'll have plenty of time to talk tonight."

I sigh. I suppose she's right.

But I still can't seem to shake the feeling that something is wrong.

DAEMON

Some days, I wonder what the hell I'm doing here.

Some days, it's easier to remember that there are hundreds of lives at stake, including my own. Other days, I'm not sure any of the courtiers' lives are worth saving. Why should I care about them when they're all so incredibly vapid. Why the fuck am I in this castle, trying to play nice with my brother and force Alix into a marriage that I'm growing increasingly certain will kill me?

I'm standing against the wall of the ballroom clutching a glass wine. All around me, the entire court is dripping in silk and jewels, dancing and talking as if they have all the time left in the world.

*I hate these damn things.*

I didn't realize until now, but not everything about Dyaspora was so bad. There were no balls for one thing, and I never had to dress up and pretend to be interested while some court lady talks my damn ear off as if I haven't already heard the story ten times.

The court was small to begin with even before the curse. Now it's even smaller—only a few hundred noble families left in all of Vernallis. No one can travel anywhere because of the curse, almost no one from the other kingdoms ever visits, and hardly anyone has had any children in the last century. No new people or new experiences means there are no new stories. Yet, at events like this, after a few glasses of wine, it's like everyone forgets how bored they are.

Not me.

I'm one of the only people who actually does have new stories to tell, but I don't want to waste them on the court.

I glance sideways at the woman standing next to me. It's one of Claudette's sisters—Laurette or Paulette, I can never remember which is which. She's talking at me with a level of enthusiasm I wouldn't be able to muster for the happiest day of my fucking life, let alone for some inane small talk.

"Do you see the man with black hair over there?" I interrupt her to point across the room at Jett.

Paulette turns around and looks. "Yes."

"Why don't you go talk to him. I'm sure he'll find this story fascinating."

I don't wait for her to reply and stride away toward the bar. Rude? Yes. Do I care? Not at all.

I make my way over to the bar and ignore the servant offering me more wine. Instead, I grab the bottle myself and fill my glass to the brim.

"You alright?"

I turn around at the sound of the voice behind me, expecting it to be Kastian. He's tried to corner me into talking twice since letting me out of the bathing room several hours ago, but I don't want to talk. I don't know what to say and I don't want to hear whatever he's thinking.

I'm surprised and grateful when I come face-to-face with Fox behind me. I plaster on a grin and pass him the bottle of wine. "Yeah. Of course, why?"

He just stares at me with calculating eyes before taking a sip of wine directly from the bottle.

See, this is why I like Fox. He's not quiet because he has nothing to say—I'm fairly sure he's the smartest of all of us. I'm damn fucking sure he's smarter than me. But rather than rubbing that in everyone's face he just observes.

"I don't want to be here," I tell Fox—not that he precisely asked. "I hate dancing."

He looks sideways at me, like it *didn't seem like you hated it the other night.*

I finish my wine.

I don't hate a lot of things that would be far easier if I did.

What I really can't stand is the triviality of something like this. There are mere nights left until the curse becomes permanent and Thorne is throwing parties. Maybe he doesn't care about himself, but doesn't he care about all the people he's potentially dooming along with him? I don't fucking care about myself either, but I've been scheming since day one to save as many of my friends as I can. You'd think the damn king would try to top that.

As if my anger had somehow summoned him, the enormous double doors suddenly open, announcing the king's arrival. The sound of trumpets fills the air and a servant's voice echoes through the room, demanding everyone's attention be directed toward the stairs.

If only out of habit, I raise my gaze to the sweeping golden steps.

Thorne stands at the top of the stairs surveying the court, but he isn't alone. Beside him, Alix stands stiffly, looking slightly unsure of herself. She's wearing a long red gown with a slit in the wide skirt, high enough that the tattoo on her thigh peeks through.

She's fucking beautiful.

*She's mine.*

I feel myself taking an involuntary step forward before I slam into something hard in my path.

"Don't," Fox grumbles under his breath.

I blink a few times, trying to clear my head. I realize that the thing I walked into was Fox's arm holding me back. *Gods.*

I step back, shaking my head roughly and shove Fox's arm away. "I wasn't doing anything."

This time, his silence feels judgmental.

As Thorne sweeps Alix onto the dance floor, the crowd parts to give them space in the center. The trumpeters fall silent and the string quartet takes over, their music swelling as Thorne and Alix move gracefully toward the middle of the room.

It's impossible to keep from thinking of our dance the other night.

I fucking hate dancing—I wasn't lying about that—but I hated watching her dance with Kastian more. Which, I know, is exactly why he did it. Kas likes Alix just fine, but he's not hanging on her every word like I am, or obsessing about trying to keep her safe. None of my friends are doing that, which makes it harder and harder to convince myself that my interest in her is nothing more than physical attraction.

Any asshole can see that Alix is beautiful, but not everyone wants to cut off the arms of anyone who touches her—literally. Inspired by that thought, I stare at Thorne's hand on Alix's lower back and imagine severing it from his body.

*Fuck, I need to get out of here before I do something stupid.*

For once, I'm not worried about keeping a constant eye on Alix. Actually, I'm the biggest danger to her at the moment because the longer I watch her, the more ideas swirl in my mind. Painfully stupid ideas, like how I'd happily damn the entire fucking kingdom and let the curse take over just to have her all to myself for the next fortnight.

I step back from the dance floor and begin making my way toward the door. I keep my gaze trained on the doors avoiding looking at the dance floor, yet I see them anyway. I catch the reflection of the dance in one of the wide dark windows, just in time to see Alix turn in an elegant circle, her dress fanning out around her.

I don't know whether I'm imagining it or it's just the angle of her reflection in the window, but for a second, I think she's looking right at me. Our gazes lock in the dark reflection, and the compulsion to turn around and rip her from Thorne's arms is so overwhelming that I stop short, my nails digging into my palms.

Fucking hell, what is she thinking right now? Is she remembering everything unhinged possessive thing I said to her yesterday when I thought she was in danger? Did I scare her?

*I'm fucking scaring myself right now.*

My heart races, thumping wildly in my chest. My skin itches and my face feels hot, just as it did when he kissed her in the throne room. I'm practically shaking, and any rational thought flees my mind, replaced by an incessant chanting. *Mine, mine, mine.*

"Daemon!"

I glance at the sound of my name coming from somewhere to my right and find Claudette pushing her way toward me. *Fuck me, not right now.*

"Where are you going?" Claudette asks, her blonde curls bouncing with every word, "You're not leaving, are you? The dancing has barely begun!"

I can't reply. I'm positive that if I open my mouth to say anything right now, I'm going to lose all control and blurt out what I'm thinking. *She's mine. I have to have her. I think I lo—*

"Lords, ladies, friends, it's a pleasure to see you all here tonight!" Thorne announces, his voice booming out over the crowd and penetrating even my tangled thoughts.

I don't even know when the song ended or when they stopped dancing. I didn't register the change, and I still feel like I'm in a daze.

"We were all fortunate enough to welcome Lady Isabelle back to Vernallis a mere two weeks ago," Thorne continues, "and soon she will be the one who finally lifts our curse after a hundred years of suffering. Everyone here has been endlessly patient and hopeful, and for that, my rose and I want to thank you."

The man knows how to make a speech, I'll give him that much. If only anything he said had any substance. His speeches are gilded lies, just like everything else at this court.

"They look nice together, no?" Claudette says.

I shake my head again. "What?"

"The king and Lady Isabelle. They look nice together."

I don't answer. Against my will, I turn around to face the dance floor again. Without meaning to, I glance at Alix and suck in a breath when I meet her gaze, finding her already watching me. Maybe it's my twisted imagination but I swear she's begging me with her eyes to save her.

Why does this feel like torture?

I shake my head, but it doesn't clear.

Something is wrong with me. I don't feel sick, I feel *off.* Like something is shifting around in the back of my brain, rearranging itself and the movement is making me dizzy.

Thorne grins broadly, raising his arms as if to embrace the entire room. "Tonight, I wanted to present a gift to all of you, as well as to Isabelle, and I believe I have found a way to do both."

My brow furrows. What gift?

I don't have to wait long for the explanation. At that moment, two elven servants appear, carrying a golden violin case between them. Alix audibly gasps.

"Holy shit," she mutters, seeming to forget for a moment who she's supposed to be. The corner of my mouth ticks up at that.

Thorne meets the servants on the edge of the dance floor and lifts a glittering gold violin from the case. He holds it up to the crowd, nodding proudly as if he himself was the one to forge it, then walks back over to present the instrument to Alix. "For you, my rose."

I can't hear her reply, but I watch her mouth move. She says something, then laughs—looking genuinely happy.

I'm torn between pleasure at her happiness, and nausea knowing I wasn't the one to cause it. I should have been the one to give that to her. It was my goddamn idea. He doesn't know anything about her. He doesn't even care...

Thorne must direct Alix to play, because she moves easily to the center of the dance floor, standing in the shadow of the enormous golden chandelier, and raises the bow to the strings.

I know what song she's going to play before she even starts, and I'm not disappointed when the first notes of the ballad ring out over the crowd. As I'd expected, there's muttering and excitement from the crowd.

Alix doesn't realize it, but she's playing the ballad of the first king of Vernallis. It's a celebratory song that hasn't had much reason to be played in the last century. It's hopeful. Triumphant. Everything the court needs to hear and everything their king isn't.

I was so shocked when I heard Alix playing this song in the tavern, it almost overshadowed my shock at seeing her come alive through her music. She's a different person when she plays, just as beautiful but more sure of herself, more honest than I've ever seen her otherwise.

I know I should leave, but now I can't. I'm fascinated. Mesmerized.

As I watch her, the light in the room shifts. The candle light flickers, casting shadows across Alix's face.

My gaze drifts upward to the chandelier hanging over her head. It's rattling slightly, its crystals trembling, as if a tremor rocked the room. No one else seems to have noticed.

I only have that brief second to wonder if something is wrong before things get exponentially worse.

The enormous golden chandelier suddenly breaks free of the vaulted ceiling and falls. A scream goes up across the room, but Alix doesn't notice. She's too engrossed in her music, her eyes closed and swaying, standing directly beneath the plummeting chandelier.

Just like all the times before, I don't realize I've moved until it's already too late to stop. Without thought, I shove Claudette out of the way and launch myself across the room. I feel like I'm flying, then I crash into Alix, tackling her to the floor, before blinding pain seers through my back and the chandelier crashes on top of us.

I'm shaking, my back straining from holding the weight off her. I can't even see through the pain in my back, yet somehow I look down at Alix's face.

Beneath me, she lies flat on the floor. The roses in her long hair are crushed, and her eyes are wide, like she's barely yet processed what's happened.

Shielded from the crowd by my body, she turns her wide blue eyes to mine and for a split-second our gazes lock. For a breath, I can't even feel the pain in my back.

The haze on my mind clears, and whatever has been shifting in my brain finally stops, locking into place.

"I'M FINE," I GROWL, EVEN AS PAIN STABS THROUGH MY BACK and shoulders.

"Are you sure?" Alix asks, a hint of panic in her voice.

"I keep telling you, Peaches, we're not like you. A few flesh wounds aren't that bad."

I'm lying; *it's bad.*

Twelve identical stab wounds mar my back. Most didn't pass all the way through, but there's a bloody hole on my right upper chest that makes me think I came very close to being pierced through the heart. Even for Fae, that would be nearly impossible to come back from. Blood loss can be recovered, skin can knit back together, but a knife through the heart will stop nearly any creature—magical or otherwise.

We've left the ballroom. Alix trots alongside me, holding her enormous ballgown off the floor. Despite nearly being crushed by a two-ton chandelier, she's completely fine, which is the only reason I don't regret the nearly unbearable amount of pain I'm in. I have one arm thrown over Kastian's shoulder and he's supporting at least half my weight as we make our way down the hall toward the barracks.

*Worth it.* Even if I had been stabbed in the heart, I wouldn't regret saving her.

"Why isn't it healing?" Alix demands. "I thought you'd heal instantly."

"We don't," Kastian says, clearing his throat. "We heal faster than you do though, as long as the wound doesn't get infected or pass through something vital."

"Stop fucking worrying. I just need some bandages, I'll be fine by morning," I growl.

Kas looks at me suspiciously, and I'm sure he knows I'm downplaying the severity for Alix's sake.

"Is there anything I can do?" she asks.

I look at her again and my chest aches in a way that has nothing to do with my wounds. This is the first time we've spoken since I left her room at dawn, and I'm dying to know what she's thinking. I'm dying to drag her back upstairs and pick up where we left off. *I'm dying…*

"You can go back to the ball and act like Isabelle," I say flatly.

She reels back, a combination of fear and frustration crossing her face. "Go back to the ball? Seriously? But you're hurt."

"He's right," Kastian grumbles. "Soldiers get hurt all the time. None of the other nobles care enough to be here. You need to go back and act like you don't care or Thorne will be more suspicious than I'm sure he already is."

Alix glances at me. "I'm not sure that's true. If he was paying attention to me at all, he'd already be beyond suspicious, but I don't think he cares."

I nod sharply. I know what she means—despite my efforts to keep her at arms' length, I haven't been exactly subtle about my growing interest in her. And if I'm honest, she's just as blatant. "I know, but just try. We've come too far to blow it all up now."

For once, Alix doesn't argue and turns around to go back to the ball.

"Kas," I begin. "You should go with her. I—"

"Don't start," he grumbles. "I need to look at your back. You know it needs to be healed and no one else has that much magic."

I grit my teeth, but nod once. "Fine. Fox, make sure nothing else happens, then walk Alix back to her room before dawn."

Fox nods once and departs. I expect Jett to go with him—those two are just as close to each other as Kastian and I—but instead, Jett stays, hovering behind me.

As soon as Alix is gone, I let out a breath.

I'm pretty sure the wounds in my back are worse than I'd like to believe. I won't know until I get my shirt off to look, but the stabbing pain in my chest and the way my breathing feels labored tells me that one of the metal spikes on that chandelier might have done some damage to my lung. No need to tell Alix that, though. She'll view this through her human lens and panic, distracting me from what I really need to focus on.

"That had to be intentional," I mutter. "What the fuck is going on in this castle?"

*And more importantly, what does it have to do with Alix?*

"Agreed." Kastian nods grimly and adjusts my arm on his shoulder to better help me up the stairs. "There have been far too many near-death encounters lately. The train crash, and everyone waking up to the sound of the bells."

"Then there was Foulo in the library," I add through gritted teeth.

"What happened with Foulo?" Jett asks. "I noticed he wasn't at the ball."

I freeze. Fuck. I didn't tell them about that. Partly because there hasn't been a lot of time to chat between maiming Foulo, pulling Alix from the ice, and spending the day locked in the bathing room of the barracks. But it was partly also because I don't know how to justify my reaction to Alix being in danger.

I guess now I don't have to justify it. The entire fucking court just saw me risk my life to protect her.

We reach the barracks. Thankfully, it's empty, as everyone is either upstairs at the ball or using the absence of the nobles as an excuse for a night off. Jett holds the door open while Kastian half-drags me over to the nearest bed.

I hiss in pain as I sit. "It's really not that—"

"Shut up," Kas scolds.

Being from Hydratta, he is unusually attuned to healing magic. Still, I have to grit my teeth and dig my nails into my thighs to keep from yelling as he begins working on the largest wound.

Jett crosses his arms over his chest and leans against the wall, watching while Kastian examines the wounds on my back. "So are we going to talk about this?"

"About what?" I growl through gritted teeth.

"Come on, Ashwater. You know what everyone's thinking."

"I'm not thinking fucking anything right now except how badly this—Ow!"

"Sorry," Kastian grumbles, not sounding sorry at all. "Some of these are going to take a day or two to heal."

"A day or two is nothing. It's worth it. It would have killed Alix instantly."

"Yeah, but that's what I was trying to say," Jett interjects. "How many times have you saved Alix's life now?"

"I'm guarding her, that's the point," I snap. "And I've already said I think it's suspicious how many near fatal accidents she's had in only a few weeks."

"Do I really have to be the one to point out the obvious?" Jett blurts out. "She's your bonded."

He says this so matter-of-factly, without any shred of doubt or concern that it knocks me back. A weight seems to clamp down on my chest, and for a moment, I can't think of an answer.

"That's insane," I growl.

But even as I say it, a voice in the back of my head disagrees. Is it insane?

Soul-bonds aren't predestined—at least, most Fae believe they aren't. They're formed, usually through shared experience or extreme emotional upheaval.

"I can't be bonded to Alix," I grit out, hoping my friends attribute my expression to pain from whatever Kastian is doing to my back.

"Why?" Jett asks casually.

I glare at him. I love Jett like a brother, but in moments like this, he's so fucking annoying, I could—and often have—hit him. "Because...I'd know."

"You sure?" Jett asks. "I wouldn't say that self-awareness is one of your strongest qualities."

"I've already fucked her, remember?" I growl, trying to sound as detached as possible. Like spending the night with Alix wasn't the best night of my fucking life. "Everyone knows it's impossible to sleep with your bonded and not realize it."

"You sure?" Kastian asks. "I know everyone says that, but what if the bond wasn't formed yet?"

I growl low in my throat, as much from anger as from the pain in my back. "I'm fucking sure. Alix isn't for me. If I were bonded to her, I wouldn't be able to handle her marrying Thorne, would I?"

Jett frowns, rubbing the back of his neck. "Not to kick you while you're down, Ashwater, but you're *not* handling it. At least, not very well."

"You locked yourself in the bathroom all night," Kastian interjects.

"Yeah," Jett adds. "And you throw a fucking tantrum every time the king touches her. You're lucky your brother is such an asshole and mostly ignores Alix, or don't you think it would have already blown up in your face?"

I scowl, but I can't help thinking of Foulo writhing on the ground, or the blinding rage that hits me whenever Thorne touches her. I remember the moment in the ballroom when I looked at Alix and felt as if my mind was truly clear for the first time ever.

*Fuck, are they right about this?*

"Dessa thinks so too," Jett adds. "She said she's worried your feelings for Alix will expose all of us."

"Since when do you talk to Odessa?" Kastian growls, speaking up for the first time.

Jett shrugs, glancing distractedly at Kastian. "Dunno. Why shouldn't I?"

Kas doesn't answer him. He swallows loudly, then walks around the side of the bed to face me. "That's as much as I can do for your back tonight. You should let Fox guard Alix while it's light out and get some real sleep. I don't know how it's possible, but you look worse than you did in Dyaspora."

"Thanks," I snap, reaching for my discarded shirt. I hold it up and scowl at the bloody holes marring the fabric. "Does one of you have a shirt I can wear?"

"Sure, let me just leave you with this." Jett pushes off the wall and walks down the length of the room, keeping his eyes on us the whole time. "If you're really expecting Alix to marry the king, what are you going to do on the wedding night?"

Without warning, a spike of adrenaline rushes through me. My pulse beats faster and black dots appear on the edge of my vision. I feel as if I've caught fire and I'm burning from the inside out, the urge to smash something, to tear the room apart is so strong, I could kill...

"It would be fine," I grind out. "She's perfectly welcome to do whatever with whomever she wants."

Jett just rolls his eyes and goes to find a shirt.

I glance up, catching Kastian's eye.

He looks at me apologetically. "Sorry, mate. Believe me, I know. An incomplete bond makes you feel fucking crazy."

I just nod, even though that makes no sense.

Kastian hasn't formed a bond with anyone yet. And hopefully, neither have I.

Despite what I said to my friends, I barely make it four hours before I can't tolerate being away from Alix any longer. I heard Kastian's suggestion that I sleep in the barracks tonight, but I can't. I feel...itchy.

I'm sure the ball is over by now. It's not quite dawn, but the barracks is already silent.

Inside my head though, it's far from quiet.

I can't fucking stand knowing that something strange is going on in this castle and that Alix might be in danger, any more than I can stand knowing I've left Fox to guard her all night.

I need to be the one protecting her. I need to know she's safe. I need to... I don't know. Talk to her?

A voice in the back of my head keeps demanding that I seek her out immediately and confess how I can't think when she's around. How watching her dance with Thorne felt like I was on fire. How I'm terrified that Jett and Kas are right, and she's my bond.

I argue half-heartedly with that voice even as I climb the stairs in the dark echoey castle. I don't know what I'm going to say when I get to Alix's room, but I know I need to say *something*.

I find Fox on the floor outside, and he looks up at the sound of my approaching footsteps. "Is she still awake in there?"

He shrugs and gets to his feet. "Not sure."

I run a hand over the back of my neck. "Right...well, you can go. I've got this."

He looks me up and down, but just nods and strides away. I've never been so glad for Fox's selective silence, because I couldn't fucking handle having to explain what I'm doing. I can barely explain it to myself.

I wait for Fox to turn the corner, then approach Alix's door and knock. I just need to see her and then I'm sure everything will be clear.

There won't be any bond or unusual connection, and I can go back to trying to get over my infatuation in peace.

I wait with bated breath, but I don't hear Alix's usual invitation to come inside. Maybe she went to sleep after all?

I knock again and a second later, I hear something.

It's not a scream, but it's disconcerting—like a high-pitched buzzing in the back of my head.

The hair on the back of my neck stands up.

"Isabelle?" I knock loudly; for once remembering to use her supposed name in case anyone is listening. "Isabelle? Are you alright?"

Alix doesn't answer, and a feeling of dread washes over me. I unlock the door with a wave of my hand and step inside.

For a moment, I don't see Alix anywhere. The room is dark as if she'd gone to bed, but she's not in her bed and the bathing room door is wide open. "Alix?"

I turn and spot the doors to her balcony standing ajar. Dashing over, I push them open wider and my heart leaps into my throat.

Alix is standing on the railing, her bare feet dangerously close to slipping off the edge. Her arms are outstretched and her hair and nightgown whipping in the wind. As I lunge toward her, she teeters, swaying as if to music that only she can hear.

"Alix, no!"

I don't waste time wondering what's going on. I grab her outstretched hand, pulling her and catching her in my arms. She struggles, kicking and thrashing her arms. Finally, I realize that her eyes are closed—like she's sleeping.

I sink to the floor of the balcony, Alix cradled in my arms. I tap her face lightly. "Alix! Wake up!"

# CHAPTER
# TWENTY-ONE

ALIX

My eyes flutter open, and I stare up into Daemon's bright green gaze.

For a moment, happiness and excitement swell in my chest. I feel safe, content, home... and then he's jostling me and nearly screaming in my face. *What the—*

I sit up and blink several times. I don't know where I am and it takes a long second to process that we're out on the balcony of the castle. It's still dark out, and I think I can smell just a hint of rain in the air. *How did I get here?*

Daemon cradles me in his lap as if I fainted. I tune into what he's saying and pick out words like "sleepwalking" and "jump."

I shake my head. "I don't sleepwalk."

"Yes, you fucking do. You could have killed yourself and it would have taken hours for anyone to notice."

Seriously? Could my nightmares have really gotten so bad that I was about to fling myself off the castle balcony? "I don't even remember falling asleep."

Daemon glowers down at me. He's sitting flat on the stone floor of the balcony, as if he collapsed as soon as he pulled me back from certain death. His back is up against the columns of the railing, and I'm draped across his lap.

I try to sit up and can't help but smile slightly which only makes his scowl turn darker. If I didn't know better, I'd think he was really angry with me, but I think I do know better...or I'm starting to.

"This is the last fucking straw," he rages, more to himself than to me. "How many ways can you nearly die before—" he breaks off, looking down at me with blatant pain on his face.

My breath catches and there's a swooping in my stomach as if I'm falling from the balcony for real. "I'm fine. You saved my life...again."

"But Alix—"

I don't want to hear whatever he has to say next. I'm sure he wants to go over and over this latest accident with a thousand questions and no more answers than we started with. I'm sure he'll tell me that he's just doing his job guarding me, and that there can't be anything between us.

But I know better.

I saw his face in the ballroom, and just now when I woke up. He looks how I feel—like I'm dying every time we're together and not touching. He makes me feel crazy—but he likes crazy girls.

I shift closer. He looks at me in wonderment when I scramble into his lap, straddling him, my knees touching the cold stone on either side.

I feel him freeze as I put my hands on his shoulders and lean in to press my mouth against his. I run the tip of my tongue over his bottom lip and hear his breath catch.

"Alix, we need to talk about this," he says against my mouth.

"Later."

"You almost died twice tonight."

Yes, and isn't it clear that's exactly why I want to fucking do something? I don't want to talk or wait or wonder anymore if there's something real between us. No more back and forth or avoiding each other. I want him, and I'm positive he wants me too.

As if he can read my mind, Daemon leans forward and presses his mouth firmly against mine. His hands trail up my back and pull me more tightly against him. His fingers tangle in the fabric of my long nightgown and begin to inch it up my thighs.

I moan and rock into the hard length of him, straining against his trousers.

He pushes my nightgown up until it pools around my waist and glances down.

"Fuck, Peaches."

I almost laugh at how his pupils dilate when he sees I'm not wearing anything under the thin nightgown. Ellender has a lot of things going for it that the human world doesn't, but they don't seem to have mastered comfy and functional underwear. Right now I definitely don't mind being without my cotton hip huggers.

I rock against him, providing delicious friction between my bare thighs. My clit brushes against the rough fabric and throbs, the beginnings of an orgasm already starting at the base of my spine.

I close my eyes and tip my head back, a moan escaping my lips.

He tears the rest of my nightgown off and dips his head to take my bare nipple into his mouth, only making me moan louder. It's not lost on me that I'm entirely naked while he's still fully clothed. Before, or with anyone else, that might make me feel vulnerable, used, but right now, it's the opposite. I feel powerful, like all of his attention is mine, and I'm the one in control of what happens next.

The tingle at the base of my spine grows until it's a small fire licking up my insides and burning in my lower belly. He groans deep in his chest as I rock against him. His hands trace over my bare skin and skate along my breasts while his hot tongue drags across one nipple, then the other. Flicking back and forth until I think I might scream.

I'm wound so tightly that just another minute and I could probably come from this alone, but that's not what I want. "I want you inside me."

He groans again, somewhere between satisfaction and pain. "Whatever you want, Peaches."

I reach between us and fiddle with his belt. He leans back harder against the stone railing to watch, then stiffens. A hiss of pain escapes his mouth.

I stop and look up, concerned. "I forgot about your back. Are you okay?"

He blinks at me incredulously. "Am I *okay*? Fuck, Peaches, I think you're going to kill me."

"Sorry!" I pull my hands back.

He shakes his head, still looking half bemused, half in pain, and whips a large hand out. His fingers tangle in my hair and he yanks my face back to his to whisper against my mouth. "I hope you do kill me. I can't think of a better way to go."

I let out a sigh and a breathy laugh as he wraps an arm around my waist and stands, taking me with him. My legs instinctively wrap around his waist and he sits me back on the edge of the railing. His large hands clamp down on my thighs, holding me safely in place before pushing my legs wider apart.

I reach for his belt again, and he bats my hand away. "Not yet."

He sinks to his knees in front of me and doesn't hesitate before pressing a hot kiss to my inner thigh. His fingers skate up the outside of my thighs, dancing closer to my hipbones.

My entire body shudders at the first hot lick of his tongue over my center.

He presses his tongue flat and drags it up and down, languishing me with gentle pressure. I squirm, the fire in my belly building higher.

He finally moves to my clit, sucking it lightly into his mouth and letting his teeth scrape lightly. Heat radiates through me, but I try to push it back. I want him inside me when I come. I want to ride my pleasure out together and feel how hard he grows watching me.

My hands land in his hair and twist, forcing his face up to mine. He licks his lips and smirks at me. "Something wrong, Peaches?"

I feel like I'm having an out-of-body experience. I'm so hot, my skin seems to hum with awareness. I think it's probably cold out here, but I can't feel it. My gaze is fuzzy, but through all that, I still know what I want. "If you don't fuck me right now, I really will kill you."

He laughs and gets to his feet, simultaneously pulling his shirt over his head. The bandages from when he saved me the first time tonight cross over his tattoos, hiding the designs from view.

I keep my legs spread, and he stands directly between my legs and begins to undo his belt. I wrap my arms around his neck and drag my tongue over his jaw, his neck, up to the point of his ear.

His belt hits the ground, the metal clanking against the stone. Then he flips open the button and pulls his cock out.

I wrap my own fingers around his. A low growl emanates from him and he lets out a hiss as we both guide him toward my entrance.

I'm still so sensitive, so close to the edge, that as he presses into me, I begin to shudder and my legs shake. He grips them tightly, holding them open as he slides slowly into me.

Jesus fucking Christ.

He doesn't move for a moment, just pulsing inside me, and I can't breathe. Every nerve ending in my body is turned on and alert. I feel like I'm dancing on the edge of a knife about to fall—in more ways than one.

"Fuck," he swears.

Then before I know what's happening, he's lifting me up and striding back into the castle, his cock still lodged firmly inside me. I wrap my arms and legs around him, helpless to do anything as he kicks the balcony door closed and marches me toward the bed.

"What are you doing?" I gasp.

He lowers me to the bed and braces his hands on either side of me, never pulling out. "I want to fuck you so hard my cock will form a permanent imprint inside you, and I can't do that while making sure you don't fall off the balcony."

Before I can think of anything to say to that, he straightens. Gripping me on both sides where my hips and thighs meet, he looks down, watching as he slowly pulls out of me and pushes back in again.

We both take in the sight as he slowly fucks me. My breath hitches, and I hold it. I feel like I'm waiting for something, but I'm not entirely sure what.

The orgasm that I've been fighting since the moment he first touched me starts building again, but this time it feels deeper. Stronger. Not like a sudden spike of pleasure, but like a wave rolling in and growing.

I let out the breath I was holding in and gasp. "Oh my God," I whisper, my voice hoarse, my breathing uneven. "Give me more. Please."

He growls again and abruptly pulls out of me, flipping me over on my stomach. Before I even process the shift, he's sliding back into me again. "Fuck, you're so wet."

I press my face into the blanket, whimpering with pleasure as he slides out again and hammers into me, building that wave inside me higher and higher.

He grips all my hair in one fist and pulls, yanking my head roughly to the side, then leans forward, his chest pressing flat against my back. Out of the corner of my eye, I can see him as he bends to capture my lips again.

"You're so fucking beautiful, Alix," he says—not like he wants me to hear it but like he's thinking out loud. "So perfect. So mine."

I whimper, suddenly remembering him saying something like that on the day I learned about the curse. Does that mean it was an instinct even then?

It can't get better than this, right?

But it does.

"Oh my God, Daemon," I breathe.

"Say it again."

Keeping one hand in my hair, he presses even deeper inside me, so deep I swear I can feel it in my stomach. With his free hand, he reaches around to rub my throbbing clit, and I let out a sharp half-scream. Stars twinkle on the edge of my vision, and for a moment, I wonder if it's possible to pass out from pleasure.

"Say it again," he repeats more urgently, his breath hot in my ear.

"What?" I gasp.

"Say my name."

"Daemon," I gasp. "Please."

My body finally gives out, unable to hold back the wave any longer. I squeeze my eyes shut, my mouth falling open in a silent scream as every muscle in my body tightens around him. My vision blurs, and I'm so overwhelmed I barely hear it when he growls it in my ear.

"Mine."

# CHAPTER
# TWENTY-TWO

ALIX

Throughout the day, it rains.

I never thought I'd be glad for more darkness, but the rain means that Daemon never has to leave my room and I come apart with him inside me twice more before I finally fall asleep.

When I wake again, there's a bubble of excitement growing in my stomach. I roll over and find Daemon wide awake and staring at the ceiling, his face the definition of *brooding*.

"Don't tell me you're going to freak out now," I say. "Please don't be that fucking basic."

He looks over at me for a fraction of a second his gaze flares to life. "No," he says, shaking his head. "I'm just thinking."

"About?"

"Everything," he grumbles, unhelpfully.

*Right. Okay, moody...*

Before I can settle into what I can already tell will be a frustrating conversation, I need to pull myself together a little.

Standing, I grab a robe from the wardrobe, then duck into the bathroom for a minute to ward off UTIs and clean myself up. One look at myself in the mirror is humbling to say the least, and I splash some water on my face and pull a brush through my hair before returning to the bedroom.

I swear to God, Daemon hasn't moved a single muscle. It's like he's turned to stone.

"Are you going to tell me what's wrong?" I ask. "What is this 'everything' you're so fixated on?"

"Mostly how I'm the biggest fucking hypocrite in Ellender."

"What do you mean?"

He rolls over to look at me. "I mean I hate Throne for not trying harder to save his kingdom, but I'm here willing to let them all burn if it means I can have you for just a minute longer. I'd bargain with every life in Vernallis to keep you."

My mouth goes dry and my heartbeat speeds up, pounding so hard against my chest I can barely hear myself think over the thrumming.

I can't think of what to say—I don't have words important enough to match his casual declarations—but I don't have to say anything. In seconds, Daemon's face crumbles back into self-loathing. "I don't know what I'm going to do in a few nights when nothing changes and the kingdom stays cursed forever."

Oh. Right.

I'm embarrassed that for a moment, the curse completely slipped my mind. All I could think of last night was him. My biggest worry right now is the messy situationship we've got going on, but that's incredibly selfish when there's an entire kingdom of people whose lives hang in the balance.

I let out a breath. "Okay, logically, what are the options here?"

"Meaning?"

"Are there ways to escape that don't include Thorne? Just hypothetically, if you went to the human world, would you stay cursed? You said lots of Fae escaped there years ago to avoid it, right?"

"I thought of that," he says darkly. "But it's not so simple. From what little time I spent in your world, it's clear that things are different now than they were a century ago. Plus, I can't ask my family to give up magic entirely, and I don't know if I could leave them."

"Do the guys use magic? I don't think I've seen any besides the wings."

"They all do, especially Kastian, and he's never had the experience of losing the majority of his magic the way I have. He'd lose his mind."

He looks conflicted, tortured, and my heart pangs. Clearly he's thinking about it—leaving all his friends to stay with me. But I don't want that either. They feel like part of him, like a pack.

I walk around the bed and climb up, kneeling on the end by his feet. "Okay, then breaking the curse is the only option, right?"

"If it were really an option, then sure," he grumbles.

"I mean...I could be trying harder to make the king like me. I obviously haven't been putting any effort into it, but I could...."

He looks up sharply. "No. Absolutely fucking not."

I shrug. I can't believe I'm even suggesting this. Do I actually have Stockholm syndrome, or am I just so incredibly cockstruck that I can't think clearly anymore. I shake my head hard. "I'm just saying it's a possibility. If I could save you, and all I'd have to do is seduce—"

"No," Daemon growls, more aggressively this time. "I'm not letting that happen."

"But if it could help, then—"

"No!" He looks up at me with dark fire in his eyes. "You've nearly died practically every other day since arriving here and Thorne barely seems to care. Not only would the curse not break anyway, but he clearly can't keep you safe."

He stands abruptly and strides toward the door.

"Where are you going?" I demand, also jumping to my feet.

"To talk to Thorne. I want him to explain to me what he's planning to do about the curse. Since he obviously doesn't care to keep you safe, even he must realize that marriage won't solve anything."

"Wait!" I blurt out, jumping off the bed after him. "At least wait for me to get dressed so I can go with you."

He looks back at me and huffs an angry breath through his nose before giving a tight nod.

BARELY HALF AN HOUR LATER, DAEMON AND I RACE DOWN AN unfamiliar corridor.

"I know I haven't spent much time exploring, but where are we going?" I ask.

"To his private wing."

"What? But he said never to go there."

"I don't really care what he wants, Peaches."

I purse my lips, worry washing over me as I practically jog to keep up with Daemon. The king seemed pretty adamant that I shouldn't go anywhere near his rooms—honestly after what I've heard about him and how he hasn't pursued any sort of physical relationship with me, I assumed that's because he keeps mistresses in there. But maybe pissing him off isn't the best way to start this conversation.

At the end of the corridor is a large wooden door. As we approach, the door opens and King Thorne walks out. His eyes immediately narrow at the sight of us. "Where the fuck do you think you're going?"

"To see you," Daemon barks.

Thorne's eyes flick to me and there's quiet anger simmering there. He shuts the door behind him with a click that resonates down the hall. "I was just on my way down to the throne room. Walk with me."

The three of us walk down to the throne room together in seething silence. Well, seething on Daemon's part. I just feel uncomfortable, and maybe a little nervous.

"Did you enjoy your gift?" the king asks.

It takes me a long second to realize that he's speaking to me, and another second to remember the gift in question—the last twenty-four hours have been so crazy, I practically forgot about the golden violin. I'm surprised he remembered it. I would have thought his ball being destroyed by my near death and his brother saving me would take higher precedent in his mind.

"I did," I say after a long pause. "I hope someone was able to retrieve it from the ballroom after the incident."

Thorne presses his lips tightly together, looking angry. "Yes...let's hope."

"That's what I wanted to discuss," Daemon demands. "You have to realize that was intentional."

"Intentional?" Thorne echoes.

"She was standing alone in the middle of the damn room right under that chandelier. That thing is over a thousand years old, and it happens to fall when she's right under it?"

"As you said, it was over a thousand years old," Thorne says flatly. "Unfortunate, obviously, but not entirely surprising. Isabelle was lucky you moved so quickly—though I suppose I can't say the same for you. How is your back?"

Daemon ignores him and barrels on as if the king didn't speak. "What about all the other times she's nearly died?"

"Such as?"

"The train crash. There was no one driving that thing I checked, and every other passenger car managed to break off and slow down long before ours."

Thorne's eyes are cold and his tone clipped. "An unfortunate accident of course."

"What about the bells mysteriously waking the entire court? What about Foulo attacking her?"

"What's this about Foulo? I haven't seen him in several nights, did something happen?"

Daemon continues, his rant picking up steam and volume as he goes. "And there was the wolf when she first arrived, the ice breaking, then the chandelier, and—" He breaks off.

I know he's thinking of the sleepwalking incident last night, but for whatever reason doesn't want to explain that. Even without that as evidence, though, he's making a good point. I assumed Ellender was simply dangerous, but could the attacks be pointed?

"Clearly, someone is targeting Al—" Daemon coughs, catching himself. "Isabelle. Someone is sabotaging *Isabelle*."

Thorne looks thoughtful. We've come to a halt in the entrance hall in front of the doors to the throne room, but he makes no move to open them. Instead, he strokes his chin, thinking.

"You're right," he says finally.

Daemon falters, clearly shocked. "I am?"

"Yes. I agree, someone is obviously trying to prevent my wedding in an effort to stop the curse from breaking."

I raise an eyebrow and can't keep myself from interjecting. "Who would want to do that?"

He shakes his head. "There's no way to know, but in the meantime, we must make sure you're kept safe until the moon."

"How?" Daemon demands.

Thorne frowns. "If the person attempting to harm my rose is a member of the court, then it stands to reason we should remove Isabelle from the vicinity until the rose moon."

"Why not move up the wedding instead?" I blurt out before Daemon can stop me.

I feel Daemon's hard gaze on the side of my face but I ignore him. If it means saving his life, I'll do anything. Even break my own heart.

"Weddings are always held on rose moons," Thorne says, someone the coldness in his eyes thawing a fraction. "I don't want to risk changing anything when so much is at stake, and regardless, the ceremony is barely a week away."

"Oh, now you fucking care," Daemon growls under his breath. "That also means you only have days left until your whole kingdom is potentially doomed, but by all means, let's focus on the reception decor."

"What was that?" Thorne looks dangerously at his brother. "Don't fucking test me, Ashwater."

Daemon sets his jaw. He keeps his mouth shut but is clearly close to boiling over. Thorne smirks smugly. I swear the happiest I ever see him is when he's needling Daemon.

"Is your estate still empty?" Thorne asks.

Daemon coughs. "Mostly."

"Good." Thorne claps his hands together as if it's settled. "Then we'll all travel there immediately."

Daemon stiffens, looking stunned. "What?"

"We'll all travel to your estate," Throne repeats. "I thought you agreed that if Isabelle is unsafe at court then surely leaving the castle is the best option."

"But why my estate?" Daemon growls.

Throne sneers. "Why not the estate of my Commander and most loyal brother? Unless there's something you wish to confess..."

Daemon shakes his head stiffly while anxiety churns in my stomach. I don't dare catch his eyes. Instead, I focus on the king. "Wait, when you say all of us—"

Thorne looks back at me. "I'll be going, obviously. You and I have hardly had the chance to see each other since your return. It might even be...fun."

I highly fucking doubt that, but all I can do is smile.

King Thorne's word is law.

The moment he breathes a word about traveling to the Winter Palace, every one of the dozens of servants jumps to attention. Within an hour, the entire court has packed, and before I know what happened, Odessa is ushering me outside to a long procession of carriages.

These are the sorts of vintage fairytale coaches I expected to see when we first set off for the Winter Palace. But why are there so many of them?

We make our way across the lawn and stop in front of a long line of horse drawn carriages. There must be four dozen of them, parked in a long winding line down the path that leads up to the castle. Each are painted black with intricate wooden carvings or flowers and birds on their heavy wooden walls. A red banner adorns each coach, every one sporting a different golden crest.

"I thought the court was staying here?" I hiss under my breath.

Odessa looks sideways at me. "Most are, but I don't think King Thorne knows how to travel without at least a small entourage. It won't be a large group going with you—twenty or thirty courtiers at most."

I laugh. "I barely know twenty people at home. He knows this defeats the purpose, right? Any of those people could be the one trying to hurt me."

She huffs. "I mean, you and I know that, but no, I don't think he realizes the problem."

"Amazing," I mutter sarcastically. "So we're about to saddle poor Beatrix with thirty surprise houseguests and it's not even going to keep me safer."

"Are you scared?" Odessa asks.

I bite my lip. "I'm not sure honestly. I guess I am in an abstract way, but I try not to think about it. If I think about any of this too hard I'm pretty sure my brain will melt, so..." I trail off, then shake my head roughly. "Anyway, I don't think Daemon will let anything happen."

Odessa looks sideways at me again, this time with more of a question in her gaze.

"What?" I demand.

"Just noticing that you two have gotten closer lately."

I flush, remembering how she walked in on our kiss the last time we visited the Ashwater estate. "Something like that."

"Are you sure that's a good idea? What with you leaving soon."

I bite the inside of my cheek. I know what she means but I pretend not to. "It's no different than you and I becoming friends. Speaking of which, would you feed Sushi for me?"

She nods, but still looks a bit worried.

Despite my original insistence that I didn't want to make friends here, Odessa was right. I have gotten comfortable around her in a very short span of time. Maybe not best friend level closeness, but I could see it happening if for some reason I wasn't able to return home next week. Still, I don't exactly want to talk to Dessa about my messy drama. Not that I think she wouldn't listen, but Daemon is practically her brother and it feels weird.

Fortunately, I don't have to because she doesn't get any more opportunities to ask about it as at that moment, we reach the front of the line of carriages.

The nobles stream out of the palace around us and make a beeline for their coaches. I wave as I spot Claudette and her sisters among the crowd. After last night, I feel far more comfortable with practicing my non-toxic Zen attitude toward them.

To my surprise, Claudette shoots me a wounded look and turns her nose up before flouncing into her carriage.

I turn to Odessa. "Um, what was that?"

"I think it's my fault," a low familiar voice sounds from behind the second carriage, and Daemon walks out to greet us. He rubs the back of his neck and looks down, slightly embarrassed. "Don't worry about it."

I scoff. "Oh, please. I've never not worried about anything in my life. What happened?"

He shrugs. "I think she was trying to talk to me while you were playing last night. I may have shoved her out of the way to get to you."

Odessa shakes her head. "Good lord. Be more obvious, would you?"

I smile as a smug sense of satisfaction washes over me.

Okay, so maybe I'm not as Zen and evolved as I wish I were, but whatever. At least Daemon just basically admitted he's not thinking about anyone but me, and despite knowing how dangerous that is, I can't help but glow with pleasure.

"You'll be riding in the second carriage, behind the king," Dessa says, jerking me violently back to the present.

"Oh. I thought I'd be in the king's carriage."

Daemon's eyes narrow. "Did you want that?"

"Uh, no, not really. But shouldn't *he* want to?"

I feel like I'm beating a dead horse into dust, trying to make anyone else worry about how the king doesn't seem to care about Isabelle. Or maybe they all know, but they just don't know what to do? Initially I wasn't worried about this at all, but now that I've grown closer to everyone, I wish I'd tried harder in the beginning to help.

But would that have mattered?

Is it stupid to feel responsible for not breaking the curse when I probably never could to begin with?

"No one rides in the king's carriage," Daemon says, startling me. "To do so would imply equal status."

For a second, I forgot what we were talking about, my mind is such a jumbled mess. "Oh..." I shift uncomfortably. "Will I be alone in my carriage as well?"

Daemon's eyes dart over me, humor and heat flashing in his expression. His mouth quirks up into a smirk. "No. As both the head of the guard and brother to the king, the second carriage is mine. I hope you don't mind *getting to* know me instead."

I feel a flush rising to my cheeks. *No. No, I don't mind one bit.*

Beside me, Odessa looks back and forth between us. She lets out an exasperated sigh and throws her hands up before walking away. I think I hear her mutter something about "hopeless."

THE CARRIAGE LURCHES AND BUMPS ALONG THE ROAD, THE wheels creaking ominously as we all trundle toward the Ashwater Estate. I now realize why we rode horses last time. The carriages are slow, made even slower by how we have to move in such a large group.

The carriage has two identical benches on either side, and Daemon is sitting on the opposite. We haven't talked much since the procession started moving.

I sit stiffly, peering out the tiny window. "Are you okay with this?"

Daemon looks up from his lap. "With what?"

"With Thorne deciding to use your house without asking your permission."

He grimaces but only grunts in response.

I have no idea what his fucking problem is.

"Are you mad at me?" I ask, unable to take the silence for another minute.

"Why would you think that?"

"I don't know, maybe because you're not talking to me? And not to harp on about the obvious, but every time you seem to let your guard down just the tiniest bit, you get weird and moody afterward and I don't see you for days."

He narrows his eyes. "I don't do that."

"Yes, you do," I insist, my voice raising slightly.

"Shhh!" he hisses, glancing behind at the wall of the carriage behind which the driver is sitting.

He leans in close to me and lowers his voice to barely more than a whisper. "I'm not ignoring you, Peaches, I just have no fucking idea what to say to you right now. There are dozens of people all around us, and these coaches aren't exactly soundproof. I can't talk about Thorne, or anything that might sound strange if overheard...like this, for example."

"So you can't just make small talk with me," I hiss, slightly offended.

"I thought we were at least at the point where we could hold a conversation."

He shakes his head. "Not like this. I'm trying to pretend you're not you, and I refuse to have a conversation with you while pretending you're someone else, and anything I would say to you, I definitely wouldn't say to *Isabelle*."

His explanation sends my mood into a ninety-degree turn, and suddenly I'm so much happier. "Really?" I ask, the corner of my mouth tipping up. "What would you want to say to me?"

"Alix," he intones, his voice full of warning.

I grin. "Just tell me one thing. I promise, no one will notice."

He shakes his head.

A small rebellious part of me seems to wake up and sniff the air. I reach across the carriage and make as if I'm fixing his collar, while actually grazing my thumb over the exposed skin of his tattooed collarbone. "We could always *not* talk."

I feel his sharp intake of breath the moment my skin touches his. "Alix, don't. You think if I can't even talk to you with others around, then this is better? I'm not allowed to touch you."

My mischievous grin widens. "But you're not. I'm touching you, so you haven't done anything wrong."

He shakes his head and leans back, gently lifting my hands off his shoulder. "Good fucking god, you're trying to kill me. *Literally*. I've already made enough mistakes with you to get any other guard executed without trial. If anyone saw this, we'd better hope I manage to kill Thorne before he kills me."

My breath hitches. I hear what he's saying, but the small rebellious part of me that I've kept hidden for so long has been unleashed.

A surge of excitement and bravery shoots through me. "What if you didn't touch me, then," I breathe. "What if you just looked?"

With a boldness I definitely didn't have a few weeks ago, I slide across the carriage and onto his bench. His eyes widen, and he glances quickly behind him again as I climb into his lap, my knees pressing into the bench on either side of his thighs. My enormous dress fans out around us and his hands come up to my waist on instinct.

I lower myself down onto his lap and find him already rock hard against me. I press down harder, teasing.

"Alix," he warns. "I'm not fucking joking. The driver is right behind me, and Thorne's carriage is right in front of us."

"So we'll be quiet, then. My dress covers everything important anyway."

He tips his head back against the wall, looking almost in pain. "You were born to torment me."

The tendons in his neck strain, and I'm sure that he's so close to the edge it would only take a breath to push him over.

I reach up and take hold of the ribbon holding the front of the dress together and give a deliberate tug. It falls open, spilling my breasts out directly in front of his face.

The carriage passes over a particularly large bump right then. "Fuck."

I bounce on his lap, and he hisses, grabbing my waist harder and pulling me down against him. Our gazes connect, and then he's stretching up to press his mouth to mine. I gasp, excited.

"Fine, you win," Daemon growls against my lips. "If Thorne finds out and executes me for this, it will not matter, you're killing me anyway."

A warm tingle passes over my entire body, stealing my breath as Daemon moves his mouth from my lips, down the column of my throat. He scrapes his teeth over my skin, nipping softly, and finally makes his way to the top of my breast.

I drape my arms over his shoulders and hang on, bowing my back to give him better access.

His hot mouth covers one nipple while he rolls the other between his fingers. Sparks of pleasure shoot through me and land between my thighs.

I rock against him without really meaning to. "God," I moan softly. "I could fucking come from this."

He looks at me and pulls back, my breast sliding out of his mouth. "From what?"

I rock my hips against him again to illustrate my point and lean over to whisper against his ear, "This." I rock again. "Last night I was so, so close even before you touched me. I feel like I'm always on edge lately."

He lets out a breath. "Fuck, Alix."

I roll my hips against him again, the scratchy fabric of his trousers doing delicious things to my throbbing pussy. I press down, rubbing against the ridge of his hard cock in his pants. "Do you still think you'd get in trouble if you didn't even fuck me but I still come all over your cock?"

He mutters something I can't understand and it takes me a moment to realize it wasn't English. "What was that? I think your magical translator failed for a second."

He lets out a harsh laugh that's more of a sigh. "I said, 'you're so fucking sexy it's like torture.' But you're wrong about the translator."

"Hmm?" I press another kiss to the side of his sharp jaw, not even caring that the stubble scrapes against my skin. "What do you mean?"

He leans his head back against the wall of the carriage and watches me almost lazily, still fondling my breasts as I grind against him. It takes him a second to answer my question, clearly distracted. "I mean I'm always speaking English to you."

I gasp, as the fabric scrapes just right against my clit and a little jolt of pleasure shoots through the base of my spine. "I know. Fox told me, we can magically all understand each other."

"That's true—" he groans softly as we go over another bump and my rolling hips bounce even harder against him. He swears under his breath and starts again. "That's true, but I also speak English. I was banished to the UK, remember? How do you think I was able to talk to you in your world if I didn't speak English?"

Oh. I hadn't really thought about that. Maybe that's why he has a different accent than the others, because he's actually speaking to me and it's not filtered through whatever magical weirdness is translating everything.

I lean back for a second, distracted. "So what language would you speak if not English?"

He moves his hands down to the point where my thighs meet my hips and holds me through the fabric of my gown, his thumbs digging into the soft flesh below my hipbones. He yanks me forward and I have to cover my mouth to stifle a moan.

"Vernali," he answers finally. "It's very similar to your French language. I'm sure there was some Fae influence somewhere back in your history to make the languages so similar."

"Show me. I want to hear it."

"Now?" he asks, pointedly, scraping one thumb over my peaked nipple.

I nod. I'm not sure if he'll be able to show me, or if Ellender will translate these words like all the rest of them, but I want to try. For some reason, I really want to know what he'd sound like in his native language.

I reach between us and rub him through his trousers, the back of my hand brushing against my own wetness. I'm so fucking turned on right now that if I undid his belt, he could slide into me without even trying.

Daemon groans low in the back of his throat. *"Tu es tellement belle que je ne peux pas me contrôler en ta présence."*

"I like it." Panting, I rub him harder, resuming trailing kisses along his jaw.

"Alix, don't," he says in English, trying to push my hand back. "My control is so low right now and I absolutely can't fuck you in this carriage."

"I mean, you could." I cock my head. "Say something else in your language."

He does, the words coming out on another moan as I flick the button of his trousers open. *"Je suis amoureux de toi, mais tu vas être ma mort."*

"What does that mean?"

"It means you're a beautiful demon sent here to torture me."

I can't tell whether he's being serious or not, but regardless, I snake my hand below his waistband and drag my fingers over his hard length. "If you really want me to stop, I will. But otherwise, I'm going to wrap my hand around your cock and drag it against my clit. And then I'm going to impale myself on it and ride you until we both come with all those people right outside—"

"For the love of Gods, Alix."

"Or I can stop."

He pulls me even tighter against him and lets his head fall forward into the crook of my neck. He growls low in his throat, opening his mouth to sink is teeth into my skin. "Don't you fucking dare stop."

I do exactly as I promised—I reach beneath my dress again and wrap my hand around his cock and pull it out, squeezing lightly and running my thumb over the tip. He hisses, and I smile as I guide his head to my entrance, running it over my throbbing clit a few times first. Then, I line him up, and slide down in one swift motion. Daemon curses again in Vernali.

"Quiet," I remind him. "Wouldn't want Thorne to hear you."

He closes his eyes and presses his face against my neck again, to muffle his voice as he continues muttering under his breath.

Feeling immensely powerful for once, I lift my hips and begin a new rhythm. Heat starts building again, radiating from the base of my spine, down my legs, and into my toes, making them curl inside my shoes.

*"Tu te sens tellement bien Pêches. Je ne désirerai jamais personne d'autre que toi."*

A whimper escapes me as our bodies meet again and again, and I can feel the orgasm just out of reach.

Daemon grips my hips and helps me go faster, lifting me up and slamming me back down so hard I'm practically crying from the pleasure of it.

He grabs the back of my head with one hand and pulls my mouth back to his, kissing me and stifling my scream just as white-hot pleasure finally courses through me. Every muscle in my body squeezes and I feel him tense as my release pushes him over the edge.

*"Je pense que tu es mon soul-bond,"* he says, breaking our kiss.

My entire body is loose and lazy, but at those words, my eyes widen and I pull back from him again.

"What's wrong, Peaches?" he says in English.

"Um, nothing," I breathe. "Just thought I heard something, but it's fine. I don't think anyone heard us."

He nods, placated by that.

It's not nothing, though.

I don't know how the magic works or why I can understand some things but not others, but evidently, there's no direct translation for "soul-bond" because I heard that word as clear as day.

And I'm afraid to think how I feel about it.

# CHAPTER
# TWENTY-THREE

ALIX

It takes far longer to travel to the Ashwater Estate by carriage than it did by horse, but I can't say I mind.

After several long hours, our procession arrives in Storia, and I scramble to the window to peer out at the lovely village. It's raining, which isn't quite as picturesque as the snow, but the village still looks nearly perfect. "I still can't get over this place. It looks like an actual fairytale."

Daemon smirks at me. "As opposed to the rest of Ellender, which looks like...?"

"Oh, shut up." I toss him a teasing smile. "I just like it here, okay? Is that a crime?"

He's quiet for a moment. "I'm glad you like it."

My heart squeezes, and my stomach somersaults. I can't even lie to myself about why. *I don't want to.*

DAEMON'S EVER ERRATIC MOOD TURNS DARK AND STORMY again as soon as we arrive at his estate.

Just like our last visit, Beatrix comes running out of the house to see what all the commotion is. Daemon quickly brings his mother up to speed, and the next thing I know I'm watching a procession of servants filing into the house, dragging more luggage than I would expect to see at baggage claim.

King Thorne steps out of his carriage looking happier than I think I've ever seen him. It's in direct contrast to Daemon, who looks like he's contemplating violence, and Beatrix who is clearly nervous.

To my relief, there's no confrontation outside the house. It's growing late—or rather, early—and Beatrix offers to host the king and his entourage for dinner, which he accepts before following his courtiers inside.

"Where's Kastian?" Daemon asks the moment Thorne is out of sight.

Beatrix wipes sweat and flyaway hair off her forehead. "Inside. He arrived about an hour ago."

"Why is Kastian here?" I ask, looking up at Daemon.

"I sent him ahead to warn that we were coming. Thorne has dozens of properties, most closer to the palace than Storia. The only reason he'd choose to come here is to fuck with me and I'm not about to help him do it."

"Let's hope that's all it is," Beatrix says, shooting a nervous glance at the house.

Daemon gnashes his teeth together, but softens slightly as he throws me a look. "I'm going to find Kas. Do you want to—"

"Isabelle can help me in the kitchen," Beatrix announces, reaching out and gripping my arm tightly. "You wouldn't mind, would you?"

"Um, no, of course not."

Daemon hovers for a moment, watching me, before he finally gives us a nod and strides around the side of the manor toward the garden. Clearly, he thinks I'll be safe with his mother, but personally, I'm not so sure.

"I'll warn you, I'm a bad cook," I say to Beatrix as we stand side by side at the long ceramic kitchen counter. "I'm a microwave kind of girl."

As soon as the words leave my mouth, my stomach drops. *Shit, should I not have said that?* The real Nana is also a box mac and cheese and frozen vegetables kind of lady, but what was she like sixty years ago? I'm sure I'm drawing unnecessary attention to myself.

To my relief, Beatrix doesn't say anything about it; she just picks up a knife and begins slicing carrots.

I steal a glance at her again. Daemon doesn't look like his mother any more than he looks like King Thorne. Her hair is far darker than his and her eyes are hazel. But now that I'm looking for it, I do see a bit of Odessa in Beatrix's side profile. There's something about her jawline and expression that's similar.

I'm still struggling to wrap my mind around how slowly the Fae age. Beatrix looks about forty to me, but Daemon said he's 121 so she's got to be at least a few decades older than that. 150? 200?

"Did you make dinner the last time we were here?" I ask, realizing I've been staring at her for too long.

She shrugs. "I helped. If I'm honest I won't do much in the way of cooking this time either."

I look down at the platters of ingredients on the counter in front of me, and the plate in my hand I was about to use for hors d'oeuvres. "Then what are we doing?"

"I just wanted to talk to you." Beatrix puts her knife down and turns to me, wiping her hands on her apron. "I know you're not Isabelle."

I drop the plate I'm holding with a loud clang. It lands on the floor and rolls on its side across the room, landing under the table with a clatter. "Oh shit, sorry!" I chase after the plate, dropping to my hands and knees to crawl under the table and retrieve it.

Behind me, she makes a clucking noise with her tongue. "Just as clumsy, though..."

"Sorry," I repeat, crawling out from under the table.

"It's fine, dear. I have much bigger things to worry about than a plate."

Right. Of course she does.

I narrow my eyes, scrutinizing her. Surely if she wanted to tell King Thorne, she would have done it after my birthday. Does she want to blackmail me?

"Don't look at me like that," she scolds gently. "I'm not trying to hurt you."

"How did you know?" I demand, a little more aggressively than I intended to.

She laughs. "Aside from the fact that you're nothing like her? I met Belle several times when she was here. I assume you're a relative?"

"Granddaughter," I say sheepishly.

"Ah. I'm glad to hear that Belle got her happy ending, after all."

I pause, biting my lip as I grab another plate.

I'm not sure she did, actually. It's taken me thirty years to notice, but I'm pretty sure my grandparents' marriage was miserable and my mom's childhood was really weird at the best of times. I think that despite all Nana's success, she's unhappy and I don't know exactly why.

Not that any of that is what I should be worried about right now.

"How did you meet her?" I ask. "She never came here. I'm sure of it, or it would have been in her book."

Beatrix picks up her knife again and resumes chopping carrots. "I used to be the lady in waiting to all the potential royal brides," she answers, not meeting my eyes. "By the time Belle arrived, I'd already moved out of the palace and back here. Dessa was grown and filling the role of lady in waiting, but I still dropped in occasionally. Just to check on her."

I want to hear more about Nana. To know if there's anything she can tell me that might help explain the king's behavior or make my performance more believable, but I'm not sure this is the best time. We're hardly alone.

As if on cue, the king's voice rings reverberates through the house. I glance over my shoulder toward the closed door to the dining room. Next, Daemon's loud voice booms over the rest of the chatter. I guess he's back from talking to Kastian and it sounds like he's arguing with Thorne—*again.*

"Should we really talk about this right now?" I hiss. "No one else has noticed I'm not really my Nana. Well, except Odessa."

"But my son knows."

It's not a question, just a statement, but I still nod in confirmation. "I wouldn't be here otherwise."

"Hmm. Are you really planning on marrying the king?"

"No...it's complicated. Sometimes I'm not really sure what I'm doing here anymore."

I can't tell what she's thinking. Is she angry? Or perhaps worried? Does she think any of this was my idea?

"I wouldn't if I were you," she says. "And not just because I saw that dance the last time you were here."

I flush. I can't tell if she's trying to say she wants me to be with Daemon instead of Thorne, or that she thinks I'm not good enough for either of them because I'm lying about who I am. "Just to be clear, I didn't mean for any of this to happen. I wasn't even going to stay, but I don't know how to get home without help, and—"

"There's a portal in the garden," she interrupts.

I blink at her. "Excuse me?"

She sighs. "My son is an adult, and the gods know I barely even know him. I don't want to intrude on his business, but if he's keeping you here against your will, you should know that there's a portal to the human world in our garden. If you walk through the roses to the stone wall at the back, there's a small pond. Wade into the pond, and once you're there, I promise, you can't miss it."

"Um, thank you."

I look out the back window and even though the darkness prevents me from really seeing the garden, knowing it's there is overwhelming.

Now, what do I do?

Do I want to just leave? Could I walk out there now before anyone even realizes I'm gone?

But then what? I'd never get a chance to say goodbye to Dessa, who was right when she promised that we'd become fast friends. Then there's the guys. Since they've been guarding me, I've grown fond of all of them; even-tempered and rational Kastian, ridiculous Jett, with his ever-present smile, and silent, looming Fox.

And of course there's Daemon. If I leave now, I'll never see him again.

A sharp pain jolts through me at that thought, and I shake my head, my mind reeling. "What did you mean you don't really know your own son?"

She sighs. "Ninety years is a long time, even for the Fae, and even before that I didn't see him often after he went away to school."

"When was that?" I ask, in spite of myself.

"He must have been about eight? Daemon's father—my husband, I mean—was a strong presence and he was never all that fond of Daemon for obvious reasons."

I nod slowly. I guess this is what Daemon meant about having to form his own family. If he left home at eight and was banished to the human world at seventeen, only to come back and get sent to prison—my heart aches with combined sympathy and anger for any child that had to grow up so fast.

"You think I'm a terrible mother," Beatrix says flatly.

"Oh no, I don't," I say quickly. "I assume there weren't a lot of good options for you either."

She grimaces. "I don't know where you're from or what kind of world you grew up in, but here, if the king tells you to go to his bed, you do it."

"That's horrific," I snap. "That kind of person shouldn't be king at all."

She laughs. "Wouldn't it be nice if we could choose our rulers, but alas, that's not the way things work. I was young and not long married when King Florian first took interest in me. When I got pregnant, I assumed the baby was my husband's, but as time went on and I never had more children and Daemon looked so much like the king...it was clear what happened. I don't think my husband would have minded so much if no one but us knew, but it was fairly obvious to anyone with eyes. The former Baron of Ashwater wasn't nearly so handsome."

I nod, not really sure what to say to that.

"I would have felt guiltier except that I always wanted children, and clearly my husband wasn't going to be providing me with any. In some ways, I feel lucky."

I nod again. That much, I do understand. I wanted children for years, but it just didn't happen. Now I wonder if I dodged a bullet. It would be so much harder to leave my marriage if we had kids. But still... there's always the what if.

"Anyway," Beatrix says briskly. "I just wanted to say that I don't think you should marry the king if you can avoid it. He's a lot like his father, and both were unfaithful and cold to the women they claimed to love. Even if somehow you break our curse, which I hope you do, your life would be difficult."

"But would that matter to you?" I ask. "I mean, sorry...I just meant that my life being difficult doesn't really matter if the trade-off is saving the entire country, right?"

It's not a rhetorical question; I'm really asking her if she thinks that's true, because lately I can't tell. I want someone to explain to me exactly what to do to fix everything and let everyone get exactly what they want.

I want a happily ever after.

Except, I know life doesn't work that way. In real life, things could always be worse.

"Have you met Aurelia?" Beatrix asks suddenly.

I'm thrown by her sudden change of subject and my brow furrows. "Yes...the last time we were here. Why?"

"If you decide to stay, you should speak with her again. She won't join us for dinner, but if you wanted to find her after everyone else has gone to bed, you could knock on her door. She sleeps in the little tower at the back of the house."

I nod, my mind still spinning. "Thank you for the warning. And for telling me about the portal. I really appreciate both."

She steps back, clearly sensing my unspoken plea to end the conversation. "Oh, can I ask, what's your name?"

"Alix," I say dully.

"It was nice to meet you, Alix. If you do decide you want to go for a walk in the garden, I'll make sure you have a few minutes before anyone comes looking."

"I hope no one waited for me," I say with mock cheer as I step into the dining room.

All eyes flick up to me. Beatrix looks satisfied, Daemon relieved, and King Thorne just as inscrutable as always.

I stood in the kitchen for a full five minutes, considering what would happen if I walked out to the garden and left without a word.

The short answer is *nothing*.

Nothing would happen to me. I'd return to my life completely different, but materially, nothing would change. I still wouldn't have enough money to leave Ryan. I still wouldn't know how to stand up for myself. And worst of all I'd be alone, knowing that everyone I've come to know here is suffering far more than I am.

I still don't know what my purpose is here and I haven't figured out exactly how to help, but I'm not ready to give up yet. At least I'm going to talk to Aurelia as Beatrix suggested and see if she has any insight.

Dinner is a strange and stiff affair. There are many unfamiliar courtiers around the long dining table, and they do the majority of the talking, leaving me free to stew in my own thoughts. The entire time we're eating, I feel eyes on me. Several times I look up, expecting to find Daemon watching me, but every time it's Thorne instead. Maybe I should be glad to finally have his attention. Scratch that, I should definitely be glad to finally have his attention, but I swear his eyes on me feel like insects crawling up my skin which makes my stomach churn.

Finally, a servant clears the last of the dessert plates and everyone begins to file upstairs to bed.

If there's one positive thing about everyone being cursed during the day it's that there are never any 'late nights.' My sleep schedule has never been so regulated.

The king and all the courtiers have already visited their rooms to change for dinner, but I haven't even seen the second floor of the manor. "Um, which room am I supposed to use?"

"I'll show you," Daemon mutters under his breath, grabbing me by the elbow and pulling me toward the stairs.

Out of the corner of my eye, I spot the king watching me closely, his hard gaze on Daemon's hand on my arm. Quickly, I shrug him off. "Directions will be fine. I assume I'll have the room next to His Majesty?"

Daemon's eyes narrow for a second and I see anger flash across his face before he quickly represses it. His posture shifts, back to the lazy self-assured stance I've come to realize he only adopts when trying to draw less attention. "Exactly. Thorne, you can show Isabelle to her room, right? I know it's probably beneath His Majesty, but since you said you never get to spend any time with her..."

I know I was the one to start this, but why is he pushing it further?

Thorne glares at Daemon as he holds out his arm to me and leads me up the stairs. I have no choice but to follow even as my heart is pounding so loud in my chest I think everyone must hear it. All I can think of is Beatrix saying, *"Here, when the king invites you to his bed, you go."*

"IT'S A QUAINT HOUSE," THORNE REMARKS SNIDELY AS HE leads me up the stairs. "But I suppose that's good for our purposes. No one would ever expect to find me here."

I nod, even as I firmly disagree. To him, the estate might be "quaint" but I've never seen anything more beautiful.

The upstairs of the Ashwater Estate is just as lovely as the rest of the house. It's homier than the palace, with dark wood floors and deep red patterned wallpaper. The grand stairs lead up to a landing which splits in two directions, with long halls on either side, undoubtedly leading to many guest rooms. There are at least thirty courtiers here and Beatrix didn't seem the least bit concerned with fitting everyone.

Thorne walks me stiffly to the end of the hall and stops in front of a door. He turns in, caging me against the wall with his body. "I regret not spending more time with you since you've arrived, Isabelle."

Inside, I'm screaming. *You regret not spending more time with the one person you think could save your kingdom? Yeah, I think you've finally got something right. You should feel like shit, you cold, inscrutable asshole. What the hell were you thinking?!*

Out loud, I say, "I'm sure you were busy."

"I intended to spend all of yesterday with you." I blink at him in evident confusion, so he adds, "At the ball."

"Oh, right, of course. If only your court would stop trying to kill me..."

I don't really mean it as a joke, but he chuckles anyway, leaning slightly closer.

Instinctively, I look up, trying to maintain eye contact.

Whenever we eat dinner, we sit so far from each other that I can't really read his micro expressions, and yesterday when we were dancing, I was just trying not to trip. Now, I scan over his face closely for the first time since the day I arrived. Objectively, he's absurdly handsome, just like the character I always pictured. His jaw is sharp, but perhaps too square. His eyes are pale blue, but there's no heat in them.

After a second, I realize I'm not actually looking at the king for him; I'm looking for similarities to Daemon.

My stomach gives another unpleasant lurch, like the feeling I used to get if I didn't finish my homework on time.

Whatever barrage of insanity is flying through my head, the king doesn't seem to be suffering from the same problem. His pale eyes track over me, and for the first time since the day I arrived, he actually seems to *look*. "Fortunately, now that we're away from the palace I have nothing but time to time to dedicate to you."

I suck in a breath. "That's amazing."

Thorne flashes me a satisfied smile. He opens the door to his room and motions for me to follow him into his bedroom. "Come inside."

Real panic wells up in me and my heart starts racing. "I'm actually really tired from the trip, so..."

"Too tired for a nightcap?"

Internally, I roll my eyes. Come in for a drink? While I'm at it, I think I'll jump into his white van to see a puppy. "No really, I'm fine."

Annoyance colors his expression for a moment, but he quickly hides it. "At least let me say a proper goodnight."

He leans his arm against the wall, boxing me in.

*Oh my God.*

*Okay, stay calm...this is good, right?*

I want King Thorne to be interested in Isabelle. I want him to fall in love with her. But that's only an abstract thought where "Isabelle" is basically Rose from *A Kingdom of Thorns*. She's not me, she's a character...this nebulous concept of a person and not me or my Nana.

The scent of the king's cologne overwhelms me and my heart starts pounding so loud I know he can hear it. I'm sure that he's about to kiss "Isabelle." Except, I, Alix, feel like I'm going to throw up. Or faint. Maybe both at once.

Thorne leans closer and suddenly a sharp pain stabs through my head. Like a migraine, but concentrated all at once right behind my right eye. I let out a yelp and I quickly jerk my head to the side, narrowly avoiding his lips.

My hand flies to my head, just as Thorne pulls back and glares at me. His large hand snaps out and he grips my chin, forcing my face up to meet his.

A crash, like breaking glass, shatters through the quiet of the house.

I jump and spin around, searching for the source of the sound.

"What the fuck was that?" Thorne barks, his face twisting in anger.

"Um, I don't know," I stammer, my heartbeat still pounding out of control. "Probably a sign I should go to bed, though. You never know— the rain could be slowing down, and I wouldn't want to be around for that."

"No..." Thorne says slowly. "We wouldn't want that."

I duck out from under his arm, immensely relieved he doesn't try to stop me. "Well, goodnight!"

Without another word, I open the door behind me and slip inside, shutting it with a snap. The room smells familiar and inviting, like cedar and cinnamon. I let out a long breath and lean against the door, my eyes closed with relief. The pain in my head is gone just as quickly as it came, but I still feel a bit dizzy.

After a long second, I open my eyes and push away from the door.

The room is large, with vaulted ceilings and wooden beams criss-crossing overhead. It's more masculine than the rooms I've slept in at the palace and seems sturdier somehow, with thick rugs, dark wood, and a Tudor-style canopy bed in the center of the room.

I jump in surprise as my eyes dart over the bed. My eyes fly open in shock, and a little shriek escapes my mouth. "Daemon! Fuck, you scared me."

Daemon is sitting on the bed, head bent. He's so still that for a second, I didn't even see him, the red fabric of his jacket blending well with the oxblood curtains around the bed.

As I step closer, he looks up at me. "Did he touch you?"

I'm a little taken aback by the look on his face. His eyes are blazing, with anger or...something else I don't quite understand. "How did you get in here?"

At my question, Daemon jerks his chin toward something to the right. I glance over and spot a shattered window. "You couldn't have just opened it?"

"Didn't feel like it."

"Right..."

*I guess that explains the noise...*

I sigh and turn to lock the door behind me, then stride over to the edge of the bed.

"Did he touch you?" Daemon asks again, more forcefully this time.

"Not really," I mutter.

Growling low in the back of his throat, he gets abruptly to his feet. "Be specific, Alix."

"No. He tried to kiss me but the window breaking startled him and I left. You know what's really fucked up though? He's not doing anything wrong in his mind. Isabelle is supposed to be marrying him, not you."

Daemon stalks toward me, his gaze dark with fury. "Don't you think I know that?"

"Of course, I just—"

He grips the back of my head, tangling his fingers in my hair. He jerks my face up to his. "Don't you think it's killing me to have to sit here and wait for you instead of—"

"Instead of what?" I ask urgently.

He doesn't respond, and I have only a second to suck in a breath before he's spinning me around and pushing me backward against the bed. Daemon lands over me, his arms straining as he holds himself off me. "I'm going out of my fucking mind here, Alix. The only thing that has kept me from blowing up this entire damn thing is that Thorne hasn't shown that much interest in you. But now—"

I laugh, almost nervously. I'm not afraid of him, but I'm afraid of whatever stupid thing is about to come out of my mouth. If he keeps talking like this, looking at me like he can't live without me... "I never would have gone into his room, if that's what you're thinking."

"But you said before that you'd marry him."

"Yeah, but..." I break off.

"But what?" Daemon demands, his face still mere inches from mine.

I shake my head. "Nothing."

I can't say it—that I only said that so I could have stayed with him. I can't even think it because not only would marrying Thorne so I can stay here with Daemon be morally fucked and unfair to everyone, I'm not even sure it would be possible. The Fae are possessive, and didn't Daemon say they biologically can't cheat on their partners? Would this count? Ugh, I'm going out of my mind.

His eyes track my face, like he's trying to memorize every single detail. "You make me feel fucking crazy."

My lips part and my chest heaves with every breath. "Likewise."

Pointedly, his eyes fixate on mine, and he lowers himself more deliberately over me. He reaches down and cups me between the legs.

I let out a hiss as his fingers brush over me.

"What's wrong?" he demands.

"Just...sore."

I haven't had so much sex in such a short period of time in...ever. I've never done this, not even when I was first married. And I've certainly never had sex several times in a row without being able to shower in between.

Like he can read my mind, Daemon nods and pushes off me, standing straight.

For a moment, it's all I can do not to whine in protest, but then he reaches down and scoops me up.

"What are you doing?" I demand as he carries me bridal-style off the bed and across the room.

"You need a bath. And frankly, I need to calm down before I do something I can't take back."

I bite my lip. I really want him to explain what he means by that, but maybe it's better not to hear it. Daemon carries me across the room in two strides and shoulders open a door I hadn't noticed before.

We're standing in a bathing room, smaller than the ones in the palace but no less immaculately decorated. The floor and walls are polished red marble while the bathtub is made from what looks like solid bronze.

"You certainly seem to know your way around the guest rooms," I mutter, for lack of anything else to say.

Daemon puts me down and bends to turn on the faucets. "This isn't a guest room. This is my room—or, it was, when I lived here."

I blink in surprise. I'm not sure what to make of the fact that he wanted me to sleep in his room, even expecting that he wouldn't be in here with me. I don't know what to make of it.

Actually, that's a lie. I know exactly what to make of it.

I know exactly what all of these tiny gestures added together mean, but I'm afraid to voice it out loud because the second I do is the second it becomes real.

Daemon straightens, standing in front of me as the tub begins to fill. I tip my face up to his again, my gaze meeting his in invitation.

He reaches out, slowly, and grips the ribbons holding my bodice together. I suck in a breath as he tugs, and the front of the dress pops open, cold air brushing against my skin.

"You're giving me a complex," I whisper, reaching up to run my hands over the lapels of his jacket.

His voice sounds ragged when he replies, "Why?"

"I'm always naked around you, and you're always so put together."

He growls a low sound. "If you were inside my head, you wouldn't think I was put together. The opposite, actually. I feel like my brain fractures around you. I'm a fucking mess."

My fingers trace down to the button of his jacket, and I play with it for a second before sliding it through the loop. "If I ask you to stay, are you going to argue with me about how someone might hear us?"

"I don't care anymore if anyone hears us." He reaches up and circles my wrists with his large fingers, holding on to me as I finish unbuttoning his jacket. "I should care, but I can't make myself walk away from you."

My chest squeezes. "Good."

My heart pounds, and heat drenches my core as we finish undressing, and I step into the bath. After a moment's indecision, Daemon sinks into the water behind me and pulls me back against his chest.

The moment our skin touches, I feel my entire body relax, even more than it did from the hot water alone.

For several long moments, we sit there, saying nothing.

*I could do this every day.*

I know I'm not supposed to think like that, but I can't help it. I could easily see a future where I spend my evenings sitting in comfortable silence with Daemon, not feeling the need to fill the air with anxious chitchat. It's a future I want, and yet, I can't see any world where that would be possible. Maybe if he came back to the human realm with me? He's lived there before, it would be hard but possible.

But what about his friends? Odessa and the guys, who are slowly becoming my friends as well?

"What are you thinking?" Daemon asks.

"Way too much," I breathe.

He chuckles softly, and I feel the rumble of his chest through my back. Without seeming to think about it, he raises a hand and draws it lazily down the length of my hair.

"Do you think the king did this on purpose?"

I feel him shift, and can hear the frown in his voice. "What do you mean?"

I trail my fingers in the water, unsure of exactly the right words. "I mean...you hate each other. Do you think he wanted to come to your house and finally wanted me to go to bed with him—"

Daemon growls, cutting me off. "I don't want to think about that."

"Well, exactly," I insist. "Do you think somehow he knows about this? Is he trying to piss you off?"

"I doubt it." He sighs and wraps his tattooed arms more tightly around me and presses his face into the crook of my neck from behind. "I'd like to think Thorne cares more about his kingdom than to waste the last days he has to save them playing some juvenile mind games to fuck with me, but I don't think that highly of him. He was cursed because he doesn't care about anyone but himself and apparently a century wasn't enough to fix him. He doesn't care about the court."

"So why don't you think this was about you?"

"Because if he knew I cared that he tried to fuck you, he would have done it at dinner in front of me."

I choke. "What?"

"Sorry," Daemon says, not sounding apologetic at all. "But bluntly, when the curse first began, two thirds of the most brutal attacks were his doing. His instinctive self is violent and brutal."

"Like a beast," I mumble, thinking of *A Kingdom of Thorns*.

I can easily picture the king doing horrible things while under the influence of the curse. Even though he's never been violent toward me, unless you count yelling, there's something off in his gaze. An instinctual feeling that would make me turn around and walk in the other direction if I saw him on the street, no matter how handsome he is. If King Thorne had been the one outside my door the day I found out about the curse, I know it would have turned out differently.

On the other hand, there's Daemon, who didn't seem much

different at all while the curse was active. Who looked at me just the same as he always does. Who just wanted to protect me...

"How do soul-bonds work?" I blurt out.

He stiffens behind me and his hand stills in my hair. "That's a fucking abrupt change of subject. Why?"

Actually, it doesn't feel that abrupt to me. It feels like exactly what I should be asking—what I should have asked days ago.

"Just answer the question. You brought it up before but you didn't really explain it. How does it work?"

He shifts once more, running his fingers down the length of my hair several times, like he's using the movement to cover his thought process. I could swear it feels like the air hums between us.

"No one really knows," he says finally. "The general consensus is that bonds aren't fated or pre-chosen, they're formed over time—usually from emotionally intense connections or shared experience. Not everyone who is married in Ellender is bonded, but most are, either from the start or after a while. We can date or have casual partners, but if a bond doesn't form, most Fae will move on and keep searching."

"So once bonded, you can never be with anyone else?"

"I don't think anyone bonded would want to try it, but I've heard it causes extreme disgust and often pain if you try."

"What does it feel like? The bond I mean?"

He's silent for another long second, and I hear him suck in a breath. "You'd have to ask someone bonded. I could only guess."

My heart squeezes.

I don't know whether I want to believe he's lying, or I'm glad he didn't blurt out something crazy...like maybe that I'm his soul-bond.

# CHAPTER
# TWENTY-FOUR



I lie on my side in the semi-darkness, listening to the rain pelt a steady tempo against the windows. My internal clock is beyond fucked up by now, but I think it's like 2PM, which makes it roughly two in the morning, Ellender time.

Like the rest of the house, Daemon is asleep. He lies on top of the covers facing me, like we could be talking, except for his closed eyes and steady breath. I can't help but notice that he doesn't sleep deeply. His eyes move behind loosely closed eyelids, and I get the feeling that if I made any sudden movement, he'd be up in less than a second. He's constantly on edge, never fully relaxed.

*Did prison do this to him or was he always a light sleeper?*

I sigh and begin slowly edging toward the far side of the bed. No sudden movements.

I swing my legs over the side of the mattress and onto the floor, then look back to check that Daemon's eyes are still closed. They are. My trip across the room takes longer than it should, because I stop every few feet to make sure I haven't disturbed him.

I don't know why I'm so nervous about this—I'm not doing anything wrong. Except that I assume if Beatrix wanted me to bring Daemon with me to talk to Aurelia, she would have said so. Since she warned me about the portal and told her story, I trust her.

Miraculously, Daemon never opens his eyes as I ease the heavy door open and step out into the hall. I throw one nervous glance at King

Thorne's door right beside mine, and hold my breath as I tiptoe down the hall.

Because of the rain, I'm not afraid that Thorne or any of the courtiers he brought along will wake up and attack me, but I still don't want to be alone with any of them, especially the king.

I'm not sure how to reach the tower that I've only seen from the outside of the house, but I doubt it's hard or Beatrix would have been more clear in her instructions. Sure enough, I find a second staircase at the end of the hall, this one thinner and obviously only meant for one person to walk up at a time.

My entire body tingles with anticipation as I ascend the stairs. I stop when I come to a closed wooden door with little purple flowers painted on the worn wood.

I raise my fist to knock, then pause.

I can't help but be aware that the gate is right outside. No one is around. What would happen if I didn't knock. What if I turned around and left right now? Part of me wonders if everyone would be better off.

With a deep breath, I knock twice.

Immediately the door swings open. I jump in surprise, especially when I see that no one is waiting on the other side.

"Come in," Aurelia's high pitched voice rings out from somewhere out of sight.

My heart still racing, I step into the room and the door swings shut behind me.

I'm standing in a perfectly round room. The walls are covered in colorful paintings and shelves with hundreds of knickknacks and lovely treasures and there are rainbow braided rugs on every inch of the floor. On one side of the room is a round table and a tiny kitchen, like the fairytale version of a hotel kitchenette. On the other side, bookshelves filled with thousands of volumes rise from floor to ceiling. Between the shelves is a ladder, which I assume leads to a bed.

"Be right down!" Aurelia's voice rings out from above. "Make yourself comfortable, Alix."

I bite my lip. This is weird, but I guess no more weird than anything else in Ellender. I doubt the same girl who painted kittens on her windowsill is coming down here to slit my throat. So I cross the tower and take a seat at the little table.

A second later, Aurelia's feet appear on the ladder. She's wearing bright pink genie-style pants and a matching pink blouse with blue stars embroidered on the collar. Her short hair is pushed back from her face with a ribbon.

"Hi," she says, grinning as she reaches the floor. "Beatrix said you would come by."

"She did?" I laugh. "I wasn't sure myself."

Aurelia just smiles and dances across the room to the little kitchen. "Do you want some tea? I was going to make myself some."

"You don't have coffee, do you?"

She shakes her head. "I don't think so, but I can give you an extra teabag."

I smile. "Sure."

She returns my smile, then turns toward the sink and fills a kettle with boiling water, then rather than putting the kettle on the stove to warm, she flicks her fingers at it like I've seen Daemon do before. Instantly, condensation appears on the sides of the kettle and steam begins to rise from the top.

"You do magic," I comment, pointing out the obvious.

She nods. "Most everyone does. It's only Vernallis who have had their powers so diminished by the curse." To illustrate her point, she flicks her fingers again and the unlit candle sticks on the table flare. The plates and bowls stacked on shelves along the wall come to life, spinning and dancing for a few seconds before falling back down, quiet and inert.

I gape at the unmoving plates, then look up at Aurelia. She crosses the kitchen again, now holding the steaming kettle. Two mugs fly off the shelf of their own accord and land on the table in front of us, then with a final flick, she makes the tea pour itself. "Sorry, I never get the chance to show off. Almost no one ever comes to the house, and I think you're the first person ever to visit my room—aside from Beatrix, that is."

I swallow against my dry throat. I'm still working through the shock of the dancing plates. But then again, nothing should really surprise me anymore. "So you're not from Vernallis?"

She shakes her head. "I was born after the curse, but my mother crossed into Thermia to have me."

I nod, taking a sip of my tea to hide the fact that I have no idea what to say. Clearly, Aurelia knew I would be coming to talk to her and was waiting for me, but I don't know how to begin and she isn't exactly taking the reins.

"Beatrix told me I should come talk to you," I say finally.

"She's meddlesome like that, but in this case, she's right. There's things you should know before you sacrifice yourself to end the curse."

I swallow another mouthful of the scalding hot tea. "I already know this situation is weird. When I first agreed to it, I didn't know marriage was part of it, and now I'm only considering it because of the curse."

"Do you really think you can break it?" she asks.

I open my mouth, starting to say "I don't know" but stop before the words come out. Instead, I say, "King Thorne clearly doesn't love me, no matter who he thinks I am, and I don't love him either, so...no. I don't think I can break it."

It feels like I'm admitting to something terrible. Saying out loud that I don't think there's anything I can do feels final in a way that fills me with a mix of grief and frustration.

"I want to tell you a little story." Aurelia fiddles with the sleeve of her blouse, her eyes cast down at her tea. "It's not long, I promise, and I'm not great at storytelling anyway, but I still think you should hear it."

I nod, taking another sip of tea. "Shoot."

"I've lived in this tower my entire life," she begins. "Beatrix isn't my mother, but for the last ninety-nine years, she's the only family I've ever really known. Did she tell you she used to be a lady in waiting at the palace?"

"Yes."

"Beatrix was the companion assigned to my mother when she arrived in Vernallis to marry the future king. Prince Thorne had spent years searching for the perfect bride, and the entire kingdom was shocked when he chose a commoner rather than any of the noble women from one of the other three kingdoms."

My breath catches, remembering the story that Daemon told me. "So your mother was the one to cast the curse?"

She smiles a little bitterly. "Eventually. The king chose her because she was a powerful sorceress, and though she wasn't noble, she came from a long line of strong magic. The king also has strong magic."

"I've never seen him use it," I interrupt, my heart starting to beat faster.

Aurelia shrugs. "The curse drains the power from the land little by little—not inherently, but because Fae were never meant to live in constant darkness. We need the sun to thrive, which incidentally is why Dyaspora is such a brutal punishment. The cold and forced labor aside, that far north, the sun only shines for a single hour a day. It makes a perfect breeding ground for the types of creatures that thrive in darkness and weakens the Fae prisoners."

"You seem to know a lot about it."

She gestures vaguely to the thousands of books on her shelves. "Being alone all the time, I've had a lot of time to read. Anyway, King Thorne chose my mother because she was likely to have powerful children. He'd grown up surrounded by doubt in the line of succession and desperately wanted a strong son to put all questions to rest."

"What about you?" I can't help but ask. "I'm assuming he's your father."

"He is," she says, like it's no less important than commenting on the weather. "But he doesn't know I exist. And anyway, Vernallis practices male-primogeniture. Women can only inherit the throne if there is no male heir, and in this case, there is."

I blink, confused, until it clicks. "You mean, Daemon? But he's illegitimate, right?"

"It doesn't matter. If King Thorne were to die, Daemon would immediately become king. It's just how things work here." The corner of her mouth tips up in a mischievous smirk. "I guess I could always fight him over it."

My stomach lurches. "Would you?"

She grins. "Probably not. I doubt I'd win anyway, but it doesn't really matter. This is all hypothetical and not the point of my story."

I wave my hand at her. "Sorry, go ahead."

"My mother traveled to the palace from her home in Solistine expecting to marry a prince. Beatrix told me how sad my mother was when she realized that there was no instant connection between them and no soul-bond. She thought maybe she could force the bond to appear, but instead she ended up pregnant ahead of her wedding and the king carried on with his mistresses up in his private tower."

"Asshole," I mutter.

Aurelia cocks her head to the side, like *tell me about it*. "Obviously my mother was shattered and she left Vernallis with the help of her lady in waiting."

"So she cursed the entire country?" I ask.

I try to keep the note of judgment out of my voice but it's hard. Just like the last time I heard this story, my immediate thought is that it's understandable to curse the king, but why punish thousands of other people along with him? They didn't do anything.

"I don't know why she did that," Aurelia says quickly, obviously following my train of thought. "At least, I don't think she meant to curse everyone."

The cup in my hand shakes. "Is she still alive somewhere? Maybe we could ask her?"

Her expression shutters. "She died giving birth to me. She had to know she would die when she decided to cross into Thermia for the birth...they have their own issues in that kingdom. But she still did it, and gave me to Beatrix for my safety."

My heart drops. "She didn't happen to leave you a detailed journal or something, did she?"

"No, sorry, but I do know something that might help you." Aurelia grimaces. "She cast the curse in front of Beatrix, and I've memorized it after all these years. She cursed the kingdom to be judged on the content of their true character and show on the outside who they are on the inside. She said that the curse would only break when the King of Vernallis admits he is powerless and sacrifices whomever he loves most."

I blink at her. "Wait, that's exactly what it says?"

She looks equally confused. "Yes..."

"I thought he had to find true love?"

"He does...and then he has to sacrifice her."

I jump to my feet, spilling what's left of my tea in the process. "Oh my God. So you're saying it's never been about the love. He's been marrying all these women over the years to...sacrifice them?"

Aurelia looks startled as she stands too. "Yes. Didn't you know that? I thought that's what we were talking about."

"No!" My heart starts to race, and my palms sweat. I need to get the fuck out of here.

I stride toward the door, not entirely sure where I'm going, but then stop and whirl back around. "Wait, you said you could help me. If you thought I already knew I had to 'sacrifice' myself, what did you mean?"

Aurelia rubs her palms nervously on the sides of her voluminous pants, like her palms are sweaty. "I was going to tell you that my mother cast the curse to punish the king, not to punish the court. I'm sure she wasn't expecting it to last one hundred years. So, I have to assume that the person she meant for him to sacrifice would have been someone she knew. Someone who was already in Ellender at the time the curse began."

"So, not my Nana," I conclude.

"Right. I could be wrong. As I said, I never knew her...but if I'm right, then there's nothing you can do either way. If you die, it won't matter, so if I were you, I'd walk away now."

"Walk away?"

Aurelia leans forward, her wide eyes seeming to convey more than her words. "Don't wake anyone up and don't say goodbye, just leave. There's a portal in the garden."

I chew on my lip, watching her without really seeing anything at all. I'm shaking and my pulse is thrumming way too fast. Is that what I should do? Just walk away now without saying anything?

"Thanks," I mumble distractedly. "For telling me."

"Alix!" she calls after me, a hint of anxiety in her voice. "What are you going to do?"

I don't answer her, because I don't know yet. I'm running on adrenaline, following my heart rather than my head down the long stairs.

I just hope my heart knows where it's going.

DAEMON

ALIX REACHES DOWN TO SHAKE ME AWAKE, but I'm up before any words come out of her mouth. "What's wrong, Peaches?"

She leans back, startled, as I sit up abruptly. "I was going to say, wake up."

"Yeah," I prompt her. "I'm up. What's wrong?"

I can tell there's something wrong immediately. I can't smell her actual fear, but I might as well be able to. The scent of sweat on her palms and the back of her neck is strong, and she's shaking more than when I pulled her out of the icy lake.

"I met Aurelia," she says.

I blink, startled. Whatever I was expecting Alix to say, it wasn't that.

I know my mother has been keeping Thorne's daughter here; I guess this family has a soft spot for secret bastard children. I met her once when she was a young child, over ninety years ago, but haven't seen her since I've been out of Dyaspora. She's my niece, technically, but I have no idea what she looks like.

"What happened?" I ask, after a moment. I can't understand why meeting Aurelia would cause Alix to panic, but my adrenaline is high knowing she's upset, and instinctively, I want to destroy whatever's hurt my...whatever Alix is to me.

"I'm a fucking idiot," she mutters, wringing her hands. "I shouldn't have woken you up because now I know it's going to turn into this whole dramatic thing, but I couldn't just leave. Not without at least warning you that the curse isn't going to break unless we do something."

My heart pangs, and before I realize it, I'm standing too, blocking Alix from pacing and forcing her to look at me. I don't know what's going on, but all I heard was the word "leave" and now I feel just as panicked as she looks.

"Slow down, Peaches," I say, trying to keep my voice steady. "What happened with Aurelia?"

"You know who she is?" Alix asks. "She's Thorne's daughter...which I guess makes her your niece. That's kind of weird, but—"

"Get to the point," I growl.

"She told me about the curse and her mother. It was never about the king getting someone to fall in love with him. The curse is only broken when the king sacrifices the person he loves most."

My eyes widen, and then it's like a lead ball drops into the pit of my stomach. The beginnings of horror start to dawn on me, but still, I need her to be specific. "Tell me everything."

She nods, launching into a play by play of her conversation with my mother and later with Aurelia. There's a buzzing in my head as she talks, and it's all I can do to let her finish before I lose it completely and drag her outside to the portal whether she wants to go or not.

I can tell there are holes in this story—probably ones she has no way of filling with her limited knowledge of Ellender. That's a problem I can deal with later. Right now, all that matters is getting her out of here.

Without a word, I reach out and grab Alix around the waist, pulling her into my arms. She seems to think I'm trying to embrace her and she goes limp for a second, before realizing my intention.

"Daemon! Put me down, what the fuck?"

I ignore her, instead crossing the room in two strides to reach the window. It's the same window that I smashed mere hours ago and repaired with magic before falling asleep. The glass splinters again as I march toward it and launch into the sky, barely even aware of the rain as I fly down to the garden.

There's a portal to the human realm behind the Ashwater Estate. It's likely the entire reason my ancestors built the house there, and it's the one I used to use to help Fae escape from Vernallis. It won't drop Alix back in Ironhill, but it will at least send her to the same continent. Even if it didn't, I wouldn't care. The middle of the fucking Pacific Ocean would be safer for her than Vernallis.

I swoop low over the house and the rose gardens and finally land next to the stone wall at the very back of the property. We're secluded here and invisible from the house—though I'm all too aware of our proximity to Thorne.

Anger surges through me again at the mere thought.

I allowed him to come here and left Alix alone with him. I brought her straight to him without even questioning why. This is my fault, but now I'm going to fix it...at least, for her.

"Daemon, stop it," Alix barks, covering her face from the rain. "I'm trying to talk to you."

"I heard you," I growl back. "And now you're leaving."

I put her down, and she stumbles on the uneven ground. Instinctively, I throw out an arm to steady her. She looks over my shoulder toward the pond, and her eyes widen.

"What?" she blurts out. "No. That wasn't why I told you. If I wanted to just leave, I would have."

"So you want to stay and be 'sacrificed?' I thought I told you, you can use as many fucking euphemisms as you want but they all mean the same thing. He's going to kill you."

"I know," she spits, obviously growing angrier by the second. "I'm not fucking stupid."

"Good, then you're leaving. Let's go." I try to herd her toward the portal, not even taking the time to think about what this will mean. Never seeing her again feels impossible, but it feels worse to consider letting her stay for another second.

Alix plants her feet on the half-frozen ground, refusing to go another step. I could move her, but I'd have to pick her up again. I let out an angry breath. "Don't you understand that I can't let you stay here now? It wouldn't help anyway."

She raises her chin to glare at me. "No! What about the curse? Aurelia said—"

"I don't give a fuck what anyone said, I only care about you. You just told me Thorne is the one trying to hurt you, Alix. What were you expecting me to do with that information?"

"I-I don't know. I thought you'd know what to do. I told you because I think we can fix it. Aurelia thinks the curse wasn't meant to last this long and that the person Thorne loves most would have been someone her mother knew."

I shake my head. "Maybe that's true, but I have no idea who that would be."

"But we could at least try to find out."

"No." I run my hand through my hair. "I will try to find out, I promise I won't give up on this, but you're not going to be here for it. You need to go home. Now."

She glares at me, clearly plotting her next argument.

I don't understand why we're fighting about this. I don't understand how she could want to stay knowing that the danger she's in isn't abstract, it's sleeping right next door.

"You owe me," she insists, her voice cracking slightly.

My heart sinks. I forgot about her money. I glance over my shoulder toward the house. "Wait here for a second. There're hundreds of priceless things in that house, I'll go grab you—"

She makes a small fist and punches me hard in the chest. "I don't care about the money, you fucking asshole."

"You don't?"

"No!" she chokes. "I mean, you owe me more than just sending me back home without even thinking about it. Things have changed, and I—"

I close my eyes, unable to keep looking at her, and tilt my head back so the rain pours over my face. "All this changes is that I can't keep pretending it makes sense to keep you here. I should have let you leave the moment I realized you weren't Isabelle, but I was selfish. Then, when I knew there was no chance Thorne could ever truly love you—because if he did, he wouldn't have been able to just stand by and watch every time you got hurt—I should have let you go."

"Then why didn't you?" she demands.

I swallow thickly and look back at her. She's soaked, just like I am, and I can't tell whether the water pouring down her face is tears or raindrops.

I know exactly why I couldn't let her go. Because I love her, and I deluded myself into thinking I could keep her here with me.

Odessa's warning echoes in the back of my head, taunting me.

*You'll fall in love with her and you'll risk everything to keep her, but I don't know if she'll love you enough to stay.*

Well, fuck Dessa, she was wrong.

Because I did risk almost everything to keep Alix, but I'm not willing to risk her, and I won't let her stay.

I realize I'm been standing in silence for too long, letting her question hang between us. She glowers at me, clearly thinking I'm unable or unwilling to acknowledge the truth of my feelings for her. Nothing could be further from the truth, but telling her now, right before I send her away will only hurt her and I can't do that.

Alix shoves past me and marches angrily toward the house. "I'm going to get Aurelia, and you can talk to her and—"

I grab her arm and pull her back to me, dragging her into my arms. Before she can protest, I bring my hands to her cheeks and pull her face to mine.

She gasps in surprise against my mouth, but I don't let her go—exploring her lips, her taste, for the last time.

Alix relaxes into the kiss, and I walk her back away from the roses, never breaking our kiss.

At the edge of the pond, I squeeze my eyes shut tighter and pull back. "I'm sorry."

And then I shove her back into the glittering pond.

# CHAPTER
# TWENTY-FIVE

ALIX

"Excuse me, what's the date?"

The teenage gas station cashier looks at me and his expression goes from bored to shocked in the span of a second. His mouth falls open, gaping at me.

"What's the date?" I repeat.

"Uhhh, it's June 10th."

"And the year? Ugh, never mind, just hand me one of those magazines."

He grabs a magazine from the rack beside him at random and shoves it at me, never taking his eyes off me. I take it eagerly and flip it over, then let out a sigh of relief. Okay thank God—it really has been only just under a month. I know that's how long it felt like I was gone, but I've read enough fairytales that I was worried enough to double check.

"Can I use your phone?" I ask.

The cashier doesn't even bother arguing with me or asking where my cell is. Probably because I'm dressed like a renaissance fair escapee and asking what year it is. I'm giving crazy vibes, and it's always best not to argue with crazy.

The kid hands me the phone and I quickly dial.

*"911, what's your emergency?"*

"Uh, hi. My name is Alixandria Knight. I think I might be missing."

· · ·

Understandably, the police have a lot of questions. Where have I been? Am I aware of how worried my family is? Why am I dressed like a theme park princess?

Fighting my tendency to bow to authority, I refuse to answer even a single question. I remind them that I'm an adult and completely free to go off the grid if I want to. As long as I'm not under arrest, there's no reason to talk to them...but also would they please call my mom?

The police officer calls my mother—the only number I can remember off the top of my head from years of childhood conditioning, and I wait. Six hours later, I'm sitting in the rundown local police station, drinking a cup of bitter coffee and bouncing my leg against my chair.

"Get out of my way!" a familiar voice barks from somewhere down the hallway.

"Ma'am, you need to calm down," rumbles one of the officers.

"The next person who tells me to calm down is getting punched in the nose."

*Huh. I guess that's where I get it from.*

I get to my feet. "Mom?"

Dressed in a navy blue pants suit and a perfectly quaffed French twist, my mother storms down the dingy, fluorescent-lit hallway, past the police officers, clearly trying to contain her, and barges into the office where I've been waiting. She doesn't wait for me to say anything; she just launches herself across the room and envelops me in a hug. I feel every muscle in my body relax.

After a long second, she pulls back and brushes a single tear from one eye before fixing me with an angry stare. "You better have a good excuse for this."

"Excuse me?" I splutter. "That's the first thing you want to say?"

"I thought you were dead. We all thought you'd been kidnapped by some deranged lunatic. Ryan is beside himself, did you call him yet?"

"Uh...no, not yet, but I do have a good excuse."

She finally looks at me and spots my dress. She gasps. "Oh my God, it's a cult. You got taken by one of those exercise sex cults! Please tell me you did not become someone's eighth wife, Alixandria."

I pinch the bridge of my nose and close my eyes. "Let's just go home, Mom. We can talk in the car."

"I hope you know I am not prepared to listen to any nonsense about worshiping aliens or secret bunkers."

"Yup, sure, I got it."

. . .

THE PORTAL DROPPED ME SOMEWHERE NEAR THE BORDER TO New York and it takes several hours for my mom to drive us back to her house in Philly. She seems to take it as a given that her house is where I want to go, and I almost argue with her until she mentions that Nana is still staying with her.

"Of course we didn't have time to find her a retirement home after we realized you'd gone missing."

My heart skips an excited beat. I've been dying to talk to Nana since the moment I arrived in Ellender, so at least that's something to look forward to. A very small something by comparison to everything else I'm feeling.

Just like when I arrived in Ellender, being back doesn't feel quite real. I'm caught somewhere between shock and devastation.

It feels like when you accidentally stub your toe or slam your thumb in the car door and there's a tiny fraction of a second when you don't feel it yet but you know the pain is coming. I'm stuck in that fraction of a moment, when I've been hit but the pain hasn't struck yet, and I know that no matter how I brace myself and wish it wouldn't hurt, it will. And the pain will be a thousand times worse for having been delayed.

"So, are you going to tell me what happened or leave me in suspense?"

"It wasn't a cult," I grumble.

"That's hardly helpful, Alixandria. Now I'm imagining the worst possible scenarios. You weren't grabbed by one of those prostitution rings, were you?"

I look sideways at her, furrowing my brow with annoyance. "If I was, does it occur to you that maybe I wouldn't want to be put on trial about it within hours of escaping?"

She blinks at me, the nuance of victimology obviously lost on her. "So, you were taken?"

I sigh and put my head in my hands. *Jesus fucking Christ.*

Even though I had hours in the police station to think about it, I hadn't decided if I would tell my mom the truth. Five minutes in the car with her, though, and I know for sure that I can't tell her. She won't believe me, and she'll probably drive me straight to the nearest hospital for a brain scan. *Yeah, no thanks.*

"I caught Ryan cheating on me with my best friend," I say, my face still covered by my palms. "I had no idea it was going on, but in retrospect, I realize that definitely wasn't the first time. So I kind of lost it, okay? I just needed to get away for a while. I'm sorry I didn't call and that you worried, I didn't mean to upset you."

I brace myself for an onslaught of judgment or maybe a lecture about how marriage is supposed to be forever and I need to be more forgiving. Instead, she lets out a harsh breath. "Shit."

I glance up, startled. My mother doesn't swear, so even that small exclamation is noteworthy coming from her. "What?"

She takes one hand off the wheel and runs it over her face without even bothering to care that she's smudging her makeup. "Ryan is at the house."

"Excuse me?"

"Well, you were missing! And he's your husband, it just seemed to make sense to have everyone together in case we got news." She reaches into the center console and fishes around for her phone. "Look, it's no problem. I'll handle it. Let me call Kevin now, and maybe—"

I reach out and put a hand on her arm, stopping her from dialing my stepfather's number while she's driving and inevitably veering into oncoming traffic. "Mom, stop. It's okay."

She blinks at me. "Oh, Alixandria. Are you sure?"

I'm strangely touched by this very out of character show of support —even if it is coming at the eleventh hour. "Yes. I have a lot to say to Ryan. I might as well get it over with."

When we step into the house, there's an immediate flurry of activity.

Everyone must know that I was found because they don't seem surprised that I'm back, but there's still an explosion of noise. I turn my head, slightly overwhelmed. My husband is here along with mom's husband Kevin. My gaze darts over Ryan for one uncomfortable second, and then finally I find whom I'm searching for.

Nana is sitting on the couch in the living room, but jumps up just like everyone else when I walk in. She's dressed simply in a blue sweater and slacks with her long hair pulled back in a low ponytail. My light eyes lock on her dark ones. Her gaze darts pointedly down at my dress and the corner of her mouth ticks up in a half smile and in a split second I know that she knows exactly where I've been.

"Baby, oh my God!" Ryan yells, pulling my attention away from Nana as he strides purposefully toward me.

My stomach churns, and I step back, putting obvious space between us. Ryan stops short, several feet from me. In that second, I feel a palpable shift in the room, as my family immediately turn from relieved to suspicious.

"Ryan, what are you doing here?" I ask, calmly.

He blinks at me, confused. "I—Well, you were gone. I was worried about you, what happened?"

I take a deep breath, closing my eyes for a second.

In my mind's eye, I can see a version of how this conversation could go. It's the way it would have gone if I'd stayed to fight that day I walked in on him and Jenna.

I'll demand an explanation and he won't have one. He'll tell me that the problems in our marriage are because I don't give him enough attention and because he's sick of pulling all the weight. I'll point out that I do everything around the house even before losing my job, and he'll throw the job issue back in my face. I'll end up screaming, trying to get him to care at all about how he's hurting me, and he'll just fixate on my shortcomings. Eventually I'll lose track of what the argument is about and walk away, and that's how he'll avoid ever having to explain his cheating or take accountability for anything. Later, I'll feel guilty for losing my temper and end up being the one to apologize.

I've played this cycle out so many times with various different fights, it's like a play where I know my lines and choreography by heart.

Or, this time, it doesn't have to be like that.

It doesn't have to be a fight or a back and forth about what he did. I don't have to keep begging for a shred of attention, or wasting my energy on someone who can't and won't reciprocate. I can just say my piece and leave. "Do you want to step outside with me for a moment?"

Ryan looks even more confused, but he follows me outside. Behind me, I can see my mom wringing her hands—probably worried that we're about to embarrass her in front of her neighbors by fighting in the lawn. But miraculously she doesn't say anything.

We step outside onto the front walk and for a moment I just look up at the sky, enjoying the midafternoon sun.

Ryan tries to step toward me again, arms outstretched. "Alix—"

Once again, a wave of nausea passes over me. I put a hand up to stop him "Don't touch me. I don't feel well."

He furrows his brow, but stops in his tracks. His gaze rakes over me. "What are you wearing?"

I glance at my dress. "Don't worry about it."

His eyes narrow. "Well, what the fuck, Alix? Where have you been?"

I shake my head. "It doesn't matter. I don't want you here. You should go home."

"C'mon, baby, don't be like that. I came all this way because I was worried about you. When we talked on the phone..."

"You mean when I told you I wanted a divorce and you tried to trap me into financial abuse?"

He grins nervously. "I don't remember it like that."

"Oh? How do you remember me reacting to you cheating on me with my best friend?"

He shoves his hands in his pockets and rocks back and forth on his heels. "Alix, look. It was a mistake, okay? But what you did is so much worse. Everyone thought you were dead. Do you realize how fucked up and manipulative that is? If you wanted attention, you didn't have to go this far to get it."

I close my eyes again. "I'm not going to fight with you. It's over. I told you I wanted a divorce and I left. I don't have to justify my time to you anymore, and you being here right now is not okay."

"Is this about another guy?"

I can't help but bark a laugh. The hypocrisy is staggering. "No, it's not. It's about me. I'm unhappy and I'm not willing to settle for '*just okay*' anymore. I want to be with someone who supports my dreams and isn't annoyed by the things I like, and who doesn't feel burdened by being my partner."

"Oh, so it's all my fault now? You were this perfect little wife and I'm the bad guy?"

I shake my head. "I definitely wasn't perfect, but I'm sick of being the only one who ever worries about how my behavior affects the people around me. I'm sick of constantly apologizing and never getting any respect back."

"You want me to say I'm sorry? Fine, I'm sorry you're so unhappy and that you don't seem to want to even try to work on it."

I step back. "Okay, I'm really done here now. I deserve to be happy, and as much as it kills me to say so because I have totally fantasized about cutting your fucking arms off, you deserve to be happy too."

He reels back. "My arms? What? That's fucking sick Alix, you're—"

I turn around and walk the two steps back up to the door, before glancing over my shoulder at him. "Oh, and can you give my best to Jenna please? Tell her I wish you both all the happiness you deserve."

"We're not..." He frowns and shoves his hands deeper into his pockets. "We're not together anymore. It didn't work out."

I laugh for real this time. "I guess she realized we're both too good for you. Have a nice life, Ryan."

With that, I walk inside the house and close the door behind me with a snap. I turn to lean against it and find my entire family still standing in the living room almost exactly where I left them.

"Um, Ryan had to go," I mutter.

"Are you okay?" my mother asks.

I open my mouth but nothing comes out. A huge lump bubbles up in my throat, and I try to swallow it, unfamiliar with the feeling.

Am I okay? No, I am not fucking okay, but it has nothing to do with Ryan or Jenna. When I realized my marriage was over, I was angry, but not about losing my husband. It was never about him; it was me. I was mourning for the loss of my life and the plans I'd made.

Now, I don't feel like that. There's an acute sense of loss, of emptiness in my chest. Like something—or, someone—is missing.

My eyes and nose burn, and there's a ringing in my ears.

And suddenly it all hits me. Everything is over and worst of all I'll never see Daemon again.

I look at Nana, silently begging for help—with what, I'm not even sure. She pushes past my mom to reach me. Without a word, she throws her arms around me and doesn't let go.

And finally, for the first time in twenty years, I sob.

# CHAPTER
# TWENTY-SIX

ALIX

That night, I sleep in my childhood bedroom surrounded by neon-blue and lime-green bedding, *Pottery Barn* artwork, and fifteen-year-old TV posters.

There's a voice in the back of my head that tells me it should be comforting to be here, but the reality is that I was never comfortable in this room. I'm not sure I've ever been completely comfortable anywhere.

I'm not surprised when I wake up in the middle of the night screaming from a nightmare. I suck in steadying breaths, but can't seem to make my heartbeat slow down. Still shaking, I swing my legs over the side of the bed and tiptoe out into the hall.

The house is asleep, but I'm used to walking around in the dark by now. I tiptoe down the hall to the kitchen, and stop when I see the glow of a light on.

Nana is sitting on a stool at the kitchen counter, an enormous mug of tea in one hand. She looks up when I enter and smiles. "Good morning."

I glance at the dark windows. "It's not morning."

She shrugs. "I've never cared much for timekeeping anyway. Morning can be whenever you wake up. Do you want some coffee?"

I sit in one of the island stools across from her. "Um...tea, maybe?"

"Sure."

She gets up and crosses the kitchen to mom's Keurig and pops in one of the single use packets. I watch her in a daze. I don't even know what to say. There's so many questions I have, so much I'm bursting to talk about, but I can't think how to begin.

"How did you get the idea for Ellender?"

Nana hands me a scalding hot mug of tea and sits. She smiles. "I like to say it was a dream. I've been asked that so many times over the years and I always knew exactly how to answer. Until recently, as I'm sure you know."

"Yes, I saw. What happened at the signing?"

She shrugs. "I think when you've been telling the same lie for so long that you start to believe it yourself, sometimes the truth has to force itself out, even at the worst possible time."

I take a tiny sip of my tea and it scalds my tongue. "So you were lying, then. It wasn't a dream?"

She looks down her nose at me. "Why don't we be frank with each other, Ali. You're not a kid anymore, we don't need to beat around the bush."

I take a calming breath. "Okay, fine. How did you first find Ellender?"

She leans back on her stool, settling in. "I lived in Ironhill my entire life. When I was growing up it was by no means a wealthy area, but the mining industry was thriving and the town was comfortable. It was also a superstitious area, and everyone knew and believed every legend about the creatures that would come out of the woods or lived in the mountains.

"My father—your great grandfather—worked in the mines, as did pretty much all the men in the area. He was a foreman, and he was always trying to invent ways to make work faster and easier for his crew.

"When I was about twenty, I was still living at home. I wanted to go to college but it wasn't as common as it is now. It would have been easier and more expected for me to take some typing classes and work as a secretary for a while before ultimately getting married. I'd known Gerald —your grandpa—my entire life and he'd asked me to marry him several times. I knew that was the simplest path forward, especially if I wanted to move out of my parents' house."

"So what did you do?"

"Nothing." She sighs. "I didn't know what to do with my life so I didn't do anything at all. I stayed in the same town with all the same people acting as if I could stay frozen in time forever. I was stuck."

I take another sip of my scalding tea. I wish I didn't empathize so much with what she's saying—how it's easy to stay in a life that's just okay because it's so much harder to figure out where to go next.

"One evening, my father didn't come home from the mine. Our house wasn't far, so I took his truck and drove there to make sure he was alright. In retrospect, that was stupid. I could have called someone for help, but at the time it felt like the right thing to do. I went down to the mines, and I figured I'd just walk a few feet past the entrance—just to see if there were still lanterns lit or sounds coming from inside."

"And you found the gate?" I finish for her.

"Yes. Before I knew what was happening, I'd arrived in another world entirely."

"What palace were you at?" I ask, unable to contain my questions. "Summer or winter?"

"I don't know. Summer, probably, as that's what time of year it was. In any case, I quickly discovered that my father had also fallen into this other world and he'd been captured by the faerie king. I met King Thorne and offered to take my father's place."

"Why would you do that?" I burst out. "Why not try to help him another way, or—"

"I wanted to," she cuts me off. "I wanted to help my father of course, but I was also enchanted by the land I'd just found. I'd discovered that magic was real, and there was this impossibly handsome king willing to let me live in his castle. Compared with my life, it seemed like a fantasy come true."

"Oh. Yeah, I guess that makes sense."

"Wasn't it the same for you? When you discover that this magical place exists, how could you not want to stay?"

"Um, not exactly. I took a little longer to warm up to it, but finish the story, we'll get to mine later."

She smiles and leans forward against the kitchen island. I could swear there's something light in her posture. Like maybe talking about this after so long is lifting a weight of secrecy that she's been living with for sixty years.

"Well, for a while, I was in heaven. I'd never experienced living in a place so nice. There were servants and I wasn't expected to do anything at all. Sleeping during the day was odd and the king was generally cold to me, but he gave me a kitten to keep me company. A little loneliness didn't seem like a bad trade for the ability to spend all my time in the library."

Immediately, the image of the beautiful library pops into my mind, except I can't focus on it since she mentioned the kitten. "Oh my God, Sushi!"

She smiles. "What about him?"

My face falls. "I left him at the palace with Odessa. Oh my God, how—"

"Shhhh," she soothes. "That cat came from Ellender."

I narrow my eyes. "Wait, are you serious?"

"Very. Of course I had to keep renaming him every couple of decades to make it less strange that I had a sixty-year-old cat. *Sushi* was originally called *Pooka* because he had this magical ability to always turn up right where I needed him. I'm sure he'll make his way back to me eventually."

I stare at her, eyes wide, my head spinning. Part of me thinks she's fucking with me, but of course, this entire conversation is unbelievable. What's one more crazy thing to add to the list? "Er, right...okay, I guess we'll come back to that. So at first you were happy at the palace, but when did things start to go wrong?"

She sighs and pushes a tendril of gray hair out of her face. "Eventually, I got bored and started to become more curious about the palace and the king. What was this mysterious curse that made them sleep all day? Why wasn't I allowed to enter the north wing of the castle? What did King Thorne want from me?"

"And did you find out?" I ask, leaning forward as my heartbeat picks up.

"Yes. The king and I had been eating dinner together for some time. I'd started to know him a bit better, but he was still an enigma in most ways. That's why it was such a surprise to me when he announced our wedding to the court."

"Wait, he didn't ask you?"

She shakes her head. "No...I didn't know what to make of it. I was sure we'd had a misunderstanding. In some ways, I wasn't opposed to it. I'd be a queen, and get to live the same elegant life I'd been living for the last three months."

"But you didn't love him?"

She shakes her head. "I didn't know him well enough to love him; he was always distant. He'd shower me with gifts, but not attention. Everything felt forced, like a performance for the court."

I nod. I know exactly what she's talking about. But I also know that this revelation is huge. If Nana never loved King Thorne, she could have never broken the curse anyway. The king was wrong.

I bite my lip. "Then what?"

"I didn't want to stay and get married to someone I barely knew so I made up a story. I told him my father had been chronically sick my entire life and that he only had a few months left. I said I wanted to go home to see him before he died and that I'd come back soon for the wedding." She shakes her head. "It wasn't a very good story. I don't know why he believed me—"

"Because the king is a narcissist," I fill in. "He assumes everyone loves him. Even if you had years of resentments and a thousand reasons to hate him, he'll assume the crumbs he feeds you will be enough to earn undying loyalty."

She frowns, thinking. "I suppose that's right. I hadn't thought about it like that."

"I've seen it," I grumble. "Most people would assume that throwing an innocent man in prison for ninety years would make him hate you, but Thorne thought he should be grateful to have been let out."

Nana shrugs. "You'd have to elaborate on that, I think, but I know what you mean generally and yes, I think you're right. The king truly believed I would come back, and maybe he was right too. I admit I was conflicted...I didn't want to get married but I didn't want to leave Ellender either. I thought I might get more clarity back home. I could see if I missed the place, you know?"

I nod. "I get it."

"Anyway, he gave me an enchanted necklace." She nods at the necklace around my throat. "He had a ball and gave me the gift in front of everyone, then promised to take me to the portal the following day since it was nearing dawn. I went to bed as usual, but overnight I grew curious."

"Curious how?"

"I realized that if I was really going to be able to decide if I wanted to come back for the wedding after my *trip to see my father*," she makes air quotes with her fingers. "I'd have to know everything. I was going to get married. I couldn't still have questions about what was truly going on in the castle. So later that night—or rather, day—I ventured out of my room to see what was so secret. I snuck into the king's private wing, and there I discovered this...room."

"What, does he have a personal brothel back there?" I scoff, rolling my eyes.

She grimaces, a look of old horror passing over her face. "No... worse."

I sit up straighter. "What's in there?"

"It's a crypt, I suppose you'd call it. A display room for the bodies of all the wives who'd come before me. They're kept in cases on the wall, like butterflies pinned behind glass."

"Oh my God..." I breathe, unable to find the right words to express my horror. "Holy shit. I can't even picture that, why—"

"Don't try and picture it, Ali." She shakes her head, her expression full of long repressed horror. "In any case, I ran out of there as fast as I could. I must have screamed when I saw all the bodies. I don't remember, but something woke the king. He ran after me and burst through the door to his wing just after I'd made it back out into the hall.

"He hadn't seen me in the room with the bodies, but he had to know I was snooping around, and now I knew why he was so furious about anyone going in there. I tried to explain what I was doing, but it was daylight and he was...different. Monstrous. It was like no matter what I did, I couldn't reason with him or make him understand me. He'd turned into—"

"—a beast," I finish for her.

"Exactly. So I ran. I made it down the entrance hall, but then he inevitably caught up with me. I grabbed the sword from one of those big suits of armor he's got and stabbed him with it."

"Nana!" I exclaim, startled. "Holy shit."

She laughs lightly but without humor. "It was the closest thing, and it did seem to slow him down."

"I didn't see any suits of armor," I muse.

"Maybe he got rid of them after I left. I would have. Anyway, I ran all the way out of the castle. It helped that it was finally light out and I could see where I was going. I took my horse and rode as fast as I could back to the portal where I'd arrived, but I was sure that the king would follow me. In my panic to keep him from finding me, I set fire to the mine and destroyed the portal."

I gape at her, startled by not only this revelation but the possible meaning behind everything else that happened since.

"So you caused the fire in Ironhill."

She nods, looking pained. "I didn't know what would happen—that it would take jobs from thousands of people or destroy the town. I wasn't thinking about any of that, but even if I was, I can't say I wouldn't do it again."

Shocked, I can only gape at her.

This isn't exactly the story I was imagining. I'd thought Nana's memories of Ellender would be more like the happy fairytale she wrote in *A Kingdom of Thorns.*

"So how did you come to write the book?" I ask.

She laughs again, with a real smile this time. "After I returned, I was half certain that none of it had been real. I had the necklace, but it took years before I knew if it worked. It was easy to convince myself I was going insane. I wrote the book to keep a record of it. Like a narrative journal.

"Quite a few years later after I was already married with a baby, my life wasn't turning out the way I wanted. I don't think it's a secret that your grandfather and I had a difficult marriage. I had the idea to stash away extra money—just in case I ever wanted to leave Ironhill. I sent the book to a publisher, not really expecting to hear back, but I did almost immediately. They loved it, they just had one request—that I give the story a happily ever after."

I realize I'm leaning forward, hanging on to her every word. "But why did you never leave Ironhill, even after you made all that money and the town was destroyed?"

"I don't know. I just felt...stuck there. Like I had to stay and bear witness to the destruction that I'd caused." She frowns, then shakes her head. "It's a good thing I did, though, or you'd never have been there. Was your experience at least better than mine?"

I heave a sigh. "I think I will take some coffee now. Maybe with some whiskey, if mom has any lying around."

Nana smiles. "I think I can make that happen."

IT TAKES A SURPRISINGLY SHORT AMOUNT OF TIME TO explain to Nana everything I've been through for the last month. She smiles at the mention of Odessa and Beatrix, but doesn't interrupt me until I get to the part about meeting Aurelia and Daemon shoving me back through the portal.

"So he loves you," she says, matter-of-factly. "I suppose that's something. It means not all is lost."

I blink at her, startled. "No, he doesn't. That's kind of the whole point, the king doesn't love me. We don't know who he loves."

"Not the king, dummy." She reaches across the counter and gives me a playful smack on the side of the head. "The man who was supposed to guard you."

"Uh, no. I don't think he does either." I feel my face flush. "And anyway, is that what we should be focusing on?"

"What else is there to focus on? That's all that matters."

My chest squeezes. I wish that were true, but nothing is ever that simple.

"That's nice, Nana, but there are real problems here. The curse isn't broken, and Thorne has tried quite a few times before. According to you, he's got an entire shrine of attempts to break the curse, and nothing has changed."

"But now you know the truth of how the curse works, right? That changes things."

I sigh. "That's what I said too, but Daemon didn't think so."

She purses her lips and steeples her fingers in front of her, elbows on the counter. "Tell me how the curse goes again?"

I sigh and brush my hair back from my face. "The curse will only break when the King of Vernallis admits he is powerless and sacrifices whomever he loves most. But we have no idea who that is. It's obviously not me—or you, I guess."

She purses her lips. "Hmm. I don't know, Ali. I wish I could give you some wisdom right now, but in my experience, men like Thorne never love anyone more than they love themselves."

"Yeah," I mutter glumly. "That's pretty much what Daemon said too."

I sit in depressed silence for a long second, feeling her eyes on me.

"If you could break the curse tomorrow, would you go back to Ellender?"

"Yes."

"What if it never broke?"

I pause. That's harder to answer. "I don't know. Despite everything, I loved it there—especially whenever I got to see what was outside the castle. I made friends I'd want to spend every day with, but..."

"But what?"

"But I wouldn't be happy without Daemon, and if the curse isn't broken, he wouldn't really be there."

"Then you should go back," she says flatly.

"What? But he told me to leave."

"Yeah, so?" She rolls her eyes. "Men say a lot of things they don't mean, especially when it comes to protecting women they love."

I close my eyes. She keeps saying that—the L word—as if it's set in stone. But it isn't. We never said that to each other.

Except, maybe we kind of did. Not in so many words, but...

*I'll die before I let anyone hurt you.*

*I can't stop thinking about you.*

*You're mine.*

"Ali?" Nana interrupts the explosion of realization going on in my mind.

I shake my head. I don't know how to explain to her the shift going on in the back of my head, like some pieces are falling into place, and yet so many more lay scattered on the ground, face down and impossible to fit into place.

"Maybe if I knew what to do," I muse, more to myself than to Nana. "If I had some way to fix things, I'd have to go help Daemon, but I don't know the answer. The king doesn't love anyone enough to sacrifice them. The only person he loves is himself."

And then, in a sudden blinding second, I get it. The missing puzzle pieces right themselves in my brain and fly into place, showing the entire picture so clearly that I can't believe it took me this long to understand. "Oh my God," I blurt out, unable to think of a single more eloquent thing to say.

Smiling slightly, Nana stands from her chair and pats the counter in front of me with the palm of her hand to get my attention. I look up at her with wide eyes, still reeling from my revelation. "I'm going to leave you to think," she says. "I'm sure you have plans to make and not a lot of time to make them."

I nod, my mind still reeling. "Thanks, Nana."

"Oh, and Ali?" she says, already moving toward the hall. "Even if you don't come up with the perfect plan overnight, don't cut yourself off at the knees. Take it from someone who dreamed her entire life about a happily ever after and never really found one. Love and family are the only things that matter. Everything else is temporary."

BY THE TIME I'M FINISHED TALKING WITH NANA, THE SUN IS coming up for real. For once, the sight of pink in the dark sky doesn't mean the end of something, but the beginning.

I don't know whether I'm excited or delusional, but I feel almost giddy as I dash back to my room to shower and get dressed.

The only things here are the rejects from my high school wardrobe that never made it out when I left for college and ultimately got married. I try pulling on a pair of ripped skinny jeans and can barely get them over my thighs. The PINK leggings are somehow worse, and stretched so thin over my ass I'm sure it's worse than the wet T-shirt I wore in Ellender. I sigh and march down the hall to my mom's room.

Mom's clothes aren't my style any more than the rejects from the early 2000s, but they at least fit and I have to admit that her *Lululemon* workout leggings are pretty damn comfortable compared with the stockings Odessa always gave me to wear.

When I'm dressed, I borrow some cash and the car keys from my mother and drive down to the twenty-four-hour Walmart, stopping only once on the way for coffee. If things go well, I won't get to drink ice coffee with aspartame syrup and whipped cream anymore, so I might as well go all out now.

At Walmart I grab a cart and make a beeline for the hardware aisles.

In less than twenty minutes, I think I've got everything I need, plus a huge canvas backpack to hold it all in. I look like I'm about to go backpacking across the world—which I guess isn't the worst analogy ever.

I go back to mom's house long enough to drop off the car and grab my Ellender dress and shoes. To my immense relief, Nana is the only one there.

"Kevin drove your mother to work," she says when I walk in. "I told her you took the car because I asked you to pick up my prescription."

"Do you need a prescription picked up?"

"No. I don't have any, but your mother never asks questions if I sound elderly. Honestly, I think that her going to 'work' is code for 'touring retirement communities.' She didn't even complain that you took her car. Clearly, she's up to something."

I shake my head. "Do you need me to stay for a couple of days and help you talk Mom out of buying you a house on Cape Cod or wherever?"

Nana shakes her head. "Don't worry about me. I can handle my own daughter, Ali."

"She's going to sell your house."

"Let her." Nana scoffs. "I think I'm finally going to do something with all that money I've been holding on to. Maybe I'll travel. Who knows, I might come visit you. Christmas might be fun in Ellender. Assuming you're not all cursed, obviously."

"Wait, what? Come visit?"

She smiles mischievously. "I think you're forgetting that it doesn't have to be only one world or the other. You could always come visit us, and I could go there."

That actually hadn't occurred to me. It feels like the choice is here or Ellender, but could it really be both?

"But Nana," I begin. "Are you sure, I mean traveling like that is stressful and maybe Mom isn't totally crazy to be thinking about retirement..."

"Pfft," she interrupts me with a scoff. "Please. I have another three or four decades coming to me. If anyone should retire, it's your mother."

I raise an eyebrow. "Nana, not to be morbid, but...are you sure? You're in your eighties."

She smiles at me conspiratorially. "I wore that necklace for years, Ali. How do you think I look so good for my age? Don't tell your mother, but I think she's older than I am now by a few years, at least."

My jaw drops and I have to force myself to close it again. I take a sip of my nearly cold coffee. "Yeah, you're right. We can absolutely never tell her that."

NANA PROMISES TO EXPLAIN MY ABSENCE TO MY MOTHER, and honestly, I'm just relieved that I don't have to do it. I have no idea what she's going to say, but better her than me.

Then with one last hug and a promise to visit, I take my backpack and walk out the door, ready to return to the portal.

For once in my life, I'm not worrying about what anyone else thinks. I'm doing this for me—and maybe, for the chance of happily ever after.

# CHAPTER
# TWENTY-SEVEN

DAEMON

"How could you let this happen?" Thorne roars, swiping everything off the dining table with one arm. "Do you have any fucking idea what you've done?"

"Nothing? You knew someone was trying to hurt Isabelle."

"And you were supposed to fucking watch her," he rages.

"What did you want me to do, never sleep for an entire month? Or maybe I could have chained her to the wall to prevent her going outside for some air."

He bares his teeth at me, looking more like an animal than a man.

I don't know what the fuck he's so angry about. As far as he knows, Isabelle is dead. Which is exactly what he wanted.

It's so obvious to me now that it was him all along behind the attacks on Alix. Probably he made me guard her because after the train incident, he realized he could take out two birds with one stone, and I might die too—either protecting her, or by accident in whatever new catastrophe he'd set up.

"You failed to protect her until the wedding," he carries on, completely unaware of the irony in his rage. "I should send you back to Dyaspora for this!"

"Do it."

He looks at me, startled enough to shake the rage off his face. "What did you say?"

"I said fucking do it. I don't care anymore."

Thorne evidently has no idea what to say to that because he just looks at me. Any other time, I'd enjoy striking him speechless, but not now. I won't ever enjoy anything again.

I sigh and step back, turning around to leave. "If you decide to send me back, let me know. Otherwise, I'll be in the barracks until the rose moon."

Apparently Thorne doesn't feel like bothering to send me back to Dyaspora, because no one comes to find me for an entire twenty-four hours.

I find Kastian and explain everything to him, knowing he'll tell the others. Then, as promised, I return to the barracks and don't return. Even during the cursed time, I don't move from my bed. Evidently, grief is also an instinctual emotion.

Before I sent her away, I was almost sure that Alix was my soul-bond. Now, I'm positive. Being without her is physically painful, like I cut off my own right arm and let the wounds fester.

*Ironic.*

I can't even force myself to care about the curse. I know I should be using the information that Alix got from Aurelia to find the answer. I should care that there are only hours left before I'll lose all my free will, but I can't bring myself to care about anything. I underestimated how painful it would be to break a soul-bond. Or maybe I just didn't want to think about it, because if I'd known I'd end up in agony I might not have gone through with it.

The only consolation is that males almost always form the bond first, and Alix is human, so it's likely she won't be in as much pain—if any at all. I have to hold onto that thought because otherwise the drive to protect her from that pain wars with the instinct to protect her by staying away, and I feel as if I'm finally losing my mind for real.

"Daemon!"

I barely look up at the sound of Kastian's voice or the many footsteps behind me.

"Come on, Ashwater. Get up," Jett says, with a forced note in his usual humorous tone.

"Fuck off," I mutter.

I know I sound juvenile, but they don't understand. None of them have ever found their soul-bond, let alone lost them. They can't realize how painful this is.

"Daemon, seriously." I feel the end of my bed dip as Odessa sits. "Don't you think you should at least say goodbye?"

"To whom?" I growl.

"To us, for one," she snaps, clearly unable to keep her sympathetic tone in place even at such a dire moment. "And what about your mother?"

I want to say "what about her" but that sounds too juvenile even for my mood. Instead, I roll over and finally look at them all. "I said goodbye when we left Storia. There's nothing else to say."

Kastian, Jett, and Fox stand over me like sentries, while Odessa is perched on the far end of the bed. I notice she's wearing a traveling cloak, but I can't find it in me to ask why.

"It's chaos in the palace," Kastian says, crossing his arms over his broad chest.

"That's not unexpected," I grumble. "Even the dumbest courtiers must have realized that if Isabelle is gone and the curse hasn't broken, there's no time left to find a solution. They put their faith in a selfish asshole who didn't care about them a hundred years ago and certainly doesn't now."

"Exactly," Dessa says. "They're scared. They need someone to take control and lead them."

I lie there for a long second, uncomprehending. Then finally I realize what they're getting at. "You can't seriously expect me to go up there."

"People listen to you," Jett says.

"No, they don't. Not anymore. I've been gone for years and since I've been back, I've barely interacted with the court."

"It doesn't matter," Dessa insists. "Everyone remembers how it was before you went to Dyaspora, and most remember your father."

"I'm not him," I growl. "Any more than Thorne is. He's the fucking king, go tell him to pull his head out of his ass."

"Impossible," Kastian growls. "He's been in a rage as long as you've been lying here, depressed."

I narrow my eyes at Kastian. "You want someone to play king? You do it. You have more right than me to wear a crown and you won't be effectively dead in thirty-six hours."

Fox and Jett look sideways at Kastian, obviously distracted by my near revelation.

"Why do you have a right to the crown of Vernallis?" Jett asks.

"I don't," Kastian snaps. "I'm from Hydratta, you know that."

"Why don't you tell them who you were in Hydratta?"

Kas glares at me. "If you weren't so pathetic right now, I'd hit you."

"Do it," I sigh, lying down. "I don't care anyway."

There's another long silence. None of them seem to know what to say. I hope they'll just leave.

"I keep trying to think of what the sorceress must have been thinking," Dessa says, as if continuing a conversation we'd already been having.

"What do you mean?" Kas asks.

"Don't you think she had someone in mind when she cast the curse? At first I thought it would be Aurelia, but why would she want to kill her own daughter? It must be someone else."

"If she did, she was wrong," I say bitterly, my back still to the group. "Thorne doesn't love anyone except himself."

"There must be someone. A friend? Maybe a mentor?"

"There's no one!" I bark, my voice ringing around the room.

"Don't fucking yell at her," Kastian growls under his breath.

Odessa glances at him, clearly startled. I don't understand either. Odessa is my sister, not his. What the hell does he care if I offended her? Anyway, I thought they didn't get along.

Regardless, now I feel like an asshole. I shoot Dessa an apologetic glance. "Sorry. I just mean I've thought about this and there's no one. I'm the only family he has. If I thought killing myself would help anything, I would, but he fucking hates me."

"Don't even say that," Dessa hisses. "You can always get Alix back. She's not dead, and if you don't die, then things could still work out."

I start to try and deny that Alix is the reason I'm such a mess, but what's the point anymore? It doesn't matter who she is or who she was pretending to be; she's gone and despite what Odessa says, I don't think I'll ever get her back.

I close my eyes and tip my head back against the wall with a thump. "I agree with Aurelia that the sorceress had someone in mind when she cast the curse, but I have no way of knowing who that is. We're no better off than we ever were, so if you all don't mind, I'd like to spend my last hours in peace." *Or at least as much in peace as is possible when it feels like a thousand knives are piercing my chest over and over.*

"No," Kastian grumbles.

I glare at him. "No?"

"No. You're in charge, mate. We follow you, not just because we owe you our lives but because you're a good leader. Usually. But I'm not signing on for this. You're fucking up, and we're not going to just watch it happen. You need to pull your shit together and get up, or I'll drag you out of here."

"I'll help," Jett says, raising a hand behind Kastian's back.

"I don't need help," Fox grumbles. "I could drag all of you across this fucking continent with one hand."

I glare at my friends, torn between anger that they're fighting with me and feeling emotional that they care.

"What are you expecting me to do?" I mutter. "Getting up won't miraculously make it so I know who Thorne needs to kill."

There's a silence, where clearly everyone is thinking. Gloom begins to descend over me again, a hopelessness that is much more difficult to stomach than any anger.

"What does Thorne keep in his stupid tower?" Odessa asks after some heavy pondering.

I shrug. "I dunno, why?"

"We should go search it. It can't hurt. Maybe he has something up there that would point to who he cares about."

"He doesn't let anyone up there," I grumble.

"Yeah, but he's also pretty preoccupied right now," Jett says with the ghost of a smile. "Come upstairs, you'll see what I mean."

I look around at all of them once more. They're not going to leave me alone, are they? And anyway, with all of them here I feel slightly less horrible. Like the knives in my chest are only half as sharp.

Running my fingers through my hair, I sigh and get up. "Fine. Let's go."

I'm surrounded by four wide grins and I can't even pretend to find that annoying. Instead, I look down at the floor, feigning indifference.

"You lead the way, Ashwater," Jett says happily. "We're right behind you."

MY HEAD POUNDS AND MY CHEST STILL FEELS LIKE IT'S going to crack open as I march upstairs. Stepping into the entrance hall, my jaw drops.

*Fucking hell.*

Jett wasn't exaggerating, this place is a goddamn disaster.

The entrance hall is in shambles just like the day after the curse took over the court. Windows and statues are smashed, there's ink and food and other things I don't want to consider smeared on the walls. Smoke fills my nose and the noise is deafening. People are yelling outside, on the upper levels, and down the long echoing corridors.

As we stand frozen in the doorway to the staircase, shattering glass pierces the air and I duck instinctively, shielding my face. "What the fuck is going on?"

No one else looks surprised—though, I suppose they wouldn't. I'm the only one who's been in hiding for the last day and a half and therefore didn't realize the extent to which the court has lost their minds.

"They're punishing the king," Kastian says without inflection. "Before the curse takes hold they want him to know what they think of him."

I grimace. In a way, I understand that and I hardly blame them, but—

A loud smash, like stone against stone rattles the floor and I stiffen. "Let's get out of here before we get crushed."

With sounds of agreement, my friends follow me across the entrance hall to the wide sweeping marble staircase. I jog up a few steps, stopping only when I hear Thorne's voice echoing from the throne room.

"Stop them!" He's shouting at someone. "Where are all the soldiers? Find me Foulo!"

The corner of my mouth ticks up in a smile. At least we know he won't be in his chambers while we try to search it.

As long as I can remember Thorne has kept his tower private from outsiders. Even back when King Florian was alive and Thorne was merely the heir, no one entered. I never thought much of it—he's a controlling asshole and keeping people out of his space is the sort of thing he'd do. But now, as we dash up the half-ruined stairs amidst shouts and screaming, my heart pounds with anticipation. *What is he hiding in there?*

We march down the hall that leads to Thorne's tower. Ahead, a group of five or six red-jacketed soldiers guard the door. I stop mid-stride and curse under my breath. I guess Thorne didn't leave his precious tower unguarded after all.

"What do you want to do?" Kas mutters behind me.

"Kill them," Fox says without inflection.

I ignore them, not wasting my time explaining myself.

"Hey!" I step away from my friends and shout to get the soldier's attention, raising a hand as I stride closer. "Get out of the way."

The nearest guard looks at me nervously, while the one slightly behind him stiffens, readying for a fight.

"We were told to guard the king's quarters." the nearer guard mutters.

"Told by who?" I snap. "I never ordered you to do that."

"The orders came from me," a familiar snide voice sounds from the back of the group.

I blink, peering between them. Foulo is shorter than then most Fae and wasn't immediately visible, but the guards part to let him through and he steps in front of me, a glint of hatred in his eyes.

"Oh, it's you," I say, forcing my tone to remain casual.

"I'm giving the orders now." He spits. "I hear you've been sniveling and crying in your bed ever since the king took your job away."

I don't react, keeping my face neutral—almost friendly. "You're right, Foulo. I have been feeling off since finding out that the king betrayed the entire kingdom and has no way to break the curse, but I'm glad you stepped up in my place." My eyes dart to the empty right sleeve of his jacket which is pinned up out of the way. "Thanks for lending a hand."

He grits his teeth, and his face turns red. He reaches toward his sword with his left hand.

"You don't have to take orders anymore," I bark at the soldiers as I dance back out of Foulo's reach. "Look around you. This place is going to hell. Do you really want to spend your last hours guarding a fucking door?"

For a moment, no one moves. Then, four out of the six guards drop their weapons on the floor with a smashing of metal on stone. Without a word, they shoulder past us, and march down the corridor. I glance meaningfully at the last guard, and he too drops his weapon and scampers away, leaving only Foulo.

I grin. "I suppose we're going to get a rematch, Foulo."

He stares at the retreating soldiers, then to my friends behind me. His neck works and he swallows thickly, but when he speaks his voice is steady. "Five on one?" he sneers. "Is that the only way you'll fight me?"

"Big talk coming from the man with one arm. None of them needs to help me destroy you. In fact, would you prefer I use one hand, just to make it fair when I slit your throat? The only reason you're still alive is because I promised I wouldn't hunt you down."

"You—" he hisses and spits with rage, unable to even form a sentence as he launches toward me.

I draw my own sword, but before I can advance Kastian knocks hard into my arm. I whip my head around.

"Don't waste time on this," he barks, eyes fixed on Foulo. "I'll handle him. You have to search that tower."

I glance back at him, hesitating. A part of me really wants to stay and take on Foulo myself, but there's so little time left. Kas is right.

Foulo comes for me again, and this time I dodge left, darting around him. Kas raises a hand and from nowhere a jet of water blasts Foulo back against the stone wall.

Out of the corner of my eye I see Odessa freeze, watching the water drip onto the floor. I snatch at her sleeve. "Let's go."

She shakes her head and jogs after me, Fox and Jett through the door into Thorne's tower, leaving Kastian and Foulo behind.

The door swings shut behind us and for a second I think there's something wrong with my ears. All sound in the castle beyond—the deafening shouting, the clang of weapons and splintering wood and glass—cut off in an instant. It's perfectly silent, like being underwater.

"Woah, eerie," Jett says out loud.

"It must be a spell. Come on, let's go."

Thorne's tower turns out to be larger than I expected. It's multiple stories high and there are rooms on every level—an armory, an office, a small private dining room that looks like it's hardly ever been used. We stop when we nearly reach the top of the tower and find ourselves in his bedchamber.

"It looks normal," Odessa says dejectedly, turning in a circle to take everything in at once.

Unfortunately, I agree. There's a four-poster bed with red linens and various dark wood furniture, but nothing...personal. There's no art on the walls or books on the shelves. You'd think it was a guest room for all the personality Thorne has put into it.

"There's another level," I say with a sigh. "I'll check up there but I'd bet it's just storage."

I feel frustration and depression washing back over me, and once again the agony in my head and chest throbs to life. The pain was dampened, though never gone completely, while I was focused on other things, but now it seems to flare even hotter than before.

I press my hand to my chest, wincing slightly as I climb the winding stairs alone to the very top of the tower. I'm hardly paying attention as I reach the top, but then I look up and my eyes go wide. "Fuck."

"What is it?" Jett yells from down below. A second later he jogs up the stairs and peers around me to look. I feel him go stiff. "Fuck."

I step slowly into the room, my entire body vibrating with horror and the beginnings of rage. I don't turn around when I hear Odessa and Fox come up the stairs behind Jett and their gasps when they finally see what we're both looking at.

*Bodies.*

Or, at this point, the better word would be *corpses.*

Lining the walls are six desiccated corpses, each encased in pristine glass cases like precious artifacts. The bodies are ashen and withered, their skin resembling aged leather stretched taut over their skeletal frames. Their faces are hollowed, with gaping mouths that seem to silently scream into the void.

It's obvious that the corpses were once female. Long straggled hair still clings to one or two scalps, and each corpse is adorned with a crown and an immaculate glittering gown, which drapes over their skeletal forms, hanging loosely, as if trying to preserve what's left of their dignity.

Most grotesque of all, each of the corpses has a dagger plunged deep into its hollow chest. The daggers are identical, short with twisting wooden handles that remind me of the thousands of rose bushes all across Vernallis. It's as if Thorne has speared each of them with a true thorn to the heart.

"I'm going to be sick," Jett gags, and I hear his quick footsteps retreating down the stairs. Fox follows silently.

Odessa comes up beside me and puts a hand on my arm. I flinch, as if she struck me, my entire body vibrating and on edge.

"It's the wives," Dessa says in a quiet, broken voice.

I don't answer. A roaring, like the wave Kastian conjured in the corridor, is growing in the back of my head.

I knew what it had to mean when Alix told me that the curse was really about sacrifice rather than love, but seeing it displayed is so much worse.

I reach out a hand to steady myself on the nearest wall. *He was going to do this to Alix.*

"I've seen enough," I growl, stepping backwards and marching down the steps after Jett and Fox.

"Wait!" Dessa says. "We still need to search. We need to find out who he loves."

I shake my head. "No. Don't you get it? No one who does this could ever love anyone. He's not a narcissist, he's a sociopath. A monster."

"But without knowing who he loves—"

I turn my back. "Thorne doesn't love anyone except himself."

My ears are still ringing as I march down the stairs. I don't know what to do now, and the urge to return to the barracks and ignore everything is so strong I can hardly resist it. I'm fucking sick of thinking things might change, and getting my hopes up for even a second. First when I left Dyaspora, then when I thought I'd found Isabelle, when Alix agreed to help and when I thought for just a second she could be mine.

Each time the disappointment is worse, and turns to cold rage all the faster.

"Oh my god," Dessa blurts out behind me. "You're right."

I stop short. "What?"

She almost laughs. "You're right. Don't you get it?"

I can't fucking deal with another epiphany that will only lead to more disappointment. "I don't know what the fuck you're talking about."

"You just said it! Thorne only loves himself. He never soul-bonded anyone even though he's been married multiple times. He didn't even seem to care for his parents. You're his brother, and he obviously doesn't love you."

"Half-brother," I grumble, wanting to put as much distance between myself and the owner of this room as possible.

She doesn't care, and starts pacing, gnawing on her lip. "The curse is broken when the king of Vernallis admits he is powerless and sacrifices the person he loves most. Don't you get it? He has to die. He has to admit he's powerless and sacrifice himself to save the kingdom."

A cold wave of clarity crashes over me as her words sink in.

*That's it.*

Her argument makes perfect sense, each point clicking into place like pieces of a puzzle. My heart pounds as the truth settles in, undeniable and unavoidable. She's right. She has to be right, but what do I do now?

Dessa claps her hands. "It's the only thing that makes sense. Why would a sorceress who just had her heart broken want to punish another woman? She wouldn't. It's not about his partner, it's about him."

"Do you think he knows?" I ask.

"I don't know."

I run a hand through my hair, my mind reeling. "I need to find Thorne."

"Are you going to ask him about the sorceress?" Dessa asks, dashing after me.

I shake my head. Suddenly the pain that has been plaguing me for days eases, which only reinforces my certainty that I'm on the right track at last. There's only a few hours left until it's too late, but that'll have to be enough.

"I'm not going to ask him anything," I growl. "I'm going to force him to listen. If he doesn't already know how the curse is really broken he will in a few minutes."

Jett cocks his head to the side. "And what if he already knows? What if he realizes the curse has always been about him and he just doesn't care?"

"That's easy." I throw the tower door open and march out into the hall. "Then I'm going to kill him myself."


I charge back out of the tower, nearly running straight into Kastian. There's a gash across his right cheek and he looks tired, but otherwise unharmed.

"Find anything?" he asks without preamble.

"Yeah," I grumble darkly. "What happened with Foulo?"

In answer, he jabs a finger over his shoulder. Behind him on the floor in a puddle of red-tinged water, Foulo is lying on the ground with a blade sticking out of his chest. My stomach churns for a moment, thinking of the knives stabbed deep into the corpses of the dead queens.

"You're hurt," Odessa blurts out, looking past me at Kastian. Her eyes have a strange glint to them.

Kas reaches up and touches the cheek. He pulls his fingers away and looks down, startled by the blood. He wipes his hand roughly on his jacket. "It's nothing."

Odessa gives him another strange look, and seems to debate whether she should say something or not. Then she just nods stiffly, and turns to me. "What are we standing around for? It's not as if we have much time."

I scoff, but of course she's right. The sky outside is dark and it's been that way for some time now, which means we could have little more than hours left before the curse takes its final hold.

I navigate the winding corridors of the dilapidated palace, guiding us back to the grand entrance hall. The building is in worse condition than we left it, with more stone and plaster crumbling from the walls and the air thick with dust. The shouting in the corridors is growing louder, and it sounds as if more chanting has started up outside.

I strain my ears and finally pick up what all the distant shouts are saying: *Kill the king! Bring down the beast!*

I grimace. It might have taken to the eleventh hour, but the entire kingdom is finally on the same page. I just hope it's not too late.

The once-open doors to the throne room now stand firmly closed. A throng of about a dozen courtiers jostle and push each other, their faces ranging from furious to desperate as they fight to get inside. Blocking their path, eight guards hold the line, arms crossed and feet planted firmly on the marble floor. I suppose not everyone has abandoned their loyalty to the king just yet.

"Thorne must be in the throne room," I mutter. "The fucking coward is hiding from his own damn court."

"We'll handle the guards," Jett says, garnering nods of agreement from Kas and Fox.

"I'll go in with you," Odessa tells me.

I'm about to tell her no, but before I can, Kas beats me to it. "Absolutely fucking not."

She glares at him. "Who the hell are you to tell me what to do?"

He looks a bit flustered, but carries on anyway. "You're not a fighter, how the hell are you supposed to help? You're just going to be a distraction."

She bristles furiously and opens her mouth to retort, but this time I cut her off. "He's right. All four of you stay outside, preferably together. If this doesn't go well then soon the rioting will get far fucking worse and you'll be the only ones unaffected. I'd tell you to start running now, but I know there's no point..."

"You're right, there's no point," Kas says, clapping me on the shoulder. "We're staying with you until the end, no matter what."

I give him a nod, silently communicating so much I wish I'd said sooner. If I don't come back out I know he'll take Odessa and the others to Hydratta just like he promised me back in Dyaspora. No matter what happens they'll all be safe. Alix will be safe, and that's what really matters.

I descend the grand staircase, my boots echoing on the marble steps as I approach the massive, intricately carved doors of the throne room that stand stubbornly shut. Kas and Fox surge past me. Their swords gleam under the chandelier's light, catching the eye of the guards stationed at the entrance. The guards tense, hands instinctively reaching for their weapons.

With a shout that echoes through the grand foyer, Jett launches himself off the last five stairs, landing with a thud on the marble floor. He snatches up a jagged piece of a fallen marble statue, its cold weight solid in his hand. With a swift, powerful swing, he hurls it toward the enormous arched window, sending shards of glass crashing down like a sparkling waterfall over the entrance hall. Grinning, he bolts down the corridor, the sound of his footsteps echoing as he leads the soldiers on a wild chase, his diversion successfully clearing my path to the doors.

I don't waste a second, and run toward the doors, unlocking them with a wave of the hand as I go.

The doors swing open. Beyond, I can see the enormous opulent throne room with the golden carpeted aisle and Thorne's throne at the end. I launch myself inside, bracing for a fight—as if Thorne might be hiding behind the door waiting to strike.

The doors swing closed and I stand in silence, my heart thundering with adrenaline.

But after a long moment, nothing happens. Finally, I turn on the spot, looking around.

The room is empty, and Thorne is gone.

# CHAPTER
# TWENTY-EIGHT

ALIX

I gasp for breath as my head pops through the surface of the pond. *Holy shit, I'm soaked. And not in a fun way.*

My teeth chatter, and of course it's pouring rain, making the whole thing so much worse. Still, I let out a breath of relief and wade out of the water and onto the muddy bank. The scent of roses mingles with the rain and fills my nose. I swear I've never smelled anything so comforting.

I reach back into the water and drag my Walmart backpack wrapped in two layers of thick black trash bags out onto the bank beside me, then take a second to catch my breath. I sit on the muddy ground, panting, as a smile spreads across my face. "See, I'm not crazy," I mutter to myself. "It was real."

*And thank God, honestly.* Because otherwise, I would have taken two Ubers and a bus to the New York state line and walked into a pond on the side of the highway for nothing. And then I really would be crazy.

It was hard to know what time it would be when I arrived, but I think I've prepared for anything. Even if the king and his courtiers are still staying at the manor, I can handle it. At least, I hope I can.

I reach for my bag and tear off the trash bags I wrapped around it to hopefully protect everything inside from getting soaked with pond water. It looks dry enough, except for the raindrops now making dark spots on the canvas. I stuff the trash bags into the side pocket, then dig into the backpack for a can of bear spray and a hammer and brandish one in each hand as I start creeping through the roses toward the house.

I stifle a giggle, laughing at myself. If anyone could see me right now, I'm sure I look deranged. Then again, anyone out in the daytime really would be deranged, so maybe I'd better not jinx it.

I reach the edge of the patio and the door bangs open. A shriek startles me, and I'm just about to lift my hammer when I realize it's Beatrix running toward me.

She ignores my weapon and launches herself at me, sobbing into a handkerchief just like I saw her do to Daemon.

"I'm so glad you're alright," she sniffles.

I pat her back, unsure what to do with this level of raw affection from a maternal figure. "How did you know I was here?"

"I told her." Aurelia appears at the door behind Beatrix. She wiggles her fingers at me. "Magic gives you really good intuition."

I raise an eyebrow. Damn, I could use some of that, especially right now.

Beatrix and Aurelia usher me inside, and within what feels like seconds, a steaming teacup is shoved into my hand and they're pushing me into a chair at the kitchen table.

"The court left pretty much the moment you did," Aurelia says, her voice rising to something between excitement and nerves.

"Which was when?" I ask, swallowing a sip of my tea. "I just want to make sure the time is the same between here and my world."

"About two nights ago," Beatrix replies anxiously. "Daemon told everyone that you died."

I splutter. "What?"

"He did." Aurelia nods along, looking aghast. "The king got so angry I could hear it all from my window. He yelled for a while, then his wings came out like he was going to start a real fight, but instead he just flew off."

"He probably knew he'd lose," I grumble.

"Maybe. He didn't come back, though, and a little while later, Daemon told all the courtiers to get back in their carriages and they all disappeared."

"They went back to the Winter Palace," Beatrix says, disapproval strong in her tone. "I think it was the first time most of them realized what's happening. You'd think they would have tried to leave or save themselves, but no. Time is almost up and only now the court has figured out the position their king has put them in."

I grimace. "I think denial is a pretty common reaction to hearing the world is ending. Next, they'll riot."

Beatrix nods gravely. "Undoubtably."

We sit in thick silence for a second, processing the weight of everything going on. Finally, I break the tension. "You guys don't seem that surprised to see me."

Aurelia smiles. "I had a feeling you'd be back."

"But you were the one to tell me to leave."

"And I was right, you should absolutely have left!" Her eyes widen. "But soul-bonds are impossible to ignore."

I cough, the air in the back of my throat getting caught on the inhale. *God, did everyone know but me? Do I even know for sure that that's what this is...a soul-bond?*

If somehow everything works out in the next day or so, I'll have to come back and ask her exactly how that intuition thing works.

"Listen, I don't mean to be rude, but I should probably get going. I have no idea how long it's going to take me to get back to the castle, but I need to get there before the rose moon...which is tonight, isn't it? When does it start?"

"At sundown," Beatrix says quickly. "It will be dark for an entire day and night, and when the sun rises again, the curse will either be broken or...not."

"I think I know how to break it. At least, I hope I do. I have an idea."

Beatrix's eyes widen with excitement. "Then you're right, you'd better go right now."

"I think you should wait to leave until it gets dark," Aurelia interjects. "That's only in an hour or so."

"But then I'll have an hour less time to reach the castle, and I still don't fully know what I'm going to do when I get there."

"I know...but you should wait anyway. If you're traveling alone, it's best to make sure you're safe. What if the rain stops and the sun comes out?"

I start to argue with her, but Beatrix interrupts, "Can we at least get you some dry clothes? You must be freezing."

"Can I just duck into your bathroom for a minute to change? I brought my own clothes in here." I hold up the backpack.

"Of course," Beatrix gushes. "And while you change, we'll get one of the horses ready. Then you can leave whenever you want. Now, or you can wait until it's dark, but either way you're ready."

"Oh...no. That's okay."

They give me odd looks. "How are you going to get to the palace without a horse?"

"I figured I'd walk? Or maybe there's someone who could drive me in a carriage."

Aurelia laughs. "You must be joking, you can't walk all the way to the palace."

"I know it won't be comfortable, but I think I could do it. It would probably take a little longer than the carriage ride, so five hours maybe?" I push my hair behind my ears and shrug. "That's possible."

"But there're wolves out there," Beatrix gasps.

"Yes, but—"

They ignore my protests and go outside to the stables, leaving me alone. I close my eyes; I guess I'm facing all my fears today.

I duck into a bathroom to change and reemerge ten minutes later. As I stride toward the stables, Beatrix and Aurelia stare. I don't have to wonder what they're looking at.

The clothes in Ellender are beautiful, but not super practical as far as the women are concerned. I figured if I was going to risk my life, I might as well not worry about a corset.

I'm wearing my mom's black yoga leggings, two pairs of new waterproof socks, and old hiking boots I haven't worn since high school. On top, I've layered a sports bra, an *Under Armour* top, a heavy mesh vest from Walmart that I'm pretty sure could stop a bullet, and mom's *North Face* jacket. I've got fingerless gloves that turn into mittens, a headband to keep my hair out of my face, and a rain hat that looks impossibly stupid but will probably make it easier to see. Honestly, aside from the hat, I think I look pretty good—in an outdoorsy mountain-girl sort of way.

Aurelia looks me up and down, then reaches out and pinches the fabric of my leggings. "What are these made of?"

I laugh. "If I come back, I will totally introduce you to the wide world of *Lululemon.* You're gonna love it."

The smile slides off my face as I take in the horse that they've gotten saddled and ready for me. It's a mare, I think. She's chestnut colored with a black mane and looks friendly enough...as far as horses go, that is. It's like picking out the least deadly looking scorpion.

"What's her name?" I ask in hushed tones.

"Marie," Beatrix pats the horse's neck.

I grimace. "I don't think we're on a first name basis yet. Maybe once she proves she isn't going to buck me off."

"She's very gentle."

I don't believe that for a second, but I somehow find the courage to thank Beatrix and take the reins from her.

I step up beside the horse, looking her in her black glassy eye. "I'm going to need you to work with me here. I cannot deal with another traumatic incident today, you know?"

The horse snorts and paws nervously at the ground. I grit my teeth and straighten my spine. I'm going to choose to see that as a good omen...because I don't really have any other choice, and as much as I hate to admit it, Beatrix and Aurelia are right. Walking five hours in the rain isn't the best idea. I'm not conceding about waiting until dark, though. I'm leaving now.

I hold my breath as I climb onto Marie's back, and we venture down the long cobblestone path toward the village.


RIDING THE HORSE PROVES TO BE JUST AS TERRIBLE AS I feared, but amazingly I don't fall off. I can't figure out how to make her go fast, and even if I could I probably wouldn't want to, so we move along at a slow canter.

I ride the narrow cobblestone streets of the village of Storia, the wooden shutters of quaint cottages closed against the chill. As I leave the village behind, the path into the woods becomes tangled with brambles and underbrush, the rain pelting down in icy sheets that sting my skin. Despite the harsh weather, the deep grooves in the muddy ground, left by the heavy wheels of royal carriages, remain visible, guiding me through the dense forest and back toward the looming silhouette of the palace.

Marie mostly does the work herself, seeming to follow some instinct and sticking to the path. Eventually, I grow the tiniest bit more comfortable and loosen my death-grip on the reins—just a little.

Finally, the rain shifts to an icy chill, transforming into sleet that pricks my skin like tiny needles. My breath puffs out in frosty clouds.

"We're almost there," I mutter, though, only Marie is there to hear me. The horse huffs a breath, and this time, I'm sure it's a response.

I spot the castle turrets against the darkening sky in the distance and feel instantly braver. I dig my heels into her flank, finally urging her to go faster. She does, and soon, I'm riding out of the tree line and toward the little village.

My stomach sinks, and I pull back on the reins to stop Marie, gaping in surprise at the village in front of me.

It's...chaos.

All along the main street buildings are burning, animals run around free, and angry villages march through the dark streets. Some brandish torches while others carry pitchforks, daggers, or whatever else they might be able to use as a weapon. I watch in horror as more and more people—Fae, goblins, and whatever else—stream out of houses and from the alleys between buildings. They form a mob, marching toward the castle.

Shouts of *"Find the king!"* and *"Kill the beast!"* echo through the streets, reverberating back over and over, as the chant is picked up by more and more people.

My hands tighten on Marie's reins. I expected chaos, but this is all far too real. I guess it's too late to turn back now.

I don't want to get caught up in the mob, so instead I grit my teeth and urge Marie to ride around the outskirts of the village. Thankfully, there's not much more than a handful of houses off the main street, and we're able to slip by in the darkness, past the flickering flames reflecting off stone walls. Soon, we reach the town square.

I crane my neck over my shoulder. The mob is close and growing closer by the second, but they haven't quite reached the palace steps.

Without thinking twice, I jump down from Marie's back and tether her to a post outside the stables. "Wait here. I'll be back...hopefully."

I guess my fear of Marie is nothing compared to my fear of losing everything I've come to love.

I swing off my enormous backpack and fall to my knees in the street, rifling through it for the weapons I brought.

*Weapons* is a loose term.

Nothing I have was ever meant to hurt someone—I don't know how to shoot a gun even if I'd wanted to bring one, and it's not like Walmart is selling medieval broadswords in between the car parts and the flat screen TVs. Still, I'm not worried as I grip my bear spray in one hand and a blow torch in the other.

I don't want to hurt anyone, but I have no problem defending myself if it comes to it. I'm sure that mob wouldn't think twice about bowling me over on their way to the king, and if that's what's going on in the streets I don't even want to know what the nobles and the soldiers are doing.

Armed and feeling a little braver, I swing my bag back over my shoulder and dash up the first few marble steps, bracing myself for an uncomfortable climb. The stairs are endless and my legs burn after only a few seconds, but there's no other way to reach the castle—not unless someone happens to fly by and wants to give me a lift.

As if on cue, a dark shadow falls over me, as if something has moved in front of the moon. I look up instinctively, squinting through the misty rain that still hangs over the city.

A tall muscular figure with wings glides across the sky over the village. My heart picks up speed, beating hard against my chest. Even at this distance, I recognize his stature. "Daemon!"

I raise a hand, waving and shouting for him to stop.

Daemon cranes his neck and looks back at me. I shield my eyes from the rain and peer after him as he flies in a circle overhead, turning around in midair and coming back toward me.

My pulse quickens, and a rush of warmth spreads through my chest. Memories flood back, each one laced with joy and anticipation, causing my heart to expand with a mix of excitement and deep emotion.

But then, the bubble growing in my chest pops and dread washes over me as the figure draws nearer. *It's not Daemon.*

King Thorne draws closer, landing a few steps above me. The menacing backdrop of the castle rises over him and my mouth falls open. For a second, all I can do is stare at his wings.

They're black and feathered, but don't have the same red tips that Daemon's feathers do. Instead, each feather looks like the blade of a knife. He's less like an angel and more like a bird of prey, preparing to strike.

The king cocks his head at me and his lip curls up in a sneer. "Isabelle...back from the dead so soon?"

A shiver travels up my spine. I glance behind me. I've climbed at least three flights worth of stairs, and falling backward would definitely kill me. Worse, there's nowhere else to run.

I step slowly back, feeling my way down the stairs. At the same time, I hold my bear spray out in front of me. "Stay back. Don't touch me."

Thorn's smile tips up even more, and with a tiny flick of his finger the can suddenly zooms out of my hand, flying backwards to clatter against the street far below. My breath catches, and my fingers tighten around the blow torch still clutched in my other hand. I raise that too, and it meets the same fate, flying out of my hand and into the thicket of snowy roses bracketing the steps.

My heart sinks into my stomach.

Thorne laughs and stalks toward me, dragging his enormous wings behind him. His expression is that of a cat stalking a mouse, and right now, that's exactly what I feel like: a pathetic mouse who thought a blow torch and a six dollar can of bear spray could hold off the world's most powerful cat.

"What are you doing out here?" I demand.

He laughs. "I should be asking you that, but it hardly matters now. I'm glad to see you, Isabelle."

"O-oh yeah?" I stammer, still edging down the stairs. *I have to keep him talking. Buy myself a second to think.*

"Certainly." Thorne drawls, almost like he's enjoying himself. "See, I thought you died and yet there was no change to the curse. Imagine my frustration realizing you weren't the one after all. I'd wasted so much time."

"You still wasted your time," I say through gritted teeth. "You don't love me."

He cocks his head, his smile turning frightening. "Don't I? I spent years thinking of you, remembering how you left me. Imagining what I'd do to get you back."

"That's not love. That's control. You knew you'd been tricked and it became an obsession but it was never about me."

His face twists and for a moment I think I see a spark of recognition in his eye. Maybe for a moment he realizes his mistake, and knows that he really did waste his time all these years. Then, in a blink, it's gone. "Perhaps you're right. I suppose we'll find out together, won't we?"

His hand whips out with such speed I can barely see it. In an instant, I feel myself falling backwards as if he'd shoved me with both hands.

A part of me expected this, and I brace myself and try to curl inward, protecting my neck as I fall backward against the stone. My huge backpack takes the brunt of the fall. Still, pain shoots through me, rattling every nerve and bone in my body as I tumble back down the stone steps. Thorne stalks after me and all I can see are his boots and the tips of his black wings before my eyes close against the blinding pain radiating through me.

I land in a heap on the bottom step and force myself to crack my eyes open. I'm alive and everything hurts, which doesn't feel like a good thing but at least probably means I didn't break my neck.

I sit up, wiping blood from my mouth.

Through watering eyes, I see Throne grinning down at me.

My head pounds with pain and through my haze I hear the shouts of the mob growing closer by the second. Maybe if I can just stay alive for another minute or two, the mob will reach us and Throne won't be able to kill me before they see him?

Evidently unconcerned about the mob, Thorne raises a boot and presses it deliberately against my chest, forcing me back to the ground. He reaches into his belt and draws a smooth-hilted black dagger. "There's no time for a wedding first, but I think the Gods will have to forgive me that. I only wish Ashwater could see me kill you."

I glare up at him, strangely defiant in the face of death the way I've never been before. "No matter what, it won't work. You'll stay cursed forever because you're so fucking stupid you never even realized that the only person you love is yourself. You never even realized that I'm *not* Isabelle."

Thorne reels back in confusion. He takes his foot off my chest and I don't waste a second, scrambling backwards.

In that same second, I hear a shout rise over every other sound. Both Thorne and I turn and see Daemon rushing out of the castle. He doesn't bother with the stairs, spreading his wings and launching himself toward us. For a moment, my heart flies too. Soaring, as I know everything will be alright.

Then, with another wicked grin, Thorne whips back around and throws the dagger in his hand directly toward my heart.

# CHAPTER
# TWENTY-NINE

DAEMON

The world slows to a crawl as Thorne's dagger slices through the air and embeds itself into Alix's chest with a sickening thud.

My body seizes, an icy paralysis gripping me as my eyes lock onto hers across the yawning fifty yards that separate us. Her wide blue gaze goes impossibly wider and she lets out a sound somewhere between a grunt and a scream. Then, she falls backwards into a heap on the dirty street.

A sharp, searing pain explodes in my chest. My heart pounds erratically and my vision blurs as a wave of terror grips me. My legs tremble, nearly bringing me to my knees.

Without thought, I launch myself down the stairs, uncaring if my wings have spread to break the fall.

I need to reach her, catch her, roll back time and stop the dagger from ever piercing her heart.

I don't fucking understand what's happening. One moment, I was searching for Thorne, who slipped out of his throne room like the snake he is. The next moment, I find him, but he's not alone.

I don't know what Alix is doing here or when she came back. All I know is that now she's lying still in the street and I need to get to her.

I expect her to move. Stand up and smile at me, or scowl, it doesn't matter. I'd even take a twitch of a finger. Anything, if it means that she's alive.

But she doesn't move.

Alix is here. She came back to find me...and now, she's dead.

I descend from the sky in a chaotic whirl of feathers, my breath coming in ragged gasps, and land in the empty city square. The relentless downpour drums against the cobblestones and the only noise aside from the screaming in my head is the distant shouts of furious villagers. Thorne is about ten feet from Alix's crumpled body, blocking me from reaching her.

I open my mouth, letting out a sound that is mostly animalistic roar. Thorne stiffens, and the smug expression on his face falters for the briefest second before he turns to me and smirks. "I was just saying it's too bad you weren't here to see her die."

I take a heavy step toward him. The pain in my head from the last several days suddenly feels like nothing. Nothing compared with the agony surging through my chest. My throat tightens, and I nearly double over from the twisting in my gut.

I can't seem to form words, all that comes out is "Why?"

His smirk morphs into more of a sneer, his eyes turning cold while his posture remains casual. "You think I didn't see you lusting after her? You always wanted what was mine."

I'd laugh if I could find any humor left in the world. "You don't know fucking anything."

He thinks I was just lusting after Alix? He thinks I want anything he has? He's never understood that I want to put as much space between us as possible, because I've always known what a twisted evil monster he was behind his cold exterior.

"You don't even understand the irony of this, do you? You killed her for nothing. You don't love her, if you did—"

If he did he'd feel like he was dying. *I'm sure I'm dying.*

Thorne says nothing, his eyes darting to the side. As I look at him, another awful truth washes over me. "You know that, though, don't you? You know you don't know how to break the curse. Is that what you were fucking doing when you ran into her, running away?"

His prolonged silence is answer enough.

He was running away—not just from the angry mob, but from the kingdom. Maybe to one of the portals to the mortal realm as I considered doing so many times. It hasn't even occurred to him to sacrifice himself. Instead, he's putting his own comfort and safety over everyone and everything else, and ripping out the hearts of Vernallis in the process. I should have expected nothing less from the king who kept his dead wives as trophies.

Before either of us can move another muscle, a shout echoes down the street.

Thorne turns and glances over his shoulder toward the heart of the city. He tenses, his hands curling into fists. I follow his gaze toward the ever growing mob marching toward us. In mere seconds, they'll be close enough to recognize the king. A large part of me would like to see what happens when they do.

"Your people are turning on you," I taunt Thorne. "They know that you abandoned them. How does it feel to know that every single being in Vernallis wishes you were dead?"

He turns back to me and attempts to keep the sneer on his face, but it falters. Satisfaction washes over me when I spot the real fear in his gaze.

His enormous black wings unfurl glistening with rain drops and without a word he launches into the sky.

I tilt my head back to watch him ascend, the cold rain splattering against my face and blurring my vision, making it difficult to track his silhouette as he vanishes into the stormy sky. If I don't follow now, I'll lose him in the storm.

I look at Alix, still lying immobile on the ground and another wave of agony nearly crushes me. My heart screams to stay by her side, yet the empty void gnawing at me whispers that she isn't going anywhere. *Ever again.*

Meanwhile, there's only hours—maybe minutes—left to go after Thorne.

A sharp pain grips my chest, but I refuse to let it take over. I clench my fists, feeling my heart pound like a war drum. I let the energy course through me, transforming the ache into a fiery rage that propels me forward.

It feels as if my body is splitting apart, a searing sensation coursing through me as my wings unfurl with a powerful whoosh. I launch into the sky.

Ahead, Thorne veers sharply, changing course, his silhouette a dark streak against the sky. I trail him, both of us heading back toward the looming silhouette of the castle.

Thorne lands with a splash on the rain soaked palace terrace. I follow, my feet touching down just seconds later on the wet stones. Above us, the enormous circular window of the throne room looms against the castle wall casting a sharp ray of light over the dark castle ramparts.

"What happened?" I hiss as I stalk after my brother, kicking up water with every step. "I thought you were fleeing for a portal? Decided to stay and see the end of your court after all?"

Thorne grits his teeth and doesn't answer.

I don't think he knows what he's doing anymore. He doesn't know where to run where I won't follow him, and he must know deep down that the curse isn't going to break.

He's trapped—imprisoned.

I know exactly what that feels like and it makes me smile to know he's suffering a fraction as much as I am.

His face twists in contempt as I approach, forcing him to back up against the nearest stone pillar. He glances back at the ground far below, and there's a tiny hint of fear in his face when he turns back to me. "What do you think you're doing, Ashwater? Spend your last moments however you want, don't waste your time fighting me."

"You just killed the only person I'd care about spending my last moments with. Now the only thing I have left is the pleasure of watching you die.."

"You can't fight me. I beat you ninety years ago and I'll do it again now."

I let out a bark of humorless laughter.

He beat me ninety years ago because he caught me off guard and had dozens of soldiers with him.

"Do you know how much fighting goes on in Dyaspora?" I shout over the sound of the rain. "Think about it for a fraction of a second. I've had decades to become far stronger than you in every conceivable way."

I lunge for him but he ducks. My hand closes around the air rather than his throat. I strike again, this time catching him across the cheekbone with my fist.

Somewhat to his credit, Thorne doesn't back down. He charges at me, catching me across the chest. With a wet thud, we go tumbling across the stone balcony grappling for control.

Thorne's face twists with rage. "I never should have let you out!"

"No, you shouldn't have. But that's always been your fatal flaw, Thorne. You're so in love with yourself you think everyone else must be too."

The freezing rain pours down in sheets, instantly drenching me to the bone as Thorne and I tumble and slide across the slick surface. Drops of icy water sting my skin and plaster my hair to my face as we struggle to regain our footing on the wet balcony tiles. The roaring wind whips through our hair and feathers, threatening to knock us over once again.

I land on my back, Thorne above me. He raises his fist and brings it down forcefully toward my face. I roll away just in time, causing his fist to slam into the stone. The balcony's stone cracks under the impact, and he cries out, shaking his hand in pain. I don't miss the opportunity to roll out from beneath him and reach for the sword in my belt.

Thorne staggers back to his feet, his eyes wild and his breath ragged. He spins with a ferocious intensity, and before I can even unsheathe my blade, his shoulder slams into me like a battering ram. The force of the impact sends me stumbling backward and he chases after me.

Our breaths become ragged, each inhale sharp and shallow as we grapple with each other across the rough stone of the terrace. At times, we teeter dangerously close to the edge. Thorne's left fist connects with my jaw in a brutal arc, and the metallic tang of blood fills my mouth. Worse, my right wing is bent and throbbing, yet I refuse to yield. A deep gash mars his cheek, oozing crimson, and his right hand is swollen and misshapen, the fingers bent at unnatural angles.

Thorne wrenches himself from my grip, glaring at me with manic fury as he backs up, framed against the enormous round window beyond which lies the throne room. "I always knew I couldn't trust you." He spits. "You think if you kill me you'll be king for five minutes? How pathetic."

"Of course you would think this is about the throne. I don't care about the crown and I never have," I growl, darting around him trying to find an opening. "But you couldn't understand that because you'd never give up power. Even now when you could save everyone, you won't. You'll take us all down with you."

He staggers backwards and for a moment I think I see a glimmer of confusion on his face. Maybe he really doesn't know that to end the curse all he would have to do is sacrifice himself. If he doesn't know, that's somehow sadder.

I lunge towards him, my hands closing around his throat.

Thorne's face flushes a deep crimson as he desperately scratches at my fingers with his injured, swollen hand, but I maintain my grip. Each breath I take is labored, my chest rising and falling heavily, while sharp pangs radiate from my aching jaw and even more intensely from the ache in my heart.

My hand clamps firmly around his throat as I force Thorne backward, step by step, until he's teetering at the brink of the balcony. Below us, thousands of feet down, the outlines of thorny rose bushes are barely visible in the rain-soaked darkness.

Thorne's face turns red as he struggles to breathe, his feet dangling over the edge of the balcony. I hold him firmly in place, his eyes widening with fear as he realizes how close he is to falling.

"I just want to know. When you killed all your wives, did you feel any guilt? Did it ever occur to you how it wasn't a sacrifice since you didn't love them?"

If he's surprised that I know about the queens he doesn't show it. "I did—" he coughs. "I do."

I shake my head. Part of me thinks he believes that. He has no idea what love is, or what a real sacrifice feels like.

I squeeze his throat tighter, only my arm keeping him from plummeting to the ground below. With my other hand, I pull a knife from my belt, intending to plunge it into his heart before letting him fall.

It feels almost poetic. He'll die with a blow to the heart, just like he killed all his wives. Like he killed Alix. Like he's killed me along with her.

I raise the knife.

But as my hand raises I shake, my arm coming to a sudden halt. My eyes widen with a startling realization.

Killing Thorne, as much as I want to, won't fucking matter. If I kill him, it's just as meaningless as how he killed Alix—for the slightest chance of affecting the curse, but more for revenge. His revenge on her for defying his control and against me for being born.

What I'm doing is no fucking better.

And more, Alix wouldn't want me to do it. I remember her in bed after falling through the ice. *Please don't murder Foulo. Unless he attacks you first, then, I guess it's self-defense. Just don't hunt him down. I don't want that on my conscience.*

Alix wouldn't want this.

"Take it," I demand, shoving the dagger into Thorne's broken fingers. He lets out an involuntary sound of pain as the hilt of the blade presses into his twisted hand, but I don't relent. "Take the knife!"

His pale eyes meet mine. His face is read from lack of oxygen and his pupils are dilated with rage, but he shakes slightly as he closes his fingers around the knife.

"Stab yourself," I tell him with no feeling in my voice.

The glimmer of a smirk passes across his features. "Are you out of your mind?" He rasps, the words sticking in his throat.

I ignore the question. My arms shake from the effort of holding him and not allowing myself to crush his throat. "Stab yourself in the fucking heart. It's the best thing you'll ever do for the kingdom. If there's a shred of decency in there somewhere you'll do it."

His gaze is calculating, watching me closely while the knife trembles in his loose grip. After a long heartbeat, his eyes narrow. "I'd sooner burn the entire city to the ground."

I feel as if a door slams inside my mind. There's a finality to those words that can't be changed. He would destroy the whole kingdom before himself—he already is.

I close my eyes and release my fist.

Thorne falls. For a second I know he believes he's about to plummet to the ground far below, because he gasps in a shaking breath when instead he lands back on the stone balcony, the knife still in his hand.

I push rain soaked hair from my face and step back.

"What are you doing?" Thorne demands.

"You saved my life once. Consider this my returning the favor. Enjoy your last moments, as short as they'll be."

My hands curl into fists at my sides and I turn away. It's the hardest thing I've ever done, and at the same time, it's easy. Easy because if I only have minutes left I want to return to Alix's body and spend them with her. I won't do that with blood on my hands.

Thorne's ragged breathing is loud behind me, barely drowned out by the pounding of my deliberate footstep as I walk away.

There's no peace in letting Thorne go, only certainty. Certainty that it's over. Fate or the gods or the fucking sorceress will have to decide where to go from here because I'm done fighting the inevitable.

All the rage flies out of me in a single whoosh, leaving only pain behind. My adrenaline flees my body and my wings disappear. I stalk back across the balcony toward the round window to the throne room. With one flick of my wrist, I smash the window. Glass shatters everywhere, but I hardly notice as I make to climb through the jagged opening into the throne room.

A shout erupts behind me, shattering the eerie quiet in my mind. The air shifts, and I know what's happening even before I hear the footsteps or the swish of a blade.

Instinctively, I pivot on my heel as Thorne lunges, driving my own dagger toward my back.

My vision turns white and I don't even think about it.

With both hands, I seize his face in a vice-like grip and twist with all my strength.

His eyes lock onto mine, first filled with contempt, then morphing into fear as he realizes the inevitable.

And finally, there is nothing in his gaze. The sound of cracking bones and tearing flesh fills the air as I twist his head around and forcibly rip it from his shoulders and his lifeless body crumples to the ground.

* * *

I don't waste a single second with Thorne's body.

I climb through the shattered window and march across the opulent throne room. Outside in the entrance hall, it's as if no time has passed. The building is in shambles, the guards and the nobles are brawling, and I see my friends among the throng fighting for order—fighting to give me time to handle my brother.

While barely any time has passed, I feel decades older. There's a weight pressing down on me and I know with absolute certainty that weight is the loss of my bond.

My heart beats sluggishly, like it wishes to just give up and sleep.

It's all I can do to stride across the entrance hall toward the open double doors.

"Daemon!"

I hear Kastian shout behind me and don't turn back. All I want to do is get to Alix. Lie next to her in the street and close my eyes.

"Where's the king?" Kas demands, catching up with me.

"Dead."

There's a beat where I feel his gaze on me, surely taking in my bloody hands.

I speed up. I don't want to explain anything to Kastian or anyone else.

I force my way through the front doors and back out onto the steps.

It feels impossibly poetic that I'm back where I started. I've made a circle, coming back to the exact point where I saw Alix fall on the street far below, and while everything feels different nothing really has changed.

I peer through the rain toward the base of the stairs. My pulse skips and my stomach lurches with nausea. I don't see Alix anywhere.

I take a staggering step forward. Where is she?

My heart beats sluggishly, like it wishes to just give up and sleep. It's all I can do to stride across the entrance hall toward the open double doors.

I look feverishly around the grounds and the city below for Alix. I'm about to fly down to the street again, when my gaze lands on a bedraggled figure in a wet black jacket, slowly climbing the steps. I squint, and my heart thrums back to life when I recognize the human fabric and construction of the coat.

A fleeting hope alighting in my chest, I rush down the stairs, stopping short when I reach her.

Alix tilts her head up to meet my gaze. Her face is pale, her hair soaking wet beneath her muddy jacket, but she's here, alive, breathing, and glaring up at me like I'm everything that's wrong with her world.

"I've said before I think these steps were intentional torture," she grumbles, "but, seriously, did no one ever think of elevators?"

My words get caught in my throat. My mouth gapes open as slowly I feel the life flooding back into my chest.

"What are you doing here?"

"Hi," Alix says, a little awkwardly. "This isn't how I pictured our reunion, maybe—"

My heart soars and I reach for her, gathering her up in my arms. "Alix…"

"Ow—" she hisses.

I let her go, horrified to have hurt her. "What happened?"

She presses a hand to the back of her head. "Sorry. I'm fine. I hit my head."

I suck in a breath, the vice on my chest loosening slightly. I can't even think of what to say to her. I love you. I need you. Please stay here with me.

All that comes out is: "How?"

She rubs the back of her head. "When I fell."

"No," I choke. "You got hit. I saw it."

"Oh." She grins at me and unzips her jacket. "I thought ahead. I had no idea Walmart sold bulletproof vests, but I figured it couldn't hurt."

I blink at the thick black garment she's wearing under her coat. I'm not entirely sure I understand what it is, but it doesn't matter. She's alive…and here.

"What are you doing here?"

"I had to come back," she breathes. "I'm probably fucking crazy, I know it was way too dangerous, but I couldn't stay away. I had to tell you, I think I know how to break the curse. Thorne has to die, and—"

I don't let her finish. I reach out and grab the back of her neck, tug her toward me and slam my mouth down on hers. She gasps, the warmth of her breath colliding with mine, and I kiss her deeply, channeling every ounce of longing and anger into a single moment. The blood on my hands smears her cheeks, but seconds later it gets washed away by the rain.

Alix pulls back looking breathless. "So, is that it? He's dead, right?" I wipe the last of my bloody hands on my jacket and nod. She smiles. "Is everything going to be okay, now?"

I look at her, hope and excitement clear on her face and I wish I could tell her everything was fine. I want to lie, if only to have a few more minutes of happiness before nothing ever feels right again.

But I can't.

I shake my head. "I don't think so, Peaches. He didn't sacrifice himself. I killed him."

Her face falls. "Oh. So, now what?"

I look behind her at the open door, beyond which I can see chaos still carrying on. "Now nothing. We wait for the sun to rise. And judging by that—" I point at the sky where there's pink on the horizon. "There's not long to wait."

Her face falls. "What? No..." Her words die as she chokes and tears appear in the corners of her eyes. "That can't be it. There has to be something else we can do."

"If there was, Peaches, I'd do anything to stay with you." I shake my head, my chest squeezing as if I've been clamped in a vice. "You'll be fine. Kastian will help you. And Odessa, Fox and Jett. They'll all make sure you're safe."

"Do you think I'd be here if I was worried about being safe?" she demands, tears now freely pouring down her face.

I have nothing else to say to that, so I just reach for her and pull her to my chest.

# CHAPTER
# THIRTY

ALIX

Daemon and I barely get a few seconds alone before—as it so often does—things get worse.

He lifts me and carries me up the rest of the stairs, and together we stride back into the castle. Kastian meets us at the entrance, and I manage a faint smile in his direction just before we find ourselves in the midst of chaos.

If I thought the riot would have subsided just because Thorne is gone, I was wrong. The entire room is buzzing with violence and explosive anger, like the impending sunrise is feeding the courts fury.

I see Odessa over by the stairs. She meets my gaze through the crowd and her violet eyes widen. Immediately, she starts pushing her way toward us. Beside me, Kastian stiffens, like he's holding himself back from something.

Daemon turns to Kastian, drawing his attention. "Take Alix and leave now."

"No," Odessa says as she finally reaches us.

"There's no reason to wait any longer. This is the end." Daemon gestures behind him at the rainy but rapidly lightening sky.

"But it's raining," I begin. "It's dark, so—"

"It won't matter," Daemon growls. "The curse becoming permanent means the sun is irrelevant. You all need to run. Better yet, fly. Put as much distance between yourself and Vernallis as possible."

"We're not leaving you here, Ashwater," Fox says.

I glance behind me. I don't know when he arrived, but his seldom used words pack a punch.

"Yeah!" Jett cries, as he fights his way out of the throng and lands panting beside Odessa. "I'm not leaving either."

"You promised you'd go," Daemon growls, more to Kastian than the others.

"We will," Kas assures him, "But not yet. We want to stay with you until the end. We—"

"No!" Daemon bellows, making everyone go silent. "No. You're not waiting here with me."

"But if there's only a few moments left..." I start, my throat constricting with unshed tears. "What's the point of running now?"

It's too late anyway. I know it's too late because the sun is rising and the first light of dawn is creeping through the open door and shattered windows. It steams across Daemon's face, illuminating his eyes as he stubbornly glares down at me.

"The point is that you'll be safer." He insists, as if he can't see the sun. Or, perhaps he can, but that's only making him more certain. He reaches out and brushes a tear off my cheek, tipping my chin up so my gaze meets his. "I fucking love you, Alix. I love you—" he looks back at his friends "—I love all of you, but I can't protect any of you. I've exhausted everything I can think of and it wasn't enough, so you have to go. I'd gladly sacrifice my last minutes with you if it means you're safe."

Before anyone can respond, a deafening boom reverberates through the castle causing the stone walls to quiver. I instinctively throw my arms out to steady myself, struggling to maintain my balance as the floor beneath me trembles violently. The chandeliers sway precariously above, and the ground feels as if it's alive, shifting and convulsing with a forceful intensity.

Daemon reaches for me, his arms closing around me as we all fall to the floor, knocked over by the force of the earthquake.

Daemon's strong arms draw me even closer, his lips brushing against my ear. "I love you," he whispers, sending shivers down my spine.

Before I can respond, he captures my lips in a passionate kiss, stealing away any chance for words to escape. The taste of him is intoxicating, like honey and fire and everything in between. I don't pull back until the shaking ground finally quiets. When we break apart, I feel the warmth of the sun on my face.

I look behind me. It's still raining, but the sun is breaking through the clouds in some places, sending an array of rainbow colors dancing across the sky.

My heart pounding out of control, I turn my face back to Daemon. He blinks back at me, confused. "What's going on?"

"Do you feel okay?" I ask nervously.

"Fine," Daemon says, eyebrows pulling together.

I glance around the destroyed castle entryway. All around us, the Fae nobles are also looking at each other with bewilderment. No one is acting animalistic—in fact, they all seem far more civilized than mere moments before.

Pushing himself off me, Daemon gets to his feet and walks stiffly over to the nearest beam of sunlight. He stands still, the rainbow beams of light reflecting off his handsome face.

We collectively hold our breaths.

"You feel like yourself, Ashwater?" Jett calls. "What's my name?"

"Fuck off," Daemon growls.

Jett grins. "That's exactly right. He's fine."

"Oh my god," I blurt out, happiness starting to rise in my chest. "Did it work? Did killing Thorne fix it?"

Daemon shakes his head frowning deeply. "Impossible. Nothing happened when I killed him. I'm sure that wasn't it. He didn't make any sacrifice. The curse said—"

"—the curse will only break when the King of Vernallis admits he is powerless and sacrifices whomever he loves most." A feeble voice interrupts.

I whip around, searching for the speaker and find myself staring directly into the face of a feeble old man.

He stands hunched, wearing a ragged servants uniform and a torn and muddy cloak. He's Fae, I can see that from his ears, but he's old and withered in a way I've never seen another of the Fae before. I can't even imagine how old he must be.

"What did you say?" I ask, unsure if this old man was really the one who spoke.

"Hey," Daemon says sharply. He comes up behind me and puts a protective hand on my back all the while scrutinizing the old man. "I remember you. You were in Dyaspora with us, I—"

"You freed me," the man says with a slight nod, as if he's tipping an invisible hat. "Thank you for that."

Daemon falls silent behind me, evidently as confused as I feel. I plow on, determined to understand what's happening before I let myself feel hopeful. "Do you know what's happening? You're right about the curse, but it's impossible. The king is dead and he didn't sacrifice anything."

The man smiles. "There's this interesting thing about monarchies. The king can never really be dead because the very second one ruler dies, the reign of his heir begins. There is *always* a king of Vernallis."

And then, I get it.

"It's you." Everyone turns to look at me, but my gaze is only on Daemon. "With Thorne dead, you become the king, right? Wasn't that why he hated you? That means that technically your reign began an hour ago."

Daemon's expression goes blank. It's like he's looking at me, but seeing nothing. I'm sure the realization is hitting him just as it's hit me, but still I voice it. "From our first conversation you told me you didn't care about yourself. You knew you'd be cursed forever, it was about saving your friends...and me, sacrificing your final moments with us."

Behind Daemon, Odessa laughs, throwing her head back in some exclamation of relief and joy. Kastian's usually serious face splits into a manic smile, and even Fox looks happier than I've ever seen him as Jett starts dancing an erratic jig in a circle around them all.

"I love you too," I blurt out. "From before. I just wanted to respond...so, there it is."

Daemon's piercing gaze is fixed on me, his expression a mix of shock and delight. Suddenly, his face breaks into a wide grin, revealing his perfect white teeth, and in the same second any awkwardness or doubt flees my body.

A spark of excitement ignites within me, building to a crescendo with each passing second. Until in one swift motion, Daemon scoops me up in his strong arms and spins me around, holding me so close it's as if he never intends to let go.

IN THE LIGHT OF DAY, NO ONE KNOWS WHAT TO DO.

The palace and the city are in shambles, and somehow the courtiers themselves are worse. Since they'd never expected to see another moonrise, no one knows how to react knowing they'll not only live but have to live with whatever they did in the days leading up to the crisis.

Daemon holds my hand tightly and leads the way back into the throne room where we find the majority of the court standing around the ruined throne room looking a bit lost.

"I guess they're regretting destroying everything now," Daemon grumbles.

I squeeze his fingers. "You need to say something to them."

He reels back, looking disgusted. "Me? Why?"

"Because you're their king now, asshole," Kastian replies, grinning.

Daemon shakes his head. "I don't want to be."

"Tough shit, Ashwater," Jett beams. "Who else is going to do it?"

"I don't know," Daemon growls. "Anyone."

"Not just anyone can rule people," I say gently. "Dominance and leadership are instinctive traits. Look what happened when a bad leader was in charge." I gesture vaguely around the ruined room.

"Anyway," Odessa smiles. "I think it's got to be bad luck to turn down the crown after you just ended a century-long curse."

Daemon still looks dubious, but I really don't think he has much of a choice in the matter.

As we've been talking, the court has begun moving closer. There's a crowd of forty or fifty nobles, all straining their ears to hear what we're saying. And behind them, more people are streaming into the entrance hall. Soldiers, nobles, even the occasional peasant or goblin-like creature. All faces are turned to Daemon, looking for answers.

"It doesn't have to be a long speech," I prompt. "Just tell them what happened and that everything is going to be fine soon. We're going to make sure it's fine."

I grab his hand tighter and squeeze. "Don't overthink it. You were literally born for this."

His back stiffens, but as I squeeze his hand more tightly a determined look passes over his face and he turns to the rapidly growing crowd.

"The king is dead," Daemon begins.

There's a ringing silence following his proclamation, then someone cheers. Soon hundreds of voices join the chorus and the entire court is yelling their approval.

"I don't think they mind," I mutter out of the corner of my mouth.

Daemon shakes his head, looking worried, despite the fact that everything seems to be going in his favor.

"What's wrong?" Kastian asks.

Daemon puts up both hands to quiet the crowd. "Thorne's death means the crown falls to me, but I don't want it. That is, not unless you want me to have it. For far too long none of you have had any choices. I won't begin a new reign by stripping you of more autonomy."

The crowd falls silent for a moment, then all at once the cheering begins again.

"I think that's a yes," I mutter. "Congratulations."

"I have no idea how to be king," he replies, looking slightly dazed.

My modern human brain is already thinking about getting everyone into emergency therapy and how to set up social safety-net programs, but clearly that's not the sort of help the court is looking for. At least, not for the immediate time being. "I'm not sure anyone knows how to be a king. Maybe just do what feels right."

"Instinctive, you mean?" he asks, the corner of his lip turning up.

I grin sheepishly. "Exactly. First, I'd probably help restore the town and the palace, help people find their families and rebuild their homes."

"Good idea, Peaches." He smiles for real, the grin lighting up his entire face. Then he gives my fingers another squeeze, then strides away from me to talk to the nearest courtiers.

Odessa comes up beside me, taking Daemon's now vacant place at my side.

"That didn't take long," she observes.

"I see what you mean now," I say. "I mean, I did before, but now it's really clear."

She furrows her brow at me. "I don't know if you're picking up bad habits from us or what, but you really need to work on explaining yourself better."

I laugh and jerk my head toward Daemon, who is now standing with a large group of soldiers on the opposite end of the destroyed hallway. Daemon is explaining something emphatically to the group, while Fox looms behind him, arms crossed. The soldiers look equal-parts inspired and terrified, which I'm sure is the point.

"He's a good leader. I think he'll make sure everyone recovers."

"So will you," she points out.

I nod, smiling slightly. I hope she's right.

IT'S EVENING AGAIN BY THE TIME DAEMON AND I GET another second to talk. We walk the familiar path back to my bedroom together, and Daemon shuts the door behind us.

I let out a sigh. "It's weird being in here again." Daemon doesn't answer, and I glance back at him. He's leaning against the door and for a second, he just stares. The glowing smile he's been giving the court is gone, and now there's so much going on behind his eyes that for a moment I falter. "What are you thinking?"

His fingers flex at his side, curling into fists and back out again. "I'm trying to decide if I should yell at you for risking your life, or just be grateful you're alive."

I bite my lip. "Both?"

He lets out a growl low in his chest. "This isn't a fucking joke, Alix."

"I know it's not. I really meant 'both.' Don't you think I'm upset that you risked your life, too?"

His eyes flash with something unfathomable and he pushes off the wall, stalking toward me and closing the space between us in two strides. I back up, and he ends up caging me against the side of the four-poster bed—a familiar position for us by now. My pulse picks up, despite the hard look on his face.

"You're mad that I was in danger?"

"Of course."

"Even though there was never a chance I would lose?"

I bite my lip. He's lying to himself, or maybe just to me. That fight was far closer than I would have liked it to be—then again, now that it's over, I suppose there's no one else to worry about.

"With that logic, there was never a chance I'd get hurt either," I breathe, tipping my face up to his. "I was wearing the vest that whole time."

He makes another low rumbling growl. "This could go on forever."

"Then let's not let it. Let's just be grateful."

He lets his head fall forward until his face is pressing into the curve of my neck. His shoulders relax and he inhales deeply, breathing in my scent. "I never thought I'd see you again."

My stomach twists and my chest seems to squeeze, a combination of emotion and longing and fear all at once. Unsure how to voice that, I reach for the familiar defense mechanism and try to brush it off. "Oh, I'm sure you would have gotten over it. I bet there are thousands of Fae women who would love to throw themselves at a king."

He stiffens and pulls back, looking me dead in the eye. "No. That would never fucking happen."

"I know. Sorry, bad joke, I—"

"No, I need you to understand this." His fingers tangle in my hair and he holds me still, forcing me to keep meeting his eyes. "There will never be anyone else for me. Ever. That's how bonds work. I can't ever leave you and I won't want to anyway, but if it hasn't kicked in for you yet you could still go. You don't have to—"

My eyes widen and I feel my breath catch. "You're saying I'm your soul-bond."

His eyes go impossible wider and he swallows, looking confused for a moment. Then his eyes darken.

## DAEMON

I still can't fully believe she's standing here in front of me. I wouldn't believe it, except that the hole in my chest has closed and the thousands of daggers that had been stabbing at me, picking like thorns, are gone too. All that's left is a warmth, a pulsing beat in my heart urging me to finish this. To claim her fully as mine forever.

"I didn't realize I'd never told you," I say, not really sure what I'm going to say next. "I somehow thought that you knew. You must know, because I can't think of anything else."

"I did...I do know," she says, her voice shaking slightly. "But say it anyway."

I move even closer, pressing my entire body against hers and plastering her back against the bedpost. "You're mine, Alix. Forever. I'll never think about anyone else, never want anyone else. I'll follow you anywhere for the rest of my fucking life."

Her mouth parts on a gasp and she stares up at me in wonder. I can feel her heart beating against my chest.

Alix is smiling, clearly picturing our future and I love that she's thinking about it. I love her, but I can't think about the future right now because we're still standing so, *so* close. I can feel every inch of her against me, and the bond in my chest is riding me, needing to be completed. Consummated. I need to sink inside her and feel her squeeze around me, knowing that she's completely and entirely owned.

My already hard cock pulses, and I press my hips harder against her stomach. Alix shivers, her gaze turning hooded and she draws her tongue over her lips.

I reach down and run my hand up her thigh in her tight black leggings. "Have I told you I like these?"

"No."

I trail my fingers over the curve of her ass. "I like them."

"Maybe I'll wear them sometimes," she says a little breathlessly. "Do you still have that leather jacket? Cause I'm sure we could work out some kind of a trade."

I laugh under my breath, and let my head fall into her shoulder, pressing my lips against her hair, her ear, the curve of her neck. "Let's negotiate later, Peaches. If I'm not inside you in the next five seconds I'm going to fucking die."

She moans and shifts against me. I step back a fraction, letting her turn around so her ass is pressed firmly against my cock, her forehead against the bedpost. She raises her hands in the air and reaches up, clasping her hands around the post like she's trying to climb it. She arches her back, pressing more firmly against me.

I don't waste a second reaching for the waistband of her trousers and yanking it down, baring her ass.

She makes a sound somewhere between a moan and a hiss when the cool air hits her bare skin, but I won't let her be cold for long. I can already scent how wet and ready she is. I don't bother undressing fully or even taking off Alix's shirt. I just undo my belt with one hand and free my painfully hard cock before fisting myself, lining up with her entrance and thrusting inside.

Alix gasps loudly and stretches, arching her back and somehow taking me deeper.

"Fuck, Peaches," I gasp, closing my eyes against the black dots appearing at the edges of my vision.

This isn't going to be gentle. I'm aching, starving for her, and there will be plenty of time later to take her again slower. To trace my mouth over every inch of her body, to look her in the eyes and tell her over and over how much I love her, until I eventually stop worrying she's going to disappear again.

But not now.

Now, I start to move, thrusting in and out of her hard, getting high off her high pitched whines, and holding her hips so tight I know my fingers will leave bruises.

"Harder," she says breathlessly.

I raise a hand and bring it down hard on her ass and she cries out, something between a moan and a scream.

I already know my wings are out before I see the feathers out of the corner of my eye. I should have known Alix was mine from the beginning—from the first moment I flew while holding her before I'd even known her for three hours.

I was taught that bonds aren't predetermined. That they can snap into place at any time of shared heightened emotion, but if that's the truth, then how would I have been showing signs of the connection before even leaving the human world? That doesn't feel random, it feels like fate, and maybe I've never believed in fate before but I like the idea that Alix was always meant for me.

Suddenly I want to see her face.

I pull out and spin Alix around again to face me. She stumbles, her leggings holding her knees together, and I grasp her hips to steady her before falling to my knees in front of her.

"What are you doing?" she gasps, slightly out of breath.

In answer, I hold her by the hips, my face aligned with her bare cunt. I lean forward and press my mouth lightly against her clit, while at the same time I drag my hands down each side of her thighs peeling her leggings down her legs.

Alix gasps, her hands falling to the top of my head.

I drag the flat of my tongue over her, slowly, then faster. I switch to nibbling at her clit, sucking it into my mouth and swirling my tongue until she's trembling and close to falling over the edge. Then, at the last second I release her and drive my tongue into her hot entrance instead.

I have to lift one of her legs up to get the leggings over her foot, and I use the opportunity to spread her wider, pushing her knee to the side and licking her from ass to clit. She whimpers, her fingers tightening in my hair to keep her balance.

"Daemon," she hisses. "Please."

"'Please' what, Peaches?"

"Please. I can't take this, it's too much."

In my opinion, too much is a good thing. I smirk against her, still using every inch of my tongue to make her legs shake and her entire body contact.

"Please," she begs again. "Fuck me. I want you back inside me."

I almost moan at that. I want to be back inside her too, but I want her to come first. I want to taste it when she falls apart, then sink into her while she's still shaking.

Alix tips her head back and fists her hands in the fabric of her shirt.

"Take it off," I demand as I finally free both her feet from her leggings and toss them behind me.

"What?" she asks, eyes hooded with lust.

"Take the shirt off. I want to see every inch of what's mine."

She grips the hem of the shirt and pulls it over her head, then does the same with the tight black undergarment she's wearing underneath. Her tits bounce as they're freed, and I groan then toss her legs over my shoulders and go back to eating at her pussy until she starts trembling once more, and finally screams, bucking her hips against my face.

Before the echo of her scream has even died in the room, I pull her down to the floor with me. Her body is loose and languid and she falls easily, sitting in my lap so she's straddling me.

I push her hair back from her face and bring my mouth to hers.

Her lips part immediately, tracing her tongue over mine and undoubtedly tasting herself on my lips.

She wraps her arms around my neck and her forearms brush against my wings. She stops, reaching out to draw a finger over one of them. "I love these. You look like how I always pictured angels."

"You're the fucking angel, peaches. And I'm glad you like the wings because you're going to be seeing a lot of them. I can't ever control myself around you."

"What if you wanted to lie on your back. Would it crush the wings or would they disappear?" She shoves lightly against my chest, read-justing so her knees fall to either side of my hips.

I force the wings to vanish and lie down on the rug looking up at her. Her hands rest of my chest, while mine fall against her splayed thighs. She adjusts slightly, dragging her perfect pussy against the length of my nearly dripping cock until the head nudges at her entrance.

She raises her hips, then slides down the entire length of my cock.

We both groan as she sits down fully once more. Then finally, just when I think I'm going to die if she doesn't move, Alix rolls her hips.

I let out a hiss, and her mouth quirks up, clearly enjoying her payback. I'm enjoying it too-there is no such thing as too much of her.

First she braces her hands against my chest as she moves slowly up and down. Then I see a bead of sweat on her hairline, and her breath starts to grow erratic again. She leans back, her palms landing just above my knees, and opens her entire body up for me to admire as she rides me.

I lick my thumb and reach out, rubbing it against her clit as I watch myself disappearing in and out of her, faster and faster as she starts to lose the rhythm.

The heat that's been pounding at the base of my spine since the second we entered this room reaches a peak and finally I can't take it anymore. I pinch Alix's clit between two knuckles and rub up and down. She closes her eyes tight, her body tensing around me once more, and opens her mouth in a silent scream.

And then as she pulses around me, I finally let go, looking up at her face as I erupt inside her.

An eternity later, Alix collapses, slumping forward against my chest.

For several long minutes we lie there in silence. The sun streams through the high windows and I watch the dust swirling in the air as I play absently with Alix's hair.

"I get it now," she breathes.

My hand stills in her hair. "What?"

"Happily ever after. I never really knew what that meant exactly. Like what happened after the story was over, but I get it now. It's just this. Us."

"That's right, Peaches. And thanks to Thorne's necklace, that's going to be a really fucking long time." I press my forehead to hers. "You and me for the rest of our immortal lives. Think you can handle that?"

She grins. "I can't think of anything better."

# EPILOGUE
## SIX MONTHS LATER

ALIX

“Take a deep breath. Crossing over can be disorienting.”

Nana glares up at me from where she landed on the muddy ground. She swats away my outstretched hand and pushes herself to her feet. “Stop treating me like an old lady. I’m not dead yet.”

I purse my lips. “And we’d like to keep it that way. Don’t you think—”

Nana holds up one finger to silence me. Only then do I notice the stiffness in her posture and her wide eyes as she stares dazedly around the garden. You’d think she’d never seen roses before.

Then again, the garden looks especially beautiful during the day, and I suppose Nana has never seen much of Vernallis in the sunlight.

“Um, this is just the yard,” I tell her quickly. “Wait until you see the house. Come on, let’s get you some dry clothes.”

I grab Nana’s hand and pull her through the overgrown garden. It’s taken me a few tries to get used to navigating the endless maze of flowers, but I can do it almost perfectly now. It helps that Sushi has no trouble getting lost in the garden and often greets me when I move back and forth through the portals.

Since moving to Ellender permanently, I’ve passed back through the portals several times—mostly just to use my phone and so my mother doesn’t think I died. This time, it was to pick up Nana and bring her back here for Christmas.

It turns out that humans can't usually access the portals on their own—at least, not on purpose—but that was another welcome side effect of King Thorne's necklace. I'm wearing so much magic on my chest that I can pass back and forth whenever I want. Thorne was useless in almost every way, but his necklace has really turned out to be a life-saver—*literally.*

"It's warm here," Nana comments, glancing down at the soaking wet winter coat clinging to her slight frame.

"Yeah. It's been warmer since the curse broke. I'm not sure if it's going to stay that way forever, but I've honestly just been enjoying being outside in the sun. So has all of Vernallis, with the sun back their magic is getting stronger by the day."

"Interesting," Nana comments. "I can't wait to see that."

Nana peels her coat off and throws it over her arm as we march through the garden. Ahead of us, an enormous gray cat prances out of the bushes and bounds straight for Nana. He rubs up on her leg and she squeals in delight, sounding at least thirty years younger than she is. I pause and watch as she picks him up and he barely squirms in her arms.

"Oh Pooka," she coos, bouncing Sushi up and down in her arms. "I think he's gained weight, Ali. What have you been feeding him?"

I roll my eyes. "That's not our fault, believe me. The house had so many mice when we moved in he was having a gourmet feast every single day."

Nana puts Sushi down and raises a brow at me. "Alright then, let's see this rodent infested mansion of yours."

I flush. "There's no mice anymore. We're still working on fixing the house up, but it's been going pretty quickly. Especially now that we've officially moved out of the palace."

It only took hours after King Thorne's death before Daemon and I realized that we didn't want to live at the Winter Palace, where every winding hall felt haunted by the curse and Thorne's horrible reign of terror. Still, it took us over a month to disentangle ourselves from the noble court and move into the Ashwater estate.

Nearly as soon as Daemon became king, we realized there's a whole lot more to running a functioning country than having the blessing of the court. Clearly Thorne hadn't been doing anything for the country for over a century and the kingdom had stagnated under the effects of the curse. With the end of the darkness however, came a new dawn for Vernallis—literally.

All of a sudden advisors and courtiers popped out of the woodwork looking to cement their places in the new court. Letters and messengers started arriving from the other courts, and soon we had to bring in some advisors if only to help take on the workload. Officially, Kastian, Odessa, Jett and Fox became the first and only members of the King and Queen's inner circle, and the first thing on our agenda was to move the capital of Vernallis to Storia.

The second thing on the agenda was opening a music store in the village.

"This is the estate," I announce proudly, pushing through the last of the rose bushes until we're standing on the edge of the patio. "So, what do you think?"

Nana looks awed. "I think it's the perfect place for your fairytale ending. Are you going to show me around?"

I grin and grab her hand. "Yes of course, come on, we'll start in the kitchen."

I GENTLY GUIDE NANA OUT OF THE GARDEN AND ACROSS THE patio to the house where Beatrix is busy preparing afternoon tea. As we approach, I catch Beatrix's eye through the window. She sets down a delicate teacup and waves enthusiastically. Her gaze shifts to Nana, and her face lights up with delight. She dashes to the back door and bursts out onto the patio. "Belle!"

Nana gives Beatrix a warm hug, her eyes crinkling. I hover in the background while they catch up.

Before Ellender I never could have imagined living in the same house as my mother-in-law. But then, I never had a mother-in-law like Beatrix, who was overjoyed to welcome me into her family from the very moment I arrived. She loves having her house full again, and is constantly hinting that she'd like a grandchild or two to dote on.

*Soon*, I always think. *Soon, but not yet.*

Thanks to my necklace I no longer feel like I'm on a deadline and I'm excited to spend a few years just getting to know myself and my new life.

"Have you seen Odessa, yet?" Beatrix asks Nana excitedly. "I'm sure she'll be ecstatic that you're here."

"We just arrived," I explain. "But I bet Dessa is outside. Come on, Nana, I can show you the rest of the property while we look for her."

"I'll have tea ready for all of you when you come back inside," Beatrix calls after us, waving merrily and bustling back into her kitchen.

I take my time looking for Dessa, showing Nana around the entire property first.

We stop by the stables, where my horse, Marie, now has the best kept stall on the premises and gets to enjoy taking me out for daily trail rides. Then we walk through the courtyard, where we find Fox and Jett play-fighting with long wooden swords. They have quite the audience— a dozen or so blue-jacketed soldiers, and Aurelia who is sitting under a nearby tree with a book in her lap and pretending not to watch. I smirk when I see her shoot a sideways glance at Jett who lifts the hem of his shirt to wipe sweat off his brow.

"Explain the tin men," Nana mutters, jerking her head toward the soldiers.

"We couldn't get rid of the guards completely," I explain, as we both stop to watch the sparring match. "I don't have any doubt Daemon and the guys could handle any threat, but we didn't want to put hundreds of soldiers out of work. Now we have them on a rotation and there's never more than twelve guards here at a time."

Nana's eyes widen. "Twelve? That's a lot, especially when you already have so many people living with you."

"I like living with so many people. The house is obviously big enough for all of us and I'm never lonely anymore. It's like constantly being at summer camp." I shrug. "And don't worry about the guards you'll hardly notice them. Now that Fox is in charge of the army everyone has gotten really quiet."

"Fox?" Nana raises a brow.

I gesture across the courtyard. "The tall blonde guy who looks like that Viking vampire from *True Blood*. He doesn't talk much. Don't take it personally."

We wave to Fox, Jett and Aurelia and continue our walk around the property searching for Odessa.

We don't have to search very hard.

On the opposite side of the house from the rose garden sprawls a vast lawn, now so overgrown with a riot of wildflowers that it resembles a vibrant meadow. At the far edge of this meadow is a serene lake, far larger the tiny portal-pond nestled in the garden. I know that the lake is exactly where we'll find Dessa, lying on the grassy bank and soaking in the sun.

I lead Nana through the meadow, stopping occasionally so she can admire an unusual flower or insect. When we're thirty yards back from the rocky shore of the lake, I raise a finger to point out Odessa's hair, which shines practically ruby red in the sun. Before I can say anything, I'm drowned out by an enormous splash and a roar of water. An enormous geyser jets up from the center of the still water, splashing back down with enough force to flood half the lawn. Moments later, Dessa's piercing scream echoes violently across the property, slicing through the air like a sharp blade.

I stop short. "Oh, no..."

Nana stops beside me. "Trouble?" she asks, her lip curling with a mischievous smile.

"No...not trouble. Just—"

I don't have to explain. As we watch, the surface of the lake shifts again, this time forming a giant wave which crashes down hard, soaking everything in a ten foot radius.

Odessa jumps up, spitting mad and soaking wet. She storms across the small beach screaming something in a language I don't understand. My gaze darts in the direction she's heading and I'm unsurprised to find Kastian, leaning casually against a tree.

"Oooph," I murmur, reaching for Nana's shoulder and turning her gently back toward the house. "Let's wait and talk to Dessa later. When the magical language filter can't even pick up what she's shouting that means she's *really* mad."

Nana cracks a smile. "I take it those two don't get along?"

"Um...I'm not really sure, actually." I answer, quickly ushering us away in case Kastian decides to flood the entire property...*again*. "I think it's more like she hates him and he likes upsetting her."

"Pulling her pigtails on the playground?"

"Yeah, I think so. I guess all we can do is wait and see."

"This place is beautiful, Ali, truly," Nana gushes as we return to the house. "I might just be inspired to write another book."

I grin. "Maybe this one will be a halfway decent movie."

Nana scowls and swats playfully at my arm. "Hush. The movie might have been garbage, but it paid for the cruise I sent your mother on so she wouldn't notice I came here for Christmas."

We walk up to the front door of the house and two blue-jacketed guards step aside to let us pass. One nods at me and I nod back, recognizing him as one of the guards who was at the gate when I first arrived at the Winter Palace a thousand years ago.

Nana waits for us to step into the foyer, then turns to me. "Should they bow to you or something?" she asks, shooting me a playful glance.

"You just want them to bow to you since you're with me."

"A woman can dream, alright? But really, why don't they call you the queen?"

"Because I'm not the queen. Not yet, anyway. Daemon is the king by birth, so he doesn't have to wait for an official coronation to be the king," I explain. "We haven't even had time to plan a ceremony yet, but the advisors say that's not unusual. I guess coronations usually happen up to a year after the last king dies, plus we've confused them all by moving in here instead of the palace, so it's taking some time to sort itself out. The villagers love having us here, though. It's brought tons of new people to the town and they're finally expanding."

"But what about you? Will you also have a coronation?"

"I'm not royal so I'll have to wait for our wedding before anyone calls me queen. I'm not in any hurry, though. I'm already doing the job and it's not like I'll get any extra benefits by having the title. I know the people respect me, I don't need anyone to bow."

"Does that mean you've decided to get married?" Nana asks, a twinkle in her eyes.

I shrug. "Eventually."

"Not to overstep, hon, but you literally moved across worlds. You're renovating a house together. What else is there to wait for?"

"You're relentless." I give her shoulder a playful nudge. "We're waiting for my divorce to be finalized, which is taking longer than it should because I'm living '*in Europe*' with bad cell reception."

She furrows her brow. "Why bother? I can't imagine that matters here."

"Because I want it finalized."

Daemon's voice echo's through the house and I turn in a circle before I finally spot him. Daemon is striding down the stairs toward us. He's smiling and dressed casually in a loose white shirt and black trousers.

"Or really?" Nana asks.

Daemon's tone remains flat, but his eyes dance with humor. "I don't want anyone claiming rights to what's mine, in this world or any other."

As if to illustrate his point, he stops beside me and throws his arm over my shoulder, pulling me in for a quick kiss.

Nana shakes her head, her mouth tipping up slightly. "As long as you're happy, Ali."

I smile and lean my head against Daemon's chest. "I am."

"Well then that's what counts, but I still expect a wedding. It should be a big dramatic affair, like Princess Diana. I don't have forever to wait, you know."

I roll my eyes. She's always telling me she's got endless time left, but then the moment she wants something it's all *"I'm mortal, I'll be dead before you know it."*

"How about you write another book and then we'll get married." I state, hoping she'll just drop the whole idea.

"What?" Nana squawks. "That's unfair! You can't put that kind of deadline on creativity."

"We're in no rush," Daemon says, smiling against my ear. "The deadline is your choice."

"Here, I'll even help you," I laugh, watching Nana fret. "You can start with 'Once upon a time' and stop when you hit 'And they all lived happily ever after.'"

THE END

# ABOUT THE AUTHOR

USA Today and International bestselling author Kate King loves sassy heroines, crazy magic, and alpha-hole heroes.

An avid reader and writer from a young age, she has been telling stories her whole life. Ever a fan of the dramatic, she lives in an 18th century church with her husband and two cats, and often writes in cemeteries.